SHADOW MOON

SHADOW MOON

FIRST IN THE CHRONICLES OF THE SHADOW WAR

GEORGE LUCAS AND CHRIS CLAREMONT

SHADOW MOON

A Bantam Spectra Book / September 1995

™ and © 1995 Lucasfilm Ltd.
All rights reserved. Used under authorization.
Cover art by Ciruelo Cabral

BOOK DESIGN BY CAROL MALCOLM RUSSO / SIGNET M DESIGN, INC.

Library of Congress Cataloging-in-Publication Data
Lucas, George.
Shadow moon / George Lucas and Chris Claremont.
p.   cm. — (Chronicles of the Shadow War ; 1st)
ISBN 0-553-09596-X
1. Claremont, Chris, 1950–   . II. Title. III. Series: Lucas, George.
Chronicles of the Shadow War ; 1st.
PS3562.U234S53   1995
813'.54—dc20   95-3613
                                                CIP

Published simultaneously in the United States and Canada

Bantam Books are published by Bantam Books, a division of Bantam Doubleday
Dell Publishing Group, Inc. Its trademark, consisting of the words "Bantam Books"
and the portrayal of a rooster, is Registered in U.S. Patent and Trademark Office
and in other countries. Marca Registrada. Bantam Books, 1540 Broadway,
New York, New York 10036.

PRINTED IN THE UNITED STATES OF AMERICA

BVG   10 9 8 7 6 5 4 3 2

For fans

of fantasy

everywhere

G.L.

To Eleanor, Betsy, Lucy and Tom

For Faith, Trust, Patience and Skill

C.C.

SHADOW MOON

PROLOGUE

IN THE MIDDLE OF THE NIGHT, WILLOW UFGOOD RODE
the back of a dragon.

It was a dream, had to be. He'd gone to bed quite a bit
later than usual after a hard day in the fields. Spring had
come late this year, the weather changeable as a courtesan's
costume; when it finally broke, he and the other farmers of
the vale had to hurry with their plows to turn the ground and
ready it for planting. He was out the door every morning before sunrise and didn't quit until the night grew too dark to
see, sowing seeds of wheat and corn and barley and then
checking the condition of the modest orchard of apple trees
arrayed in a double row up from the river to form one border of his holding. At the same time Kiaya was busy with her
kitchen garden close behind the house, with the herbs and

vegetables that would not only grace their own table but bring welcome income at Saturday market.

The whole family pitched in to help, but the children were still too young to handle stock, and as it was Kiaya's special gift to charm the green, growing things of the earth, so it was Willow's to speak to the animals that walked upon it. Occasionally, though, he considered that a mixed blessing—as with today, when his pig decided to behave like a pig and take it into its head that plowing was beneath its station. He couldn't force the beast—it stood as tall as he and outweighed him by more than he cared to think about—which meant he had to resort to persuasion. The pig, of course, chose to hear nothing that was said to it until it was good and ready, preferring to bask in the sunlight and enjoy a day that felt more like midsummer than spring.

Willow wanted to strangle the beast. He thought of glazed ham and pork roasts and chops and bacon—oh, how he loved bacon—but he knew the pig wouldn't take that threat seriously. It was far more valuable to the farm in its present occupation and as breeding stock. In that moment, and only for the moment, the world seemed to shift ever so slightly, turning back on itself a whole year: same field, same situation (though the pig then wasn't acting nearly so pigheaded), Willow tilling his soil as his father had done and his father before him and so on back as far as memory went in Nelwyn Vale, distracted suddenly by the cries of his children that they'd found a baby in the bulrushes. Such an ordinary day it had been, yet from that point his life was forever changed, and the fate of the world in the bargain. That day he'd rescued the Sacred Princess Elora Danan.

He found himself walking to the river, crouching by the spot where he'd drawn her ashore. There was a peaceful stillness to water and air that allowed him the full use of his senses, as though every sight and sound and scent stood as an individual, in stark and absolute contrast to its background, rather than being mixed together in a cacophonous blend, as was normally the case. Honeysuckle was sweet, almost cloying, until it gave way to the more delicate fragrance of Kiaya's rosebushes, winding their madcap, helter-skelter way up and over her arbor. He heard the whine of a mosquito, the deeper buzz of a fat-bottomed bee, the zizzing of a clutch of cicadas, building to a crescendo and fading away, the trill and squawk and whistle of a myriad of birds. He saw a widening circle of ripples, marring the perfect plane of the river as a fish quickly broke the surface to claim the life of an unwary bug. He beheld the pattern and order of life, in all its forms around him, and thought how a year ago that sight would have left him content.

It still brought him joy, but contentment was a word with an edge that, while it had yet to draw blood, still pressed him deeply enough to make itself felt.

The pig was up when he returned to the field, shifting impatiently from one foot to the other and glaring at him accusingly, as though it was Willow's fault this task wasn't being properly accomplished.

After supper, when the children were safely tucked abed, he retired to his workshop off the back of the house proper, half-sunk into the ground, so that he had to descend a small stairway from the washroom. Originally, it was where he stored his tools and made whatever was needed in the way of furniture for the house; now, in addition, it was where he practiced his magic. The walls were slabstone, like the house, which gave the whole structure the sense that it was an extension of the natural landscape, rather than something that had been built. There was a hearth in the far corner, for warmth as well as to heat his various concoctions. He had a comfy chair to relax in, on those occasions when his castings left him too weary to manage the climb to the main floor, and a wooden stool by his workbench. Windows for light by day, candle sconces for night. The floor itself was bare, unlike the polished wood planking of the rest of the house, because regardless of season, he preferred working barefoot, drawing comfort and no little strength from the raw, rich earth beneath his toes.

On the table was the gift he'd been making for the Princess. It was a stuffed bear, a larger version of the ones he'd made for his own children when they were her age. Its fur was golden, to match her hair, short and thick like a tabby cat's and plush enough for a girl to sink her face into. The arms and legs and head swiveled, so that if Elora hugged the bear it would feel as though the bear was hugging her back. As he'd known from the start, the face had been the main challenge. He sat in his plush, overstuffed armchair and stared, savoring the mug of cider Kiaya had poured for him, and the bear stared back. More than once over the weeks, Willow had been prepared to swear the bear's expression changed. The eyes were polished crystal that he'd quarried himself; he'd meant them to be green, to match Elora's, yet in place they appeared a rich hazel, like finely aged wood, the same as his own. The mouth would seem serious one glance, then take on a wryly humorous cast with another.

The bear had actually been finished the better part of a fortnight, time enough for even a Nelwyn messenger to carry it to Elora's home, the fabled Daikini fortress of Tir Asleen. Willow's intent had been to present it himself, but nature had little interest in such human desires or the plans that went with them. The time he'd be away would cost him the better part of this year's crops and that was a loss his family could ill afford. He'd sent apologies and regrets as soon as the weather's perversities became clear; the bear should have gone with them.

Yet here it was, sitting on his table.

He sipped his cider, thinking how quickly it had grown cold, never considering that the cause of the chill might be the length of time he'd been sitting there, and turned his gaze to the hands that held the mug. A year ago they'd been farmer's hands, and he a proper Nelwyn with improper dreams of becoming a sorcerer's apprentice. Now he was a wizard, true, and felt the power crackle within him at every beat of his heart. It was part of the fabric of his being, it reached through him and from him to everything he touched.

"Some power," he muttered in asperity, "some wizard, who can't even persuade a pig to pull a plow."

He rose to the table as he spoke, reaching out a finger to gently trace a line from the center of the bear's forehead down between its eyes and over the tip of its nose of black thread to finally tap it oh so gently on its chest, right over its heart. The stuffed animal wasn't alive, yet he felt from it a sense of . . . *be-ing*. As though the act of physical creation had imbued it with a minute portion of Willow's own spirit.

"Watch over her, little bear," he said. "Keep her safe always."

He took care not to wake Kiaya as he snugged his way gently beneath the sheets. There was a fresh scent of flowers and sunlight to the cotton, hardly a surprise, since he'd watched them billow in the afternoon breeze as she hung them out to dry. She stirred anyway, sleepily murmuring his name, and to make up for disturbing her, he gently scratched her back along the length of her shoulder blade. She immediately rolled to her stomach, flexing along the full length of her like a cat as an invitation to continue, and so he did, stroking the tips of his nails from the top to the bottom of her spine while she smiled and purred in delight. She drew him to her, one kiss leading to another, returning his caresses with her own, and passion quickly claimed them both.

Afterward, he thought it would be a long time before sleep claimed him, he'd never felt so alert and wide-awake, but the moment he stretched himself flat, he found himself yawning, fatigue sweeping like a sunset across his back and shoulders.

He beat his pillow into its proper shape and rolled over onto his side . . .

. . . to behold the whole, wide world far, far below.

He cried out.

The dragon laughed.

A louder shout burst from him, heart trip-timing in his chest more sharply than a quartermaster's drum beating the call to arms.

He was nestled in the hollow of a set of shoulders so broad they easily would have fit his entire farm, staring up a neck that all alone topped the tallest tree he'd ever seen. He didn't want to think of how far the creature stretched in the other direction. Great wings reached out from where he stood, beating only occasionally as the dragon rode the evening thermals, letting wind and air do most of the work of keeping it aloft.

The ground below was already cast in shades of velvet, dusk

having mostly turned to full night, but the dragon soared high enough to catch the last rays of the sun as it dropped beyond World's End, casting diamond sparkles off the surface of the Sunset Ocean.

In spite of himself, Willow pushed to knees, then feet, taking hold of one of the double row of dorsal spines—most resembling maple leaves in shape—that ran the length of the dragon's back, from skull to tail. At this juncture, they stood easily twice the height of a tall Daikini, which made them nearly four times his own, and he couldn't help marveling at the scale. He knew houses in his village where a single segment would have served as a good-sized wall; the only reason his didn't number among them was that he'd expanded it to a second story when the children grew old enough for rooms of their own. The dragon's line of flight put this side of the dorsals in sunlight and even that faint and fading radiance, he saw, was enough to paint the outline of body and wings in continuous flashes of crystalline fire, as though the dragon was formed of the same golden, glowing substance as the sun itself.

It was a beauty so wild, so elemental, it made him ache.

No less wondrous was the world through which they flew. Normally, heights terrified him; his wife was far better on ladders than he. Here, though, he felt no fear, and decided that was probably because it was so far a fall, his mind simply refused to comprehend. Or better yet, since this was a dream—*has to be a dream,* he told himself—there was nothing in it that could truly do him harm, so why not simply stop fretting and enjoy both flight and view?

"Why not, indeed?" the dragon said companionably.

"You can talk!"

"But you can't fly, so I figure I'm ahead of the game."

It was a pleasant voice, with a baritone's hearty resonance, the kind he'd expect to hear at the Ram's Horn Inn, telling stories before the blazing hearthfire. The dragon had turned his head all the way around for a look at him, with the same disconcertingly boneless ease of a swan.

"You knew what I was thinking!" Willow protested.

"Think more quietly, then. I'll wager there isn't a creature within mindsight of your dwelling, Nelwyn, doesn't know your every secret."

Willow flushed furiously, as scarlet as the sunset sky.

"No one ever told me."

"Did you ever ask?"

"Why should I have? It never occurred to me that my thoughts could be heard by any but me."

"Sorcerers . . ." The dragon sighed, with a bemused dismay that was altogether genuine. "The power to shape worlds and not the slightest sense in some of 'em how to use it."

"I've been learning!" Another protest.

"Parlor tricks. As you are more sensitive to the world, little magus, so is the world more sensitive to you. You took up the sword fate offered; you must measure yourself against all those who do the same."

Willow was about to ask what that meant when he caught sight of a layer of clouds ahead and gasped with the realization of the dragon's headlong speed through the air as, an eyeblink later, he found himself passing through the heart of them. There was an instant's darkness and chill, as though he'd suddenly been immersed in fog, and then they were once more in free and open air.

"I thought there'd be more to it," he mused aloud in wonderment.

"Clouds, you mean? Nope," and the great head shook back and forth. "What you see is both less and more than what you get.

"I'm Dineer," the dragon said. "Calan Dineer."

"Willow Ufgood," was the Nelwyn's reply as the dragon offered a wry grin with his surprisingly mobile mouth that revealed fangs far longer than Willow was tall.

"Savior of Elora Danan, Slayer of the Demon Witch Queen Bavmorda. You've quite a reputation."

"This is lunacy," was all Willow could find to say to that.

"Or a most spectacular dream." The dragon chuckled.

"The sun hasn't set." There was amazement in the small man's tone.

"Oh¿"

"We've been flying all this while and the sun's no lower in the west than when we started. Have you somehow magicked time to a stop¿"

"Neat trick, but also one that shouldn't be indulged in often. Time is like a great river; the more you try to manipulate it, the greater the consequences. And they're not always the ones you expect."

"Oh," Willow replied, as though he understood, when in fact he hadn't a clue what the dragon was talking about.

"We fly at the pace the world turns, which means our position relative to the sun remains constant. If I go slower, it will drop below the horizon; faster, it will appear to rise."

"And when you come to the end of the world, what then¿"

"The world has no end, Nelwyn."

"You lie!"

"Look about you, what do you see¿"

"Water." He clutched the nearest spine and looked about for a gap he might squeeze through to place himself safely between the line of double dorsals, and thereby block out the view. "What have you done with the land, monster¿"

"Look to the edge of what you can see, Willow. How do things appear¿ Or are you too afraid to try¿"

He took a brave stance—no giant lizard was going to shame him, the dragon's chuckle on hearing this wayward thought only making Willow all the more determined—and ruthlessly quelled the trembling in his voice when he replied.

"The horizon, it's"—he thought a moment—"curved."

"What's a curve that goes right the way around¿"

"A circle."

"And an object made up of nothing but circles¿"

"A ball."

"In large, by any other name, a world."

Try as he might, Willow couldn't comprehend the difference

right away, and the effort stole the strength from his legs, dropping him to his seat with his back against the dorsal spine, slack-jawed with astonishment and no little awe.

"You need not take my word for it." Dineer chuckled. "Mathematics will provide you proof."

"That's Tall Folk knowledge," Willow told him. "We Nelwyns have our own way, with little use for Daikini numbers."

"It's there, regardless."

"Where does it go, Dineer, this water?"

"To another land, only there this is called the Sunrise Sea. And beyond that land, another ocean. And so on, until at last we come back to where we started."

"Are there people?"

"Domains there, as here, all the Realms of the Veil Folk. Plus what you would call Daikini, in their mad variety. Kingdoms galore, the greatest being Angwyn, which is as far from your home, young magus, as it's possible to go."

I wish we could, he thought, with a yearning that poked him as sharply as any knifepoint. If the dragon heard, he gave no sign.

"Did Bavmorda know," he asked instead, "of these other lands?"

"A Magus—a true sorcerer, of true power—is driven to know all there is to know. From that quest comes power. There are Worlds Within and Worlds Beyond, Willow. What you behold with your five physical senses is but one among a multitude."

"Can't I be satisfied with that?"

"If you were, you wouldn't be here."

Dineer had altered course along the way; belatedly, Willow realized the sky had darkened, from the pale blue of day to the rich cobalt of twilight and lastly to the diamond-laced velvet of full night. The dragon's skin radiated a welcome warmth, but there was still sufficient chill from their headlong passage through the sky to allow him the sight of his every breath. He was thankful that the bulk of the dragon's body blocked the wind of its flight from reaching him; he had no decent handholds beyond those of its spinal ridge and sensed rightly he'd be as helpless as a leaf in a hurricane. He didn't like the road those thoughts were taking, and to cast them loose, Willow turned his eyes upward through air so clear he imagined he could see every individual flash of brilliance from each of the stars above.

He'd never given them any serious thought before. They appeared every night, so constant in shape and position they made the perfect guide for travelers. Which in turn made him consider how a bright lamp, when brought close to the eyes, tended to wash away all sight of whatever lay behind it.

"They're always there, aren't they?" he asked. "The stars, I mean. Day or night. If the world is a ball, floating in the sky, then why not the moon? And the sun as well? And if they're balls, what of all those little lights beyond? Are they balls, too? Are they small because they're small, or because they're far away? If the world doesn't end, what of the sky around it—how far does it go, how much space *is* there?"

It was more revelation than he could handle; it left him trembling with the awful sweep required of his imagination. His was a reality where the average tree was monstrous huge; celestial proportions had no real meaning to him.

Ice gripped him, heart and soul, a terror as sudden and all-consuming as the fear of his family's death. "Why aren't we falling?"

"There's no need to fear, Willow," the dragon told him. "The Mother World won't let you go."

"Balls don't hang in the air, you throw them and they fall," he cried, as close to panic as a fresh recruit in the face of his first battle. His hands closed convulsively on the edge of the nearest dorsal in a desperate, reflexive bid to hold on.

"Then don't look. Don't think about it. Be a farmer. Be a Nelwyn."

Willow felt a flash of anger. "There's no shame in either!"

The dragon shrugged, the flex of its shoulders feeling more to Willow like a minor earthquake.

"Why did you tell me these things?" There was a roughness to his voice as his fury began to turn from wayward sparks to a sustained blaze. "What do they have to do with me?"

"You're a wizard," was the reply, as if the answer was altogether obvious.

Willow was panting, flushed within, soaked without by sweat. His rage had been like a fever of such intensity that it consumed itself even as it tried to do the same to him. With a conscious effort of will he forced his fingers to open; they were white and swollen from the force he'd exerted on the dorsal and he hoped he hadn't hurt the dragon in the process.

He looked about himself, taking in the dragon, the night, the world.

"We're not falling," he said in wonderment.

Nothing had changed. And everything.

"It's all a matter of perception, really," Dineer noted, tone as casually dry as any academic's. "A ball in the air will fall. The same ball in water might float. Who knows for truth what medium the world passes through? We may well be falling, all of us together"—Dineer's mouth creased into a grin—"but who's to know until we hit something."

"I feel comforted already."

"To an ant, Nelwyns are giants. To Nelwyn, Daikini are. Everyone has their place in the scheme of things and all prefer to view that place as being the center of the universe."

"Including dragons?"

"But of course, my friend. Save that we *know* we're the center about which all revolve."

"A rare wit. I'm laughing inside."

"You're learning, young magus. Give as you get, as good as you get."

"Among the Nelwyns, the rule is to give as you would be given. There's a difference."

"The two aren't incompatible, or mutually exclusive. Situation defines response."

"Outstanding. Am I so exhausted in mind and spirit that the best my dreams can offer is a dialogue in philosophy?"

"Not what you'd expect from a farmer, or a Nelwyn, is it?"

"I am both, lizard."

"And more?"

"Why am I here?"

"Interesting question, considering where we are."

The bulk of the dragon's body obscured any view of the ground directly below, and Willow had no intention of making his way to where the curve of its rib cage turned downward for a better sight. Instead, he picked his careful way along the dorsal ridge, soon finding an opening large enough to allow him to wriggle through and continue on between the double line of spinal plates, up the shallow curve of the neck until he reached Dineer's head.

He leaned against a brow ridge, that curled back from the dragon's right eye to form a many-spiked crest that peaked above and behind its skull. He didn't understand how so huge a creature could remain aloft; the head alone would fill the entire market square of his village and he suspected that the dragon entire would dwarf Tir Asleen.

There was precious little ambient light, since the moon had yet to rise, but it wasn't needed. One of the first side effects of his wizardry was a heightened sensitivity of his physical being. He could outhear a cat, outscent a hunting hound, and his sight had no peer. MageSight, he called it, allowing him the full range of vision even in pitch darkness.

At first, nothing looked familiar.

Is that a surprise? he asked himself in a tone as wry as the dragon's. *By the way, when was it* you *last saw the world from such a view?*

A serried line of mountains, saw-toothed and jagged like the mouth of a shark, building to the ugly hollow of an ancient volcano, which in turn gave way to an ugly valley below. Willow didn't need MageSight or a second glance to tell him what stood at the head of that valley, dominating the highlands, with easy access to the plains beyond.

"Nockmaar," he said in recognition of that damned fortress, his voice a rasp.

"Bavmorda's dead," he continued. "Consigned to the doom she planned for Elora Danan."

"You should know."

"I was there, Dineer, I *saw* it." A pause. "Are you trying to tell me different?"

"There are Twelve Great Domains," the dragon said, "as much

of the spirit as of the flesh. Elora Danan is the Thirteenth that binds them all."

"I never understood the how or why of that. What makes her so special?"

"Perhaps it's time you started learning."

"Is something wrong, Dineer? Is there some danger?"

There was a rush of wind, exceptionally gentle, considering the tremendous size of the creature that generated it, as Dineer belled his wings and extended his hind legs for landing. Willow saw they were in a different valley, in a land of rolling hills, where the peaks of the Nockmaar range were reduced to bumps along a distant skyline. Where the dominant color of one was a dank slate, here was a riot of earth tones, rich greens and browns; Nockmaar stone was leached of life, the granite of Tir Asleen fair burst with it.

Willow assumed the dragon had cast some sort of glamour over the castle to mask its presence; he had no other explanation, save the rankest incompetence (which he prayed was unlikely), for the failure of any sentries to sound the alarm as the head arched delicately forward to rest on the topmost battlements.

The hint was unmistakable and Willow wasted no time clambering from his perch.

He stumbled on landing and had to take a breath to gather his legs and wits beneath him.

"I'll ask again, Dineer," he said as he straightened, "and I demand an answer—is there some da—"

He was speaking to darkness and open sky.

The beast was gone, as if it had never been.

An appropriate profanity made it as far as thought, though not to execution, before being derailed by the clash of steel from beyond the nearest corner tower and a level below.

There were torches everywhere, along the parapet and walls, arrayed at intervals on poles across the courtyards below, illuminating the bailey to a fair semblance of daylight. There was a day's worth of activity as well, a tumult of people and animals, carts and their cargo, scurrying purposefully to complete the preparations for the upcoming days of celebration. The din was awful, voices of all shapes and description—human and otherwise—trying to make themselves heard over the clash of hooves on cobblestones, the crunch of crates striking the ground, hammers on anvils. They competed in turn with a valiant band of musicians off in a corner, facing a clear space whereon couples were merrily dancing and flanked on either side by plank tables on which were laid buckets of ale and rough red wine and trenchers of breads and meats and sweets, catering to the entire assemblage. It didn't matter whether folk were noble or common, secular or clergy; for this one special night, all the arbitrary distinctions of society had been suspended, allowing people to treat one another solely as people, and everyone was making the merry most of it.

To Willow, though, it was as if all the noises he'd ever heard—up to and including the one great battle he'd fought in—had been poured into the confines of these walls, which served then to magnify them tenfold. It was a wonder anyone present could make their thoughts heard, much less their voices.

Yet once more came to him that still, pure *tang* of blade on blade, sharp and staccato, a summons as peremptory as any monarch's and as impossible to refuse.

He took stock of himself as he hurried along, mindful that—dream or no—he wanted to look his best. He'd donned his nightshirt before bed, but that was long gone, replaced by boots and breeches, a light woolen shirt, a leather overshirt that was as much a jacket. Belt around the middle, traveling pouches at his sides, he was dressed for a journey. In height, like all Nelwyns, he wasn't much to speak of, standing barely as tall as a Daikini man's hip, the length of his body concentrated more in his torso than in his legs, which gave him a surprising reservoir of strength but made walking a trial. His hair was shoulder length and full, mahogany brown at first glance but shot through with streaks of fiery russet that manifested themselves in the right light. He never considered himself particularly handsome, no matter how often Kiaya told him different—or particularly quick, or intelligent, or brave—even though, in truth, he was all these things and more. What he saw in his mirror was a plain man, whose goal was to do honorably and right by himself, his family, his friends. That was what he offered the world, and all he asked of it in return.

If he thought of himself as molasses, then the figures dueling along the parapet were wildest quicksilver.

One was dark, the other fire. Both Daikini, a man and a woman, lithe and lean with the bodies of trained warriors and the moves to match. The man stood a head taller, but the difference offered no advantage. The woman wore black, wool and cotton and leather and mail, as though ready to ride to battle. The only spot of color about her was her hair. It was the red of fallen leaves, the dusky rose of simmering coals, making her face appear all the more pale by contrast. The man's hair appeared black, though Willow knew it was laced with dark brown, the tan of his features complemented by the rich colors of his clothes. He'd contemplated no war in his future when getting dressed, that much was obvious; his fur-trimmed boots were more appropriate to the Royal Court, splendid for the dance, useless on campaign, and his pants were cut more to show the elegant shape of his leg than for actual comfort. His shirt was a bell-sleeved cotton so fine it most resembled silk, and the exertion of the duel had opened its laces to expose a fair broad expanse of chest. Over that had gone a sleeveless waistcoat. No doubt, there'd been a doublet—that was the fashion of the season, so Willow had been told when adamantly refusing a similar suit for himself—long since cast aside to allow for more freedom of movement.

Swords clashed high, low, then the woman lunged to full extension, apparently intending to impale her foe through the heart. Only that heart wasn't there to receive the fatal blow. The man spun away from her attack, making a full revolution down the length of her arm to stand behind her. As he went he caught hold of her wrist in his free hand; he lifted it, and her sword, and twisted to force her against him. Then, his other hand—which held *his* sword—pulled tight to the small of her back and he moved the pair of them as one along the length of the parapet, in perfect time to the music from the castle mainyard below.

He offered a smile, she kicked him in the knee.

"Sorsha," he cried, more in dismay than pain.

"Madmartigan," she mocked in return, matching his tone and coming for him once more with her blade.

He hopped clear as best he could, both swords moving too fast to follow as every attack—his to hers as much as the reverse—met its parry. Willow dropped to a seat where he stood; he had a splendid vantage point, and enjoyed the show. He'd never met a more devoted couple, or one more likely—at any time, for the most absurdly trivial of reasons—to kill each other.

"It's a night of celebration, woman," Madmartigan insisted in asperity.

"Well, *I'm* certainly having a wonderful time."

"Where *were* you raised?"

"You know damn well where, and by whom."

"You're a Princess, damn it. Try acting the part. *I'm* supposed to be the rogue here!"

"Oh," she said, and it was immediately clear Madmartigan had said exactly the wrong thing, because she redoubled her already considerable efforts, forcing him to drop his irreverent mask for a time and concentrate on swordplay. "I see," she continued, speaking in the same staccato rhythm formed by the impact of their blades. "You get to carouse, you get the comfy clothes, *you* get all the fun, while I wave sweetly from my window? I don't think so."

"It won't break your soul to set aside your sword for an evening and take up dancing instead?"

To emphasize the point, he somehow slipped around her guard again. Willow was looking for the move, watching with all his formidable concentration, and still couldn't tell how the man accomplished it. All Sorsha could do was fume and follow as he led her gracefully across the stone in a way Willow had never seen before.

She clocked him solidly with her sword hilt, and when he

cried out, clutching reflexively at himself, she tripped his legs out from under him.

Before his rump struck stone, she was away with the merriest of laughs, daring him to follow her up a flight of stairs and around the corner of the battlements.

He cast about, seemingly in confusion, as if unsure of which way to go. A moment later he'd launched himself into the air, describing a great arc across the bailey at the end of a halyard normally used for lifting armaments to the top of the wall. His plan was to swing ahead of her and be waiting when she emerged, hopefully winded, from the corner tower.

Unfortunately, he chose to land right where Willow was sitting.

It was a most impressive collision, despite the Nelwyn's last-ditch and frantic attempts to scramble clear.

"*Damn* you, Nelwyn," he heard as they untangled themselves, though the affection in the Daikini's voice belied the profanity he used. "What God did your kind annoy when they were handing out sizes, eh? Too small to notice, too bloody big to avoid."

"I'm pleased to see you, too, Madmartigan," he grumbled in reply.

Sorsha's contribution to the conversation was a delighted bubble of laughter, occasioned by her holding a pair of swords—hers and her husband's—crossed at Madmartigan's throat. He was sprawled amidst a jumble of collapsed crates, legs outstretched and splayed apart, while she straddled his hips, perfectly balanced on the balls of her feet; a twitch of her wrists would be all that was required to finish him.

"No fair," Madmartigan protested. "I cry interference."

"Nice try," was her response. "Better you should watch where you're going. I certainly did."

"Do you see what I'm supposed to see in her?" Madmartigan asked Willow, with an exaggerated roll of the eyes.

"Your equal?"

"Not tonight, my little friend." Sorsha smiled. The swords stayed where they were.

Madmartigan crossed his ankles beneath her, and his hands behind his head, looking like a man without a care in the world.

"I yield," he told her. "Now may we dance?"

Carefully, for the blades were honed more keenly than any razor, Sorsha set aside the weapons, rolling forward to her knees in the same motion so that her face was above Madmartigan's.

Willow looked away and didn't remind them of his presence—with a discreet cough—until their second kiss.

"What was that all about?" Willow wondered aloud as the three of them made their meandering way along the parapet to a bridge connecting it with the inner keep.

"All work and no play—" Madmartigan began, but was as quickly cut off by Sorsha, whose tone—this was evidently an old argument between them—made Willow fear the duel would start up all over again.

"I'm a warrior, Madmartigan, why is that so hard for you to accept?" Sorsha took a hefty swallow of wine from a skin Madmartigan had produced and passed it along to Willow.

"And what am I? But there's more to life, there should be more to *our* lives."

"I hate the way the King's household looks at me. They want to make me something I'm not and resent me for resisting."

"Can't you find a middle ground? I think you look lovely in a gown."

"Funny, based on our first meeting, I thought much the same of you."

The wine was a rough red, tasteful but merciless, especially when it went down the wrong way. Willow coughed and choked and nearly drowned at the memory of that wild afternoon and Madmartigan's impromptu disguise as a village wench. He almost got away with it, too, until one of the soldiery made an improper advance.

Tactfully, Madmartigan chose to change the subject.

"I thought you weren't coming," he said to Willow.

"I'm not coming. I'm not here." The two Daikini exchanged deadpan looks, choosing to take the Nelwyn at his word. "But I will say, I can't remember when I've had a more wild dream."

"How'd you make the trip?"

"On the back of a dragon."

"Sounds like a dream to me." Sorsha smiled, only to burst into a riotous set of giggles as Madmartigan swept her into his arms and down a flight of steps in another impromptu pirouette. This time she didn't hit him, or push away, but tried to match herself to the melodies of the fiddles, uillean pipes, and tiompan gaily holding forth below.

"I'll wear a gown tonight, if you'll do the same tomorrow," she challenged.

"Hmm," he considered. "Scandalous thought. Only men are supposed to show the shape of their legs."

"Probably because they're afraid of the competition."

"I don't understand you Daikini," Willow grumped aloud, because for the most part he truly didn't. "Sorsha wears pants every time she rides to battle, the shape of her legs are plain for all the world to see. Where's the blessed scandal?"

"That's practicality, Willow," Madmartigan explained. "Wearing trousers in a fight. She's a warrior, not a woman."

"At last he comprehends," she applauded.

"But at court, at a ball—I suppose you could say it's a whole different kind of battle, with its own set of rules. Men play peacock and display their charms for their ladies. Women . . ." Words failed him, which was a rarity.

"Men choose, women are chosen, that's the polite way of putting it," Sorsha finished for him, making plain her dissatisfaction with such an arrangement.

"In Tir Asleen, my sweet, a courteous guest lives by Tir Asleen's rules."

It was clear this discussion wouldn't reach its end tonight, if ever.

"As long as I'm here," Willow announced, "I'll look in on Elora Danan."

"You always call her by name, Drumheller," Sorsha said. "To most everyone else here, she's 'Her Royal Highness the Sacred Princess.'"

"To me, Elora Danan is who she is. I changed her wrappings

too often to consider her a 'Sacred Princess' anything—*what* did you call me, Sorsha?"

"Drumheller. A warrior term my father taught me, before Bavmorda did away with him." A sadness swept across her fine features, like a squall line over a smooth-surfaced lake, gone as quickly as it had arrived, helped on its way by the comforting grasp of Madmartigan's arm across her shoulders. "Part pathfinder, part stalking horse, he—or she—is the warrior sent ahead of all the rest to charm an ambush out of hiding."

"How wonderful for him. Or her."

"It's a job only the best of the best can do, Willow," said Madmartigan.

"You speak from experience?"

"Sorsha and I, we have that in common."

"You think *I'm* such a one, Sorsha? One of us has had too much wine."

"This is a dream, remember? Wine doesn't enter into it, only truth."

"If we're to talk nothing but truth, past time I was awake."

"Forgive me, Willow, it's how I've come to think of you. Showing the rest of us the way, whether we like it or not."

"Your thoughts, then, are more generous than mine."

"Damn but you're a thorny bugger sometimes, Willow," and Madmartigan clapped him gently on the shoulder for emphasis.

"At my size, words have to serve as well as knives for weapons. Unlike you Daikini, it's not so easy for us to impose our will on others. Or physically defend ourselves when things go wrong. We have to try persuasion. And diplomacy. To talk our way out of a mess."

"To charm," Sorsha repeated and, with a grace that matched her mate's, took Willow by the hands and drew him gently along the skybridge. She led the dance, because that was her nature, but imposed her will with such gentle ease that he had no problem following. She matched her steps to his, in tune to the music, letting words flow with movement as though they were all part of the same song. "The ambush out of hiding."

"You're getting too damn good at this," Willow groused in reply, but he couldn't help a wide grin of his own as she raised his arm to pass him through a full turn; a moment after, the grin was an outright laugh on all their parts as she spun herself down into a crouch so that the Nelwyn could turn her. It was all improvised, every step, yet to anyone watching it appeared as though they'd been dancing together all their lives.

They passed the wine again, exchanged some gossip, spoke a little of the world.

"Not so easy for us, either, sometimes—that imposing the will you spoke of—" Madmartigan noted, as seriously as Sorsha would allow, "—especially where it concerns the Veil Folk and the Realms Beyond. The sharpest steel is no match for spells that can change a man to stone or swallow him whole."

"I suppose you're right," Willow conceded. "That dragon I rode could smash this castle to rubble with a swipe of its tail. Nobody stands alone in the world, that's what he told me. There's always someone bigger, some force greater, as there are those beneath you in the scale of things."

"Conversations like this, my lad, it strikes me Willow's not the name for you. Bends too easily."

"All Nelwyns bend, Madmartigan, in part that's how we survive. And don't call me 'lad,' I'm older than you *and* a father."

"Explains why you're turning stodgy on us."

"Am not. I'm no different now than *ever* I was!"

But then he thought about what he just said, and noted the stifled giggles of his friends, and sighed surrender. Of that point, only.

"Whatever." Madmartigan was oh so gracious in victory, Willow wanted to stomp him on his big toe. "But anyone fool enough to take a hand to you, I'll wager it comes away bloody. You're not a good Willow, my friend, or a good Nelwyn, there's way too much steel in your soul."

Tone and eyes didn't match for that last thought; the one was jocular, the other—belying it totally—in deadly earnest, striking a sudden resonance in Willow that sobered him instantly.

"I have it," Sorsha announced, "for the duration of this dream then . . .

"Sorsha," Willow pleaded, "have a little mercy."

"Suffer, Elora's Champion. I'm Princess, Royal-born, entitled to my flights of whimsy. With the rank and privilege to enforce my royal decrees." Her voice lowered in tone, deep and rich, and she mock-solemnly intoned, "Nelwyn you may appear in form, but in substance you are something far more formidable, deserving of a title to match."

"This is ridiculous."

"For the duration of this dream—no, better yet, until We," she deliberately applied the Royal pronoun, and rolled her voice to match the court chamberlain's sonorous tones when announcing the Honors List, "deign to release you—" the music below was building to a wild crescendo, so infectious a rhythm that Willow was hard put to stay still. Yet the force of Sorsha's eyes, the strength of her voice, held him fast, commanding him with the same power she applied in battle, directing her troops over the helter-skelter clash of arms. "—shall you henceforth be known, with all rights and responsibilities due the name—"

"Between us only," Madmartigan interjected conspiratorially, "elsewise everyone will get confused. Kings don't tend to like that."

"—as Thorn Drumheller."

Faster than Willow could follow, she drew her sword. With each of those three words, she tapped him on his shoulder with the flat of her blade. Right, left, right, same as for a knightly investiture.

"You're both demented," Willow told them.

"Takes one to know," was Madmartigan's riposte.

These two fenced as fiercely with words as blades, with a skill that put even their brownie companions to shame—and that was no mean feat. In such verbal jousts, they rarely gave quarter and while Willow tried his best to match them—even holding his own on occasion—sometimes his only recourse was to simply disengage.

"Enough of this foolishness and enough of *you*," he said with finality. "I am going to Elora Danan and then I am going home and if I never see the pair of you again I swear it'll be too soon!"

He didn't mean it, of course, but that's the trouble with words spoken in haste and in heat, they come back to haunt you.

Elora's apartments were located in the Royal tower, the core of the castle, about which all its component fortifications were arrayed, in an expanding set of rough circles. The rooms were sumptuously appointed, but it was still impossible to disguise the fact that Tir Asleen was first and foremost a military strong-hold. In most cases, the walls were thicker than a Daikini was tall, the doors massive constructs of wood and iron, windows few and far between and placed more for the convenience of snipers than their view.

Elora, Madmartigan, and Sorsha shared an entire floor, right below the Royal suites, their bedroom next to hers.

"Halt, stand and deliver," he heard as he stepped across the threshold. A moment later, for emphasis, he felt the sting of a brownie arrow in his backside.

"That's not nice," he said, as sternly yet softly as he dared, be-cause he didn't want to wake Elora. The room was a clutter, though most of the toys and bric-a-brac were for show, since she was still far too young to use them. At last report, she'd just about mastered the art of walking. Her bed appeared far too large for her, the child almost lost beneath the jumbled mounds of her down comforter and pillows and stuffed animals. There was an unusual amount of light, so much so that Willow's MageSight was unnecessary, some of it was cast by the heaped embers in the hearth behind the fireplace screen; the rest came from stars and moon above, shining through a large, circular glass skylight that had been cut into the ceiling to give the cham-ber the airy aspect of a solar. Willow didn't see much in the way of furniture, but the floor bore a number of plush rugs; a sensible arrangement where a toddler was concerned, nothing to run into and a fair cushion beneath her whenever she fell.

To the casual eye, the room was otherwise empty and un-guarded. The challenge and his sore backside most eloquently proved different.

"Careless big fella, heh," said a tiny voice from behind, and

Rool strode stiff-legged into view, the whole of the brownie's body nearly masked by the weave of the carpet.

"In a rowdy humor tonight, are we?" Willow wondered.

"Looks same as always," offered another voice, this from a brownie wearing the helm and cloak of a slain mouse. "Talks different, though. Putting on airs, like some dandy from Court, looking to better himself by making nice with Elora Danan. Could be an impostor."

Willow decided he'd just reached the end of his patience with this dream. He snapped his fingers and was rewarded by a pair of outraged squawks from the brownies as a pair of fiery sparks burst beneath them, leaving tiny pops of thunder in their wake and the smell of burning air, as a stroke of lightning does in a summer thunderstorm.

"Trust me," he told them, in a tone that made clear he wasn't joking anymore, "I'm me."

"Could have simply *said* so," came from Rool.

"I'm tired. It's late. I'd like my spirit to be back home with the rest of me, enjoying a good night's sleep, is that so much to ask?"

The brownies looked at each other as though he was talking crazy, and said as much, altogether to themselves, ignoring him completely. Rool's approach was pragmatic; the posturing was left to Franjean.

Willow took advantage of their disputations to cross to the bed for a closer look at his goddaughter. In many ways, she was still one of the most beautiful things he'd ever seen, on a par with his own children. Her hair was spun gold, shot through with strands of fire that might well have come from Sorsha's own head. She was plump, but babies were supposed to be so at her age, giving the impression that her body was little more than an arrangement of circles pinned together. Round head, round belly, round arms, round legs. There was an air of peace about her, of an innocence and freshness that had nothing to do with her age. She was someone whose natural state was a smile, of delight and wonder at the world arrayed before her. It was a warm and welcoming room, the kind where it would be easy to spend some time; by her sheer presence, Elora Danan made this ancient fortress a happier place. And all within, better folk.

"Now, lass," Willow muttered, "if your charms can only work as well on the stiff-necked, stone-skulled rulers of the Realms Beyond, there may well be some hope for the world."

His foot bumped something on the floor and he reached down to recover a ball. It fit comfortably in his hand, and on an impulse, he gave it a spin, balancing it on his outstretched forefinger, thinking while it turned of what the dragon had told him. He could still feel the aftertaste of the terror of those moments, but it was fast fading before his growing fascination with this new way of looking at the world. He stopped the ball, arbitrarily labeling the place where his fingertip rested as Tir Asleen. Then he turned the ball right around in his grasp to the point opposite; he put his thumb there and called it Angwyn, and yearned to journey from one to the other.

Never happen, of course. Not anywhile soon. Too many responsibilities at home. Yet Nelwyns were a long-lived people, and in next to no time, the children would be grown. Perhaps then.

"Thought you weren't coming, big fella." Rool again, having scrambled lithely to a perch on Elora's bedstead.

"Everyone says that," he noted as he set the ball aside, with its fellows.

"Seems sensible enough, since here you are."

"It's a dream. I'm at home, Rool, asleep in my own bed. Trust me on that."

"If you say so."

"Me," Franjean said, "I say it's *guilt*!" He would have emphasized the word with a shout, had not a stern "shush" from Rool and Willow both not dampened the volume in the barest nick of time. "Elora's celebration, it is, a year tomorrow since she came to Tir Asleen. Is Willow—her savior, her godfather—coming to be part of the festivities? He says not, *he* has to tend to his precious fields."

"I don't plant now, my family doesn't eat later."

"You're a wizard, Willow," said Rool, "you'll manage."

"Does he at least send a present for the little lovely," Franjean continued remorselessly, without missing a beat. "I don't *see* one!"

"That," agreed the other brownie, "is shameful."

"I have a present."

"With you?" From both of them in perfect unison.

He was about to say no when some inspiration prompted his hand toward the traveling pouch on his left hip. These were one of his earliest successes in learning the art and craft of magic; the apparent size of the bag bore no relationship whatsoever to the volume within, or how much it could carry. Food would stay fresh, water wouldn't spill; if something fit through the drawstring opening, it could be carried inside. All he had to do was think about what he needed and reach in; if it had been packed away, his hand would instantly find it.

Which is what happened. He thought of the bear and there it was.

Oddly enough, since his last recollection of the bear was leaving it on the table of his workshop. He took this as proof positive he was dreaming.

"She sleeping all right?" he asked as he smoothed the hair on the bear's head.

"Like a baby," said Rool.

"Dolt," said Franjean, "what d'you expect? She *is* a baby!"

"Why do you ask, Willow?"

"No reason, Rool." He held the bear up before him and looked it square in its crystal eyes. "Well, here we are, you and I, about to part company. Perhaps that's the purpose of these meanderings, to deliver in dreams what I'll fail to in flesh. Forgive me for that, Elora Danan," he said to the girl. "I don't know why I waited. No doubt because, since this gift came from my hands, I wanted it to *come* to you from my hands. No strangers between us. No distance.

"Let my bear stand in my stead, will that be acceptable, Highness? All that I would be, were I here, let him represent."

"Willow."

"Yes, Rool."

"Do you know what you're doing?"

"Yes, Rool."

"I don't think so. Look at yourself, wizard, you're glowing!"

"Bless my soul, so I am."

"You're not supposed to cast spells in here."

"Death Dog's *fangs*," hissed Franjean, "you're not supposed to be *able* to cast spells in here. There are protective wards set around this room thicker than the damnable *walls*!"

"Not my doing, not my power," was Willow's reply. "It's a resonance, a reflection of Elora's."

"Im*press*ive."

"Very, actually, Rool."

"Since when is she a sorceress," Franjean said, with more than a pinch of outrage, as if he should have been the very first to know.

"In the strict sense of the word, I don't think she is."

"Don't you know?"

Willow sighed. "Franjean, we're talking *prophecy* here. When was the last time you heard of an oracle being specific? No one's sure what she can do and it's not as if she's able yet to tell. Myself, I wonder if she's like the dragons, outside all the rules and structures that define the world. That would explain their interest in her."

"Never seen a dragon, Willow," and there was envy in Rool's voice.

"It was a wonder, even if it was out of my own imagination." Willow shook his head, to bring his focus back to the moment at hand. "As for Elora Danan, I'm fairly sure wards are no use against her, nor are spells on her, she possesses a kind of natural immunity."

"If that's so," Franjean challenged sarcastically, "then how could Witch Queen Bavmorda have hoped to destroy her with the Rite of Oblivion, eh?"

"She was a baby, Franjean," was Willow's sensible reply. "Power's useless without the knowledge to properly wield it."

"She's still a baby," Rool said.

"Bavmorda's dead. And we've spent the best part of the year since exterminating her Death Dogs."

"And that leaves all the world brimming with sweetness and light? Including the trolls and ghouls and goblins and gaunts and things too foul to even own names?"

The brownie had a point.

"That's not a problem, Rool. I think I have added my knowledge to her strength, through my bear," he said with a sudden, shy smile, pleased at the rush of inspiration. "That should make her defenses as comprehensive and resilient now as when she'll be full-grown. Not much use against a steel knife, I'll grant you—that will have to be Madmartigan and Sorsha's lookout—but pure hell for a magic one. Satisfied?"

She stirred, and he feared he'd woken her, but all she did was shift toward her back in such a way that her arms flopped open on either side of her. She was all twisted up in nightgown and comforter, one bare leg exposed to the evening chill. The hearth was doing its valiant best, but even this late in the spring the nights remained significantly colder than the days; there'd be frost on the breaths of those sentries standing watch outside. Willow tucked the bear snug under the crook of the arm nearest him. As if that had been all she was waiting for, Elora rolled suddenly toward him, wrapping both arms about the bear and drawing her legs together, knees up, to ensure the stuffed animal's safe imprisonment. Her gown was a proper tangle, there was nothing he could do about it without surely waking her, so he contented himself with rearranging the covers. So taken was he with the baby's charm, that he missed a hurried conference between the brownies, in which they decided there was no way they were letting him travel home alone, in so obviously demented a state. They were inside his traveling pouch before he knew what they were about, and try as he might to get them out, they remained well and truly hidden.

"Suit yourselves, then," he told them. "I'm done here."

Not quite. There was one final obligation, as easily and happily fulfilled with Elora as with his own. He smoothed her hair from her brow and gave her a kiss and a wish for the sweetest of dreams, the happiest of tomorrows, and that was that.

The next he knew, it was morning. He woke with a start, beside his wife, where he'd known he'd been all the night through.

He was so thankful for that realization that it was a long few moments before his mind registered what his eyes beheld from the first, a pair of brownies sitting side by side at the foot of his bed.

After that, giving the lie to the still loveliness of the sunrise, with mist curling off the riverfront, the field cast in azure shades accented by the merest hint of morning rose, the quiet broken by an intermittent birdsong, the whole of the dawn as prosaic and normal as could be, he learned that while he'd slept . . .

. . . the world as he'd known it had come to its end.

CHAPTER 1

THE EAGLES TOLD THEM THE RIDER WAS CLOSE.

Thorn didn't see.

The brownies were nervous enough around the Tall Folk in their own country, but there at least they had a wealth of trees and undergrowth to mask their presence. Here, in the shadow of the great mountain range that split this continent from top to bottom, there was nothing but prairie grassland from slopes to horizon. They wanted to hide and told Thorn so, repeatedly, each more loudly and insistent than the other, volleying protests and epithets back and forth as if it was a game of tennis.

Thorn didn't hear.

The animal's shod hooves struck in a leaden cadence, her every step bespeaking a fatigue sunk deep into her bones.

She'd run as far and fast as she was able, but she was done. The scent of fear was strong from her, its cause brutally clear from the fresh wounds that scarred her flanks and haunch. A Daikini warrior sat atop her back, his own boots scored by the same claws that had slashed his mount. The parade-ground perfection of tack and armor was dulled by a thickening coat of trail dust, the curve of back and shoulders giving eloquent evidence of the toll this journey had taken.

In basic form, he looked much the same as Thorn himself, though like all his race he stood better than twice the Nelwyn's size, mostly in the legs. As a race, Daikinis considered themselves lords of the earth, and didn't share well with those—like Nelwyns and the far smaller brownies—who'd come before.

Both bow and blade were slung loose, close at hand for quick and easy use. The young man's eyes never rested, scanning the way ahead as intensely as his every other sense did the trail behind; every so often he would reach forward to stroke a hand along his mare's sweat-stained neck, then give her powerful shoulder a reassuring pat. She needed rest, as did he; even this stumble-footed pace was more than she could long maintain. Stark from both horse and rider was the certain knowledge that wherever they stopped would be the site of their last stand. The trail they followed would bring them right to Thorn and his companions; the pace they maintained meant they'd reach them near nightfall.

Thorn didn't care.

His own boots cast puffs of dirt into the air about his feet as he made his way to the edge of the Scar. Dust, without any of the weight or consistency of proper earth, leached dry of moisture, of minerals, of life itself. Dull gray to the sight, powder to the touch, the crumbling detritus of a tomb, it cast a shadow film over eyes and tongue that tainted every sensation. Scrub weeds and tumbleweed marked the landscape; those seeds unlucky enough to put down roots found no substance, either to anchor or sustain them. Most were blown away by the first rough wind; the few that remained were ugly, stunted things, with little hope of lasting a season, much less beyond.

Before him, the continental divide formed an unassailable rampart stretching to the right and left as far as the eye could see.

Except for this place.

Until twelve years ago, a mountain stood here, paramount in the range. That awful night, as cataclysms and disasters raged across the whole of the Twelve Domains, it had simply been . . . destroyed.

Thorn had seen all manner of natural disasters and each time been awed by how quickly and tenaciously nature had rushed back to heal the wounds. Here, though, those normal rules seemed no longer to apply; everything and everyone that had lived within sight of the blast was gone, as though they'd never been, and nothing had stepped in since to fill the void.

"As with all the others," he said aloud, mainly to break the eerie silence, absently winding a length of braided beard around his right forefinger as he surveyed the desolation before him. "A whole world, I've wandered, to see such sights as this. One after the other, one by one by one, the smashed and broken places." Almost as though the devastation couldn't be believed, it wasn't real, unless seen with his own eyes. This was the last. As awful to behold as the first.

His first and dominant impression of the Scar was one of smoothness, as though a terrible God had sliced the mountain from its fellows as neatly as Thorn might a fresh-baked muffin from its tin, and then wantonly smashed it to bits. The ground within had been seared to bedrock, stripped of even the potential for new life, fused on top to glass, so that the scene most resembled a shallow bowl—although this one was miles across and easily a hundred feet deep. No dust settled within the rim, creating the impression that the crater was wiped neatly and properly clean each morning by some giant cloth. Whenever there were storms, the water that fell outside the Scar rushed away downhill, each drop of rain apparently desperate to find a more hospitable place to light. Looking within, however, Thorn couldn't see even a hint of liquid, where there should have been a lake reflecting the brilliant blue of the late-spring, late-morning sky.

There was a queer beauty to the place, that he had to admit. The dominant color was black, shot through with streams and reefs of darkling shades from the palette of some mad potter.

In his mind's eye, Thorn saw another field of primal desecration, this one set amidst rolling woodlands, a place once renowned for its beauty, forever ruined. The strength of its walls, the courage of its knights, the skill of its sorcerers, none of that saved the fabled Daikini fortress of Tir Asleen. The castle and its rulers embodied the hope of the world and it had been wiped away in a single instant.

There, a dozen years ago, Thorn hadn't approached as close as this. He'd stood at the head of the valley, staring with dulled eyes as though he himself had become one of the dead, in the faint and futile hope that each blink of his eyelids would somehow restore the glory that once was, and especially the lives of his lost friends.

The memory was ice in his heart, and he folded over on himself as though he'd been stabbed, lowering his forehead as he knelt until it touched the ground. He was glad he was alone, for such a grief as this should have no witnesses. Neither brownies nor eagles ever came near these blasted, broken places—Bastian and Anele wouldn't even overfly them—they had too much respect for the dead, and for the unknown force that had slain them. Thorn's face twisted as though he'd been struck a physical blow, but no tears fell; he'd wrung himself dry that first monstrous day before Tir Asleen. For all the time that had passed, and all he'd learned since, the wound remained as fresh and raw as ever.

Its sole legacy was a resonance that led him from one site to the next, with the same inexorable attraction of a compass needle for the pole. After the first few, and especially as he honed his innate talent as a wizard, the pattern of destruction had become clear. Each location was a place of Power, a crossroads where the ley lines of energy of the physical world intersected with their counterparts in the Realms Beyond, the domains of faery, home to the Veil Folk. As a consequence, the devastation had been as great in their lands, and the scars as deep. There as here, some looked on what happened as a natural occurrence, others as a mystical sign, still others as an act of war. Each party had its own opinion as to cause and reason, each had a favorite place to lay blame, with the net result that relations between the Twelve Domains—never comfortable on the best of days—went into a steep and precipitous decline. The passage of better than a decade since the Cataclysm without any further such incidents had substantially eased fears among the Daikinis, but most of the Veil Folk lived at a different pace. To them, the human span was little better than a mayfly's and the Cataclysm a flashpoint far too fresh in memory to be ignored.

Beyond the obvious—that a force of mind-numbing power had in a single, savage moment annihilated a score of locations across the whole of the world—nothing was known. Not the nature of the force, or its origin, or its purpose. The years since brought to Thorn the realization that surprisingly few were all that eager to learn any of those answers, as though doing so would call down the same doom, or worse, upon their own heads.

It was a choice Thorn himself faced at every site. He'd known from the start what was required of him, yet in each instance found himself holding back; he was no less reluctant today.

"No," he said, face still buried from the world, giving his voice the hollow sound of someone speaking in a box. "That's not right. I'm not reluctant. I'm afraid."

He stood, walked away from the Scar for a couple or three steps before coming to the end of that reflexive impulse and trailing to a stop.

"Is this it, then?" he asked himself. "Is this what I've come to, all the work and wandering, a dozen years on the road, in hiding—all for nothing? You saved the best for last, Peck," and he made the diminutive as cruel an insult as any who'd used it against him. "The resonances of the Cataclysm are as strong here as at Tir Asleen itself; if there are answers to be found, there's nowhere better."

The part of him labeled "Nelwyn common sense" wailed, *I don't want to be here, I want to go home!* To be told in turn, *But you* are *here. So what are you going to do about it?* Then, more cruelly, *And until this is done, you have no home.*

He bared his teeth. Nelwyns were built small, so went the tales of Creation told by all save Nelwyns, because the Great Givers passed them by, their attention always caught by those of more significance. The Nelwyn purpose in the scheme of things was to provide amusement to those more blessed. But Nelwyn spirits and Nelwyn hearts and Nelwyn minds bore little relation to the bodies that housed them. With every hand against them, in a world shaped for creatures many times their size, they took on the characteristics of the land they made their home. They were tough, they endured; above all, they adapted. When faced with a threat, they got out of the way. When they couldn't get out of the way, they fought, with a strength and tenacity that had to be respected. When they had to fight—man or God, this world or any of the others—they would find a way to overcome.

The Cataclysm had left its mark on Thorn as much as on the land. He was leaner than he'd been, his body toughened by un-counted miles of wandering across the whole face of the globe— which he knew now for fact *was* a globe. No need anymore for him to take the dragon's word for it. His skin was tight across his face, highlighting the shape of chin and jaw, giving him the as-pect of a Nelwyn better than twice his age. He'd let his hair grow, and beard as well, until all that could be seen of his face was a nose, strong cheekbones, and his eyes, and even they were set between a pair of magnificently wild brows. The beard he braided like his old teacher, the High Aldwyn, but the hair he'd chosen to style in the fashion of a Daikini warrior. Oddly, while the beard had grown in the color of dull silver, his hair had lost none of its youthful hue; if anything, it had grown more autum-nal over time, making it a rich auburn—red with mahogany highlights—where before it had been the other way round. He dressed like a wanderer, in whatever struck his fancy and his comfort from the markets of every continent.

It was his eyes that marked him most, though. The hazel he'd been born with had given way to green and from there to a blue that was mixed with gray. Like sky when his mood was fair, like fresh-forged steel when it was not. They were haunted eyes, that had seen too much. But that was only on the surface. Beneath, past where even Thorn cared to look on those rare occasions when he caught sight of his reflection, was something far harder and more dangerous. The part of him that had earned him his name.

Thorn anchored a stanchion deep into the earth, with a goodly length of line tied snug about it, looped around his waist and through a metal ring affixed to his belt. He donned well-worn buckskin gloves to protect his long, sensitive hands and tossed the rope over the edge. He wanted to hesitate, but knew that if he did, he'd find a chink in his resolve, worry at it like a rat until the whole edifice crumbled. Some fights couldn't be run from.

Part pathfinder, part stalking horse, came Sorsha's voice from memory, as clear as if she once more stood before him, *the warrior sent ahead of all the rest to charm an ambush out of hiding.*

"How wonderful for him," Thorn grumbled now, as he had then.

Putting his back to the Scar, he took tight hold of his line and stepped off the rim after it.

As soon as he touched bottom and disengaged his harness, a piece of rock caught his eye, hardly bigger than a thumbnail. He picked it up, rolled it a few moments between his palms, his eyes half-closed, senses cautiously aware as they built a picture of the stone within his mind.

Great age, he felt, and yet, as the world viewed such things, this particular peak had hardly been born. Young and fresh, its stark, sharp lines barely touched by sun and wind and water, there was strength to it and special pride. This was a place of *Power.*

For all the good that had done it.

There was a keening in the air, a mournful dissonance that might be wind, but he knew better, because he felt it from the stone in his hand. He thrust the pebble into a pocket of his vest and wandered deeper across the crater. Cautious steps at first, out of concern that the surface might prove as slippery as it looked, but that wariness quickly passed. Anyone watching would perceive neither rhyme nor reason to Thorn's progress. He'd walk one way, then another, pass stones by, pick one up, toss it aside, suddenly and inexplicably go back to one he'd skipped before to add it to the growing collection in his pouch.

His ramble was a revelation, as he continued to wander this boneyard of stone, collecting bits and pieces of the corpse. From outside, the surface appeared featureless, so like a household bowl in appearance he thought it would prove as clean in fact. However, while the mountain had been smashed to bits, it had been far from obliterated. Each step brought him another flash-fire image of every aspect of the peak's existence, from birth to sudden, early death. There was no consciousness, no *life*, as he understood the term, yet it had been as alive as he, rich in its own way with yearnings and desires.

When he was tired, he simply stopped and sat. He was hungry as well, he realized, his throat parched. The gleaming smooth surface of the Scar acted like a mirror, reflecting the heat at the same time as its dark color absorbed it, giving him a painful insight into what it must feel like to be on a blazing-hot griddle. He moistened his mouth with a swallow of water from his canteen, then took the edge off his growling stomach with a hunk of biscuit. His eyes were narrowed to slits, but that wasn't any real help; the glare beat right through his skin and set the underside of his skull to throbbing. Next time, he vowed with asperity, he'd remember his damn hat.

He popped another morsel into his mouth, and spat it out almost immediately, before he could properly bite down on it and shatter a tooth. It wasn't a piece of biscuit in his hand but one of the stones he'd gathered. As he held it his eyes rose and shifted sideways. Quickly, he was on his feet and hobbling as fast as his stunted legs could carry him toward a spot marked in the mountain's memory. He remembered as he went the old saw that Nelwyns weren't made for walking because they were meant to spend their days close to hearth and home; he'd always wondered why that had never been enough for him.

Should have been paying more attention to the present, not the past, as he put a wrong step on the slick surface and one foot skidded out from under him, stretching him full length hard enough to keep him lying there a good, long minute while he recovered his wits.

He was sore, mostly about the knees and forearms, which had borne the brunt of the impact, but otherwise unhurt as he pushed himself gingerly upright, until his body blocked the sunlight enough to cast the site into a fair semblance of shadow. Nothing happened when he held out the stone, or even when he placed it on the ground. It was a piece of debris, like all the rest around him.

Didn't look right, though. Not where it was, nor how it lay. He thought a moment, without the slightest notion of what was to come next, ignoring a faint hail shouted along the breeze over-head, until his left hand moved of its own volition; he couldn't help a small smile, because even the smallest and most inconspic-uous use of his power was a delight to him.

There were no fireworks, not the slightest tingle of energy, as his mouth pursed thoughtfully and his fingers turned the stone and moved it . . . *just so.*

He stroked the tips of his fingers across his lower lip and considered what he'd done. Almost immediately, a new impulse made him draw another pebble from the pouch. This one wasn't set beside the first, however, but about a hand-span dis-tant and off at a diagonal. The movement was like popping a brick from a dam; again and again, his hand returned to his pocket, placing one stone after the other on the ground before him.

When at last it was empty, he'd built a fair-sized pile.

"Interesting," he mused aloud. "I didn't think I'd gathered so many." As he spoke he reached out to fractionally adjust the alignment of one of the components.

"There," he said. "*That's* right."

It was, too, he felt it in his bones. He was looking at the moun-tain in small. The towering central spire, a sheer drop to the plain-sward side, with two subordinate ridges binding it to the range beyond, plus the cols that flowed off them; this was a proud and arrogant piece of creation, no easy conquest for the man foolish enough to try.

He looked around, aware once more of that wailing undertone of anguish he'd sensed earlier.

"If stones could cry . . ." He took a breath, let it out slowly, hearing a voice calling from the distance and paying it no mind.

"I'm sorry," he said to the cairn. "I wish I could undo what's been done."

A furious gust of energy from out of the heart of the mountains struck upward through the soles of his feet and rocked him back off his heels, hard enough to knock him flat; as he fell, senses reeling from this onslaught—a wild, almost incoherent mix of rage and betrayal—he wrapped his arms protectively about himself, like a boxer losing the ability to defend himself.

Thorn spat blood, watched it strike his miniature mountain and then be absorbed into the very stone. The fused earth beneath it began to bubble and boil, as though being eaten away by some ferocious acid, with secondary fissures radiating outward from his peak to mar more of its polished perfection. The cairn was no longer an accumulation of stones and pebbles; it was hardening visibly before his eyes, taking on the cohesion and solidity of the mountain it had once been even as it once more forged its link with the earth from which it had been raised. There was the taste of grit in his mouth, and as the tiny bits of pumice ground across his teeth, he felt a sudden flush of heat shoot through him from the soles of his feet, with such force that he was consumed before he could utter a sound. It wasn't pain, at least that resembled any he'd felt on those occasions when he'd been physically burned, but it was very nearly more than he could bear. He was sure he was glowing, that every object around him was either melting or bursting instantly to flame, because that had to be what was happening to him.

Hard on the heels of the incredible heat came a delicious chill, sinking to the heart of bones and soul from the outside in, locking him in form and place. There was a strange duality of perception, akin to what he felt when his InSight merged his consciousness with the eagles' to allow him to see the world through their eyes, an awareness that he retained the potential of movement while becoming ever more firmly rooted to this spot. He turned his head, his body following—moving not as it used to, through the articulation of his limbs, but seeming instead to flow. Parts of him would liquefy and recast themselves once more when he chose to come to rest. And if each time he looked a little different—an arm lost here, a leg impossibly stretched and bent, a face increasingly devoid of human features—that didn't matter. His essence remained true.

However, as he surveyed the stony boneyard, there was a form and structure to the landscape that he hadn't perceived before. His wish had been granted, as he realized he could now complete consciously what had been begun solely on instinct; there *was* a way to make amends and set things right. He could pick and choose among the broken remains, to gather the pieces and restore them in their proper sequence. It wouldn't be an easy task, rebuilding a mountain by hand, but he had no doubts he would be up to it. As for time, he sensed he was no longer bound by Nelwyn or even Veil Folk constraints. His span was mated to the world itself and measured its days on the same terms. An age to him would encompass the rise and fall of a continent, from the dawn of his kind to long past its sunset.

Even as these thoughts came to him (and that wasn't so very quickly, for his mind was resonating in tune to his body, casting aside all unnecessary memories and focusing solely on the task at hand) he caught sight of the next stone to add to his construction and began his glacial trek toward it.

With every breath he became more content. This was peace. This was fulfillment.

He felt a swash of air as something large passed close by overhead, the impact—very faintly felt—of tiny feet on his shoulders.

The next he knew, equally small fingers had grabbed a respectable handful of nose hair. The brownie tugged and Thorn popped back into his own head with an outraged yelp and a tremendous sneeze.

"Talking to you, sirrah," cried Franjean, brimful of an outrage to match the mountain's, before he could say a word.

"*Saving* you," echoed his companion, triumphantly brandishing his prize in one hand while holding on to Thorn's shirt with the other.

"Fool's errand, if ever there was one," Franjean finished, so close to Thorn's eye that his face filled the Nelwyn's vision even though his body didn't stand as high as many meadow flowers.

"Can we go, now, please?" Rool demanded, after a shallow nod of acknowledgment. "We really aren't welcome here."

"Hang on, Rool," cried Franjean, and then the eagles were upon them.

Two great sets of claws sank themselves deep through the fabric of padded vest, wool overshirt, and cotton shirt, closing firmly enough to hold him secure without doing any harm. Thorn felt the backwash of two powerful wings, a span that surpassed the height of a tall Daikini, and cried out as he was summarily yanked from the ground. It wasn't the physical separation that caused him pain—throughout his ordeal he'd felt like he was melting; in actuality his body hadn't changed shape in the slightest—but the severance of his psychic bond with the mountains.

"Careless," said Bastian, not bothering to hide his disdain as he muscled his limp burden skyward.

"A fledgling's mistake," sniffed his mate, Anele, holding guard position just off Bastian's left wing, a little behind and below, to catch whatever might fall should Thorn start struggling. "I expected better."

"Easy for you to say," protested Thorn feebly in his own defense.

"Speak when you remember how," Franjean told him from just outside his left ear.

"When you have something worth the saying." Rool, from his right.

Thorn couldn't think of anything, so he cast his awareness outward to join Anele, a far safer choice than distracting Bastian. As always, the view took his breath away. For those first moments he luxuriated in the caress of air across his skin—personalizing the sensations even though he knew they were really hers—

aware of every twitch and tickle that signified an adjustment of feathers and pinions as she soared. Though they hadn't risen all that high above the ground, the air was significantly cooler. The first time he'd merged senses with the raptors, it had been as great a shock as plunging into a winter stream; he'd broken the link immediately to lie shivering in a heap, his body tucked in tight to itself, terrified he'd never be able to take another breath because the one before had frozen him inside and out. Paradoxically, the sun lay across the eagle's russet-gold back like a quilt, a furnace without to complement the one within, stoked by Anele's heart, which sent blood racing through her body far faster than Thorn's did through his own.

"That wasn't very nice," Thorn grumped, stifling another sneeze as he was unceremoniously deposited on the ground close by their campsite, the clearing mostly shrouded in sunset shadows. He tried to stand but instead flailed uselessly with arms and legs, as though he'd forgotten how to use them. He moved like a baby at first, but each random gesture cast another line between spirit and flesh until—after what seemed an eternity, although it really wasn't very long at all—the wayward pieces of himself were once more bound tightly and properly together.

"Compared to what, may I ask?" came Franjean's arch riposte, mocking the manners of courtiers he'd seen in their journey.

"Tried to get your attention," Rool said, in a more pragmatic tone.

"Called until our voices broke."

"But did you listen?"

"Did you care?"

Then, in unison: "I think not!"

Thorn made a face. He'd seen goddesses with less hauteur than these diminutive creatures. They'd walked the world together, these brownies and he, and he had the inescapable feeling that he was still being taken on sufferance. Truth to tell, he was always more comfortable with the eagles; they were killers when they had to be, but they lacked the brownies' instinct for the verbal jugular. The eagles hadn't landed themselves but instead returned immediately to the air, beating quickly to altitude until they were lost from sight against the darkening eastward sky.

"I didn't hear," he told them all, voice to the brownies, mind-speech to the eagles.

"Too busy spirit dancing," scoffed Franjean.

"We could have left you, Drumheller," chided Rool.

"Should have."

"Madness enough that you go gallivanting into the heart of such an accursed place."

"Don't expect us to come save you again."

"I know it was hard—" Thorn began, but Rool cut him off.

"Sometimes, wizard, you know *nothing*," he said sharply. "About what is needful. And especially about what's hard."

Thorn nodded. "I ask your pardon, Rool," he said formally. "And yours, Franjean. I offer my apologies to you, and Anele and Bastian. This was wrong of me. It's one thing to risk my own life; I had no right to make you do the same."

"Find what you were looking for, did you?" asked Franjean with a practiced air of malicious glee.

He knew that was coming, and answered like a schoolboy before his headmaster, a sensation he thought he'd put behind him ages ago. "No," was his flat reply.

"Are we surprised?" The brownie threw up his hands in a too familiar gesture of exasperation.

"Franjean, I had to try."

"What, you refuse to believe the fire is hot until you're burning?"

"I know the fire's hot, but I need to learn the nature of whatever set it alight."

"You've looked for ten years and more, Drumheller. If you haven't learned by now, when?"

He had no answer and so made none, which only provoked an even more acerbic outburst from the brownie.

"What *is* the use, Drumheller, I ask you? Far be it from *us* to offer the slightest hint of criticism, O mighty wizard, or place the slightest impediment in the way of your quest, but is this to be the pattern of our lives? Are we fated to wander the Twelve Domains until we drop while you continue your compendium of the sites of the Cataclysm's greatest disasters?"

Franjean was right. His search had taken him across the face of the world, to lands and peoples he'd never dreamed of, yet he felt no closer to his answers today than when he set out. It was a realization that had been growing in him for a long time, with a bitterness that ate at his insides like an acid poison—that he had doubly failed, not only to save those he loved, but also to avenge them.

"Are you quite finished?" he demanded.

"Will you ever be?"

Rool spoke up. "This isn't the time, Franjean." There was a different shading to his voice, as though something had tripped an alarm in his head. Thorn caught the shift and his own focus sharpened accordingly; Franjean didn't.

"Will it ever be?" Franjean snapped in return.

Over the years Franjean had grown into a veritable peacock, with nary a stitch out of place regardless of circumstance; he always managed to convey the sense that his outfits had been constructed that very morning, for someone who lived on the cutting edge of fashion. Thorn could never decide which amazed him more: the sheer variety of the brownie's designs or how he managed to come up with them in the middle of nowhere.

Rool, by contrast, was the more practical of the pair, possessing a sobriety of manner that was echoed in the style of his clothes, which were so comfortably broken in they seemed like they'd be part of him forever. In this instance, buckskin mainly, trousers and pullover tunic, with hard-soled boots that tied snug to the leg at the knee. Thickly woven cotton shirt beneath the tunic and an ankle-length canvas coat that swirled out from his body like a cloak when he walked, to protect him from the evening chill.

"The *Daikini*," Rool reminded his companion, with an edge to his tone that matched the keenness of the blades he wore at his belt. There was no ornamentation to him; his hair was far longer than Franjean's, the color of richly polished cherrywood, falling past his backside, swept straight from the face and gathered in a leather sleeve that was anchored at the base of the neck by a leather clip chased with drops of silver that Thorn had made him.

"What Daikini?" Thorn asked.

Franjean cocked a dismissive eyebrow. "The one we've been screaming at you about all the livelong day." He rounded on Rool. "Should have scared the brute away ourselves! Make that stupid Daikini's stupid horse think it wandered into the land of angry hornets, *hah*!"

"If they could have passed us by," Rool told him, "they would have. They've no more liking for this accursed place than we do." Then, to Thorn: "This is someone I think you should see, Drumheller."

"As you wish."

There was no ease to his movements as he followed the brownies through the scrub brush and tumbleweed. The memory of his struggle with the mountains had sunk past thought and deep into his bones; he couldn't cast himself loose of the images, which in their turn lashed him with the sting of a sorrow so awful he had no words for it. The mountains had left their mark on him, a hole straight through his own heart to match the one through theirs.

The Daikini had chosen as good a defensive position as could be managed on this barren, broken land, on the steepest slope with a fair rise of rocks to his back. He'd stripped a good-sized clearing—to give him a broad and deep field of fire—and used the gathered tinder for an impressive fire to warm his bones and give him light to see by.

Thorn's InSight revealed a wandering zephyr, a ghost of a breeze, so faint it barely tickled the distant grass, thrown into turmoil as it came close by the violent updrafts of the blazing campfire. The Daikini slumped on the far side of the flames probably wasn't even aware of it, yet to Thorn it was like sitting ringside for a fierce back-alley brawl. The zephyr seemed aware of his sympathy, as it swirled up on him from behind to stroke him top to toe; he had to clench his teeth to keep from laughing at its touch and was certain the struggle flashed across his face like an alarm beacon.

Yet the Daikini didn't notice. All remained still.

The man's horse snuffled, shifting from one hobbled hoof to the next, not quite nervous but no longer wholly calm. Instinct told the mare she should be somewhere else, but she was too worn-out to care. Moreover, in the recent past she'd taken a nasty wound from which she'd never truly recovered. A glance told Thorn all he needed to know. Death Dogs. They carried no poison, but their bites were ferociously septic; if they drew your blood, you were sure to sicken from it. All too often, that infection killed. He could smell their poison within her, even though she'd fought it to the point where it now lay dormant. This night's rest was welcome, but while she might manage a plodding walk in the morning, the first decent, sustained run would be the end of her. She knew that, too.

He turned back to the zephyr, but that little wind was too faint and fickle to be of any real use. Wouldn't matter anyway; if Death Dogs were coming for them, it would be from dead downwind, following the scent of their prey.

"Deserves it, he does, that's what I say," Franjean said in his ear, without bothering to hide his disdain.

"So quick to condemn?" Thorn replied, his own voice softer than the zephyr's, pitching his words around to the brownie hunkered below the curve of his head.

"To fight a pack of Death Dogs and not expect them to follow? Too stupid to live, y'ask me." A dismissal emphasized by the flick of delicately laced cuffs from silk-soft doeskin sleeves.

"Death Dogs, you say?"

"Obvious from the cut of the wounds," Rool said quietly, "if not the stench of their poison." His two swords were carved from the fangs of a Death Dog they'd slain, and in among the tribal tattoos that decorated his face and torso were a set of scars left by that battle. He'd been thrown from the neck of one hound and another had taken a snap at him in midair, breaking skin and bones with a snaggletooth fang that came within a hair of ending his life altogether. The fact that Rool could still walk at all, much less with his old grace and ease, was due solely to the Nelwyn's talents as a healer.

"Leftovers from the old days, perhaps?" Thorn wondered. "A long way from home, if so."

"As are we," Franjean retorted.

"I'll keep watch," Rool volunteered, and was gone before the sound of his words had faded, skirting the periphery of the firelight as he made his way toward a higher perch on the far side of the clearing.

"I thought we were done with them," Thorn mused. "That those few who survived Bavmorda were long slain." From all accounts, that hunt had been a brutal, bloody business, and while he had no love for those hell-touched beasts, he was also glad he'd had no part in their extermination.

"Evidently not."

"Might just be a rogue band of wanderers."

"Like us, you mean, wizard?"

"Except, in all these years, in all our travels, we've seen no evidence of them before now."

"Drumheller—this land has Daikini, like our own. They ride horses, they herd livestock, they farm crops, just like our own. Some of them, they call the Veil Folk by different names, but Cherlindrea's scattered her groves across this part of the world, same as she did across our own. With so much else in common between us, why not Death Dogs? And if they *are* here, I for one wish to be someplace else."

"You're too harsh on the boy, Franjean. He knows they're following. Look at his choice of campsite; he's defended himself as best he can."

"He's asleep, isn't he?"

"He's human. Subject to human frailties."

"True enough there, Drumheller." A huge and mocking grin split Franjean's face. "Some warrior, *ha!* Didn't sense brownie fingers twist his hair to tangles or pick his purses clean."

They were remarkable thieves, he'd discovered that right at the start, with skills to shame magpies and pack rats both; if something could be carried, it could be stolen, and what they could carry often bore no relationship to their diminutive stature. In that regard, they were as much a surprise as Nelwyns.

"Find anything of interest?"

"Scraping of field rations," was the quick reply. "More for horse than man. Him, he's been living off the land."

"Lean pickings, then, if our own experience is anything to go by."

"No ease with letters."

"How so?"

"Nothing to write with, nothing to write on." A sharp contrast to Thorn himself, who was always scribbling in a dog-eared notebook. He'd taught the brownies during their travels, only to realize too late that he'd provided them with another means of expression, which they enthusiastically put to a use that was as eloquent as it was outrageous. They had as little respect for property as for person and many were the walls, and reputations, that had suffered for it. "Straight-ahead sort of man," Franjean continued, "what he sees, is, an' there's the end to't. Much like you."

"I'll take that as a compliment, thank you."

"As you like. See the device on his coat? He's sworn to somebody's service."

"The King in Angwyn." Thorn nodded. "Another wanderer, then, far from home."

"Oh joy, that we have so much in common."

Thorn looked away from the fire and the mountains. "Angwyn's mainly south from here, and west. It's never had a presence in these parts, the few settlements don't acknowledge its sovereignty. What's he doing here?"

"Ask him, why don't you?"

"Franjean, you think he's following us." The brownie neither spoke nor gestured in response; he didn't need to. His certainty was as rock solid as the ground beneath their feet.

"Drumheller." There wasn't the slightest attempt to leaven the full measure of scorn heaped onto that single word. "We're here, he's here, the Death Dogs are here. Coincidence? I think not."

"Will the pair of you be *silent*!" cried Rool, returning hurriedly from his scouting post on the far fire of the encampment. "Wood of the Maker, *I* can hear you, that wreck and ruin of a horse can hear you, the *Daikini* can hear you—except he's too ignorant to comprehend it and far too happy in his dreams. Damnation, Franjean, why do you always have to make a speech?" His friend lifted his eyebrows most eloquently, as if to say, *Look who's talking?* "You're not impressing anyone, we've heard it before, you're only going to make matters worse, can't you just say what's what and have done with it?"

Franjean continued as if no one else had said a word. He liked his dialogue and was determined to speak it through to the end.

"A pair of fools, that's you," he finished in Thorn's face. "The one cleaving to the other, a toss to tell which is the greater."

Thorn knew better than to press the point until some time had passed, enough for passions to cool. It wasn't the first time the brownies—one or both—had gotten upset with him; he'd long ago realized that the size of their bodies was no limitation to the magnitude of their emotions. Quite the opposite in fact.

"The eagles are quiet," he noted, taking temporary refuge in a discreet change of subject.

"The eagles don't want to give anything away," Rool told him. "These Death Dogs don't just follow their noses."

"What do you mean?"

"It isn't a wild pack, Drumheller. They move with unnatural purpose. They've been trained. They're being led."

"By two legs or four?" he asked, using the eagles' own terms.

"Bastian, he's not sure. Him and Anele, they're staying *very* high unless things here turn bloody."

"Is the pack closing?"

"Not sure of that, either. Strikes me, though, that these beasties are as patient as they are stubborn, holding off maybe until they're all gathered together."

"*Very* well trained, then. Why are they after the Daikini?"

"Who says they are? There's just the one path."

Thorn tweaked the side of his mouth. Point to the Wee Folk, yet again.

"The mare can't defend herself," he said.

"That's the way of it sometimes." Bastian's voice sounded quietly in Thorn's head. "Those who cannot fight and cannot flee . . ."

"She deserves better," was his reply in kind, silent to all save the eagles.

"So do we all," agreed Bastian. "How often are such entreaties granted?"

"Her lucky night, then."

"That is *so* rude," declaimed Franjean.

"Bastian called me," Thorn tried to explain.

"It's rude to leave us out. If those poseur pigeons—"

"Say that to their face."

"—want to talk to you"—he wasn't fazed in the slightest by Thorn's challenge, any more than he was by the eagles' beaks and claws—"they can fly right down and open their big beaks like decent folk. You don't see *us* using mindspeak."

No, Thorn thought, but thankfully kept his mouth shut, *you're too much in love with the sound of your own voices. Mindspeech is too private, there'd be no audience for your wit.*

He sensed no direct awareness of the Death Dogs but knew that meant nothing. They were bred to hide themselves from adepts of any kind—woodsmen, warriors, and magi. That, and their unbelievable ferocity, was what made them such fearsome hunters.

"The Daikini has to be warned," he told his companions, and stepped clear of the crack in the rocks that had been his hiding place. Though out of habit he moved as silently as he knew how, the moment Thorn stirred, the Daikini was out of his bedroll and into a combat crouch, drawn saber at full extension. It was a handsome blade, Thorn saw that right off, but as untested as the man who held it, without even the faintest taste of blood along its curved edge. Same went for the knife, at least as far as battle was concerned; it had slaughtered its share of dinner over time.

"Stay your distance," the Daikini challenged.

"You're being followed." Thorn overrode his words, his arms open, hands visible, to reassure the warrior that he meant no harm.

"Them damn wolves again." The man rose to his full height. Thorn hated that; it guaranteed that even the most casual conversation would give him a cricked neck. He'd been assessed as a potential danger and dismissed, the warrior turning his focus to the preeminent threat. "Took care of 'em the first time, do the same again."

As he spoke, the Daikini gathered up his crossbow; the weapon was built for cavalry use, an artful blend of power and portability. He braced it against one palm and pushed the cocking lever to draw its string to full extension, before nocking a wedge-shaped broadhead bolt into place. The feathers would make the projectile spin as it shot through the air so it would strike its target like a corkscrew, allowing the barbed triple head to do the worst possible damage.

As he worked, the Daikini shot Thorn a sideways glance, followed by a chuckle rich with self-mockery.

"Damn me," he said, "ain't it always the way? From yer trail, small steps an' all, figured yeh was some young'un, got cut loose from the family. Figured maybe them damn wolves done fer yer folks, figured I'd get ta yeh first. But yer no kid a'tall, are yeh, graybeard?"

"Not for a good while. I'm sorry."

"Not to worry, little fella," the Daikini told him, with a confident wave of his bow. "One good hit's all this lovey needs. Broadhead bolt don't kill right off, it'll sure make the mark wish it had."

All well and good, was Thorn's answering thought, *assuming you get that hit. And assuming the Death Dog bothers to even notice.* They didn't live as normal creatures and, Thorn knew from brute experience, in no way died as them.

"Ones I tangled with, figured 'em f'r outriders, like," the Daikini continued. "They were proper raiders, 'steada dumb beasties, I'd call 'em scouts. One caught my girl a wicked slash across the rump." He patted his left leg. "Damn near got me in the bargain. Pretty sure I did for him with a bolt, pretty sure I did for

'em both, but my girl she din't want ta stick about ta make
Put the frighteners into her, they did, never seen an anima'
fast, all I could do to keep my seat. Bin walkin' 'er slow,
make up for it. Got my doubts, though. Think she's b

Not quite, thought Thorn, *she's stronger than you k* *she's
on the edge.*

Aloud, he said, "They aren't wolves."

He thought of casting wards but didn't s   nse. The
hounds would simply wriggle through the   the energy
fields. Or worse, turn out to be immune.   both happen.

"Are they coming?" he heard from R   mpanied by the
click of fang swords being drawn from   bbards.

Thorn didn't reply, though he'   and to forestall further questions. In memory was the   f the Death Dogs he'd
killed; he tucked it around his sp   ng on the essence of the
beasts in the same way he v   coat, dimly aware of the
Daikini losing his own balar   mbling away in startlement
as a roiling cry burbled fr   ewhere below the bottom of
Thorn's throat. The Nelv   't need a mirror to know that his
eyes were glowing,   hey'd turned a milky amber. He
knew it was illusion   still couldn't help reflexively tucking
his tongue back in   uth as his teeth appeared suddenly to
grow much long   whole lot sharper; in concert, he flexed
fingers that se   end now in wicked claws. His heart quick-
ened to a dr   pace—this, regrettably, no fantasy—and felt
every scra   about him, arrayed in his mind's eye as portions at   ast.

Wit   jerky motions—as though the commands were
bein   to a wholly different body—he described a circle,
rig   e he stood, surveying the campsite. The Daikini was
s   ng to his feet, bow leveled, but Thorn ignored him as
           nd filled with a score and more of ways to slaughter him.
It   asn't a physical transformation, but a spiritual one. It
wouldn't help him detect the hounds; instead, it allowed him
for this brief while to think and feel as they did, to view the
world through their eyes and as a consequence perhaps antici-
pate their actions.

The moon was occluded behind a scudding line of clouds, turning the landscape light and dark in a random sequence, blurring further the distinction between what was and was not. This was the time, he knew; the hour was right, the sky was right, the energies were right.

With a wrench, Thorn tore himself loose from his trance, tasting copper as he spoke from a slice taken out of the inside of his cheek by teeth that his thoughts were trying to manipulate as though they were in the mouth of a beast.

"They're here," he croaked, using that knowledge as a goad to bully himself into motion. He scrambled around the fire, making for the Daikini's mare, cursing the fact his stunted legs forced him to take a score of frantic, waddling steps where the Daikini could have been there in two.

He'd barely begun when the poor animal shrieked in terror and pain, but mostly, he realized, defiance, and he heard a solid thud as her rear hooves struck home. Knew in that moment, as well, that it had been her hooves that had done the damage during the initial encounter, not her rider's well-intentioned bow shots.

A Death Dog sprang into view, charging straight up the slope, announcing its attack with the gobbling snarl that was their trademark. Part of the Daikini's equipment was a scabbard of short spears; Thorn pulled one free, slamming the butt home against the earth as he'd seen soldiers do in the face of an enemy charge and used his own body to brace it in place. The hound twisted desperately in midair, bending itself worse than any cat, in gyrations that should have been impossible for any creature with a skeleton, and Thorn was swept by the sick surety that it would dodge him.

Bastian stooped right then, throwing his wings wide to pull out of a tremendous dive; they struck the air with a resounding slap that Thorn felt as much as heard. It always amazed him that any living creature, even the eagles, could fall so far and fast and still survive. At the same time, Bastian lashed out at the dog with his claws. Not a fatal contact, the lunge was mostly to get the creature's attention.

It worked. The Death Dog took a fatal snap at the attacker from above, even as Bastian muscled himself safely out of reach. A moment later, as it realized its mistake, it impaled itself on Thorn's spear.

The beast still had life enough in it to make a try for Thorn, but he was already pitching his spear sideways, and the Death Dog with it into the heart of the bonfire.

Across the way, the Daikini put a bolt into the breast of another, the force of the impact tumbling the beast onto its forelegs. Thorn was there before it could rise again, to hammer the point of another spear through its skull.

"Your sword," he bellowed to the Daikini. "Sever the head!" He wanted to tell the man to hurry, but it turned out there was no need. With a two-handed strike, the deed was done. The trooper's blade had taken its first life.

A Great Hunt numbered thirteen. Thorn prayed they didn't face that many; if they did, they had no chance. Two more exploded out of the darkness while he raced toward his own bedroll. He heard the *tunk* of the Daikini's bow, followed by the *kilk-klatch* of the string being cocked, and allowed himself a small marvel at the young man's poise. He stood his ground, he fought as he'd been trained, with a speed and accuracy that would do many veterans proud.

Something bowled him over from behind, and he reflexively tucked arms and legs and head tight to his body, taking on the aspect of a hedgehog to roll like a ball before the Death Dog's onslaught. He managed to catch it by the fur below the knob of its jaw, where his arms could hold its fangs clear of him. Its teeth sounded like metal as they crashed together, while it scrabbled for purchase with hind legs on the ground and forelegs on his tunic; its breath made him gag, its spittle burning like acid as it sprayed across his face. The creature was so intent on him that it didn't notice Rool working his way over the crown of its head until the brownie reared back, fang swords in both hands, to plunge them into its eyes.

Maimed, the Death Dog sent everyone flying, lashing out in its frenzy even at its pack mates. Thorn's questing hands found his own sword and brought it around to thrust it to the hilt down the shrieking hound's throat.

He'd lost count of how many they'd killed. The battle was so fierce, and desperate, he hardly had time to think, certainly none to plan. Every act, every move, every response had to flow from the one before, the parry that blocked one Death Dog becoming the lunge that slew another. Here and now, his size proved an invaluable asset; he met the pack on its own level, able to thrust straight-on where the Daikini always had to stab downward. His short, strong arms could maneuver more quickly than the much larger man, and he was a far more compact target.

A yowl to the side announced one he'd missed, as it collapsed onto its haunches with a severed hamstring. He didn't need to see the brownies to know they'd saved him yet again, but knew as well he'd be hearing about it the rest of his days.

He used his sword to finish the job, then had to scramble for his life as the Daikini's mare reared so high over the brambles she had been tethered to that she lost her balance and crashed full-length onto her side. It was as though a mad painter had gone to work on her coat, she was splashed all over with blood, no color to the image, none to the entire scene, only blotches and smears of glistening indigo under the moon's unblinking glow. There were two Death Dogs on her, one at the neck, the other scrambling for her belly to disembowel her. She'd made a magnificent effort for her life and it would count for nothing.

Thorn spun himself full circle to build up speed and let fly with his sword. He would have preferred another revolution or two for better effect, but the mare didn't have the time. The gleaming blade appeared to leave a trail through the air, a silver streak to match the light falling from above, the throw as straight and true as any javelin.

It missed. The Death Dog saw it coming and got out of the way. Then it had to scramble as the mare lashed out with every leg, snap-arching her back like an acrobat to regain her feet. The dog trying for her throat was taken by surprise—like Thorn, it hadn't thought the mare had such resistance left in her—and found itself pitched into the air.

This time the eagles didn't pull away from their attack. Bastian struck with the force of a battering ram, full to its spine, raking the Death Dog open to the bone. The creature let loose a horrible shriek as it found itself caught in midair and tossed even higher, spinning a lazy little circle to expose its belly. It knew what was coming, but there was nothing it could do. Nothing below its shoulders worked anymore. Thorn knew from a glance that it was dying; the fiery structures of its life force had been savaged as cruelly as its flesh. The eagles took no chances. The Nelwyn had his perceptions of death, they had theirs, they knew which to trust best. Anele stooped as quickly, as powerfully, as her mate, her own claws savaging the Death Dog from breast to hip, doing to it what had been intended for the mare. She ripped out its heart and cast it on the fire.

It was a magnificent sight; Thorn couldn't help watching. An almost fatal mistake. The hounds he'd missed came looking for retribution. The Daikini had problems of his own, he'd lost bow and sword and spears, he was fending off a pair of attackers with a battle-ax whose haft had broken. There was no sign of the brownies, but that came as no surprise. With all the bodies charging hither and yon, they'd go to ground until it was safe; the peril of being *too* small. The eagles weren't in view, either, probably climbing back to altitude. Which left him alone.

He was close by the fire. He scooped up a brand, using a scrap of concentration to shunt the flames to the end of the wood and fan them to peak intensity. The Death Dog didn't mind, it actually seemed to appreciate the challenge. He wove the torch back and forth to keep the beast at a distance. It dodged the flames easily, once or twice offering a perfunctory snap of the teeth, but it wasn't trying to get him. Merely hold his interest.

It was as though Thorn's realization was a cue. The dogs facing the Daikini made swift, twisting, diving moves, using all their fabled quickness and guile; one went for his throat, the other began racing full tilt for Thorn. The Daikini reacted with equally impressive speed. His foot booted the one trying for him, and with that same movement he threw himself after the other, extending his lanky form full-length, casting the ax in a long, overhand sweep that buried its head deep in the loamy soil. All he'd managed for his effort was to crop the tip of the hound's tail. By so doing, he'd left himself wholly open to an attack.

Thorn couldn't worry about that, he had problems enough. He charged a breath with a streamer of Power, huffed it down the length of his torch, and flames exploded outward from the burning tip. This, his Death Dogs hadn't expected. One of them backpedaled furiously, right into its charging fellow, the collision sending the pair of them into a tumble of legs and fangs. They recovered almost instantly and immediately took up the chase, for Thorn was on the run, as fast as he could manage. Out of the campsite and across the boulder-strewn field. The ground sloped slightly upward and was furrowed in a random, messy pattern. A Daikini—or the Death Dogs—could streak right over the uneven terrain and hardly be slowed; not so, the Nelwyn. His slim lead vanished with every step.

His advantage was that he hadn't far to go.

At that, it was a near thing.

The mountains sensed his approach. They wanted him still, more than ever. He was counting on that.

He fed more Power to the fire, until his torch blazed so brightly in his grasp he had to narrow his eyes to slits to avoid being blinded. Another portion of Power he used to mask this from the Death Dogs. Only a half-dozen steps to the edge of the crater. He imagined he could feel their breath on his neck and then it wasn't imagination any longer; they were on him.

He spun in his tracks and pulled the "hood" that hid his torchlight, flashing the solar radiance full in the Death Dogs' slavering faces. At the same time his next step hit empty air; he'd reached the Scar.

He let himself go and the torch as well, thrusting out his hands to grab for purchase as he crashed down against the crater wall. The Death Dogs couldn't see and were following so close behind, they were so bound up in the chase, there was no chance to notice how he'd deceived them. Even if they had, there was nothing to be done about it.

They'd been pushing themselves to the limit; their leap took them a fair ways beyond him, which in turn meant a fair fall to the steep slope of the crater. They landed well, and he knew they'd be after him again the moment their feet touched the ground. His hope was that they'd have a hard time finding any sort of purchase on the wall.

He needn't have worried.

He hadn't forgotten the other forces at play here; he simply hadn't been sure they'd take an interest. But witchlights began flickering beneath the glassy surface even before the Death Dogs landed, different hues, darker textures than the ones he remembered going after him. Those had been desire, these were hate. The mountains recognized a resonance of the Power that had maimed them years before and took the opportunity to strike back with all their might.

The hounds wailed their distress, sensing what approached, and they tried to flee. Their desperate calls sounded like off-key horns; they made Thorn's nerves jangle, his heart lose rhythm within his chest—pounding too hard one set, not at all the next—and he quickly threw a calming pass over himself for protection. The smartest move would be to turn away, but he had to watch. Partly in fascination, this infuriating, insatiable curiosity that he knew would probably be the death of him; partly to bear witness.

The end was blindingly quick yet every stage found itself printed indelibly on his memory. Between one step and the next the Death Dogs turned from flesh to molten fire, retaining form and animation for a step farther until they cooled and he beheld a pair of monstrously ugly statues. In that same heartbeat their momentum caught up with them, all the impetus of their headlong flight shattering them to bits, as though they'd been struck by a hammer. Not a decent-sized pebble remained; they were reduced instantly to dust, which in turn was swept up and away by the same swirling winds and energies that had earlier entrapped Thorn.

He felt breeze touch his bare face, then the nape of his neck as he deliberately looked away, saw sparkles all across his field of vision as the mountains turned from what they'd destroyed to what they desired. He didn't have strength to fight them, and knew there'd be no help from the Daikini. Assuming the man was still alive.

He heard a Call and set his face as he breathed a reply.

"I can't," he said, though he wanted to. So easy, so tempting, to take himself out of the game, to once more have focus and home, to spend his days at a simple, straightforward task and never a need to worry about the consequences. A life with limits.

"I won't." There was real sorrow in his voice, for himself as much as the mountains.

"I'm pledged already," he went on. "You're not alone in this; others have suffered as well, in equal measure." *And all,* he thought, *cry out with equal force for vengeance.* "I offer you what's rightfully due them, a chance for justice."

He felt a tingle beneath his toes and a flush of true fear that they weren't going to take no for their answer. But the pressure of his weight slackened on his fingers as he found himself with a ledge to stand on, and another just above it, making an easy climb up his body length and over the edge of the Scar.

He rolled to his seat, and from there stood wearily erect. Then he took a breath to gather himself and make a proper, formal obeisance. He had been treated at the last with kindness and respect, he would do no less in return.

That gesture just about finished him. He'd heard the stealthy pad of feet approaching from behind but was so exhausted his brain hadn't processed the information; the sounds had no meaning, until it was nearly too late. He didn't try anything fancy in response, he simply dropped and rolled, hoping to upend whoever was after him. This attacker walked on two legs, and wasn't that much bigger than Thorn himself, impressions noted in passing as Thorn thrust out a leg to act as pivot and brace and recovered his feet. He hadn't emerged unscathed, the other had taken a slash at him as he leaped over Thorn's tumbling body, leaving a burning trickle of dampness along the length of the Nelwyn's back where the tip of the blade had cut him.

It was a face Thorn knew, and the recognition of it almost got him killed a second time.

"Faron," he called, more question than acknowledgment, because he truly didn't believe his eyes, though InSight as well as Out told him it was so.

Then the knife flashed again, for his heart this time, and there was no more opportunity for conscious thought. His body reacted as it had been trained to. One hand to block the thrusting blade, another to clutch the boy's tunic, Thorn's body giving way under the onslaught, feet presenting themselves to Faron's solar plexus as Thorn's backside touched the ground. The Nelwyn rolled onto his back, building speed as he went, pulling with his hand, pushing along the whole length of his legs, sending the boy into a flying somersault. Faron tried to land like a Death Dog, on his feet and facing his foe, twisting himself in the air so wildly Thorn was sure he'd break his back, but he didn't have height or agility enough to succeed. His body hadn't yet grown sufficiently to fulfill those demands.

Faron struck hard, shoulder first—that impact costing him his hold on the knife, which Thorn immediately kicked over the edge of the Scar—but came up quickly nonetheless, favoring his sore side but determined to continue the fight.

He bared his teeth and it was as though Thorn had been shot through the breast. The boy had long fangs, creating the impression that a Death Dog's teeth had replaced his own. When Faron flexed his fingers, OutSight caught the gleam of claws where human nails once had been. What had been illusion with Thorn when he took on the aspect of a Death Dog, was reality for the boy.

"Faron," Thorn pleaded, "no!"

A waste of breath; he knew that when he spoke. The boy sprang, expecting Thorn to try to duck away somehow. Instead, the Nelwyn stood his ground, and caught Faron's hands in his own. The boy snapped his teeth, trying for Thorn's throat, but Thorn had a slight advantage in arm length and put it to good use, pushing up and away, stretching Faron's arms to full extension.

There was blood on the boy's breath, the stale smell of lives gleefully taken; he was screaming as well, might have been words, or more likely his equivalent of the gabbling noises his hounds made; Thorn was beyond listening.

He knew there was no hope, a foregone conclusion the moment Faron had tasted blood, tasted death, but he turned the full force of his InSight on the boy regardless, praying to find some small remnant of the lad he'd brought into the world a decade ago.

As he did so, his fingers tightened their grip, his hands began to twist, forcing the boy down to his knees where he couldn't bring his legs around to strike out with them. The boy's struggles became more frantic as he finally realized his plight, but he'd have better luck trying to break a set of iron manacles than the Nelwyn's hold. It was a common misconception. To most, especially among the Daikinis, size and strength went together; lack one, you had to lack the other, especially when the odd proportions of Nelwyns were thrown into the mix. In Thorn's case, folk saw a figure that barely reached a grown man's hips and accorded a child's ability to go with its stature. Little notice was taken of the breadth of his chest, and the power of his arms and shoulders was generally mistaken for the bulk of his clothes. In the right circumstances, he was a match and more for those three times his size.

Thorn bent the boy more and more until, at last and with an awful crack, Faron's back broke.

It was like slicing the strings on a puppet; all the tension fled from the boy's body and he collapsed to the ground, little more than a collection of sticks. He wasn't yet dead, his eyes moved, his mouth still worked; he made no sound, though, for his lungs had lost the capacity to draw in air, as had his heart the ability to beat. Thorn dropped beside him, gathering the boy gently into his lap, as though he were handling a piece of the finest porcelain. There was only blind hatred in Faron's eyes, the lust of a Death Dog eager for its kill, and his teeth made a feeble *klak* sound as he brought them together as hard as he was able in a vain attempt to draw more of Thorn's blood. Dying as he was, the boy remained true to the nature that had been grafted onto his soul.

It was more than Thorn could bear, far more than the boy should have to, and so he swept InSight about the pair of them and cast his spirit face-to-face with Faron's. The boy was broken in his soul as well, a mirror to his corporeal state, the radiance that was his life dimming with every passing moment. Thorn had thought that here, at least, he'd find a last vestige of Faron's essence, but all that lay before him was the shape of a Death Dog amidst the shattered remnants of its feast. The boy's human soul, every part of him that was decent, had been utterly consumed.

Such was the way of things with Death Dogs. Stories abounded as to how they were creations of the foulest sorcery. Like all such tales, this one had some truth to it. The hounds themselves were animal, creatures of flesh and blood and bone and sinew, just like those they hunted. The leader of a hunting pack, however, had to be human, and embrace this abominable path as an active choice. Someone willing to cast off all that separated two legs from four, most especially humanity, in return for the power and passion that went with running with the Death Dogs. It wasn't true shape-shifting—the few Shapers Thorn had met were by and large honorable folk—but a deliberate and malefic twisting of something decent. A corruption of the flesh to complement that of the spirit.

Thorn took the phantom beast by its throat and peeled away the layers of its memory to determine who had brought it into being and to this place. The images came easily, a pathway he was meant to follow, leading to a mazelike catacomb of the soul that was enshrouded by a darkness the like of which he'd never known. There was no true light here; Thorn found his perceptions defined by degrees of Shadow—and his expression tightened at how naturally the ancient word for evil came to mind.

Physically, Faron had been taken by force—Thorn felt resonances of riders as dark and deadly as this vault in the boy's memory—but he'd accepted the ChangeSpell willingly. Without question, without hesitation. No true sense remained of the sorcerer responsible, both face and spirit were wholly cloaked, only the boy's reactions to him were there to be read. And they were wholly at odds with what had happened. Faron had been unafraid, certain to his core that this was someone who would never do him harm. It was a deception as absolute as the boy's faith—he was told that evil was good and so embraced it with all his heart—to his final moment, he never realized how he'd been totally betrayed.

The spirit hound uttered a growl that might have been a laugh of triumph, at the Nelwyn's inability to save yet another that he loved, and Thorn cast the last scraps of radiance from that haunted place and put out its light forever. When he looked again through his own, physical eyes, there was no movement to the boy's body and his eyes had lost their luster. Thorn closed the lids and gathered the child's head close to his breast, rocking back and forth in tune to his heartbeat, wishing for tears from eyes that had long ago gone dry, wanting to howl like a man demented, yearning with a passion that frightened him for the power to re-pay this murder a thousandfold and bring to the creature respon-sible such pain and more as he felt now.

The walk back to camp was an interminable slog. He didn't worry about the details, he focused on placing one foot before the other, content that eventually he'd reach a destination.

The carnage should have shocked him. There were bodies everywhere, Death Dogs skewered or decapitated or outright burned. Too many of those for the fire to properly handle; it had been reduced to smoldering coals, the pile on top charred meat. The stench didn't make him gag. It was as though he'd gone be-yond physical sensation, that in slaying the boy he'd cut out some small but crucial piece of himself.

The Daikini lay beneath a hound that was almost as tall as he and more powerfully built. Thorn had no idea if the man was still alive, nor any desire to use InSight to find out.

It took two tries and a major grunt of effort to push the corpse aside. Thorn wrinkled his nose at the sight and smell beneath and started to breathe a prayer for the Daikini, until a closer examina-tion revealed that the mess was mostly of the hound's making.

It hadn't been the Daikini who killed it, either. The creature bore the small but lethal mark of brownie blades.

"Lucky for you," Thorn grumble-muttered, hooking his arms around the beast's massive shoulders and attempting to move it, offering as foul a set of comments as he could give thought to at the difference between their respective sizes. He could remember easier times clearing rocks from his field, and tree trunks.

The ground gave way beneath him and he slipped forward to put his face in the muck.

"Too much effort," he heard in casually disdainful tones, "too little reward."

He exhaled a hard puff and Rool yelped in protest as the brownie suddenly found himself blown onto his own backside.

"Thorn." Mindspeech, from one of the eagles, sorrow mingling with reproach. For an awful moment he thought one of them had been hurt.

It was the mare.

She lay on her side and he marveled that she still had strength to breathe, that there was blood enough within her for her noble heart still to pump. She'd given a magnificent account of herself, that was plain from the bodies scattered about her; her hooves had broken legs and backs and heads and the crimson stains across her muzzle were from the bites she'd inflicted. But she'd been alone. In the end, that had proved the difference.

She responded to his presence as he knelt beside her. Nostrils flared and she tried a nicker of greeting that faded into a gargling cough. He stroked her neck, offering all the warmth within him, poised to wipe away her pain, then snip the last frayed cords that bound her to the world.

He couldn't. It enraged him to feel her misery. She hungered for life as much as any he'd known, she'd earned it and more, and all he had to give in return was quick, convenient oblivion.

"A kindness, folk call this," he said, more to himself, "a mercy," and he could hear the acid in his voice, heard as well the laughter of the spirit hound within young Faron's soul.

"I've lost enough friends, damn you. If there's a chance—the smallest hope—*never again*!"

He cast loose his own spirit and with ghostly senses—his In-Sight—reached deep into the mare. For those first moments he almost wished he hadn't. Bad as she'd looked from without, the damage within was significantly worse.

"This will hurt, I'm afraid," he told himself, as much as her. "Nothing much for that. Too much to do, too little time, too little strength. Haven't the energy to spare to keep the pain of healing at bay. We'll just have to endure together."

They merged, and in that moment he understood the transcendent physical glory of running. That was the heart of her being, the center of life and joy; to race, to eat the endless miles with flashing hooves, to feel the breeze of her own making stretch out her mane like a banner. The old tales said those with eyes ahead were hunters; those with eyes aside, prey. The mare didn't consider herself either. From first breath to last, existence was speed.

Thorn made a noise that put the howls of the Death Dogs to shame, guttural and harsh, baring teeth as icefire flayed him from the heart out. Life pounded in his breast like a hammer, harder and faster with each breath, demanding ever more of him to sustain the wounded mare he was trying to save. He took that energy and sent it surging from her own heart, refusing to hear the protests of muscles already pushed past endurance—his own as much as hers—ignoring the spiked bands gathering snug about his chest, as about hers. This was as much a battle as the other, with the Death Dogs and with Faron, and one he was as determined to win.

She uttered a cry he'd never heard from any horse, couldn't help a twitching specter of a grin as he recognized it as her version of the bellow he'd just made. Her feet spasmed, eyes rolling, his own body making a feeble attempt to match hers. There was poison in her system; he cleansed it. There were bones chipped and broken; he smoothed them back into place. There were slashes, deep and shallow, across her body; he stitched them closed. All the while he kept her blood burning through her veins, until her skin felt hot to the touch and she seemed to glow in the shadow light of the waning moon. Not fever so much as fire, a cleansing blaze that made flesh malleable as a forgeflame made metal.

At the same time he grew ever more cold. His skin paled, lips and fingertips turning slightly blue, as though he'd been sketched with ice. His heart thundered, each beat like a blow, yet there was no sense of movement within his chest, not a hint of blood at any pulse point. Life remained with him solely as an act of will, all else was devoted to his patient. It was the most delicate of tightropes to dance across, the slightest misstep would doom them both. Yet he didn't hesitate and didn't falter. He actually grinned, with an excitement and exultation he hadn't felt in a long while.

Light flashed across his vision and he blinked desperately to keep from being blinded. Before him, the sun popped over the distant horizon into a sky unmarred by even a hint of cloud. The air was still bitter chill and would be for some while.

He wanted to move, but found he couldn't. There was a terrible ache across his chest and for a brief moment he feared his heart had burst. Not quite. It was merely upset at the effort demanded of it, as was every other muscle in his body. He'd thought himself exhausted after the battle with the mountains, and later with the Death Dogs; they were nothing compared with this. Stone was more lively.

He let his head loll forward. The mare's head lay in his lap, her eyes closed. He knew she wasn't dead, she still radiated his cleansing warmth and he drew on that gratefully to restore some sensation to his frozen hands. The awareness that the balance between them was shifting woke the animal; she gazed sleepily at him, warm and content, safe in ways he knew she hadn't felt since she was a foal. He did nothing to disturb that feeling, for once she regained her feet and her proper self, she'd never feel it again, the price demanded for her natural speed and grace. Truth to tell, he didn't mind basking in its glow himself.

At last, however, this good thing came to its end. The mare whickered, bending her legs gingerly at first, as though to reassure herself they were still attached and functional. That done, she tucked them under herself, roll-twisting from side to belly and from there to her feet. She was a little wobbly, one hoof landing perilously close to Thorn, followed by an immediate projection of shame and apology.

"Windfleet," Thorn said, as though knowing her name was as natural as knowing his own.

She leaned her great head down and puffed warmth into his face. She bent lower, forelegs splaying awkwardly until she was hunkered down enough for him to latch an arm over her neck. Then she gently lifted and supported him until he could trust his own limbs to hold himself in place.

He ran a practiced eye along her flanks. She wasn't pretty any-more, the wounds had been too deep and too many and he hadn't the strength to tidy after himself when his work was done. She didn't mind; these were the sigils of a battle won and a friendship forged; she'd wear them with pride for as long as she drew breath.

"Tough lady," he muttered. And staggered back a step or three as she shook out her mane. His own legs were stiff as posts, they seemed to have forgotten how to bend at the knee, and he went through an entire choreography of gyrations to keep from falling, much to the mare's amusement.

She was bigger this morning than he remembered, his head barely surpassed her knees, and she carried herself with the eager confidence of one who couldn't wait to discover what this new day would bring.

He sensed a change in the mood as he turned from her to the Daikini, pausing along the way to wearily pick up a stray bit of tack, her bridle. Windfleet wasn't happy to see it, and as he turned the construction of leather and steel in his hand, he felt his mouth twist in sympathetic memory, a resonance of the bond he and the mare had shared. She had accepted the bit as she had her rider, because she'd had little choice. She'd seen what happened to those who fought and had no desire to have her spirit broken as well. She liked the man, after a fashion; he was a decent enough sort, with gentle hands and a calm, unflappable manner. From the beginning, though, she'd sensed an underlying dissatis-faction; the Daikini always seemed to be on the prowl for some-thing better; whatever he had, whatever he *was,* wasn't enough. He wanted more.

Now so did she.

Thorn flicked the bridle aside, then turned to the mare with a shrug of the shoulders and a questing lift of the hands, as if to say, *What, you're still here?*

She cocked her head a little to the side, with so human an expression of perplexity on her features that he had to laugh out loud. He repeated the gesture, with more exaggeration, making a game of it. She drew herself to her full height and he let his smile fade, matching her assumption of formality with one of his own. He offered a bow, which she returned.

With a cry of pure delight, she wheeled on her hind legs and sped from the campsite, picking her way unerringly along a path only she could see, until she reached the open plains. And he learned that her name had been well chosen.

He didn't watch too long, although one of the eagles kept an eye on her from on high, until she crossed the visible horizon and safely made the grasslands where the wild ponies ran. She'd have a good life there. His stomach was growling something fierce, but he thrust that awareness from his mind; this was no place for a meal.

"Brilliant move. A veritable masterstroke."

He ignored the words and the brownie and concentrated instead on gathering his belongings, and those of the Daikini.

"I swear, it's a stratagem *I* certainly never would have thought of."

Thorn rounded on Franjean, who stood his ground with a monumental lack of concern, leaning against a stone, legs crossed, idly examining his fingernails as though he stood at Court and not in a wildlands battlefield.

"You have something to say?" Thorn challenged.

"Heaven forfend."

Thorn turned back to the task at hand. Franjean didn't let him take another step.

"Why should I criticize in the slightest the casting loose of our sole mode of transport?"

"Forgotten how to walk, have you?"

"We're none of us giants, Drumheller. In a world designed for the likes of them"—Thorn didn't need to see the gesture or the expression that went with it to know the brownie meant the Daikini—"we need all the help we can get. I for one would prefer putting as much distance as possible between us and this place."

"No argument."

"You could have *asked,* for precious' sake."

"She needed to be free, Franjean. The Daikini wouldn't have allowed that. Or would you have our next scrap be with him?"

The Daikini coughed.

"We've managed this far on our own," Thorn finished patiently.

"You'd think some of us would have learned some *sense* along the way!"

The Daikini yawned. Big mouth. Lots of teeth, mostly straight. He made noises, blinking himself blearily awake, taking no notice of Thorn hunkering down just out of arm's reach. He scratched himself and shivered with genuine cold; the sun was higher but the ground hadn't noticed.

He tried to speak, only to come out with worse sounds than before, all colored by the rasping croak of a dry throat. Thorn had a water bottle at hand; he tossed it over and the much bigger man took a monstrous swallow, followed by a heartfelt sigh.

"By the Blessed, I *needed* that!"

He flopped onto his belly, but didn't try for more, rubbing his hands over face and skull as though to reassure himself that all the pieces remained. He cast a glance at the creature stretched beside and behind him.

"Damn, tha's one huge puppy. Thought I was done fer sure when it come at me. Figured I was slashin' air, for all the harm I did."

"It's their breeding. They're a warped branch of the line of warhounds the Veil Folk raised, more resistant than most to the touch of cold iron, to defend their holdings against you Daikini. You work steel, same as we Nelwyns and the Forge Folk; the Veil Folk can't bear the touch of it. They thought it only fair to come at you with creatures who were substantially immune to it."

The Daikini levered himself up to a sitting position.

"The Veil Folk have truck with such as this?"

Thorn shook his head. "This is a bastard breed, as I said. Tainted. I thought we'd seen the last of them."

"Oh. Who are yeh, then? Got a name, have yeh?"

"Thorn," was the reply. "Thorn Drumheller."

CHAPTER 2

THE DAIKINI'S NAME WAS GERYN HAVILHAND; RANK OF trooper, serving with the Royal Angwyn Pathfinders, attached to the outland garrison at Bandicour.

He wasn't happy about the horse.

His mood wasn't improved by Thorn's insistence that they be gone before sunset. Not that he had any objections to leaving, he just didn't want to walk.

To Thorn's surprise, Geryn's gear proved to be a lot less trouble than it looked. With surprising ease, the saddle was modified into a fairly serviceable backpack, the equipment attaching itself to the man as freely as to his mount.

"What?" the Daikini grumped, when he caught Thorn watching. "You think this in't the first animal ever got lost or kilt? Tack's expensive, an' it weren't no small job breakin' it in, neither. Nor," he finished pointedly, "my horse."

Thorn said nothing. He had his own tasks to perform.

He hooked his hands under the armpits of the last of the hounds and backpedaled toward the Scar. He hadn't asked for help, and once Geryn had seen what he was doing, the Daikini hadn't offered. The effort of disposing of the slain had consumed pretty much all his remaining strength; every few steps, he had to stop for breath and each time it was harder and harder for him to get going again.

Clothes and beard and hair were stiff with caked blood and mud and filth, and although his nose had long since grown numb and senseless, he knew he stank abominably. He had the feeling he could wash himself from now until the sun grew cold and never again believe himself wholly clean.

At the edge of the crater, standing where his hands had left imprints in the fused rock when he'd pulled himself back up over the top after the fight, he hugged the body as upright as he could manage. A challenge at the best of times, a virtual impossibility now that rigor had begun to freeze the corpse's joints. He managed nonetheless, aware that the sun was higher in the sky and he still had much to do.

There were no special words to speak; he simply gave the creature a shove and toppled him into the pit.

The body bounced once before it flamed. It never touched earth a second time.

Only one left.

"Leave it lie, Thorn," said a small voice, uncharacteristically still, with a rare use of the name Sorsha had given him.

"Let the wind take it," echoed Rool.

"No . . . decent . . . wind . . . will," he gasped in reply, needing a full breath for every word as he readied himself for what was to come.

"It'll taint whatever it touches," he finished.

"Then let it *go*," Franjean cried, with a passion Thorn had never heard from him before.

"You didn't kill him," Rool said, more matter-of-factly. "Isn't your debt, isn't your task."

"Wrong."

The body hadn't stirred from where it fell, a sad little shape as bereft of innocence as life.

"I know you mean well, Rool. . . ." he started to say as he approached the boy.

"Was the sorcerer who *made* him did the killing, Drumheller," the brownie said, as though stating a fact of nature. "There's no blame on you for what was done here."

"Doesn't matter. It's my job because the Shadow Arts are involved and I may well be the only one left with even a hope of bringing the fiend responsible to justice. And my debt . . . because mine were the first hands to touch him, and the first face his eyes saw. I breathed life into him, Rool. There's but one reason to take this particular boy and twist him to so foul a shaping—because he's linked with me."

He took the boy in his arms, ignoring the protests of his muscles and joints as he had the squabbles of the brownies, and made his way to the edge of the crater.

"I should have found you sooner, Faron," he said, voice thickening with every word. Just because he could no longer bring himself to cry didn't mean he'd lost the capacity to grieve; if anything, it made that emotion all the more keenly felt. "When there was still a chance to free a portion of your soul. For that, I am truly sorry."

He couldn't let go. The boy had to be dropped, as the Dogs were, so that not even ashes would be left to further befoul this already blighted landscape. But his arms and hands wouldn't do as they were told. Quite the opposite, in fact; the more he demanded release, the tighter they gathered the body close.

Suddenly the air about him blazed hot as a furnace. There was an incendiary breeze across his face, like the gusts that came across his working coals with each plunge of the bellows, and the smell of clean burning in his nostrils. A flash of InSight gave him a view from the brownies' perspective as he was wrapped snug in streamers of raw flame that seemed to erupt from the solid earth at his feet. They swirled around his legs, up his back, over his shoulders, down his arms, stretched themselves out full length along the body that he held until it was as encased as he.

Then, with the faintest pop of imploding air, both fire and burden were gone, the one reducing the other in a moment to less than ashes, as though it had never been.

Thorn was untouched, at least in body.

He sank to his knees and laid his palms across the imprints he'd made, inpulling his defenses as both invitation and gesture of friendship. He sensed no tangible reply, the mountain spirits were keeping a healthy distance.

He made a helpless little fiddle with his hands, not really an apology, for there was nothing he could say that could take away the hurt inflicted here and he'd already refused to do what was wanted of him.

At the last, he said, simply, "Thank you."

He forced himself to look one last time at the Scar, using all his perceptions, human and wizardly. OutSight showed him a vast, smooth depression, so dark and fathomless even beneath broadest daylight it might have been the fabled Black Water of childhood stories. He remembered his father telling him the tales, and his mother—scandalized that her beloved would frighten a child so—gathering Thorn into her arms; the thing was, though he'd squealed and cried and buried himself beneath his comforter, he hadn't been scared, not really, no more than his own children had been when he'd become the storyteller. . . .

He broke away from those thoughts, an effort that left him shaking like a rider who'd just reined in a runaway mount, and cast himself wholly into the grasp of his Talent. InSight showed him a Scar that wasn't dark at all, at least not around the edges. It was like looking at the evening sky, in the moments before night claims its full dominion; the dominant hue around the periphery was a rich purple, shot through with bands of a brighter shade, mostly reds, winding traceries that looked random at first glance, with an unsettling resemblance to the patterns of blood vessels he could see burrowing through his own flesh. They faded, in number and intensity, as his eyes moved toward the center of the depression, until they were no more. The forces unleashed here had scoured the topsoil clean and reached deep into the bedrock, purging the land not only of the Corruption that had tried to claim it but of all capacity for life as well.

Nothing in his experience, nothing in his *imagination,* had ever presented him with so barren a wasteland.

And he thought, *What price, victory, if it costs everything you're trying to save?*

He was beyond tired, he knew that. By rights there was nothing he could do, even if he was of a mind to try.

He fumbled in his pouch, one of two he carried on his belt. Provisions for his wanderings, and the tools of his trade. Came up with a handful of seeds and one plump acorn.

Interesting, he thought with a sniff of surprise, *high meadow aspens make sense, as do the rowan. This oak, though . . .*

He began to walk a rough line along the crater, pausing along the way—in the same seemingly arbitrary manner he'd used to pick up stones within the Scar—to hunker down and stab his thumb into the earth. Into each hole went a seed.

The oak was the centerpiece, the anchor for the entire copse.

For that, he returned to the clearing.

"We be gone?" Geryn asked companionably. Thorn chose to ignore the dour undertone to the man's voice; it had been a hard night for them all, no reason to expect best behavior.

"I've one thing left to do," he replied.

The Daikini wasn't much interested. With a grunt of effort, he hefted his saddle pack and moved off through the scrub. For all his talk, the site of the battle made him twitchy; it wouldn't break his heart in the slightest to see the last of it.

That feeling suited Thorn; for what he intended, he preferred to be alone.

This hole, he dug with both hands, muttering darkly as a nail tore badly enough to draw blood, then smiling—a thin, hardly noticeable tightening of the lips—in wry self-mockery at how the fates sometimes conspire to give us what we require, only not quite the way we intend. Or desire.

He rubbed the few drops of blood into the loamy earth, added some water from a bottle he'd pulled from his other pouch, feeling the texture of the dirt change around his fingers as he worked the soil. This hadn't been the best land to begin with; no farmer in his right mind would settle in the lee of a mountain range, too many different kinds of weather and almost all of it violent as a pitched battle. Few species survived here and even fewer prospered. There was no guarantee what he was planting would do either.

But there was the possibility. There was the hope. . . .

He cast his spirit self into the soil and felt all his good intentions shrivel. The brush and shrubbery of the clearing had been deceptive, as had the sparse patches of grass scattered along the slope. The elemental force that had scoured the Scar had reached beyond the crater, chasing down with a ruthless ferocity every vestige of the Power that had destroyed the mountain. It reminded him of one of the first healings he'd attempted. Less than a dozen years gone, now that he took a moment to count the days, yet it seemed to him like ancient history. A young man, one of the freebooting Cascani, viciously savaged by a pack of Death Dogs; the wounds had turned septic from the start, generating a gangrenous rot that was eating him alive from within. Thorn was flush with his own gifts then, strong beyond his dreams but sorely lacking in control. The healing got away from him; he found to his horror that he couldn't call back the energies he had unleashed. He was purging not only the infection but healthy tissue as well. It had been a hard struggle that very nearly consumed Thorn, but the man lived.

Much the same had happened here. The mountains had thought only of expunging the poison that would have ultimately killed them, not of the consequences. They'd been attacked, that attack must be repelled. To save themselves, they'd as much as destroyed the land around them.

The acorn would hatch, a sprout take root, but it would be a weak, pathetic excuse for an oak. No matter how deep or widespread the root network grew, the ground wouldn't have strength enough to anchor it. A few decent winds would yank the tree loose and hurl it away; same with all the others he'd planted.

He'd had these suspicions from the start, that the damage was so great, but he'd denied them to himself, afraid of what would be required to overcome it. Yet he couldn't walk away, any more than he could from the Daikini's horse, any more than he could from his responsibilities.

He willed a little more blood from his cut finger, felt the anticipatory tingling along his nerves that heralded each manifestation of his Talent. He desperately wanted sleep, he ached in every limb and bone, he cast the feelings aside.

He started to sing, a winter song, about the world still and quiescent, where all the elements of being tidied themselves from the previous season and gathered their energies for the one to come. He reminded the earth of falling snow, though in his telling the storms were gentle and restorative, no mention of killing blizzards or freezing cold that turned the ground hard as stone. With each refrain, each new verse, he moved the days forward, the sun staying longer overhead, its warmth gradually reaching deeper into the ground. First melting the snow, its fresh, clean water saturating the earth. At the same time he cast the mixture of water and blood that he was continually and thoroughly kneading outward from the hole he'd dug, burrowing channels of energy in every direction, as though he were the tree and this the formidable tangle of roots that sustained him. Only in this instance, he drew no sustenance from the soil but undertook the reverse, as he had with the mare, sending the essence of his own life cascading down these many pathways. His voice deepened and darkened with passion, building naturally toward a crescendo, reminding the land of spring, when it woke from winter hibernation to find life in all its myriad varieties bursting forth in glorious chaos. Life, death, rebirth, the age-old cycle. How it had always been, and should ever be.

He was sodden, top to toe, as though some cruel spirit had laid a magnifying glass atop his head to gather every wayward scrap of sunlight and focus it on him. Molten within, melting without, a race to see which would consume him first, far, far worse than what he'd endured to heal Windfleet.

No comparison between the two healings, he'd known that from the start. The mare at least had been alive. She'd fought for that life with the same determination she'd shown against the Death Dogs.

He clenched his fists, so tightly he'd crush coal to diamond then released them with a rush. He spread his fingers as wide as they'd go, a greater spread than most Daikini hands could achieve, laying his palms into the sodden earth as gently as he'd bathed his fresh-born children, no restraint now to his Casting, not a single conscious thought, trusting to blind instinct in this final effort to guide him.

He felt the raw energy course along the pathways of his nerves, couldn't help a smile as he heard squawks of alarm from the brownies as those same traceries made themselves visible under his skin. There was a style of dance in the Spice Lands on the far side of this continent, at both village festivals and at Court, where the dancers attached lengths of brightly colored ribbons to wrists and ankles; the challenge was, so long as the music played, to never let one of these streamers touch the ground or come even slightly to rest. Not so hard for the wrist-bound ribbons; something altogether different for the ties at each ankle. The dancers would prance and spin and whirl, the ribbons would stream behind them like pennants or wrap themselves around the outstretched limbs until it seemed that the figures were no longer flesh at all but composed instead of wild, flashing bands of color.

Although Thorn was still as stone, he thought he looked much the same, casting a radiance bright enough to show even against the sunlight, and then he wondered if that would bring the Daikini back for a look. He had neither strength nor thought to spare to cast a Shield Wall to keep the man away, and then wondered why it was so important to hide the full extent of his Talent. Another flash of instinct. Trust one, trust them all.

He cradled the acorn in his hands, energies coruscating about the tiny seed, awakening its own infant passion, but most of all imbuing it with a portion of Thorn's own essence. A dash of wonder, a bit of joy, a pinch of determination. Some of what he hoped was the best of himself, he passed on to the tree, and by extension to this plot of land.

He blinked fiercely, eyes suddenly flooded near to overflowing as giant blotches of fatigue swam lazily across the field of his vision.

And realized that he was done.

He looked down at the ground where he'd been working by canting his head, letting it loll forward at an awkward angle so he could properly see. The hole he'd dug was completely filled in, hardly a sign to differentiate it from any other part of the clearing.

He bent all the way over to touch his forehead to the ground and took a deep breath. He couldn't help a smile. There was a change. There'd been no smell to the land: a dry, dusty neuter before, worse than the harshest desert.

Now it reminded him of home.

His plantings had their chance.

"Whatever the hell yeh *doing*, Peck?" demanded a voice from on high, in an avalanche of gruff confusion. Diminutive term for a diminutive people, favored by those lacking sufficient wit to see beyond the obvious. He hated it.

He spared a look up the leg of the walking, talking Daikini mountain.

"Resting," prompted Franjean, from hiding, with a hiss.

"Resting?" Thorn repeated.

"Thought yeh were the one, wanted to be gone so quick?"

"Just tidying up," he offered with a groan. It was easier to sit than he'd expected. That was the ongoing irony of his Talent, one of the aspects that never failed to surprise him: the more powerful the healing, the more it took out of him; yet, at the same time, he invariably found himself restored almost as much as his patient. What was offered was returned, good for good, the balance maintained.

He hadn't cast out so much of himself, freely and without restraint, in ages, nor felt so fulfilled as a result.

He scratched himself, painfully aware once more of how un-utterably filthy he felt—*Heavens know,* he thought, *what I must look like!*—then noticed the Daikini gazing about the campsite.

" 'S different," Geryn noted.

"Oh⸮"

The Daikini shrugged, " 'S nothing."

Thorn clambered upright. "Lovely day," he said, which it was.

"Beats what could ha' been, an' tha's a fack," was Geryn's stolid response. Clearly a man who related to the world straight-on. "Had food an' water, a week's worth, mebbe, husbanded proper."

" 'Had'⸮"

The man sighed. "Damn dogs. Food was trail rations, salted proper, packed proper." Thorn knew what he meant. Standard issue for travelers, food so awful to the taste that even the eagles wouldn't touch it. "All rotted overnight," Geryn continued glumly. "Water bags're torn to shreds. None o' that left, neither."

Faron's doing. Nothing was safe from the innate corruption of the master of a Great Hunt, so stories told; given time enough, and the right quarry, it was said that such a creature could pu-trefy stone to bring down a fortress wall.

Thorn gathered up his own knapsack and followed the Daikini to the outer edge of the brush, where it faded into scrub grass and boulders. There, Geryn paused. His hands rested on his belt, an ostensibly casual pose, belied by a thread of tension run-ning through the muscles of legs and back and shoulders. His scabbards, for sword and big knife, hung low, angled for a quick, combat draw, and the Daikini stood with a respectful separation between himself and Thorn.

"Saw yeh change, Peck, 'fore the attack," Geryn said. "So yeh some sorta Shaper, mebbe⸮"

"Just a wanderer," he replied.

"Saw what I saw, an' tha's a fack."

"A seeming, was all."

"Then yeh *are* a witchie-boy!"

"Hardly." Which was as far as he dared stretch the truth, since he didn't consider himself a witch and hadn't been a boy in longer than he cared to remember.

"Wha'cha do with them bodies, hey?"

"Tossed 'em in the hole, the Scar back that way, where the mountain used to be."

The Daikini nodded sagely. "Heard tell of it, down the flat. Didn't hold much truck wi' the stories, though. I mean, mountains, they don't just blow t' bits."

Thorn made a half turn, raised a hand to present the scene beyond, as if inviting the Daikini to take himself a look.

"Yeah, well," Geryn floundered, body language making plain that he had no intention of doing so.

"It's a place of *Power*," Thorn told him, "Things happen here, things are seen here, that aren't like anywhere else." The Nelwyn held out his hand. "Believe what else you will, Trooper Havilhand, I tell you true I am no demon. Nor, I pray, anything evil."

The young man fiddled on his feet, from one to the other, as if his boots pinched. Held out his own hand, still gloved although Thorn's was bare, took the little man's in the briefest of grasps as though afraid the contact would leave him cursed.

"Whatever. Stood by me," he conceded. "Did'jer fair share on the killin' ground, only right ta grant'cha that. Scales b'tween us, they're mos' likely balanced."

"If you've a different path to walk, my friend," Thorn told him as they started on their way, "I'll not be offended."

Geryn looked back over his shoulder in surprise, then spread his mouth in a shame-faced grin. He'd automatically set a trooper's pace and in a matter of steps had left the Nelwyn behind.

"In wild lands like this," he said, as Thorn caught up, "better I'm thinkin' folks walk t'gether."

"The better to keep eyes on one another," said Franjean in Thorn's ear from a perch atop the Nelwyn's shoulder, snugged among the folds of his cloak where the brownie would be hard to see.

"Sides," Geryn said with evident pride, "I'm a Pathfinder. I'll find us the easiest way."

"Except that we *know* the way, thank you very much."

"Franjean," Thorn hissed, "be *silent*!"

"Say somethin', didja?" asked Geryn.

"Pardon?"

"Thought I heard?"

"Me, I'm afraid. Talking to myself. Daft, I know, but it's a habit I got into roaming on my own. Sort of providing my own companionship."

"Whatever," Geryn shrugged, as though this was but one more strangeness to be encountered on the road, to be recounted—with suitable embellishments—in barracks, to his messmates, over evening ale. "I'll take the point, shall I, see what's about."

"First a Daikini along a trail few of his kind have ridden," said Franjean in his ear, from a perch atop Thorn's shoulder, snugged among the folds of his cloak where the brownie would be hard to see. "Then a Great Hunt of Death Dogs. Interesting coincidence, don't you think?"

"I'd rather not think at all, thank you very much."

"Not to worry, you have Rool and me to do that for you in the main. I'm simply keeping you informed."

Rool was in the pack itself; he preferred it to Thorn's belt pouches. The pack had solid, tangible dimensions. They'd both taken refuge in his pouch the night before Tir Asleen's destruction, during what Thorn knew now was no dream; Rool came out describing it as a warehouse of infinite space, without limit in any perception. He was small enough as it was; he had no desire to spend time in a place that made him feel less than nothing. Franjean, by contrast, had claimed it for his own. It was where, Thorn suspected, he stored his own worldly goods.

"How kind of you."

"Don't take that tone with me, sirrah! You'd be *lost* without proper minders!"

I don't think so, was the thought that flashed in his brain, perfectly matching the way they so often spoke to him. Fatigue fortunately kept it from going any further.

"Don't be snippy, Thorn." Anele now, from overhead, and he

felt a flash of heat at how open his mind occasionally remained to his companions. If the eagle sensed that thought as well and took offense, she made no sign. "Listen to what he says."

"We had our back to the Scar," Franjean continued, without the slightest hint of banter to his tone, and Thorn realized the brownie was deadly serious. "That tipped the balance. Anywhere else, we'd have taken our share with us, but we'd have died."

He wanted to argue the point but had a grim suspicion the brownie was right.

"But why, Franjean? We've been traveling near a dozen years, what's changed, to provoke this adversary to make an active effort to find me?"

"If you think I'm going to do *all* the work . . . !" From Franjean's tone, Thorn knew the answer had to be plainly visible.

"No game, neither." That was Geryn, adding to his earlier observations, thinking aloud for Thorn's benefit. "Haven't seen any, large or small, since I come to these parts. No water along my back trail, leastways not that we can reach in time; they bin all fouled as well."

"Do you know this country?" the Nelwyn asked.

Shake of the head. "No reason to. No settlements up this way, not even wanderer bands. Nothin' to fear, nothin' much I ever heard of to interest a body. Rule always was, leave well enough alone." He looked around. "S'pose this is King's land, prob'ly claim it so in Angwyn, but only 'cause it's here. Ain't even been proper mapped."

"Then what brought you?"

"A fool's errand, I was startin' ta think. Was told there was a healer roamin' the high country. Bin trouble on the river, these dogs an' worse. Needed help bad, tha's what was said. I'm good on a trail, figured I'd bring him in."

"No fool you, Geryn, at least in that regard."

"Yer the healer, then?"

"Among other things."

"Had a fair chance, mounted. Afoot, hard an' bare as this country is, dunno how long it'll take ta reach the settlement."

"Three days, that direction"—Thorn pointed across the plain, a little to the left of the sunrise—"will bring us to a river, an uplands tributary of the Saranye."

"Not much use, less yeh have a boat handy."

Thorn allowed himself a smile. "You never know," he said.

Maulroon was as sour-faced as ever, as though he'd been kept waiting just this side of eternity. Not so tall as Geryn, but easily twice as broad, he was built like a barrel and was just as hard to move when he wasn't of a mind. His hair was a thicket of midnight curls, making up on chest and back and limbs for the increasing lack of it atop his head. He favored a beard, cut close along the line of his jaw to serve as a demarcation for a double chin that no amount of exercise could remove. For the first time Thorn saw sprinklings of salt among the pepper as age made its presence felt. In terms of features, there was no comparison between Maulroon and Geryn; the Pathfinder had him beaten, without question. But while Geryn had the looks, there was a charm and character to the Cascani captain that made him just as memorable to the ladies; they'd give Geryn the first glance but always return to Maulroon.

Happier thoughts, Thorn knew, of happier days. None of that was in evidence now. Maulroon had anchored his keelboat in midstream, and long before reaching the river, Thorn saw the telltale flash of a telescope being leveled in their direction. There'd be bows sighted on them as well, until the captain was satisfied of their bona fides.

From his perch on the boat's signal yard, Bastian stretched his great wings, and Thorn let his InSight bounce to the eagle for a reverse angle on the scene, then up to Anele flying high cover above for an overview.

"So the lad found y', did he, Drumheller!" Maulroon called, deliberately making his Island accent so broad it was near incomprehensible.

"Good thing for the both of us that he did," Thorn replied. "The Great Hunt came for us that very night." Maulroon used a speaking trumpet to make himself heard across water and bank;

Thorn's reply was in a normal voice, yet the captain heard him plain.

"An' then, Master Drumheller?"

"It won't be coming for anyone else."

Their trek hadn't been kind to Geryn, even though it had mostly been downhill and the country fairly gentle. Without water to wash, he was caked with sweat, so much so that Thorn tried not to breathe whenever the wind shifted around behind him, although he had to concede he probably smelled as ripe. Pathfinder uniforms tended to be far more practical than those of the other regiments of the Royal cavalry, but no mail forged is comfortable under the open sun, especially in the high country where its rays are more intense than down toward sea level. The shine had faded from his boots as well, and from the way the man had been walking lately, Thorn suspected blisters.

Maulroon and the crewmen at the oars stayed seated as the jolly boat touched shore, again to provide a clear field of fire for the archers afloat.

"You made quick passage up from Saginak," Thorn commented as he settled himself beside the captain, another moment when a Nelwyn's size worked to his advantage; he was the only one who could share a thwart with the big man.

"Y' sent y'r eagle south f'r nowt. We were already here."

The oarsmen pulled hard to clear the boat from the shore, shoulders hunched low, eyes sweeping the bank behind. Thorn saw ripples just beneath the water's surface, a few body lengths out, pacing the boat and slicing as it was straight across the current.

"Since when do the Wyrrn act as combat flankers?" he asked.

"Seemed prudent, in the circumstance. There's more t' this than those damnable dogs."

"I know." Thorn hissed, and softly hammered fist on knee.

"Aye." Maulroon nodded. "Baddest kind of business, this. Tore through Saginak, oh, three weeks back, just b'fore the dark o' the moon. Left dead and worse behind."

"Is there anything . . . ?"

"What was needful's already been done, Thorn, but I thank y'

f'r the offer. I sent the trooper after y' mainly as a precaution. Glad t' see tha' a'least turned out well."

"You were hurt in the fight." There were fresh bandages across a bare forearm and a couple of healing slashes hidden by his tunic. No sense of corruption, though, only the faint buzz he felt when nature was doing its proper work.

"Not so bad as many. My wife's brother, I had t' put the laddie down. He was the one introduced us, you t' me."

"I remember."

"Aye. They went f'r the Gifted first, y'see. . . ."

That was the way with Death Dogs; start the attack by eliminating anyone capable of curing their infections, or doing them significant harm.

"I'm sorry."

"He were a good man, he'll be missed. But tha' weren't the worst of it."

"I know. Faron."

"In all the chaos, was a while a'fore anyone realized he was missing. We were all set t' start a posse when the Wyrrn pulled us out. Never seen 'em so upset, wouldn't take no back-sass. Tried t' take the trooper as well, but bein' too damn dumb t' know better, he figured he could do the job right enough on his lonesome. Bless my soul, he was good as his word."

"I'm a Pathfinder," was all Geryn felt needed saying in response, but there was evident pride on his face as well. Maulroon didn't offer such compliments easily, and Geryn understood that.

"I dinna want t' ask, Thorn," Maulroon continued, "but the wife, she'll—"

"There was nothing left, old friend. He'd been wrapped tight in a ChangeSpell, one of the Lesser Banes, to make him leader of a Great Hunt."

"Damn." The man's lips barely moved, the word was spoken so faintly none but Thorn had the slightest inkling Maulroon had spoken, yet Thorn knew it was as though an acid lash had laid him open to the core.

"It's a while," Maulroon said after a time, "since that sorta misery's been abroad."

The Cascani were rovers, by land when necessary but preferably by water. They hailed from a group of rugged islands off this continent's western coast and, ages ago, had formed an alliance with the Wyrrn, who claimed the ocean's rocky coast as their home. Together, the two races roamed the whole of the globe and helped bind it together with trade. The structure of both societies was familiar, and it was altogether normal for Wyr children to be fostered to Cascani households, and vice versa, with appropriate spells being cast to enable the air-breathing Daikini to survive underwater. The Wyrrn needed no such aid, since they proved to be at home in either realm. Each Great Clan among the Cascani controlled a fleet of merchant vessels, and through them a network of trading posts. There were few restrictions against intermarriage between the clans, which meant over time that virtually every Cascani was in some small way related to every other Cascani, and was therefore welcome in their house, be it next door or around the far side of the world. They drove hard bargains, but they also prized honor above almost all else. To break faith with a client or a customer—or with those rare few accepted by the clans as a friend—was to bring shame not simply to the person responsible, but to the clan as a whole. In a world thick with its share of pirates and thieves, they had established themselves as the benchmark of trust and fair dealing.

Through all of Thorn's life, Bavmorda's growing power had kept them clear of Tir Asleen and the adjacent kingdoms. With her gone, and a full measure of political stability restored, Maulroon's brother-in-law had seen an opportunity for expansion. Unfortunately, en route to Tir Asleen, he'd run afoul of a random clutch of Death Dogs. Madmartigan and Sorsha slew the beasts; Thorn used his healing talents to save the man and through him had met Maulroon. They'd been firm friends ever since.

"Now I think about it clear," Maulroon continued, moving the tiller to bring the boat alongside the larger craft, "seems it was Faron's house they were for right off."

"Just dogs, Jasso?" And when Maulroon answered with a nod: "How many?"

"No proper recollection. None left t' find, so far as bodies go." A humorless twist of his face. "We've given better accounts of ourselves in a scrap, that's certes."

"It was me they were after," Thorn said quietly as Maulroon grasped a line tossed down from the deck above to hold them fast to the keelboat's hull. "That's why they took Faron."

"Razi," Maulroon bellowed to his mate, half the boat length forward, "up anchor. Let's be gone while we've daylight." Then he leaned over the side and sang a series of noises that best resembled dolphin bubbles crossed with seal barks. A sleek and shining face immediately broke surface. "Two of y' on point at all times, Daquise. Find me a clear channel and let me know, y' sense the slightest Shadow."

"As you request, sister's elder cousin's consort." The Wyr's sleek mahogany fur was plastered to his skull with the luster of fresh lacquer, which in turn made his dark eyes appear that much larger. They were Daikini-sized, as comfortable on land as in the sea, where they made their home. Of all the races of the world, they seemed the least ambitious, possessed instead of a generous and genuine curiosity about all their fellow sentient creatures. Their preference was to make friends with whomever they encountered; if that didn't work, they moved on. Many made the mistake of assuming that trait to be a mark of cowardice, a misconception that lasted only until they encountered one in a fight. Unfortunately, on such occasions, only the Wyr generally lived to tell the tale and on this subject they did no talking.

Maulroon paused a moment in the act of clambering over the keelboat's gunwale to reach back to help Thorn aboard.

"Why?" he demanded.

"Same question I've been asking myself these past days," Thorn replied. "Brownies are being obstinate, they won't tell."

"Feed 'em to the fish, then, what the hell good are they?"

Thorn ignored the squawks of protest and outrage from various parts of his person, as well as the threats of what would happen should anyone try such foolishness, but he had to smile. It was the first humorous impulse he'd felt since the Scar.

"I hate this, actually, knowing that I know the answer, that it's probably right in front of me, plain as daylight, only I can't see the blessed, bloody thing!"

"Patience, then," Maulroon grunted, watching Razi supervise the anchor detail as they hauled the hook pulled free of the bottom, feeling the current take hold of his boat. "Worry y'rself too much, it'll never come."

Thorn shrugged, clambering up to his favorite perch atop the main cabin with his back to the signal mast, where he could enjoy the warmth of the sun and not be in the way. There was a dull ache in his hips that he knew would be a fair while passing, too chronic and ingrained for a casual healing to banish and he didn't have will enough to do more. He simply wasn't designed for so much walking.

"I brought Faron into the world," he mused aloud.

"Beg pardon," Maulroon queried, though the captain's attention was mostly on his boat as he motioned his steersman behind him to keep their course in midchannel.

"The dogs."

"Aye."

"Through Faron, the Great Hunt could follow and find me."

"If y' say so, Drumheller. But who would know a thing like that?"

"Who indeed. Someone I suppose who knows the facts and faces of my life as well as I do myself."

"And maybe," he heard Rool say from snug in a pocket, "with power enough to smash a sacred citadel."

"I heard tha'," Maulroon said.

"I wish I hadn't."

"Been huntin' y' all this while, then? Since Tir Asleen?"

Thorn shook his head. "I don't think so. For one, I think they'd have caught up to us before now. For another"—he broke off a moment to mull over some thoughts—"they were too young. So was Faron."

"Say what?"

"Cast that kind of bane on a boy, you'll kill him. The body simply can't withstand the stress. But Faron had come of age, he'd begun his change of life, his growth into manhood—just enough to make the difference. That was a mistake. Had he been a little older, a little bigger, a little stronger, I'm not sure I could have beaten him. So why didn't they wait? It's been a dozen years since the Cataclysm, what's one more? For that matter, why come for me at all? I don't even know what I'm up against, wherein am I a threat?"

"Beg pardon, shipmaster," Geryn asked, not quite sure how to approach this big, bearded ruffian with the airs and manners of a pirate. There was no mistaking who was in command aboard, but the informal relationship of captain to crew evidently unnerved him. In his world, there was no place for such casual behavior. "Heard'ja mention Tir Asleen?"

"What's tha' t' y'?"

A shrug. "Heard tell of it, is all."

"Of Tir Asleen?" Thorn couldn't keep the incredulity from his voice.

"My sergeant, back in Bandicour, he bin there."

Thorn and Maulroon exchanged looks, then fixed their gaze once more on the trooper, who was beginning to wish he'd kept silent.

"T' the far side o' the world," Maulroon rumbled. "Well now, there's a rover."

The Pathfinder made a shamefaced grimace and made a show of playing with his spurs. "Weren't him alone went," he told them. "Was a triple century, so he said, sent by the King."

"Whyever for?" asked Thorn.

"Lookin' for a, whatchamacallit, Nelwyn," he said at last.

Thorn kept his tone casual. "The Angwyn King sent a force of Pathfinders to Tir Asleen?"

"An' some other place, where 'twas said the Demon Queen Bavmorda held sway."

"Nockmaar."

"That sounds right. Heard o' them places, have yeh? Thought they was stories mostly, myself. That sergeant havin' me on."

"What did they find?"

"No fortress Tir Asleen. Funny, wouldn't say more'n that, no matter how hard we pressed. Seemed scared, now's I recall. No Nelwyn neither. Found a valley an' a village, so he told us, but been years since anyone lived there. It was good land, for the most part, but empty. Like a whole country got up one day and left."

"It pretty much did," Thorn said, mostly to himself, remembering the endless caravans of carts and goats and people on foot, streaming for the borders with as many of their worldly possessions as they could carry. Even the Veil Folk had taken flight or sealed their barrows tight against all intrusion. By the time he'd made his way to Tir Asleen, to see the disaster for himself, he and his brownies were the only people walking that ancient land.

"That sergeant," Geryn said, "he said the land was cursed."

"No more than any other. But why the expedition?"

"How should I know? I weren't there. An' his Royal Majesty the King, he don't see fit to tell me." Then Geryn relented a little and gave them the only answer he knew. "But I figure they was lookin' for Willow."

"I beg your pardon," Thorn said.

"The Nelwyn sorcerer, don'tchaknow? Willow Ufgood."

"Willow Ufgood," Thorn repeated. "Now there's a name I haven't heard . . . in a very long time."

"Yeh *know* him?" Geryn cried, mightily impressed. "Damn! Wish *I* knew him. I bring him to the King, like the proclamation said"—a shy grin, as though the young Daikini was amazed at his own presumption, to aim so high—"my fortune be made. Get a posting to the Red Lions." Those were the King's household guard, culled from the best troops in Royal service, and therefore acclaimed to be the finest in all the world.

"What's he want with this Willow?" Thorn asked.

"Don't'cha know *nothin'*?"

"Humor me."

"The Ascension! This is the celebration of the Sacred Princess Elora's thirteenth birthday, a year of life for each of the Great Domains. He's her godfather an' all, i'n't he? Willow saved her from the Dark Forces, he destroyed the Demon Queen Bavmorda, he has to be there." This last, stated as an immutable fact, an article of primal faith, like saying, *The sun will rise tomorrow.*

"Oh," was what Thorn said. Then, in some amazement of his own: "I'd forgotten."

The answer, plain as daylight, as impossible actually to see. He could hear the brownies laughing and couldn't fault them for it. He should have known.

"It's been that long?" he mused aloud.

"I assumed you knew," Maulroon said.

"I must have . . . lost count of the seasons. What do you know of Willow?" Thorn asked the Pathfinder suddenly, sharply.

"He's a sorcerer." Said with a twist of the shoulders, as if that was all Geryn needed to know. "An' a Nelwyn, too—"

"Yes."

"But—meanin' no disrespect, shipmaster—din't the shipmaster here call *you* a Nelwyn?"

"Yes."

"Can't be right, then. I mean, Willow's a great sorcerer, a legend, a *hero*! He can't be anything like yeh—not sayin', y'unnerstand, yeh're lackin' courage or nothin' like that," he continued hurriedly, fearing he'd given offense, "not the way of it a'tall. 'S just—"

"You were expecting someone taller?" Maulroon suggested, almost beside himself with throttled delight.

"Well, *yeh*!" Geryn thought the captain had thrown him a lifeline.

"Tell him," an outraged Franjean hissed in Thorn's ear.

"He won't believe."

"Believe what?" the Daikini asked.

"As far as Nelwyns go, I'm as good as you're likely to find. And Willow was a Nelwyn."

"They musta got that wrong."

"The King appears to be going to a lot of trouble."

"That's gospel. Ain't been no celebration like it since the world began, so it's said." Excitement brightened the young man's tone. This was an event he dearly wished to see. "Ambassadors comin' from all the Great Domains, even those o' the Realms Beyond."

"Be a sight to behold, all right."

"Aye."

"Y'r lucky day, then, Trooper," Maulroon interjected. "Y'r out o' Bandicour Garrison, y'say?" The young man nodded. "Way these rivers run, by the time we reach a post where y' can requisition a decent remount, y'll have near the whole of the northern provinces t' cross b'fore y're home. Be just as easy an' a lot quicker t' take y' all the way down t' the Bay, transfer y' to another packet tha'll take y' where y're needful t' go. Don't think anyone'll hold it hard against y' f'r stakin' y'rself to a coupla days stopover in Angwyn proper while y' go, since it's right along the way. Y' can travel wi' me as far as the Maraguay, then I'll pass you on to a captain I trust."

His tone made his dismissal plain; as far as he was concerned, the general conversation was ended. With a shallow nod of the head, Geryn took the hint and gathered his gear, looking around for somewhere to go.

"Razi," Maulroon called, "see the lad's settled up for'ard. Show him the galley an' the head. An' the washroom, f'r himself an' his outfit. We're a working boat, mind you, Trooper," he finished to the young man himself, "so I'd appreciate it y' mind where y' walk, stay out of the way unless there's need. Y' have a question, feel free t' ask. Elsewise, get along wi' us, we'll do same t' you."

"I've no funds ta pay fer such a passage, shipmaster."

Maulroon waved the words aside. "Y' did me a service, y' helped save a friend. This is the least I can offer in return. Be off, lad, make y'rsel' comfortable."

Geryn had to restrain himself from acknowledging Maulroon with a salute, as though in those few words he'd somehow been transported back to the garrison parade ground. Then he hurried after the mate.

"Bit brusque with the trooper, weren't you?" Thorn wondered awhile later in Maulroon's cabin as he toweled himself dry. He was trembling with cold, despite his sorcerous protections against the elements, from immersion in river water that was mainly highland snowmelt and therefore not so far removed from freezing. The towel, fortunately, had come from a warming rack in the galley. He wrapped it snug about himself until the only part of him left to see was a far too hairy face, and basked delightedly in its glow.

"My nature, don'tchaknow?"

"I was hoping you'd take us the whole way, Jasso."

The big man poured himself a mug of steaming tea from a flask on his desk, then handed another across to Thorn. It was almost too hot to drink and flavored with lemon, and tasted better than what Thorn carried in his pouch. In return, Thorn rummaged about in the pouch until he came up with the remains of a sandwich, still as fresh as when he'd stuffed it into the pouch . . . and with a start, he realized he couldn't recall when that was. He broke off a chunk for Maulroon, smaller ones for Franjean and Rool, kept what was left for himself. Tomatoes and cheese, with a strip of marinated meat, flavored in basil from his own garden. Corn was the crop that always drove him crazy, he mused. It thrived in his rich bottomland, and in good years would quickly grow higher than he could reach to harvest.

He shook his head. He could no more banish memories than aches, but he'd gotten ferociously adept at ignoring both. Maulroon was speaking; he decided to focus wholly on that.

"Y're in a rare mood, Drumheller."

"What's that supposed to mean?"

"No more'n what it says. Don't think I've seen such a humor in y' since, hell, I think it was when first we met."

"A dozen years and more."

"Near enough."

"How so, Jasso?"

"Y're *alive*, bucko. Top t' bottom, in an' out. There's a sparkle t' y'r eyes, an' a passion about y'. Tell y' true, Thorn Drumheller, tha's a sight worth the wait f'r it."

"Stop."

"I'm talkin' serious, man. Knowin' y', since the Cataclysm, been like walkin' wi' a ghost. The form o' life, an' a fair bit o' the function. Precious little soul. Maybe when there's a healin' t' be done, but nonetime else. Never seen anyone build so strong an' high a wall about themselves." He sighed, a hearty gust of breath from a face dark with sympathy and sorrow. "'Course, ain't seen anyone in such pain, neither." A pause, for emphasis. "Nor fear."

"That bad?"

"Not f'r me t' say."

"That bad. It was the healings smashed that wall, Jasso. First the trooper's horse, then the land itself about the Scar. I don't think I'd ever used so much power before, or had to give so much of my *Self*. There was too much at stake, I couldn't hold back. Anything."

"Fair bargain, strikes me. Y' heal the sick, an' y'rself, all at a go."

"They were my dearest friends. There should have been a way to save them."

"Mayhap was, but y' didn't know it, is all. No crime in tha', Drumheller, not even shame. I don't expect a young'un on his first cruise t' know the taste of a rogue wind, nor how t' handle it. Nor a rogue deal an' how t' keep it from goin' wrong. Their job's t' watch an' learn. Tha' applies t' wizards, too, I 'spect. If tha's na' good enough f'r y', though"—a casual flick of the wrist sent the stiletto from his hand to the table before Thorn, with enough force to sink the blade an inch deep into its polished surface—"if y' miss y'r friends so much, then by all means join 'em."

"I'm not the only one in a rare mood, evidently."

"Not so rare, lately. Be part o' the world, Thorn, or find one more suited. Y'r friends need y' whole."

"Go on."

"There's a scent t' the air, Drumheller. A taint t' the rivers where they touch Angwyn Bay. Trouble's comin'. Those damnable hounds are part of it."

Thorn held out his mug for a refill, and said nothing.

"If it hadn't been for the attack on Saginak," Maulroon went on, opening the rear door of the cabin and stepping out onto the deck, leaning crossed arms on the cabin roof to strike an ostensibly casual pose. Watching, Thorn saw the captain's gaze sweep one bank, then the other, then the water ahead. Even the smallest ripples caught the big man's eye; every scrap of movement had to be judged, with an intensity normally reserved for wartime. "I was planning to come for you anyroad. And then close down the station."

"No more profit in it?"

"Not hardly. Each season's been better than the one before. I'm inpulling the lot. Everything."

"You're afraid."

Maulroon looked honestly surprised; the thought hadn't even occurred to him. "Aye," he said in simple acknowledgment.

"I didn't think that was possible."

"You haven't looked." And when Thorn asked for more: "There's change on the wind, everyone with a bit of awareness can sense it. All this damn babble about Elora Danan." He smiled, but there was no mirth to his expression. "S'pose I'm no different than those folk who fled y'r land after Tir Asleen was destroyed, 'cept I'm not waitin' f'r the disaster."

"Have you no faith in the Sacred Princess?"

"A working man has faith in what he can see and what he can touch. The knowledge in his head, the skill in his hands. I'm a sailor: I know the sea and I know the sky. I'm a merchant: I know goods. I'm chief o' my clan: tha' means most of all, I know people. And I've learned, these past months, I can't trust *any* of it. If there's that big a storm coming, Drumheller, I want my folk out of it. Take 'em to safe harbor an' hunker down till it blows past."

"And if there's no safe harbor?"

"Pray the worst of it passes us by. She's a *girl,* nothin' more, spent her whole damn life in tha' tower the King built her in Angwyn, trotted out when it's convenient for state occasions and the like. I know storms, my friend, and the ships I'd choose to face them in.

"She may look the part, Drumheller, good and glorious as spun gold, but I wouldn't count on her to see me through a sunset breeze."

CHAPTER 3

I N ALL THE WORLD, SO GERYN TOLD THORN WITH PAR-
donable pride, there was no city finer than Angwyn.

Certainly, Maulroon conceded, no finer harbor. Off the
Sunset Ocean, you passed through King's Gate, between a
pair of towering headlands, and into a bay that many considered a small sea in its own right. Deep water for near a
hundred miles up and down the coast behind the seaboard
range and for twenty miles inland. Three great rivers made
their terminus here—one above the Gate, the others below—allowing easy access to virtually the entire continent
west of the spinal range, and because of the depth of the water within the Bay there was no problem with silting; channels stayed clear and stable, over the course of a season, over
the course of a man's lifetime.

Gateway to both land and ocean, here was a natural place to trade. There'd been established settlements since the dawn of memory, the Daikini being merely the latest to plant roots and sink foundations. Easily a dozen cities—new and old, great and small, living and long dead—were scattered about the Bay, as well as more villages than could be counted, yet a body could still cast an eagle eye shoreward at any point and find a stretch of land as pristine and unspoiled as the day it was made.

Angwyn was where all the elements came together. Named for the ancient fortress of legend reputedly situated on the opposite headland, the city benefited from far easier access by both land and water, the one up the rangy southern peninsula formed between bay and ocean, the other across a gently sloping shoreline, hospitable to craft of any size. The same couldn't be said for its rival, the northern peninsula—a wilder, far more elemental setting, where cliffs reared straight up from the water like fortress walls, sheer, forbidding crags that topped better than a thousand feet in places. It was thickly forested, old growth and sacred, the trees as formidable as the ground they stood on. There were no man-made paths through that wilderness and permission was only rarely given to follow the trails that did exist. The folk there (none of them human) liked their privacy and had little interest in the affairs of the hustling, bustling Daikini-come-lately across the way.

Which, in turn, ceded effective control over Gate and Bay to the sovereign of Angwyn. Over generations the royal family used that advantage to build a state of unsurpassed wealth and power, renowned throughout the Daikini realms on this side of the world. They called themselves High King of Land and Sea, but if some thought that hubris, none had yet challenged it.

Thorn and his companions had a quick passage downriver, doing better in a week than Geryn had on horseback in three. The trooper proved an amiable companion; within a day, he was volunteering for odd chores—he could peel potatoes as well as any of the crew and only needed to be given instructions once—and Maulroon wasn't about to refuse the offer of an extra pair of trained eyes on sentry watch. The shipmaster kept his boat in midstream all along the upper reaches of the river, until they were well past the ruined trading town of Saginak; he didn't anchor for the night, either, but instead trusted the Wyrrn to act as pilots and keep the boat safe from grounding.

Thorn took advantage of the journey to put his own personal house in order, a task as welcome to his companions as to himself; it was long overdue. The beard was the first to go, the sight of bare cheeks and chin a startlement to him after their decade and more undercover. There were hollows he didn't remember, but likewise a strength to the underlying bone structure that was also new to him. His hair he decided mainly to leave alone, aside from a good trim to neaten its length and some serious and regular brushing to work out an ungodly mess of knots and tangles. He kept the braids as well, in memorial to one lost friend, as his hair's autumnal coloring was for the other. And for the first time in what seemed an age, he smiled—honestly and truly—at his memories of them.

It wasn't the battles he recalled, alone in Maulroon's cabin.

The evening breeze set the boat to creaking and groaning, reminding him of the little grunts and groans an old man makes trying to settle himself comfortably to bed for the night, the river gurgled alongside, keel and rudder churned a small, hissing wake behind them to mark their passing. It was their laughter that came most easily to him, the delight each took in tangling with the other, testing their wits as enthusiastically and joyfully as they did their skill with swords. Madmartigan was a hair better with the blade, but Sorsha had no equal on horseback. He could dance, but she had a way with songs that could set a room alight with passion or make a heart break. His personality shone with such blazing determination that there appeared no room in him for shadow, even though Thorn knew it was there; the shadow in Sorsha's soul, though, was plain for all to see. To outsiders, they seemed like polar opposites, with absolutely nothing in common. Thorn knew better, that in fact they were the most kindred of souls, fulfilled and made whole by the love they'd found for each other. It wasn't just happiness that sparked between them, but joy.

He missed them terribly. And yet, looking their memories full in the face after so long denying their existence, he found what he should have realized all along that they weren't really gone.

He dreamed of them that night, and Kiaya and the children, and slept more soundly and more peacefully than he had since last he saw them all.

As promised, Maulroon placed them in good hands, a close cousin, one of the senior captains of his clan; fair winds and a fast current made this last leg of their voyage from the fork of the Maraguay an uneventful echo of the first. Strangely, only a single Wyr worked this boat—a young male, the equivalent, Thorn decided, of Geryn's age, named Ryn Taksemanyin—and Thorn noted that others of his seagoing kind were increasingly few and far between in the water as they approached the Bay. The brownies saw him and Daquise—the ranking Wyr on Maulroon's vessel, who held the post of second mate—talking while Thorn and Geryn were moving from one boat to the other, a conversation punctuated by sidelong glances in Thorn's direction. There was no chance to ask what that was all about; by the time the brownies reported what they'd seen to Thorn, the two boats were well on their separate ways, and afterward Ryn kept his distance from the Nelwyn. He was always in sight, though, and Thorn suspected always watching.

Ryn's natural pose was to stand slightly hunched in on himself, thus making it hard to determine more than a sense of his true height, which Thorn guessed was also of a piece with Geryn's; sleek, lustrous mahogany fur equally camouflaged shape and strength. He had a human arrangement of limbs, although not quite in human proportions, most notable for lively, questing eyes and fingers to match. The brownies' opinion was that he was as natural a pickpocket as they, though of course in no way their equal. He wore no weapons that Thorn could see, nor clothes; his sole adornment was a satchel slung casually off his shoulder and across his body. There wasn't much bulk to him—the Daikini Pathfinder cut by far the more imposing figure—but Ryn carried himself with the ease of a trained distance swimmer, his power focused in his shoulders and legs. He was at home in the shrouds or on the deck as in the water—which was saying quite a lot—and his surface air of madcap abandon belied a fundamental maturity that far outstripped his years. His role aboard was that of a common sailor, yet from the measure Thorn had taken of him, Thorn would have assumed him to be captain or mate.

The Nelwyn took a taste of the river himself, and regularly smelled the breeze—with his own nostrils and the eagles' as well, just to be sure—but found none of the taint Maulroon had spoken of. That bothered him. Never for a moment did he doubt his friend's word, nor the big man's sensitivity—the lack of Wyrrn was proof of both—but in absolute terms his own *aware-ness* was far greater. A taint for Maulroon should have been like a stench to Thorn . . .

. . . yet he sensed nothing.

They'd thought the keelboat large but there was no comparison between it and the ocean-capable dromond they were aboard now. Three times the length of Maulroon's vessel, displacing hundreds of tons to the score or so of Maulroon's keelboat, each of its two masts supporting a huge, triangular lateen sail whose yards were themselves longer than the masts were tall, she was built to carry a tremendous weight of cargo through the roughest of seas. The line of the hull was curved like a scimitar blade, from its elegantly raked prow built close to the water up to the looming stern castle. Here, as on the river, Wyrrn normally served in a multitude of capacities: they acted as pilots, they watched the vagaries of wind and water, warning well in advance of storms that might threaten the ship or keeping it from being becalmed, they made sure to keep the hull swept clean of barnacles and other marine growth. They were an integral part of the ship's defenses and their greater-than-Daikini strength made them a godsend when it came to humping cargo. Water was their element as much as the Cascanis', where one lived and the other made their livelihood; the smartest move the two nations ever made was to forge the age-old alliance between them.

The dromond's captain, Morag, had been a sailor since she was old enough to walk a deck; she knew the Bay better than the rooms of her own house ("Hardly surprisin'," Thorn heard her husband mutter, "since she spends more time on the damn water than she does a' home"), but the absence of the Wyrrn had left her uncharacteristically edgy, and cautious.

"Anyone but Maulroon had asked," she told Thorn, "I'd na' ha' waited." Her square-cut Islander features would be considered plain by those whose only interest was cosmetic. Sun and sea had textured her skin, which paradoxically made her emerald eyes gleam all the more brightly, and years of hard work in the worst kinds of weather had left marks that no amount of makeup would hide.

"I'm grateful." He threw the bones, gathered them up.

"Been an age since I was home." She meant the Cascani Archipelago, a scattering of rugged seamounts that began two days' hard sailing up the coast and stretched beyond the Ice Lands in the far north. Hard country begetting fierce people, rovers and raiders respected by all the Domains and feared by more than a few. "Visit's long overdue."

"Maulroon said much the same." Another shake of the bones in his cupped hands, another fling onto the polished teak of the cabin roof they were sitting on.

"Don't have his knack for spottin' a storm, but I learned early to follow his lead. I'll be through the Gate with the sun."

"When will you be back?"

"Y' prob'ly know better'n me."

"Thanks to these, you mean?" He twirled a bone between thumb and forefinger, shook them out again. "Don't mean a blessed thing."

"Fortune ladies in the market, they all say dif'rent." Morag's smile told him how much faith she had in such assurances.

"The High Aldwyn gave them to me. He was a true wizard, the shaman of our vale. Didn't mean anything for him, either, but they looked impressive when he needed to buttress some pronouncement or other."

"Fake then, are they?"

"Does the crown make the King any more or less a monarch? The Power comes from within, he used to tell me. Sometimes the wielder needs a talisman to focus it through, like say Cherlindrea's Wand. Others, it's the audience that needs something, an anchor for their faith."

"They'd rather look to those wee bits than their sorcerer?"

"He has the tools"—Thorn's smile matched hers—"he must know his business. Saw a man once, wore the finest set of steel made. A blade of wonder, molded plate armor that gave him the body of a God. Put that sword in his hand, he couldn't find the wall of a barn from the inside to do it damage. Yet the finest knight I ever knew, and the finest friend I found in a crow cage."

"Myself, Nelwyn, I like a world where things are what they seem."

"No less than I, shipmaster."

"So where's y'r girl fall in all this, hey?"

Thorn looked up and over, suddenly conscious of Ryn's eyes, not for the first time during the voyage. The Wyr listened more than he talked and watched more than he listened, reminding Thorn disconcertingly of himself; when he spoke, it was all surface, glib and for effect, mainly to make those around him laugh. In truth, he said very little.

Their gaze met, and Ryn lit out for the masthead, apparently taking on himself the role of lookout, as though that had been his intention all along.

"The grace of a cat," muttered Thorn, not without some admiration, "and twice the self-possession."

"Makes y' want t' kill 'im, somewhile," Morag noted in partial agreement. "Good wi' crew, good wi' cargo, well worth his wages."

"But still only a seaman?"

"Freelancer." The way Morag said it, that was a dirty word. "Never stays on one ship long enough to make a proper place for himself. Works when he pleases, which is damnably rare. Masters an' mates have t' be more constant, like a good harness team. He has too much wanderlust in his soul." Then, without beat or pause: "Y' ne'er answered my question, Drumheller, about y'r girl." Her accent produced a word sounding more like "ghel."

"No. I didn't." But the captain wasn't about to take no as that answer. "She's the stuff of legend." That provoked a rude comment. "A dozen Realms, shipmaster, of flesh and spirit, sunlight and Veil, mortal and immortal, all claiming aspects of this life, this globe for their own."

"Been that way always, Nelwyn, so what?"

"Some races grow older, others grow up. We begin to crowd each other."

"It's a big world, man."

"You speak reality, I mean perception. In the Barrows, you hear complaints of too many Daikini; among the Daikini, why do the Veil Folk insist on placing cages about the limits of our lives? Maulroon said there's the stench of change in the air, that scares people. Too many"—and he smiled without humor—"are casting bones . . . and seeing only bones."

"An' yon girl's"—thrust of her jaw toward the still-distant skyline of Angwyn, dominated by a flat-topped needle of a tower—"going t' make a difference?"

"According to prophecy."

"Which is fine, assuming that's a contract all the parties feel bound by."

He heard, but he wasn't really listening. It was planting time, in memory, the hardest days of the year, that saw him up before dawn, in bed well past sunset, working his plow up one furrow and down the next, turning the earth, sowing seeds, a part of him wishing his growing power could do this work for him, or provide for his family without any work at all. A true temptation—wave a hand, speak the right words, and fill the house with gold enough to last a score of lifetimes.

"And cast away all this?" he remembered muttering, caked with dirt and sweat, as he muscled the plow around to follow the pig that pulled it.

It was a late evening, the night of the Cataclysm (though who was to know it then?), the moon waning as he sat beneath a shade tree by the house, muscles too stressed and weary to pro-

pel him inside, when he glanced upward to find the High Aldwyn standing behind him. He didn't think the old Nelwyn could
move so stealthily, or that he could be caught so unawares.

"You've not gone to Tir Asleen," the Aldwyn said, without
preamble. He meant, for Elora Danan's birthday.

"No."

"You were invited."

"I have responsibilities." A wave of the hand to encompass his
fields.

"Are you wizard, then, or farmer?"

There was some beer left in the jug, though nothing of supper
to eat; Thorn poured a mugful for the Aldwyn and invited him
to sit. It was a lovely night, the sky a breathtaking tapestry of
stars, its vault more crowded, each shining more brilliantly, than
he'd ever noted before. The air was warm without being sultry,
leavened by a gentle breeze that brought with it a myriad of
scents from his wife's garden by the house and the woods beyond.

"I am what I am," he said at last, because while he knew in his
heart he was the one, he refused to concede that it meant he
could no longer be the other.

"Ah"—the Aldwyn nodded sagely—"a lawyer, then."

"Is the answer so important?"

"If you're not true to yourself, how can you be true to your
power? And the responsibility that comes with it?"

"I am being true."

"You're godfather to Elora Danan."

"I was husband and father long before."

"When you were a farmer. Not a wizard."

"What do you want here? What do you want with me?"

The Aldwyn held up a scrap of cloth. It was frayed all around
the edges, like something stripped unfinished from the weaver's
loom. As Thorn watched, the threads all appeared to tear away,
one from the other, unraveling before his eyes and fading away
until all that remained in the Aldwyn's outheld hand was empty
air.

"The fabric of our world no longer holds," was the old Nelwyn's quiet pronouncement. "*Our* world, young wizard. The world of Makers, and Doers. It wears through, it tears, it ceases to be." There was a hollowness to his voice, as though the Aldwyn had looked into the Abyss, to behold something so awful that he could no more express it than comprehend it, except in vague, oblique generalities. Because to even attempt to do so would be more than any living mind or soul could endure.

"We Nelwyn are a small folk, we take up very little space—in the land or the scheme of things—content to do none harm, in hopes that the same will be returned to us." The Aldwyn's tone, the ravaged nature of his eyes, made plain his fear that those days were done. "If such is no longer sufficient to protect us, then we have no business making this place our home."

"What are you saying?"

"The farmer has his path, the wizard another. Each offers its joy, each demands a price."

"Why are you telling me this, I made my choice."

"I know." The Aldwyn leaned over to pat his hand lightly, and he snapped it back, close to his body, as if he'd been flashed by an open flame. "I just wanted to remind you. I'm sorry," he said, at the last, as a call from the house distracted Thorn. His wife, concerned because of the lateness of the hour, wanting him to come in to dinner and to bed.

When he looked back, he was alone, with nothing to mark the Aldwyn's presence save that scrap of cloth he'd held. There wasn't a mar on it, he held a perfect handkerchief of finely woven cotton, hems neatly closed, emblazoned with his own sigil.

Later that night came an explosion in the sky so great that all the village thought the world was done. Strange lights, fierce winds, a display no one would ever forget.

Thorn saw none of it. Bare moments after waking, he was struck by a pain through his heart so great he was sure he would die of it, that stretched his jaws as wide as they would go and peeled lips from teeth as though he were a beast gone mad. He made no sound, his lungs were as paralyzed and frozen as his heart. He couldn't move, either, just sat upright on the side of his bed with eyes wide and face twisted into a monster masque, like the kind the children made for trick-or-treat hauntings. Kiaya, snuggled close beside him, knew nothing of this, even when he threw aside the covers and hobbled to the window, graceless as an ancient. There was a faint acrid tang to the morning twilight that made the mist off the river seem more like the smoke of some great fire.

He knew Tir Asleen was gone, as surely as he knew the fact of his own life. He knew his friends were lost to him, as he knew his family soon would be.

The High Aldwyn met him at the door.

"Everyone's afraid," the old Nelwyn said, by way of greeting.

"Except mine," was Thorn's reply, "and that's because they don't yet know. Can you feel? The earth . . ." His face worked as he tried to wrap words around concepts far vaster than they were designed for. "By all the Blessed Powers, it's so badly hurt it can't even *scream*."

"Nor could you."

"What's happened?"

The Aldwyn bowed his head, stubby fingers working the knotted braids of his beard as though they were worry beads. "I don't know," he confessed at last. "And glad I am of it."

"I have to." And then, in that same numbed voice, with the false calm that meant the hurt and grief hadn't yet set in; "I should have been there."

"And add more graves to the boneyard; now *there's* a worthy ambition."

"I was *supposed* to be there." His voice faltered, becoming that of a schoolboy making excuses. "It's just, the harvest took longer than I thought. I knew the others would understand, I hoped Elora would as well."

He stepped over the threshold, looking at his fields, the trees that framed them on one side, the river that did the same on the other, the house that formed the centerpiece of the setting, and—he'd believed until this moment—his life.

"I thought it was a dream," he said, after filling his lungs to bursting with air that tasted deliciously sweet. He looked back to his teacher. "I was at Tir Asleen last night, I rode there on the back of a dragon, I thought it was a dream," he repeated.

"They represent the greatest of powers, dragons do, the quintessence of all that is magic," the Aldwyn said. "To see one, that's either the greatest of blessings, or of curses."

"I have to go," Thorn said.

"No," came from the other and in the shadows of the morning twilight he no longer appeared old to Thorn's eyes, but eternal, as if some primal force of nature had been suddenly made flesh. "You don't."

"I have a responsibility . . . !"

"To hearth and home, above all else, that's the Nelwyn way. We are small folk, we live small lives, we work small magicks."

"I can't think like that."

"Our strength is our community."

"I have—" Thorn began. "I guess I have . . . a larger vision of what that community is. The dragon showed me the true face of the world," he explained.

"His world. It doesn't have to be yours."

"How can I deny what my eyes have beheld? What heart and soul have learned? A friend is a friend; I turn my back on one, I turn my back on myself."

"Noble sentiments. They will cost you."

"They already have."

"You should have been content with parlor tricks."

"Better then to have never been born. I'm a wizard." His mouth worked a few moments longer, but nothing uttered forth. He'd said all there was to say.

"Your family will be safe, you need have no worries on that score." But when Thorn framed his next question, the Aldwyn held up a hand for silence. "Best you not know the how or wayfore. In your ignorance lies our sanctuary."

The old Nelwyn held out a hand, a belt with two fair-sized pouches attached, Thorn's traveling kit, plus a satchel stuffed with clothes. Thorn couldn't help a glance over his shoulder, back into the house, and with it almost went a thought to his wife, to call her to his side for a final embrace.

"Are you farmer or wizard?" the Aldwyn challenged, and there was nothing gentle in his voice, nor any mercy either. "If the one, then bind your fate to us. Accept the pattern of our ways, as they have always been . . . !"

"No."

"Then you have no place here." His words had the force of a ritual pronouncement, his mien that of a magistrate passing sentence. "And the longer you tarry, the greater the danger to all you hold most dear."

"Tell them I love them," Thorn said as he took the belt.

"If they remember nothing else about you, young wizard, that will ever remain."

"Damn my eyes," he heard loudly from Geryn to break his reverie, in a tone that mingled wonder and disbelief. He blinked hurriedly, his eyes overflowing with tears, and was silently grateful when one of the brownies pressed a kerchief into his hand. He knew without looking that it was the square the Aldwyn had given him, and thought it fitting as he wiped his cheeks and blew his nose. He'd never looked at those memories before; he'd locked away that whole portion of his life, thinking that by denying them, he might also deny what had happened, or at least deaden the awful pain. He'd opened this huge void within his heart and used it like a rubbish pit, for all the parts of himself he felt he couldn't bear, ignoring the fact that time was turning it and him to rot. As Maulroon had made plain, he'd been killing himself inside, while going through the motions of existence, in the ultimate hope that death might someday claim him altogether. Building such walls around himself that neither friend nor force could ever again do him harm.

Imagine his surprise to discover that the pain could be borne, and that with it as a balance came memories of joy.

"Not only was I mad," he muttered to himself, "I was a fool."

"An' us, hey," cheered Franjean, "we're witness to both!"

"My life, then, is complete. What's Geryn nattering about?"

Before the brownie could reply, Morag called out to the Dai-kini.

"Hoy, Trooper!" She spoke quietly, the same volume she'd used with Thorn at her side, yet Geryn—all the way across the deck and staring at the approaching shore—snapped his head around as if he were a fish snagged tight on her line.

"Ma'am!"

"Dunno how it is on horseback, but when y' ride the waves, y' be careful wi' y'r words. There's Powers a'plenty to hear a curse like that an' give y' wha's asked f'r. E'en though it's na' hardly what y' want."

"Powers I thought too great to bother with the words of a mortal," Thorn mused.

"Aye. So I used t' think m'self. But I tell y', Maulroon's friend, there's a wilding loose that bears no love to anything that breathes." Thorn sensed no specific meaning to the term she used, it may have been a force or a person; all that mattered to Morag was that it was trouble. The big woman shook her head. "Mayhap na' anything at all but me own willies. Tell me when it's safe, I'll tell y' when I'll be back."

" 'I like a world where things are what they seem.' " He offered her own words back at her.

"So, bucko, wha's the fuss then?" she demanded of Geryn, who bridled at the appellation. "Why're y' soundin' y'r mouth?"

"That column of horse along the shore road, are they who I think?"

"Aye," Morag told him, swirling a whole host of negatives through that single word. "Thunder Riders."

"Here?" Thorn noted dryly. "These days, it seems, everybody is a long way from home."

"Heard o' them, I have," and Geryn proceeded to show off what he knew. "They hail from the plains beyond the Stairs to Heaven."

Three great rivers defined the Sunset Shore, as this end of the continent was known, and two mountain ranges as well. One was the continental divide, where Geryn had found Thorn—though there was a lesser range right along the coast, giving the impression that, back when the world had yet to settle into its final form, a monster wave had hurled itself against the shore with such force that the land was shoved backward into a bunched-up jumble to form a barrier wall of phalanx peaks. The last and most magnificent, however, went the other way, perpendicular to the divide along the Sun Road from east to west, and were named the Stairs to Heaven because their peaks stood too high and proud to be believed. The greatest river in the world, the legendary Gillabraie, sprang from its heart. In a land of such natural superlatives, it was small wonder the warrior race who claimed it for their birthplace considered none that lived their equals.

" 'Cordin' t' story," Geryn continued, "they got no proper home. Born on horseback, they live with what they can carry an' no more. 'When the Thunder rides, it leaves Desolation as its trail,' " he finished formally.

They wear eagle feathers, Drumheller, Anele's voice bloomed suddenly in Thorn's mind. Her tone was cold, deliberately stripped of all emotion.

"So have others we have known, Anele," he replied, in silent speech as well.

Thorn heard her outcry, made thin by wind and distance because she was so high, and all the more passionate because of it. Grief and rage, bundled tight together. He saw a flash of movement, no more than a dark dot really against the azure canopy of the sky, no way to see details without his spyglass, and when he tried to shift to her mind he found himself blocked violently away. He sprang to his feet and hurried to the dromond's forepeak, never taking his eyes off the eagle, trusting to others to get out of his way. He had a vague recollection of a slight collision with somebody's rump and a fair scattering of profanities, but he didn't really care; his focus was wholly on Anele as she tucked wings tight to her body and stooped for the shore.

She was attacking like a falcon, only she was the size of a Daikini child, with strength and speed to match. A decent side-swipe of her wings could break bones, and she could wield her claws as effectively as a warrior could his sword.

Thorn shifted attention to the shore, thoughts racing through the catalog of options for a ploy that wouldn't actually make things worse. But when he cast his InSight toward the troop, he found himself bounced away again.

"Bloody *hell*!" he breathed in astonishment. *They have a Shield Wall,* he thought, *and a damn fine one in the bargain.*

He had no doubts he could break it. He also had no doubts that act would attract more attention than he was prepared to deal with at the moment. Fortunately, that fractional contact had given him at least a decent look at the riders' faces. They'd seen the eagle, heard her cry, were watching her madcap descent. Bows were already in hand and arrows nocked. The troop had split into three distinct sections, each moving smoothly apart from the other. One would bear the brunt of Anele's charge; they would take the casualties, and thereby leave the others a clear shot at her when she pulled up and away. Powerful as the eagle was, she was also at her most vulnerable in a climb, beating against the pull of gravity. The riders were already celebrating their triumph—eagle feathers all round!

They'd reckoned without Bastian.

He and Anele had mated young, and mated for life, and he wasn't about to lose her. He blew out his wings so close in front of her it seemed to all watching that there was no way to avoid a horrible collision that would send both birds crashing to the water. Yet she merely threw wide a wing of her own and tucked herself around him in a brutally tight pivot. Which was precisely what Bastian had intended, because the maneuver not only bled off a fair piece of her diving velocity, it also left her in level flight, headed away from shore.

The waiting troopers didn't like that one bit. A few tried their luck with arrows. None came remotely close, although when Geryn offered a raucous cheer at the eagles' escape, a small volley let fly toward Morag's dromond. One bolt struck home, right at the end of its travel, managing to snag its head in the railing within an arm's reach of Thorn.

"Bastards!" snarled Geryn, and then, much louder, "Bloody bastards!"

"If you don't antagonize people," Thorn told him, "they're less likely to throw things."

"Ain't afeard o' the likes o' them!"

"More fool you, then. We're not talking fear anyway, Pathfinder, but respect." Thorn hefted the bolt. Ironwood, a dense relative of the oak, ideal for pikestaffs and crossbows. A broad bodkin bolt, designed to penetrate both plate armor and mail. He noted barbs at random placings on the point, to tear the flesh going in. Nothing compared with the damage it would do when it was removed.

"Crisis is past," Morag told him as he returned aft, both of them watching the eagles beat their way back to altitude, Bastian making sure to keep himself between his mate and her prospective targets. "Though, if I'm any judge, he'll na' find welcome abed f'r a wee while."

"They'd have killed her," Thorn said, allowing some of his own outrage to show. "They knew how. They've had practice. She could *see* all that . . . !"

"An' it did na' matter a tinker's damn. Wild times, Drumheller. They touch us all, in ways we canna begin to imagine. If the King brought in the likes o' them"—a grim jut of her chin toward the shore, where the troop had re-formed and was now pacing them —"for his precious celebration, I'll be glad t' see the back o' him an' his precious Angwyn. Like swimmin' in a shark pit. An' if they've come on their own—be hard put t' say which is worse."

Drumheller!

"Yes, Bastian." The eagle's tone was strained, as though he was shouting his message from the middle of a fight. Which was probably the case.

I'm taking Anele across the Gate, to the forests of Old Angwyn. There are old nests, good hunting, bright water. We'll hear you when you call.

"Is Anele all right?"

He heard a rueful chuckle. *In as fine a fighting form as ever I've seen her.*

"I've never seen her so upset."

These two-legs like us for their standards.

"Common enough practice, the world over; your kind are noble creatures."

They don't merely use our image, Drumheller. They take us in our prime, they take us in blood, and use that blood to bind our spirits to their own, in much the same way the Daikini child was lashed to the hounds. To earn a feather, one of our kind must be taken alive and ritually butchered. No simple task, I grant you; only few among them would even make the attempt and even less succeed. We in our turn marked them well, and made certain our paths would rarely cross. In a hundred years, only one Maizan had claimed the prize of such a hunt, and that is the current Castellan, Mohdri. A whole nest he took, parents and offspring, with nothing but the stench of sorcery to speak of how the slaughter was accomplished. Since his accession, they have hunted us with the tenacity of Death Dogs and used any means possible to drag us down.

You wonder why we have suddenly grown so few; these riders are the reason.

"I'm sorry."

For those who ride the Thunder, Drumheller, we have no mercy.

"I understand. I'll miss your company, my friends, and try my best not to need you."

Our thanks.

"Idiot," Franjean fumed from his hidey-hole under Thorn's collar, once Thorn had passed along the news. "Better you should have asked them to take us along!"

"I'll call them back, Franjean, for you and Rool."

"Determined to play the hero." The brownie made his exasperation plain.

"I have to see how Elora's turned out."

"After half a score of years? Your concern is touching, Master Drumheller."

"And your tongue is far more cutting than usual."

"Those riders have *marked* you, mage, even if you're too headblind to notice. The boy may have been making all the noise but it was *you* their eyes were on."

"You saw that?"

"The eagles," Franjean said with prim pride, "aren't the only ones blessed with sharp sight. Go with them, stay with Morag," he hurried on, intent on making his point, "it's the same to us so long as we pass Angwyn by."

"You're afraid, too?"

"Careful," was the correction. "Cautious. Wary. At our size, a matter of survival. You're not so big yourself, you should learn from us."

"I've never heard you talk this way."

"You've never been so hell-bent on waking a bear from SnowSleep."

"Elora's as much a talisman for me as anyone. I need to see her."

"You don't even listen to *yourself* speak the truth, Drumheller, why expect anything different with us?"

"I don't understand."

"What! A revelation!" The brownie grabbed one of Thorn's braids, using it like a climber to swing outward and balance himself on the point of Thorn's chin, one hand claiming tight hold of the length of hair while he waved the other in a clenched fist. He was too close for Thorn to focus comfortably, but the intensity of the elegant little creature's fury held him in place as though he was manacled.

"Tell me, Thorn the Mighty, Thorn the Magus," Franjean challenged in a singsong tone that was an eerie parody of the High Aldwyn.

"Stop it." Thorn might have been shouting at the sun to stop it rising.

"Which finger contains the Power of the universe?"

"Stop it!" He swept the brownie free of his perch and held him, the pair of them exchanging glares like duelists crossing swords.

"You're hurting, Thorn," Franjean said softly.

"Be thankful I don't do worse."

Morag had altered course to take her dromond farther out into the channel; it may have been a lucky shot that struck, but she was in no mood to learn different the hard way. The wind had shifted as well, the lateen yards turning with it, just enough to block Thorn's view of shore from his perch on the aft cabin as he set his companion aside. He could cross to the railing, but it stood higher than he; there was nothing convenient to stand on and he had no desire to dangle from his arms like some would-be monkey, so instead he made his way to the steering post to rejoin Morag.

"Another few points to starboard," she said conversationally, " 's all it'll take to clear the harbor. Then it's through the Gate an' away t' home."

He knew Morag had seen his argument with Franjean and was thankful she'd let it pass. Generally speaking, sailors are as fond of the Wee Folk as brownies are of open water—which is to say, not at all—and out of respect and courtesy Maulroon would have told her of Thorn's companions. That way, had there been a problem, it would have been resolved long before Thorn came aboard, thus sparing all parties any undue awkwardness. By the same token, though, Thorn kept them out of sight. This had been a breach of courtesy, but he didn't know how to apologize.

"Could you spare a dinghy? That way you'd be less at risk."

She looked at him, straight on, with a directness of manner that marked both family and profession. It was how Maulroon dealt with people, and Thorn had learned how good captains did.

"Could," she agreed. "Won't. Shando," she called to her mate, who was also her husband, "break out the house colors."

"Whyfore, Morag?" Thorn asked her.

"I want no mistakes, or 'accidents.' I want all to know who's coming. That way, those riders start something, they'll know full well who they're starting it with."

There was a stiff breeze, so the moment the huge pennants were run up their respective yards, they snapped out to their full length.

"We goin' to a fight?" asked Geryn.

"Different set o' rags entire," Shando told him. "House berth, Morag?"

"We own it, don't we? Y'r as welcome at my table as Maulroon's, Drumheller."

"I appreciate that, shipmaster."

"So come, then."

He smiled and shook his head.

"Daft, y'are."

"Too damnably dumb to know better," piped up Franjean, in a voice to be heard.

"Could be the wee one has a point," Morag agreed, but her smile faded—all jollity fled—when Thorn turned his eyes on her.

"I saw the greatest fortress in a thousand ages—perhaps the greatest since Old Angwyn itself—turned to wasteland. I've seen a score of other sites on this globe, *all* places of Power, where the ley lines intersect, savaged just as badly. For all that time I'd no idea why, or what, or even if there was a 'who' responsible. Only that it happened. In the purely physical world, there are volcanoes and earthquakes and storms, why not in the magical one as well? A tragedy, but they happen."

"You wandered, you saw all that, yet you did nothing." A new voice, as rich and warm as its fur, the shape of a Wyr mouth casting the words in odd accents. Thorn cast a glare at Ryn, though he was more angry at himself for being taken so unawares, and a sharper one at Morag for permitting such eavesdropping. Surprisingly, her response was a gesture of reassurance; the Wyr was as worthy of trust as she, on that she pledged her all.

"I did nothing," Thorn said simply, in agreement. His instincts were fiercely at war within him; he'd been alone so long he'd grown unused to trust, offered or given, even from his oldest friends. Something about the Wyr reached out to him, but the resonance it struck still felt out of tune. "The walls of Tir Asleen were not just stone, and its defenders weren't armed only with wood and steel. The King had a clutch of household sorcerers, led by Fin Raziel, there were amulets and wards galore—for the structure itself and for every person within. The Veil Folk did their part as well.

"Yet they were wiped away in a heartbeat." He took a breath. "Just long enough for all to know they were utterly helpless." Another breath, the slightest shudder to it, his eyes gone hooded to hide the pain. "Utterly doomed."

"So what's changed?"

"What's it to you?"

A shrug. A hint of something beneath his facade, like a deep ocean current, the smooth surface belying a darker passion roiling far below.

"The Death Dogs," Thorn told him and Morag both. "Not natural, nor an accident. They were all young, you see, in their prime. These aren't leftovers from the old days. Someone whelped them, raised them, trained them, set them loose as a Great Hunt. Someone cast a bane on Faron to lead them after a specific target. That 'someone' may still be mostly Shadow, but now I know it's there. . . ."

"With nary a care," he heard from beneath his pocket, again in a voice loud enough to carry, "of what'll happen then!"

"Could be he has a point," Ryn echoed.

"No doubt about it," Thorn nodded. "It doesn't matter." He was thinking aloud, more for his own benefit than his companions'. "Death Dogs after me, Maizan after the eagles, with the tenacity of Death Dogs and a ferocity to match. Sorcery links them both. Maizan in Angwyn. Elora in Angwyn. Something changed the behavior of the Maizan; they were cruel to begin with, now they appear more so. You have to wonder why, and who's responsible."

"You have nothing, wanderer," Ryn scoffed, mainly to observe Thorn's response, which was a shrug as offhand as the Wyr's had been earlier. "Random elements without connection."

"Pieces of a puzzle," Thorn corrected. "Whether they belong to the same puzzle, and what the puzzle means, that's yet to be learned. Which I won't do staying on this boat, however much I might prefer it."

"Then be set wi' y'r gear, Drumheller," said Morag. "Tide'll be turning when we dock; I'm not quick away, I'm stuck till the morrow."

Nobody wanted that, and he hurried to work.

Farewells were brief, and Thorn couldn't help noticing that Morag and her husband, and the Wyr, swept the bustling wharf with the same focus and intensity that Maulroon had used on the riverbank days before. None wore swords, but there were knives in abundance and he knew the bigger blades were close at hand, discreetly out of sight. Sails were loosely furled, the ship held to its mooring by only a couple of lines, and those were fully manned. One command, and the dromond would be free.

He barely touched the dock before he heard that command given. By the time he looked around, the ship had slipped its tethers altogether and moved farther from the quay than a strong man could jump. Morag had her eyes on the way ahead, Shando on the harbor behind, ready to warn her of any attack.

Thorn shivered, feeling the intensity of their emotions wash over him like a cresting wave, a fear so real it was almost tangible.

Whatever the cause of the Islanders' apprehension, there was no evidence of it on the quay. Not the slightest bit. The crowd was bustling and excited, full of that special energy that comes from the art of commerce. At the same time there was a tremendous air of celebratory anticipation. Everywhere Thorn turned, somebody was hawking souvenirs. Banners and pennants, commemorative mugs, shirts emblazoned with silkscreened sayings and sigils, most notably one ascribed to the SACRED PRINCESS ELORA, gewgaws of every size and shape and description. Even reputable merchants had gotten into the act, as Thorn passed one shop that proudly displayed a carpet emblazoned with the date and images of the King, Elora Danan, and their respective heraldic seals. There was food in abundance and entertainers to distract the unwary while pickpockets plied their age-old trade. And constables, in turn, to give the thieves a run for their money.

The docks backed onto a row of monstrous warehouses, which in turn gave way to an equally impressive market whose boundaries were defined by the broad avenues that gave hulking transport wagons, with their eight-and ten-and twelve-mule dray teams, easy access to the waterfront. Permanent structures—four stories tall, and constructed of red brick, as modest in ornamentation as they were rock solid in construction—formed the basic layout of the plaza, these were the old, established mercantile firms; the others made do with canopied cubicles arrayed in lanes within the square. Central to the plaza was a raised platform, which at the moment was serving as the venue of some auction of dramatically patterned and colored bolts of shimmery cloth.

"Wow," was all Geryn could say as they made their way patiently through the throng.

"Takes some getting used to," Thorn agreed.

"Been before, have yeh?"

"Not here, precisely. But I've seen the like, yes."

"Could fit the whole o' Bandicour—garrison an' town t'gether—inta this market, an' that's a fack."

"From the looks of it, people in Angwyn don't know how to do *anything* small."

"Where's the palace, then?"

"Which one?"

"Get *off*!"

Thorn had to chuckle and decided to gamble on some roast meat from a vendor. A trial taste confirmed his nose's assessment; it was fresh, soaked in a deliciously spiced marinade, and then coated with a peanut dipping sauce, washed down with lemonade so strong it made his cheeks pucker. Geryn preferred a half-mug of ale and promptly made a face.

"Ain't beer," he declared.

"Hell you say," replied the vendor hotly, brandishing his license. "An' I got the certifications to prove it!"

Geryn held up his hands in a placating gesture. "Ain't *proper* beer, not the way it's brewed on the frontier."

"Then maybe you best go back, swiller. We brew for more particular palates."

"He's for a burr up his butt," the Pathfinder groused as he let Thorn tug him away. "Or better yet, a boot!"

"Different places, different tastes. The frontier isn't known for subtlety, in drink *or* manner."

Geryn laughed out loud and repeated, "That's a fack, Peck. But tell me, yeh wasn't buzzin' me about more than one palace?"

"At least one for every hill, so Morag told me, and this is a city of hills."

"The way I'm looked at, folk here'bouts must think me a proper bumpkin."

"Pathfinders are a rare sight at the heart of the kingdom, especially carrying their saddles. They're as old and noble a regiment as the Lions, Geryn. . . ."

"So yeh wonder why I've my heart set on t'other?"

"Yes, actually. I mean, it wasn't the Red Lions who were sent to Tir Asleen."

"That's a fack, certes. M' gran'da was a Lion, yeh see. We had a place up along the Madarine, no good for farmin', nothing come from that land 'cept stones an' busted hearts; m' da, though, were good with his hands, grant 'im that. Made his trade as a cobbler, boots 'n such, brought in a fair wage most times, kept us clothed an' fed. Gran'da, though . . ."

Geryn's voice trailed off and he wiped foam from his upper lip. The midday sun had turned the flagstone plaza into a searingly hot griddle, driving them to take refuge under the canopy of an open-air tavern. Thorn shifted his carryall to the ground as the two of them settled into canvas-backed chairs, spent a few moments fiddling with the laces to cover the brownies' descent from their hiding places in his clothes. He set a cup of water on the carryall and allowed himself a smile when he raised it to his lips and found it almost empty. He knew they'd prefer beer, but that indulgence would have to wait until the travelers were properly settled. He hadn't heard a comment from either since coming ashore and didn't mind a bit.

"Your grandfather?" Thorn prompted, genuinely interested.

"Aye. Gran'da, his visits, they were somethin' wonderful. His uniform was a sight to behold and the stories were even better. Always brought presents, he did, sorta bound us t'gether, jus' by bein' inna room. Made us feel we were a proper fam'ly. Made me feel proud."

"He and your father didn't get along."

Geryn looked over sharply. "How'd yeh know that?"

"A guess. A color to your tone."

"He never came when me da were home. My whole life, I never saw 'em t'gether. He wanted me da to follow him into the service, as he'd followed his—me great-gran'da—an' so on, back five full generations. Me da were his only son, but he wouldn't hold t' tha' tradition. Said he had no truck wi' takin' orders, wanted to be his own man entire, beholdin' to none. If King were attacked, that were different; elsewise, he jus' din't see the sense of it. Fam'ly came first, plain an' simple. Gran'da, he thought me da were a coward."

"Did you?"

A shrug. But the answer was clear.

"Still, Geryn, in their way the Pathfinders are just as renowned, just as elite. . . ."

"Yeh don't understand." No anger to the lad, the words came in a weary outrush of breath, as though this were an old fight. "Me da were bonded to the King's service as a boy. Pledged to a place among the Lions. Five generations, an' Gran'da was the first of us to wear that crest. An' he'd served so well he'd secured a likewise place for me da. But when the time came ta take the Oath, me da refused. Gran'da never forgave him for that disgrace."

"I'm sorry."

"Not'cher fam'ly, Peck. Not'cher problem. Dunno why I told yeh of it. Anyroad, both dead now." He grinned. " 'S a fool's dream, I know, but I thought if I could take the place m' da refused . . ."

"Perhaps I can help."

"Yer not startin' tha' bunk about Nelwyns an' the Magus, are yeh? Tha's plain daft, don'tchaknow?"

"Trust me. I'm a Nelwyn, the Magus is a Nelwyn. All you need do is present me at the door."

"An' spend th' rest o' my career muckin' stables, most likely."

"Nothing ventured . . . ?"

"Seen yeh throwin' bones on the boat, what do they say?"

Dutifully, Thorn pulled out the tiny packet and undid its leather-and-oilskin wrappings. With the ease of long practice, he rolled the bones in his cupped hands and let his eyes assume a faraway stare, not a true trance, merely the appearance of one. Then he stopped and simply held them.

"Oi," nudged Geryn, after a time. When that provoked no response, he tried a little louder. *"Oi!* Drumheller! Yeh spiritwalkin' or what?"

The Nelwyn blinked, drew his gaze back to the Daikini, but still wasn't really seeing him as he slowly moved his hands. He felt like an automaton left to rust, metal grinding so harshly on itself it was sure to break.

"My hands are cold," Thorn said, more loudly in thought than speech. Followed on its heels by an unspoken realization. *My hands are* frozen!

He set the bones gently on their bundle, stretched and flexed his fingers to restore their suppleness. The bones were dusted with hoarfrost, whose sparkles glistened brilliantly before the sun consumed them. The hands that held them felt as though he'd thrust them naked into an ice storm. He was half-surprised when he sighed to see no cloud of cold condensation on his breath, his body was so sure it was winter.

"Y'okay, Peck?"

"I know it's a common term, Trooper," he said with asperity, his body's distress provoking a sharper tone than he intended, "and I know you mean no offense, but I really don't like it."

At first, it appeared as though the young Daikini would protest the point; then he thought better of it, accepting Thorn's request with a nod of the head and an audible closing of his mouth.

"Never really thought about it, y'know," Geryn said. "Just a word, is all."

"Words have power. As much sometimes as any sword."

"So tell me, are yeh okay?"

Thorn looked about, twisting his head over one shoulder, then the other, for as full as possible a view of the plaza. Nothing had changed in the slightest, hardly any time had passed. People filled the space with their bodies and charged the air with a heady mix of excitement and joy. What skeins of apprehension there were, were buried deep. The sun shone brightly overhead, the day was warm beyond comfort.

Yet when he clutched the bones, all around him had been gray and frozen, a wasteland devoid of life where not even the hottest flame would make a difference.

"Bad Seeing, was it?"

Thorn shook his head and said, "No Seeing at all, my friend. Just a body getting old before its time. Shall we go?"

Some portion of his InSight always remained open to the resonances about him. If the image came again, or any other, he would be ready.

"Which way?"

"Biggest hill, biggest palace."

Geryn groaned. Then threw coins on the table and heaved his body to its feet and gear to his shoulder.

"Best be off, then. Probably take all day ta find it, in this warren."

He wasn't far wrong. Not so much in terms of finding the King's Palace, but in reaching it. Angwyn was built atop a score and more of hills, arrayed in a cluster about the headland. Some tall, some not, most so painfully steep that both had to pause for breath as they negotiated the slopes.

Two main thoroughfares reached out from the port. The Royal Promenade ran straight as an arrow flight to the city's main landward gate and the High Road beyond, providing the easiest possible passage for travelers following the overland route down the peninsula. Meandering the other way, along the waterfront toward the King's Gate, was the esplanade—more colloquially referred to as the "Rambles," because that was what folk tended to do when the weather was nice, enjoying both the spectacular view of Angwyn Bay and the many and varied shops that lined the thoroughfare. Both were paved highways; as were, Geryn quickly discovered to his amazement, most of the city's streets.

Clustered close about the plaza was the business district, dominated by the great mercantile houses and their attendant banks, plain, solid structures meant to inspire confidence in customers and investors both. As well could be found all the myriad establishments that serviced the port—saloons and joy houses at one extreme (proudly proclaiming that they catered solely to "quality" folk, not at all like their waterfront counterparts), chandlers and victuallers and shipwrights at the other. The neighborhood was called the Silver Square, because within that legendary square mile you could buy or sell virtually anything. It wasn't a roughhouse precinct, the Civic Watch saw to that, but that in no way meant the deals weren't just as cutthroat, the terms just as ruthless.

Most common folk lived south of the promenade. Rough trade hung close to the water; life was held more dear the farther inland you progressed. Nothing fancy there, the buildings tended to be walk-ups, four flights, maybe six, with lucky families having a whole floor to themselves. Streets were a winding, messy tangle, and what signposts there were tended to add to the confusion. There was no plan to the layout; it had the air of something made up as it went along, without a thought to the practical ramifications. The standing joke spoke of how every new monarch—or chancellor—would look down from the heights and vow to bring some order from this never-ending chaos. If anyone actually *tried,* though, they worked more subtly than any devil because none of the residents ever noticed a single change. In truth, they figured that was for the best.

North of the promenade, the lesser slopes of the lower hills were the province of the minor nobility. Landed gentry, who for convenience kept a house in the capital, and Life Peers, commoners whose titles were an acknowledgment of service to the Lion Throne. The permanent government was found here, all the departments of state. As you moved uptown, moving along the shore toward the Gate, the more formidable the hill, the more impressive the title.

Dominated, of course, by King's Mount. One of the most impressive features was Elora's Aerie, sanctum sanctorum of the Sacred Princess. This, they learned from an eager troubadour, outfitted in a costume of brilliant spangles that caught and reflected sunlight so wildly he appeared clad in flames of every imaginable hue. He cheerily offered gossip and directions and some quite marvelously filthy songs to anyone who'd paused to listen, in return for coins tossed into a proffered cap. He was a personable enough youth, but something about his smile—both lips and eyes—made Thorn nervous, a sense of being the butt of some great joke. He thought of using InSight to see beneath the surface of the jongleur's soul, and found himself dismissing the notion out of hand. It would, some instinct told him, be a mistake. He didn't know why, he knew of no way to learn, and chose to leave well enough alone.

"To some," the lad said, "a sanctuary. Others," a dismissive twist of the shoulder, "a prison."

"What d'yeh mean, wretch?" demanded Geryn, taking immediate offense. The troubadour didn't appear to mind, probably because he'd heard such comments before.

Thorn had led Geryn along the Rambles, partly to ease the strain on his own short legs but mainly to observe the unbelievable throng of people. He couldn't help being fascinated, he'd never seen so many in a single place. Eager as Maulroon and Morag had been to steer clear of Angwyn, it seemed everyone else in the country had the opposite notion: this was the ideal time for a visit.

"A cage is a cage, my friend, no matter how gilded," said the troubadour, punctuating his commentary with some sharp riffs on his guitar.

"We should all be so lucky, an' yeh ask me, to have such a life."

"Coddled and cosseted and *never* allowed out? Fun for a while, perhaps . . ."

"Elora isn't allowed out?" Thorn asked.

"Are yeh *daft*, Drumheller?" Geryn cried, aghast. "She's the *Sacred Princess*, bless all our souls! She's *holy*! Likes o' her don't mingle wi' the likes of us, ain't right nor proper. An' where's the need, anyroad? 'Tis said her tower's more luxurious than the King's own palace, an' her every necessity provided for, her every desire satisfied."

"Except freedom," the troubadour noted.

"Like t' see what body part yeh'd cast away fer a portion of such a life," Geryn challenged belligerently, punctuating his words with a rude gesture, and another for good measure to show the depth of his disgust and speed the singer on his way. Thorn slipped the troubadour a gold piece.

"She's not seen at all, then," he asked.

"The Ascension's the first time by any but the Royals and her attendants. I'd move off the road, I were you," the troubadour said suddenly, his tone flattening to an edge.

"I beg your pardon?"

"Maizan. Thunder Riders."

He was already moving, and Thorn hurried after, taking three scuttling strides to every one of his. The esplanade was wide enough for a dozen men to ride abreast with room to spare, beach on one side, buildings on the other. There weren't more than a score of riders in the unit, but their horses' hooves struck the paving stones like drumheads, making those twenty sound like ten times their number.

"I see where they get their name," Thorn said, casually pulling a wide-brimmed hat from his carryall and settling it on his head. Nothing unusual about that; the sun was high overhead and there was precious little shade.

The troubadour nodded. " 'Maizan' is what they call themselves."

Sable figures on ebony horses, as though all had been carved from a piece of blackest jet. Dark armor and horned helms. Leather overlaid with pieces of steel plate, designed as much for comfort as practicality. They were large-framed men, cast pretty much from the same mold, a stark contrast to the slim figure who led them.

She was a woman for one, not quite a match for them in height and certainly not in breadth. But she more than made up for that with the sheer force of her personality. She wore no armor, and conveyed the sense that none was needed, she was more than capable of taking care of herself without. The cut of her clothes was simple, yet the fabric was exquisite, a rich sand-colored weave that managed the flow and drape of silk while retaining the sturdiness of cotton. She wore trousers, which caused some muttering among the more conservative onlookers, that matched the color of her blouse, tucked into knee-high boots. Over the shirt was a high-collared tunic of mahogany leather, skins so fine they were as pliable as cloth, that buttoned out along the shoulder and down the side, falling to midthigh but slit on each leg below the waist to allow for complete freedom of movement. It was sleeveless, and the full, bell sleeves of her blouse billowed in the breeze set up by her mount's canter. She wore two daggers on her belt, plus a sword. The weapons and their harness were the only things about her that weren't designed for show. The leather was worn, the gloss of polish mixed with the patina of long and hard usage and the blades were hung as a warrior would, were they could be quickly and easily drawn. She wore her dark hair as a mane, gathered behind a rebellious forelock and wrapped into a broad braid that touched her backside. No jewelry to speak of, save a narrow circlet of silver that appeared to be molded to her forehead.

The funny thing was, for all her finery, she wasn't especially pretty. Looking about the crowd, Thorn picked out an easy handful of young women who matched her in age but far surpassed her in looks; from the comments, a couple of them knew it. Yet there was a presence to the rider, the way features combined with character, that would make her the focal point of any crowd, the natural center of attention. Indeed, the eyes of the crowd went naturally to her, passing over the Maizan Castellan who rode by her side. Even Thorn, who should have been looking at the man, found his gaze drawn like a magnet back to the woman.

She wasn't one of the Maizan, but she was more than a match for them.

"Anakerie," the troubadour announced to no one in particular. "Princess Royal. Her father's heir since the disappearance of her brother."

"Is that all you're going to say?" Thorn smiled encouragement when the silence stretched between them. The Thunder Riders had passed them by and the crowd begun to reclaim the esplanade.

"All there is, far as I know. Been a dozen years since the boy vanished and the Queen died. Night of the Cataclysm, it was, same night the Sacred Princess was dropped smack dab in the middle of the King's courtyard. There's some who call it a changeling switch, the one for the other, and complain Angwyn got the worst of the bargain."

"How do you mean?"

"Didn't do much good for Tir Asleen, did she?"

"Ah." And for a heartbeat, the inside of his chest felt as cold as the bones he'd held.

"Now who's hiding?"

"Not a thing," he protested.

The troubadour made a wry face. "Whatever you say, master. I've got your gold, I've no reason to complain. Your friend's found friends, though."

He followed the direction of the man's chin and saw Geryn striding purposefully through the throng in the company of a trio of Red Lions, resplendent in their scarlet tabards. The Pathfinder had the look of someone who'd just been called a liar, his companions in far better humor.

Thorn turned back with a last question for the troubadour, wondering how it was an Angwyn Princess rode at the head of a Maizan column, but found only empty space by his side.

"Gone," cried Rool from the carryall, the first he'd spoken to Thorn all day.

"Nicely done, too. I can't see a sign of him."

"Not saying much, Drumheller. From where the likes of us stand, all these Daikini look alike. Catch us up, will you?" he called, before Thorn had a chance to reply.

"We want to stay close," he continued as Thorn tucked him and Franjean under his jacket.

"Any particular reason?"

"Harder to lose your coat than your bag. Just don't giggle if we have to move."

"Don't tickle when you do, and it's a bargain."

"Drumheller!" Geryn called, in his own pale approximation of a parade-ground voice. "Thorn Drumheller!"

"I was wondering where you'd got to, Pathfinder Havilhand. I'm glad to see you've found comrades."

"See," Geryn said triumphantly, an outstretched arm presenting Thorn to the others. "A Nelwyn."

They looked, one to the other. They didn't believe.

"I am," Thorn told them. "I swear. I believe I can help in your search for the Magus."

Another set of looks, and Thorn had a sudden sense of dread that he'd said too much and all of it wrong.

"You know the Magus?" he was asked.

"Come a blessed long way, we have," Geryn said with exaggerated patience. "I found 'im out by the Scar."

If he'd had longer legs, Thorn would have run right then. But he wasn't sure of the city, or the situation; with no place to hide and no desire to reveal any more about himself than he already had, he decided to stand his ground.

"Right, then," one of the Lions conceded with a grunt. "Captain'll want to talk with you both." The decision wasn't subject to discussion. Or resistance.

Their captain had been a captain too long and would remain one until he died. Short on stature, short on wit, he compounded both with a nose for cheap wine and a belly for bad food. The only thing he had going for him in his life was his position—he was a captain in the Red Lions, though heaven knew how he'd won such a rank—and he made the most of it.

"Well!" he said, eyeing Geryn and Thorn. The Pathfinder stood at attention, spine stretched so straight Thorn thought it would pop.

"Take off yer damn hat, Peck, damn yer eyes, before yer betters, ain'tcha been taught no manners?" This came from behind—the corporal who led the detachment that brought them in—accompanied by a swift cuff to the back of Thorn's head.

The hat went flying, but Thorn caught it before it went out of reach.

"Nelwyn," the captain huffed.

"Looks like some damn Peck t' me," from one of the other Royals.

"Who the hell asked yeh?" snapped Geryn. Then, remembering where he was, he pulled himself even straighter and apologized to the captain. "Beg pardon, sir. But there's no call, they speak so. I was just doin' me duty, sir."

"Done well, Pathfinder. Be sure to mention it. In my report. Nelwyn," he repeated, in a questioning tone, fixing red-veined eyes on Thorn, who found himself resisting the temptation to use his Talent to blaze a path to freedom. "Leave him in our hands now. Good hands. We'll be responsible, see he's taken care of."

"Sir, I thought . . ."

"Not paid t' think, boy. Only do. Thinkin's for officers. Like me. We'll be in touch when you're needed. Corporal, see the lad's proper settled. Our barracks, o' course, since there's no quarters for his regiment in Angwyn. Ale from my own store, serve him up right fair."

"Yes, sir."

"And . . . Master Drumheller?" Geryn asked.

"I *told* you, boy. Now be off about your business an' let me be on with mine. Or have Pathfinders forgotten how to take orders?"

"Nossir! I mean, uh, yessir! I, uh . . ."

"Dismissed!"

He went.

The captain had fair speed for a man of his bulk and long-term dissipation. For all his gut, there was a fair amount of muscle as he swept out from behind his desk and rammed Thorn against the wall with a bone-rattling impact. The moment coincided with the door to his office closing; Thorn doubted anyone outside heard a thing and, even if they had, would interfere. The captain held him head-high, by the bunched front of his jacket, the stench of body and breath combining to make Thorn nauseous. His stare worked Thorn over as though he was some new and noxious form of bug about to be squashed.

"Nelwyn, are you?" he mocked.

"Is that a crime?"

The captain slapped him backhand. Gently for him, Thorn suspected, even though it drew blood and made his jaw ache, more of a promise of what was to come if the captain's mood changed. Then he saw the knife.

"Whatever you said to bamboozle that hick," the captain said, "won't play here. You're in quicksand, my little man, up to your nose." He tucked the point underneath Thorn's jaw and drew more blood with a calculated poke.

"What have I done?" he protested.

"Only one Nelwyn in Angwyn, Peck. Only one in the whole world, an' that be the Magus. But he warned of an impostor. A blood enemy, he said, of him an' the Sacred Princess."

"Whatever are you *talking* about!"

The captain dug the point in deeper, and blood flowed freely.

"Your lucky day you need voice and tongue to tell your story, else I'd have both out for taking a tone like that with me. We'll let you rot awhile. A night or two in the vaults, I'll wager you'll tell us everything. Haunted, they are, those dungeons. Work on prisoners better'n torture."

He tossed Thorn aside, into the arms of one of the other guardsmen.

"Please," Thorn cried, "I don't understand—what Nelwyn are you talking about?"

"Not a deceiver, then, is it? Just plain dumb, is that yer ploy? Nice try, Peck, but that foolishness won't save you here. 'What Nelwyn,' indeed." The captain thought that was legitimately funny; his deputies took the hint and laughed as loudly. "One Nelwyn. One Magus. Who the hell else would that be but the Sacred Princess Elora's godfather? Though why he's so afeard of the likes of you, I've no notion."

"Her godfather?" Impossible as it was, only one name fit that description. "Do you mean Willow Ufgood?"

"The very same, Peck. What a revelation, yer not so daft nor dumb after all! The Magus wants you alive, an' then—unless I'm much mistaken, which I'm not—he wants you damned."

CHAPTER 4

HE'D BEEN IN DUNGEONS BEFORE; DIDN'T LIKE IT THEN, didn't now. They were all of a piece, as it seemed were the brutes who worked in them. Gray, dank figures lumbering among gray, dank stones, with manners as oppressive as the architecture. Some jailers reveled in filth; the warders here actually made an effort to maintain at least personal appearances. Uniforms were clean, cells were not.

Thorn was grabbed by the scruff of the neck and hustled along at so fast a clip—for him, anyway—that he had to run. More than once along the way, impatience prompted his escort to yank him completely off the floor and carry him for a bit. Each time, though, he wasn't lowered so much as dropped. The hand on his collar wouldn't let him fall, but the stumbles were painful. He knew these humiliations were deliberate, to put him in his place and make him more tractable; that didn't make them hurt any the less.

There were broad stairs to start, but as they continued their descent the way became more difficult. Not by design, it was more a function of age. The deep substructures were far older than the ones above; successive monarchs had built new palaces upon the foundations of their predecessors. Different eras, different styles, until at the last they were winding their way down a circular stairway barely wide enough for two men to walk abreast. He had to focus all his concentration here to keep his footing; if he fell, he suspected he wouldn't stop before hitting bottom. Fortunately, the steps themselves were so worn and slippery from a slick coating of watery slime leaching off the walls—eloquent evidence that visits were few and very far between—that his guards had troubles enough keeping themselves from slipping. Thorn's relative lack of stature also worked to his advantage; his lower center of gravity and smaller feet made it much easier for him to negotiate a safe descent.

The warders brought their own torches, there were none below. Bright as they burned, the passage was dominated by a darkness so thick it seemed to swallow the illumination whole. Thorn and his escort stood in isolated pools of light, with only the slightest hints of what stood beyond. He could taste salt on the air, stale though it was, and feel a damp so profound it would guarantee sickness in any long-term resident. It was the Bay, he knew, threading its influence through the earth; they'd descended well below sea level.

"Most folks, they've forgotten all about these catacombs," the captain said, chortling. Of them all, he seemed least affected by the mood of the place. He stepped to the edge of the field of light, letting the gloom shroud his features and turn his face into a monster mask of planes and hollows. Thorn, having seen his share of true monsters, wasn't impressed but didn't let the feeling show.

"Not me, though," the captain continued. "Make it my business to know every inch of the palace underground. Can't do my job proper as captain of the guards without I know the lay of the land."

"Most commendable."

"You mock, Peck. I'd watch that, I were you, else I might forget to tell anyone you're here." To the warders, he said, "Manacles, my lads, hand and feet. Don't want the little man to go wandering. Might get himself lost. Or"—more delightedly—"stumble across something of a mind to eat him."

Three warders composed the escort. A torch was passed to the captain, who stayed behind in the passage. One warder took a watchful stance in the doorway, holding torch and drawn sword. These weren't the long, elegant blades of the Red Lions or even Geryn's Pathfinders; they were essentially big knives. Short, broad, and brutal, like the men who wielded them, as effective a club as it was a blade.

The remaining two had charge of Thorn himself. One held the Nelwyn and the last torch while his comrade set to work clamping the shackles tightly in place. They weren't gentle, speed was of the essence, and they didn't care how much they hurt him in the process. Thorn made no protest; there was no point, they wouldn't listen.

"No more smartmouth comments, Peck?" More mockery from the captain, mistaking Thorn's silence for fear. "Got some good news for you. No need to worry about rats or nothing of the like coming in the night for a snack."

Now why is that? Thorn thought rhetorically, while noting a sudden intake of breath on the part of the warder as he struggled with a rust-stiffened joint.

"No vermin down here at all, is why. Been eaten the lot, or chased away, you see, by the Demon. Stories say these vaults is haunted, reports go back as far as there's logbooks to record 'em, by a creature so fearsome it'll strip the flesh from your bones and the soul from your body."

"Sodding buggery *bastard*," hissed the warder as at last he wrenched the shackle open, and Thorn knew the curse had nothing to do with the rusty metal.

"Bad enough we're down 'ere"—spoken in a rushed whisper, almost like a prayer, as though the words themselves might keep away untold horrors—" 'e 'as to go an' throw down a bloody challenge! Don't watch *'im,*" he shouted suddenly to his companion, the reference to Thorn, " 'e ain't goin' nowhere! Watch *my* bloody back, rot cher eyes!"

"Sorry," was the shame-voiced apology, in a tone just as thick with dread.

The walls were mostly flat stone; the sudden increase in volume should have echoed through the room. Yet the sound had been deadened, consumed, as completely as the light from the torches.

With a hollow *click,* the last fetter snapped closed.

"You sure this is what the Magus wants?" Thorn called.

The captain turned back, the flames of his torch playing with the puffy rolls and hollows of his face, casting it as an ever-shifting display that managed to be both hideous and surprisingly silly.

"As a matter of fact," he said, offering the lie with a leer, "the orders were specific. This is precisely what he wants."

He stepped aside and the warder pulled the door closed.

Instant, absolute darkness.

But Thorn wasn't the least interested; his attention was focused on the rapidly fading footsteps, with one thought: *They're wasting no time clearing out, they truly believe something's down here.* The next, more important at the moment, was the realization that he'd heard no sound of the door latch clicking home, nor of the lock being turned. And at the last, stating the obvious: *This isn't what I had in mind at all.*

He opened senses wide, casting his perceptual net across the room, clipping his lower lip thoughtfully between his teeth when he received no return impression of the far walls, as though the darkness was swallowing his own abilities as it had the sound of voices.

"Well," he said aloud, just to prove he could both speak and hear.

There was no sign of life—or *unlife,* for that matter—about him that he could tell, none of the vermin that make their home in these dank, deep places, not even the faintest residual trace. This dungeon had been *empty,* to the fullest extent of the word, for a very long time.

"Drumheller," said Franjean, very quietly, right beside his ear.

"We do not like this place," echoed Rool, by the other ear.

Their voices were tight with tension, bodies poised for battle; flight wasn't an option. Not because there weren't a multitude of places for the brownies to hide, he understood, but because they didn't see any point in trying. Whatever was here would seek them out wherever they went to ground. Yet, to the best of his questing, there was *nothing* here.

He said as much. They weren't reassured. Neither was he.

"Franjean," he said, "I need some stones from my pouch." The guards had searched him before bringing him down, and stripped him to his clothes. Or so they'd believed. He'd cast a minor glamour to protect his traveling belt pouches. "Just reach in, there should be a half dozen in a little satchel."

The brownie wasn't at all happy to leave Thorn's shoulder, but he also knew this wasn't a casual request. He went down Thorn's side like a spider, with so light and delicate a touch that Thorn hardly noticed a stir as Franjean retrieved the prize.

"In my mouth, please," Thorn told him. Ideally, he'd have preferred to hold them in his hand, but the manacles were too tight, he couldn't twist either palm upward to catch the pebbles.

They were cool to the taste, some rough, some smooth as blown glass. He sucked the moisture from his mouth, ruthlessly repressing twin desires to gag and cough, and began to sing in his mind. It was a simple tune of memory; what he wanted wasn't very complicated, nothing on the order of what he'd done up in the mountains. The stones had come from a fire pit he'd laid along the trail; now his melody reminded them of what that had been like: how the flames had warmed them, inside and out, until they'd begun to glow, returning in full measure the heat and light they'd been given. At the same time he added a counterpointing undertone, to keep himself from being burned.

It was quickly done, for this had been a fairly recent fire, their last night before the rendezvous with Maulroon, and the memory was fresh. That was both the blessing and curse about working with stone; it took forever to explain what you wanted and to persuade it to comply, but once the deed was done, the imprinting lasted a good, long while.

One by one, he spit out the stones. They left burning trails in the darkness as they fell, like meteors Thorn had watched fall from the heavens, to be consumed by the air as they flashed earthward. His aim was good, and they didn't bounce far once they struck the floor; he ended up with a reasonably tight grouping a body length in front of him. They brightened with every passing moment, until all six blazed white-hot.

"Interesting," he said, when he able to speak.

"We're happy *you're* impressed," groused Franjean, not bothering to hide his agitation.

"By rights, those stones should be generating sufficient energy to heat and light a goodly portion of the cell."

"Mayhap you didn't serenade them with the proper tune, then," from Rool, with no less an edge, "because I'm still bloody *freezing!*"

"No, they're doing their part, see how they glow? It's something else."

"Now, *there's* a comforting thought."

"Yet there's nothing here."

"You could hide an army in that nightscape," said Franjean.

"I'd sense them. Or you would. I mean, there's *nothing.* A great void, as if we're the only things in this space that even exist, much less live."

"All the more reason, Drumheller, for making a speedy exit, don't you think?"

"Would you pick the lock, please? The manacle's too tight, I can't manage it myself."

There were no rude comments from the brownies, in itself a stark measure of their distress, as they set quickly to work; Rool handled the lock picks while Franjean watched his back. They chose the most rusted piece first, saturating the joints with a mixture of oil and graphite before applying shoulders and pry bars to move the inner mechanism. It was a very simple lock, the difficulty came from it not having been used in a good long time. After a struggle, however, it creaked open.

The effort cost Rool, he was trembling with fatigue. Thorn had been watching through the brownie's own eyes, so he knew now precisely how the device worked. The other manacle wasn't in quite so poor a state, and he made a fast job of it and then the leg irons.

"I remember," Thorn said softly while he worked, as though they were in the road, sitting about their campfire, only this time it was him telling the ghost stories to while away the evening and not the brownies, "old Spanyo Duguay, he said he'd met a Demon once."

"And lived to tell the tale," scoffed Franjean. "I don't think so."

"Like watching a potter work clay on the wheel, was what he told folks at the Ram's Head Inn, back in Nelwyn Vale, only much faster. Couldn't hold the same shape for more'n a heartbeat. Compared it to mercury maybe, or melting wax. Great globs of stuff, bubbling and flowing in the air before him."

"If this is meant to be reassuring . . ." Rool prompted.

"Just passing the moment—*aha!*" There was a welcome *click*. "That's the last."

"Shall we run?"

"Not much use, Franjean, if we can't see where we're going. My MageSight can make out basic shapes and forms, but my depth perception's not to be trusted. Can either of you see any better?" Silence. Evidently not. "If we aren't alone here, whatever's with us has had its chance and more to attack."

"As if it couldn't change its mind?"

"We'll have to take that risk. It's a better alternative than cracking our own skulls slipping on those steps, or worse yet, finding a pitfall or another trap."

Unspoken between them from the start was the charge, *If you'd only listened on the damn boat, we wouldn't even be in this fix!* And banging up against that, smashed and twisted together like dray wagons after a crossroads collision, the brownie's mocking recitation of the Aldwyn's charge to those who desired to be his apprentices. Thorn remembered wanting that post more than almost anything. And realizing when he'd ridden home after his first adventure that he already wielded greater Power than the Old Nelwyn had ever possessed. A bittersweet insight because even then he'd had an inkling of the eventual cost demanded of him. In the happiness of victory, the joy of homecoming, he'd refused to face it. As he had the destruction of Tir Asleen.

So easy, so tempting, to yield to the tiredness in his soul. To let himself be overwhelmed by the devastation he'd seen, those great wounds of the world. If Elora was the Light, past time she began to shine, so she could take the burden of responsibility from his shoulders. Not so long ago, that dirge of misery and self-pity would have been all he heard. Now, strangely, the feelings made him smile.

Strange, he thought, *to burn so hot and cold. To set myself as the sword of Justice on the one hand, the better to avenge my friends, and yet desire just as strongly to pass the blade on to another.*

Nelwyn nature was to be like Geryn's da, place family, hearth, and home above all, let the rest of the world follow its own road. There was a comfort in knowing your place in the scheme of things, a security in the ordinary. It was a tug-of-war within Thorn's soul that never seemed to end, and often felt like it would tear him apart. The problem was, for Thorn—and this had nothing to do with his being a sorcerer, this was part of his essential nature, that had always set him painfully apart from his friends and neighbors—what use legs, if not to take him down the road? What use eyes, if not to see what lay beyond the horizon? What use hands, if not to open doors?

He looked past the doorway. The radiance of his stones reached most of the way up the entry stairs and he found his OutSight more than sufficient to compensate for the darkness beyond. Looking back the other way, however, showed him only a gloom so deep and absolute he might as well be blind. It left him with the unassailable feeling that if he put his back to the wall and slid beyond the range of light, the rock would vanish from his touch as well as view.

He crouched down to gather his stones, then thought better of it. A sudden flash of inspiration, he had no idea what prompted it; the notion came from deep within that part of himself where his own Talent interacted with the Great Powers of the World and Worlds Beyond.

The light they cast was a small thing, against the oppressive mass of darkness, like a sapling at the foot of a glacier, with no hope or fate but to be overwhelmed. Yet it was a friendly glow, bringing a measure of warmth to a place that had known none in as long as the castle's stones themselves had memory. (And he couldn't help a shudder at the thought of how long that must be.)

He wished them well and then, to his surprise . . .

"And fair fortune to you, too," aloud, to the dark, as though it was real.

"Are you *demented?*" Franjean whispered—a rhetorical question because from the way he asked, it was abundantly clear the answer had to be, "Absolutely!"

"Can we *go!*" from Rool.

"A courtesy, is all," Thorn began as he started up the steps, but Franjean cut him off.

"Please!" Thorn had to marvel how such a little voice could project so much acid contempt, and in a single word. "Next you'll be thanking the headsman for a clean cut as you go bouncing off the execution block!"

"If he's good at his job, the compliment's well earned."

There was no reply, because Thorn misplaced his foot on the last step, landing on the tiptoe of his boot instead of the ball of the foot. There was a scummy dampness coating the stone, in the hollow worn by countless footfalls over equally countless generations. The surface was both slick and brittle. A portion crumbled under his weight, and when he automatically shifted his balance to compensate, he found himself skidding as though he was on ice. His foot went sideways, his hands went out hard to catch himself before he could crack his face. All this happened in a few split seconds.

When his bare palms slapped the stone, they burned.

A flush of heat, raw and uncontainable, his blood transformed to dry prairie grass that some fool had set alight, the conflagration racing up his arms like a runaway wildfire, consuming him from fingers to toes in a single heartbeat.

Someone had died here, a long, long time ago. Proud and angry, defiant to the end, facing hopeless odds yet determined to fight on regardless. With such a force of spirit that time hadn't faded the imprint of her personality one whit.

A javelin butt to the jaw had stunned her, a whiplash curling about her ankle upending her. She'd done a demi-cartwheel, her head striking the outer lip of the stairs with that unique, awful, fatal *crack*. The body had tumbled to the floor below.

Thorn followed, back down the steps and along the dimly lit curve of the staircase until he was directly below the doorway.

"Here's where she landed," he spoke aloud.

"An old moment, Drumheller," Rool said, thin-voiced with the struggle to master his terror. The brownies had felt the vision as strongly as he.

"Even scavengers would have left something."

"So old the body's long since crumbled to dust."

"Not the slightest residue, Rool, not physical, not psychic. The imprint of her soul is burned into the very stone up above, but this spot's totally empty. As though it had been wiped clean."

"Fine," snarled Franjean, "the 'Demon' took it. Can we perhaps make just a tiny effort not to be next?"

"It was a noble soul." Thorn told them both as he retraced his path, taking care this time to step around the spot where he'd fallen. There was anger to his voice, not so much at the death itself—she was a warrior, that came through most strongly, this was a fate she'd long before accepted—but at the betrayal that led to it.

As suspected, the warders hadn't bolted the door, and while

the hall itself was mostly night, he found his vision far more effective here than below.

"What now?" asked Franjean. "Elora?"

"Need I state the obvious, and say something's very wrong here?"

"No more than we need compound the felony by noting you just did."

He smiled. If Franjean could banter, the brownies' spirits were on the rise as well.

"Interesting," he mused as they went, "these references to her protector."

"What a concept, Rool," Franjean exclaimed to his companion, "a world not big enough for two Nelwyn!"

"Saw the circular on the captain's desk," was Rool's low-voiced response, combat tones for a combat stalk, without a trace of his companion's humor. "Fair likeness of a Nelwyn. They've been looking hard and long. Find 'em, bring 'em in. Saving grace was our being beyond imperial territory, and staying among friends since we arrived."

"Some friends," groused Franjean, "not to warn us."

"Read like the search was kept quiet."

"All the more reason to turn our questions into answers," said Thorn.

Franjean made a snort of derision.

"I beg your pardon," Thorn couldn't help challenging, afraid they were about to pick up their previous fight but unable to let the provocation slide.

"You forget, Drumheller," was the serious reply, "the one defines the other. And perhaps invalidates it."

"If you *know* something, Franjean . . . !"

"I wish it were that easy, believe you me! But it's what *you* know that matters. *You're* the Magus, remember?"

As if, he rumbled to himself, *you ever let me forget.*

Near the top of the steps, once more at the doorway to the cell, he took a moment to pull a Cloak about himself and the brownies. A passive charm, as had been most of what he'd used thus far, it made him blend with the background. Any who saw him from here on would fit him within the context of the moment; in a very real sense, he'd simply blend with the background and they'd never give him a second thought.

Looking back into the cell, Thorn was struck by a surge of disorientation. Intellect, his common sense, told him where he was and what he was looking at; yet he couldn't shake the sense, almost a certainty, that he beheld the night sky. An all-encompassing blackness that went on forever. He saw no sense of shape or boundary below him; his scattering of stones had no fixed place in that ebony void, they floated like stars and seemed almost as remote.

With a shudder, Thorn stepped across the threshold, once more into the comfortingly familiar realm where shadows were caused by the absence of light, and not of life itself.

Rool took the point, and the three of them made their wary way up the spiral staircase.

"I have an observation," Franjean offered, all business, without any of the poses struck for effect during normal conversation.

"I've noticed, too. This is a surprisingly clean dungeon."

Thorn heard a dismissive sniff. "With all due respect"—which, the brownie's tone made plain, had dropped to less than none— "it would make life easier if you'd not jump to conclusions. Especially when they're erroneous."

"I stand corrected."

"Far too often, if you ask me. Would have thought you'd have learned by now."

"There's nobody else here," hissed Rool from up ahead, having hopped down the worn slabs to meet them.

"The warders are gone?"

"No. They're grumbling over their beer. But they're it. Every level, every cell, all empty!"

"My observation precisely," echoed Franjean with an appropriate and well-deserved air of triumph. Thorn smiled a tigerish smile, hoping it wouldn't be seen by his companions, and repressed a sudden urge to murder.

"Any idea since when?" he asked.

"Long time. *Long* time. I can't smell a soul, past or present, 'cept for those two sluggos up top."

"Nor can I." Thorn nodded thoughtfully.

"Demon," said Franjean.

"How so?"

"Eaters of souls, that's what they're called, yes? Obviously this one's been having itself a feast."

Thorn said nothing. That made the brownies even more nervous.

"What?" prompted Rool. "I don't much like it, Drumheller, when you go all silent."

"A SoulEater is by nature evil."

"A creature of Shadow, absolutely spot on." Franjean, using the all-encompassing term for the Dark Realms and Forces. "And what do we have below us but a chamber of absolute shadow. The one betokens the other."

"I'm not so sure. . . ."

"Do we care? Under the circumstances, I don't think so."

They all kept silent as they slipped past the guardroom. Rool was right about the warders. Beer was their truest friend and their appreciation for what had to be the cushiest berth in the empire vied with an equally strong apprehension about what they believed lived deep below. In all their days here, this was the first time they'd been to those catacombs and they weren't happy about it. Or the prospect that, sooner or later, they'd have to return. They were praying, in fact, that it be on someone else's shift.

"Afraid, they are," said Rool, "of what they might have stirred up."

"Poor bunnies," said Thorn without sympathy.

"But not you, Drumheller?"

"I'm still not sure, Rool. I'm sorry. Evil has a taste to it. . . ."

"Perhaps it's hidden. Perhaps you're not sensitive enough to notice."

"Perhaps."

"What's our favorite saying? 'When in doubt, err on the side of caution'?"

"You talk like a Nelwyn."

Franjean, a sudden, sharp interruption: "And you're starting to act too much like a Daikini."

"What's that supposed to mean?"

Franjean chose not to answer, and Thorn not to press the point. This keep was easily the oldest structure on the palace grounds, standing alone on a neighboring hill, separated from the main buildings by a clutch of horse barns and carriage houses, with a dramatically commanding view of the city and Bay beyond, so solidly constructed that its walls appeared to be a natural extension of the hill itself. The foreslope was steep and high enough to exhaust any force making a frontal assault. The back side of the hill was much gentler and led originally to a smaller summit beyond. However, over the generations, nature had been much improved on. The hollow between two knolls had been filled in and considerably enlarged, until an artificial rise had been created half again as high as the hill on which stood the original citadel. The one had been a fortress, this was a true palace, a place of gaiety and light. It looked formidable, but just the one glance told Thorn the battlements were mostly for show. The walls were too tall and delicate, broken by far too many windows. The views were spectacular, and on a clear evening, the sight of the palace all lit from within commanding the skyline had to be breathtaking.

"*Oi!*" came a sudden bellow, catching them all by surprise. In that first moment Thorn thought it was one of the warders and nearly made a reflexive dash for the gate. But experience overrode instinct and he made himself take another couple of seconds to establish the situation before reacting.

"*You!*" The Daikini was cut from similar cloth as the warders, big in every dimension, though with far more of a belly. Thorn decided to play dumb, with a look over his shoulder as though the man were yelling for someone else, and then a querying thumb pointed at himself.

"Yes," the man cried in exasperation, "you! Short fella! Here! Now! *Hop to it!*" he finished with a roar, when Thorn didn't cross the courtyard with sufficient alacrity. He was a man for whom instant, unquestioning obedience was a state of nature. Given the way his body was constructed, Thorn felt like he was standing close by an avalanche waiting to happen.

"Godstrewth," the man complained, to every Deity worth the name, "how I'm 'spected to manage a proper celebration with the kind of help I've got I *don't* know I'm sure! Keep lollygagging like that, my little lad, the Sacred Princess Elora'll be croaked of old age before we're ready."

"Sorry," was all Thorn hazarded in reply as he clambered up onto the wagon seat.

"I hope you're stronger'n you look, I got no patience with shirkers, especially today."

"I'll pull my fair weight," Thorn assured him.

The look he got in return wasn't encouraging.

The wagon was the tail end of a convoy of goods that wound its way from the Old Keep—where the supplies came in, as opposed to the far more ornate Monarch's Mount Gate, which was for guests—to the rear of the palace. The basic lines of the overall design had been kept through this wing as well, but they were far more simplified and functional. This was the section of the palace that none but staff were ever meant to see. It had to work because they had to; adornments only got in the way. The windows weren't as big, nor were there as many; the mason stones were square and solid, lacking any of the gingerbread carvings that decorated the public facade. A triple set of doors led off the loading dock, not so tall as the main entrance around front but considerably wider; the one a function of aesthetics, to usher visitors into the palace's towering and most impressive atrium, these a matter of practicality. Made clear as the drover expertly backed his wagon into place and Thorn saw servants unrolling huge barrels of wine and beer from another in the next stall over. Obviously not the day's first delivery and he suspected the haulers were a long way from done. No one looked their best, not even close, surcoats removed and set aside, shirts unlaced and sleeves rolled up, lines of fatigue etched about eyes and mouths, bodies moving gracelessly, flat-footed and stiff-limbed. When the driver turned on his seat to look for him, Thorn stepped behind a page—still mostly boy and only half a head taller than the Nelwyn, though much lighter in the build—and wrapped his Cloak a little more tightly about himself. As far as the driver was concerned, the page was the "short fella" who'd ridden up with him; fact was, he had too much to do to waste even a thought on it. He gave orders, the boy obeyed, that was satisfaction.

Meanwhile, Thorn snaked his way through the press of people and into the corridor beyond. Along the way, he snatched himself a Royal surcoat and a silver serving tray, carrying it as though he was on the most important of errands.

The corridor itself was so wide six big men could walk abreast with room to spare, yet so crowded he had to struggle to make any headway. To his left were a line of broad, basket-handled archways leading straightaway or down ramps or flights of steps to various storerooms. Along the piers that separated each opening were crates of every size, piled higher than actually looked safe. In appearance, the scene most resembled the ultimate moving day, only not everything was packed and too many people had too many notions where the pieces were supposed to go. Confrontations abounded, men bumping bellies and trying their best to top each other's bellows—no mean feat considering the background din—with arms gesticulating wildly and faces turning red as rich wine.

"Don't tell me t' put it *there,* y' great, thumpin' pillock," he heard from one such encounter as he made his way with crablike determination as much sideways as forward through the thicket of legs.

"Can't have it blockin' road, can we?" came the equally forthright reply.

"Use yer eyes then, see f'r bloody *self*"—Islander brogue, a match for Maulroon's, thickening with anger with almost every word—"there's no more bloody *room*! It'll have t' go somewhere else."

"It can't. You'll simply have to find a way to make it fit. I don't want to hear anymore, I don't care. We're expecting ambassadors from the Thirteen Realms, there hasn't been a conclave like this in recorded memory, His Majesty wants it done *right*. Our responsibility, our job, and there's the end to it."

"Damn bloody *daft* is what I call it!"

"Fine. You go tell him. I'll send condolences to your next of kin."

"A poxy curse—"

"Don't say that!" The steward's cry topped every other voice in earshot, bouncing off walls and ceiling as the hall fell suddenly, eerily still. The man himself looked a bit abashed, as though he hadn't suspected he could make such a noise. "For *mercy's* sake," he continued, more quietly but with not a whit less passion. His voice was actually shaking, and as the import of his words sank home, the other man's face turned ashen.

"This goes for you all," the steward said, addressing everyone present. "Words have meaning. Curses have power, especially when there are those present who might, on a whim, choose to indulge them. I beg you, these next few days, with all the thirteen realms here present, be careful. In what you say, in what you *think*!"

"Be a blessing when this circus finally closes," came from nearby in the crowd. Thorn couldn't quite see from where, or who was speaking.

"We should live so long," grumbled a brownie. Only later did Thorn realize that hadn't been meant as a gibe.

He threaded his way through one of the right-hand arches to find himself in a kitchen, the likes of which he'd never seen. It stretched the whole width of this wing of the palace, a phalanx of stone hearths, each with its attendant chopping blocks and preparation tables. Between the arches opposite, set against their pillared supports, were equally impressive sinks, fed by pipes that ran down the walls from the ceiling to provide both hot and cold running water. There were racks for pots and pans, others for cutlery, others still for the makings of the feast. In one corner, the carcass of a cow was being swiftly and efficiently reduced to its component cuts, while another was occupied by a crowd of children—barely in their teens—plucking all manner of fowl. Beyond another portal was another chamber, impressive in its own right, devoted to nothing but the cleaning of all the implements. There was constant movement between the two, as scullery lads rushed implements out to be washed and returned them cleaned to where they were needed.

At first glance, the chaos without seemed replicated in full measure within, but a second look gave the lie to that impression. Thorn felt as though he was watching some tremendous human machine; there was a purpose to every action, whether it was turning a haunch of meat on a rotisserie spit or checking off the raw ingredients for tonight's feast of welcome. The staff moved with the precision of a drill team; separate tables had distinct responsibilities, as did each person working at the tables, a different section of the room for every dish and every course. One handled soup, another fowl, three varieties of meat (domestic red meat, wild red meat, domestic white), two of fish (fin and shell), salads and vegetables in abundance, plus all the attendant sauces and dressings and garnishes. The air was rich with heady scents of basil and coriander, pepper and hickory, cinnamon and chocolate. Plus appetizers and desserts and from yet another whole separate chamber, crate after crate of wine. Meats were being roasted and broiled, grilled and sautéed, fowls emerged from the oven with dark, crackling skin, while long copper pans filled with wine and fragrant herbs were set on the hob to poach fish. At the head of the room, on a long trestle table, were facsimiles of each of the planned dishes for the banquet, so the staff would have a template for their presentation, and the senior chefs—and ultimately Cook herself—an ideal to measure the actual servings against.

Thorn had never seen such a tumult and part of him yearned desperately for a seat at the tables upstairs, to taste even a portion of this feast. He was so enrapt by the sights and sounds and smells of the kitchen, he quite forgot that he was an intruder. In the hall he was one lost soul among a multitude; nobody noticed him because nobody truly knew what the hell was going on or who should be doing what. Here, because of his ignorance, he stood out.

And was as quickly marked for it.

"What's this, then?" challenged a female voice, and he yipped as fingers pinched his ear tighter than any vice.

"Sorry, miss," he gabbled. "Meant no harm, miss. Just trying to help, I was."

"Who's your master?" She started to frog-march him back toward the hall.

"Minh!" A call from the far end of the kitchen. "What's the problem?" An even more formidable woman, starched skirts hardly wilted in the ferocious heat, sleeves properly buttoned, bodice laced, hair wound into a crown as respectable as it was convenient. She wore a full apron that covered her from collarbone to ankle, and as she approached—with free-ranging and commanding strides that would do a warrior proud—she patted excess flour off her hands. The apron strings were wound round her back, tied in front, and a pair of dish towels were tucked through them; she used one to wipe her hands clean.

"No problem, Cook," was the reply, emphasized by another sharp tug on Thorn's ear. "Just disposing of someone who was where he ought not be."

"Reasonably dressed, reasonably clean," Cook noted, and Thorn wondered what vision his Cloak was presenting to her. Ideally, what she wanted most to see. "He'll do."

"Beg pardon," from Thorn and Minh together.

"It's late." Cook was already striding away. "Bring him." Which Minh did, more enthusiastically than before. "We're so backed up and shorthanded down here, the entire day's schedule's a lost cause. Bad enough His Majesty has to wait on supper, we've just had another complaint from Herself."

"Blessed fates have mercy."

"Precisely. But I won't hold my breath."

"Beg pardon?" Thorn tried to interject.

"Cart's there," Cook said to him, the best he was going to get by way of reply or explanation. Even as she spoke he realized her mind had leaped ahead to the next crisis and the one beyond. She wasn't interested in anything he had to say or do save carry out her commands.

"Through that door," she continued, with a point in the appropriate direction. "Down the hall, up the lift. Apologies for this being a cold sup. If she lays hand on you, youngster, I'll make it good."

She thought he was a boy, another of the ubiquitous serving pages. Good. Chances were she wouldn't notice him missing till she took a second look toward her precious cart. Given the natural pandemonium of the kitchen, heaven knew when that would be.

"Who's it for?" he asked.

"The Sacred Princess Elora, of course."

The cart was a struggle. It stood as tall as he did and weighed far more, with three trays laden near to overflowing. Food for a family, but a table setting for one. A glance told him the quality of workmanship of the service, a touch its provenance; each piece was unique, individually forged and shaped and painted. Nothing was used twice, not for a meal, not for a day.

Torchères at intervals lit the passage, set in polished sconces that spread their light around to eliminate any hint of shadow. It was a fair walk; new construction as well, the tower clearly the most recent addition to the palace. The flagstone beneath his feet had been intentionally sanded smooth, the seams filled in so that the floor formed one smooth plain from start to finish, and the trolley wheels oiled so that they rolled with neither squeak nor stutter. Likewise, every element of the load had been carefully packed and padded. Made sense. The china was so fine, the crystal so delicate, a harsh look might shatter it. Thorn allowed himself a small smile, realizing that in all likelihood the King himself probably didn't eat off such plate. Then he thought of the serviceable pewter that he was used to, and his smile broadened to a proper grin.

He emerged into a modest antechamber, bare of furnishings,

brick all around, with only one other door, big enough for a Daikini standing tall, obligingly open. There were vent holes high up in the curved, cathedral ceiling, too small for him (though not for the brownies) and well out of his reach. No other exits, no openings of any kind.

He stepped through the other doorway, because that was clearly what was expected of him.

The entire room began to rise.

"A lift," he murmured delightedly, once he'd put aside his initial startlement. "Brilliant."

"So glad *you* think so," groused Franjean.

"She lives in a tower, my friend. I was wondering how we were supposed to carry this load up to her."

He fished in his pouch for a comb, took a few swipes through his tangled russet hair to restore some small semblance of order, then quickly gathered it together behind his head in a thick plait. Brush went away, back into the pouch, replaced by a tooled silver pin, which he quickly fastened into place. Unfortunately, the clothes he could do nothing about; in that regard, Elora Danan would have to take him as he was.

"Heaven forfend," Franjean again, "the 'Sacred Princess' might deign to come down."

"Must be steps, though," offered Rool, "something to use in case this breaks."

"Probably another lift as well," Thorn agreed. "That offers direct access to the palace. For Elora herself. One for Royals, one for staff."

"Pretty damn tall, this place." Rool again. "We've been climbing at a fair decent pace and we haven't yet arrived."

Thorn was about to answer when he was slapped hard by a wave of bitter chill. Not the cold of wind and weather; years walking the wildlands, plus the judicious application of his powers, had inured him to those extremes. This struck beyond the flesh, a breath of foulness to coat his soul in rime ice.

He laid hand flat against the wall, but sensed nothing untoward. They were still rising, and with every moment the sensation grew more distant.

"Bugger this," growled Rool. "Franjean's right, Drumheller. I say we go, and quickly."

The brownies stood back-to-back, weapons in hand, as they had in the cell.

"It's not any Demon," he told them, belatedly noting he'd drawn a blade of his own.

"A rookery," he said. He returned his knife to its sheath, then cast propriety to the winds and poured a goblet of water from Elora's decanter. It was flavored with lemon, which managed to make it taste both tart and sweet. He took a hearty swallow, passed it on to the brownies, then spoke aloud what all three of them knew. "Night Herons."

"Hellsteeth," hissed Rool.

"Demons in the catacombs," was Franjean's contribution, "Night Herons in the tower, a wonderful home the Sacred Princess has made for herself."

"She's not yet thirteen, Franjean," Thorn snapped, "and considering what happened to her first home, it's not as if she had much choice in the matter." *Or,* he couldn't help adding, with a sudden, bitter, wholly unexpected rage that shook him to his core, more so than had the encounter with the herons, *friends to stand by her during those awful times.* One, in particular.

I had grief enough of my own, he told himself. Explanation perhaps, but no longer acceptable as an excuse. *She was better off without me.*

So he'd believed, all these years. Now he wasn't so sure.

Herons were for the air what Death Dogs were on foot. The appearance of something living wrapped around a core of rot. They possessed a dark majesty, sable with scarlet accents, so that when they stooped to the attack—with a speed and ferocity that put the eagles' to shame—it was as though a spear of blood was plunging from the sky. Far worse, though, was the inescapable sense of intelligence made evident by every move and manner. Hounds served because they were born to the role, herons because they chose to. It . . . amused them. When they killed, it was as much for pleasure as need. And while they consumed the flesh of their victims, often while the prey still lived, it was the sheer terror of those moments, the agony both physical and emotional, that gave them true sustenance. Beneath the glittering facade, bursting with pride and wealth, Angwyn had a rotten core.

The lift stopped. A door was opened.

The view was intended to take the breath away. He'd seen better and, at the moment, had more important concerns, brushing past the waiting servants and crossing to the balcony. Peering over the edge told him nothing. The top of the tower belled outward from the stalk, as though a plate were balanced atop a stick, with a diameter so wide it cut off his line of sight to the stretch immediately below, where he was sure the rookery lay. Probably nothing to see anyway, since herons, true to their name, were nocturnal.

"What is *happening* here?" he breathed. Death Dogs, Maizan, Night Herons—he found, to his surprise, that he didn't include the reputed Demon of the dungeon in this litany; whatever malevolence it represented, he suspected it had faded long before Daikini even came to this place, much less founded the current dynasty. The others, though, they were fresh and hungry forces, predators all, and he knew without needing proof that their presence in Angwyn—especially on the eve of Elora's Ascension— was no coincidence.

"The King should know of this," he continued, and felt his face go still as he considered the implications. "But he does, and doesn't care. But what about all the embassies? There are those among the Domains for whom the mere presence of a Heron is anathema, why haven't they reacted? And the Maizan as well. If the taint of Shadow on them is plain to me, why not to anyone else?" The memory of Tir Asleen touched him, and all the great powers assembled there a dozen years ago, not one of whom could sense what was coming.

He heard footsteps.

Last time he'd seen her, she'd barely learned to walk, yet these were as recognizable as his own. She'd smelled like a baby, too, mostly sour milk. Yet a single breath, the ghost of a scent as she approached stirred the air between them, and he knew it was her. He heard the *clack* of her heels on the tilework, the *shush-swish* of her clothes.

He didn't know what to say, even less what to do; he had nowhere to run.

And so, he turned. He couldn't help the shy and hopeful smile, or the words that popped out of his mouth.

"Elora Danan," he said.

"You call this food." She sneered. She had a plate from the trolley. "You call this a decent *meal*!"

Then she threw it at him.

CHAPTER 5

THE BROWNIES HAD BETTER REFLEXES. THEY DUCKED, HE didn't, partly because he couldn't believe what was happening. Fortunately, the plate only held cold meats, so there wasn't much of a mess.

Elora wasted no time rectifying that situation. She'd hauled the trolley after her and immediately grabbed for the condiment jars. He slapped aside some relish, wincing at the crash of crystal on stone; part of an artisan's life and soul had gone into the creation of that vessel, it deserved a better fate.

Of course, by then, he was decorated with a fair-sized helping of mustard. She had a good arm, matching strength with surprisingly precise accuracy, and he couldn't help the thought that she showed the skill of long practice, and realized at the same time that this explained the comparative absence of the servants he'd seen when he first emerged from the lift. This was his first brush with what for them must be a far more regular occurrence.

The brownies took full advantage of the situation to make some mischief. He caught both Rool and Franjean out of the corner of each eye, gleefully heaving goo back the way it came, placing Elora in a sudden, unexpectedly fierce cross fire that set her back on her heels in confusion.

Thorn gratefully made a break for cover, only to discover that the impromptu food fight had made the floor murderously treacherous. He uttered a gooselike squawk as first feet went flying and then the rest of him, depositing him with a thump right beside the cart. Elora responded by upending a silver tureen of cold soup over his head. He had a moment to appreciate the taste—which was delicious—before she dropped the bowl itself on top of him.

But he wasn't without resources himself, as his questing hands came up with a tall carafe of sparkling water. She thought him blinded by both soup and bowl, unaware that his InSight gave him a painfully perfect view of the scene, as she took hold of more things to throw at him. The brownies came once more to his defense, peppering Elora with the smelliest pieces of fish and cheese they could grab, while he plugged the mouth of the carafe with his thumb and gave it a hearty series of shakes.

He moved his thumb away just as she turned back to him, the contents of the carafe spraying forth as though from a fire hose, to strike her full in the face. Her eyes reflexively screwed themselves tight shut, hands waving ineffectually before her in a vain attempt to deflect the spray, but her mouth gaped wide. It was too tempting a target. Another quick shake of the carafe excited the last of the water, and then he shot it full between her teeth. She made *glug* noises, the same as if he'd dunked her underwater, then hit the flagstones herself as Franjean pulled on one ankle while Rool pushed on the other—far easier than it sounded, considering all the spilled food and drink had rendered the floor slick as ice. It was a graceless landing, hard on her bottom, and it prompted a caterwauling wail of outrage that speedily resolved itself into a cry for help.

"Guards!" she shrieked. *"Vizards! Help me!"*

Thorn considered this his cue to make a hasty exit. The girl recovered her wits with daunting speed. Fast as he moved, and for a Nelwyn he was breaking records, she hammered him full in the back with a trencher and barely missed with another carafe. He plucked it from the air just before it struck the corner of a wall, skidding down and around himself to duck out of the line of fire, cradling the etched crystal against his body as though it was a child. He found himself an alcove, where he was sure not to be run over, then wrapped himself snug in his Cloak. Any searcher—even one gifted with Talent—could stare right at him and see only bare stone.

The decanter was still mostly full, so he took a precious few moments for a drink. He felt a burning on his face and his mouth twisted with the harsh taste of vinegar and salad spices. He didn't want to consider what needed plucking from his hair.

Elora wasn't following. Too much effort, he supposed. Insofar as her targets were concerned, out of sight must mean out of mind.

"Caught you fair," said Rool, laughing. Though he'd been in the thick of battle, he, of course, was untouched, and as dapper as ever.

"Would have been worse, but for you. I'm grateful."

He started to access InSight, for a look at Elora's situation, but the brownie's words erased the need.

"She's sulking. Amazing noises, really, wouldn't have thought anything living could make such howls." Thorn nodded; his own children, even as babies, had never shrieked so. "No wonder she has Night Herons flocking to her, must believe she's one of their own."

"That isn't funny."

"Nor is she, Drumheller, though the moment had its humor."

"Why isn't anyone answering her cries?"

"After all this, you have to ask?"

"Considering what lies before her these next few days, she could be the most perishing little terror born—"

"To my mind, Drumheller, an understatement."

"—it wouldn't matter. With so much at stake, her minders would be extra-careful, not less so."

There was a flash of teeth as the little manling heaved a sack of something up into Thorn's lap. "Franjean's keeping watch, he'll call if she stirs or anyone else approaches. Not that you've any need to worry, Cloaked as you are."

"Famous last words, I'm sure."

"In the meanwhile we scavenged you a modest repast."

The sack was actually a napkin; Rool had used the silver slip ring to hold it closed. Inside was a very sloppy sandwich, mismatched slices of bread around a half-dozen varieties of meat, plus some cheese and tomato and lettuce.

"A tad messy," Rool acknowledged, "but that's only dirt. Naught I warrant to do a body proper harm."

"What, you just grabbed whatever was at hand off the floor?"

The brownie's shrug was a most eloquent reply. Thorn drew his knife, sliced the sandwich in half and then one of the pieces in half again. He returned all but a quarter to the napkin and then slipped it into his traveling pouch.

"You always do that."

"I beg your pardon?"

"More often than not, you'll take most of a perfectly good meal and stuff it in that silly bag."

"Likely to be hungry later. We *all* might." If they were, it wouldn't be the first time he'd pulled something from its depths to save them. He always considered the pouches the first practical use of his Talent; the day he'd made them was the one the High Aldwyn had given him the bones and his blessing. The day, thinking back on it, that Kiaya realized he would ultimately leave home and her. He'd wondered at her melancholy that afternoon, and for the first time she hadn't confided in him. His Talent would have easily pried the truth from her; he still wasn't sure which left him more aghast, the temptation itself or how nearly he came to yielding. And so, he came to learn that even the purest light, the most noble intent, cast a Shadow and could be used for ill. That had been the true lesson of the day.

"It's very good," Thorn said, forgetting his manners and speaking with his mouth full, "the bread especially."

"Do me a favor," he asked then, after clearing his palate with a hefty swallow of water. "While one of you watches Elora, I'd like the other to scout out whoever else is up here, servants and attendants and the like. See what we've to contend with."

"She isn't enough?"

"I'll wait here."

"Once again, we do the work, while our cruel and pitiless taskmaster . . ."

Franjean's voice trailed off. Something in Thorn's face took away the treat of mocking him.

"It's not so bad," the brownie offered.

"If you can't muster wit enough for a decent lie, it's worse by far."

"What will you do?"

"Think." A fractional pause, a hiccup of the heart. "Remember."

When last he'd seen Elora Danan, he was still twice her size and more. Round, rosy cheeks beneath a cap of unruly red-gold hair, flame-colored like a forest in high fall. Not so much fat to her frame as with most babies, but she'd had a far harder life for that first, fateful year. Two things were evident right off, an awesome strength—mostly of will at that point, since her body was still learning how to properly work—and a laugh to match. The baby had a raw delight, with everything and everyone she saw, a natural charm so fierce and overwhelming that none who met her could withstand it.

He'd loved her from the first, as much as if she'd been his own.

The strength remained, his bruises could attest to that. But not the laughter. Here was a harridan who didn't know the meaning of the word. He heard the sound of crashing and for the blink of an eye used InSight to merge his vision with Franjean's to see what was what. She'd upended the trolley and trampled the food to ruin; now she was methodically smashing every piece of plate and crystal. Breaking it to bits and then grinding each bit to powder. Shrieking all the while at the top of her lungs.

She had height on him now, standing half again as tall as he, with the promise of more to come in both leg and torso. When she reached her full growth, she'd be impressive even by Daikini standards. Unfortunately, at this point, she was plump. She'd lost none of her baby fat and put on more besides. Round face, bulging torso, as lacking of physical grace as she was in spirit. Hers was a face more used to sobs than smiles, from hurts Thorn suspected were generally more imagined than real. Her eyes were all closed and squinty, like a pig's, her mouth cast in a perpetual pout.

Where Anakerie had been dressed for comfort, Elora's costume was purely show. Layer upon layer, each wrapped and tied and buckled into place until the child could hardly move.

Doll clothes, he thought, *for a doll princess.*

"I never should have let you go," he said aloud, with a quiet sorrow. He let his head loll back against the wall. "I'd done all that was asked of me, I thought I was finished and you were safe. I thought I could go home, live my life—who was to know?"

He didn't need Franjean's ears to hear her; given the right wind, she could doubtlessly be heard on the ground.

"I hate you," she screamed. *"I hate you all!"*

"This certainly explains the tower," Franjean noted. For a disorienting moment, until Thorn disengaged his InSight, he looked up at himself through Franjean's eyes.

What a mess, was the thought that came to him. A distressingly forlorn picture, of a sad little man clutching a crystal carafe as though it was his own heart.

"You're not watching?"

"I have no stomach for it. She's wallowing in the mess—as much as that ridiculous costume will allow, which probably explains *it* as well—having herself a right proper tantrum. At this point, you don't look a fraction as awful as she." The brownie shook his head and munched on a radish, pausing after the first bite to add a sprinkle of salt. "If this is how she behaves on a regular basis, I'd want her as far from me and mine as could be managed."

"I wonder who she hates."

"Should we care, Drumheller?"

"She has a Destiny, Franjean."

"Destinies are not etched in stone, only history. And that, believe me, is mostly lies."

"You're a cynic."

"We watch the way the world works. You'd be amazed at what we see. Nobody pays attention to the likes of us, not flesh, not spirit. Like bugs, we're only squashed if we're noticed, and we've gotten very good at making sure that never happens. Always had my doubts. One girl, and Daikini-born to boot, holding the fate of all the Realms? *Please!*"

"They're all coming here to acknowledge her."

"Won't they be in for a rude surprise."

When Thorn said nothing, he added, "Just because some folk are born large of stature, Drumheller, doesn't make them smart. Quite the opposite. It's the *arrogance* of power that corrupts, the belief that because 'I' can do anything 'I' don't have to worry about consequences. When you're backed by the puissance of someone like, say, Bavmorda, you don't need to be a very good army. She'll do the work for you, or the *fear* of her will. Which is fine, until you come up against a foe who *is* smart. You know why I respect the Daikini? And fear them?"

"No."

"They have no power worth the name, not as the term is understood in the Realms Beyond. Among the Veil Folk are beings of Air and Earth, Fire and Water, who can bend those elements to their will. Firedrakes who can turn a mountain of solid steel to vapor with a single puff of breath. Trolls who can crack the ground asunder beneath your feet and open a chasm to the world's core. Elves, fairies, goblins, a whole panoply of creatures, the least of whom is a match and more for any human. The face of this globe could be cleansed of Daikini in a single nightspan, and don't think we haven't heard it proposed. But in the end no one bothers, because no one truly cares, because—in the heart of hearts of the Veil Folk—they aren't considered that significant a threat. The Veil Folk can do them so much harm, it's inconceivable they can do the same in return."

"You obviously disagree."

"We watch the way the world *works,* Drumheller. We remember. It does no good to transform your foes into an army of pigs, unless you make sure to dine that night on roast pork. Bavmorda made a mistake, it cost her everything."

"And the consequences of that act, Franjean?" Thorn's voice was very still, the words emerging on the ghost of an outbreath.

The brownie opened wide his arms, to encompass the whole of the tower and the city beyond.

Then he screamed.

What he saw, Thorn only felt. A bubbling beneath his shoulders, as though the wall had turned to gaseous muck. Of a sudden, there was nothing to support him and he felt himself teeter on the brink of some impossible abyss. A maw gaped, a dual sense of implacable resolve and a hunger that nothing could sate, so fierce that given the opportunity, it would gladly consume the world. He pitched himself forward, clawing his way up his own legs—crying a prayer of thanks as he went that *they* at least still rested on something solid—terrified the floor would begin to crumble after the wall and he would lose what little purchase, and hope, remained.

He twisted sideways, sprawling full length, noting analytically in that part of him that calmly recorded events no matter how madcap the crisis, that the stone was no longer cool to the touch of bare hands and cheek. It radiated warmth like umber sandstone after a day in the full sun, grown almost hot enough to cook on. He had better purchase now, pushing himself frantically with every limb, in a panicked log roll that would only be stopped by a collision with something in the way.

He expected that to be another wall—memory told him of one not that far away—but instead upended a pair of feet.

He used the confusion to regain his own. As one figure went

down he scrambled into an all-fours crouch, on fingers and toes, ready to spring toward whatever escape seemed most effective.

Except that there was nothing to flee from. The wall before him was no more than a wall. The person he'd tripped, however, was another matter entirely.

"Elora Danan!" he said again.

She hit him.

A clumsy sidearm sweep, mostly enthusiasm, backed by very little skill. It caught him full on the cheek and dropped him so hard he had to blink to cycle his vision back to normal. He half expected her to follow up with more, possibly even a volley of kicks, but heard only snuffling sobs.

She was huddled just out of reach, resting her weight on her hands. The reason for the tears, obvious: she was in a terrible state, so much so that he had to stifle a reflexive burst of laughter. She looked like she had battled from one end of the kitchen to the other and come away marked by every dish present. She was doused in soup and drink, relish of all kinds, smeared with egg and potato and custard, her hair matted, her gown stained to ruin. She must have gotten a particularly intense brew of spices up her nose, because it was running like a waterfall, scarlet and tan streaks of ketchup and mustard marking her face like war paint and her sleeves as well where she'd tried in vain to wipe herself clean. She tried to speak, but pepper got the better of her and she sneezed instead, spraying the floor below.

"I'm sorry," he began, "I didn't mean . . . !"

"Filthy little wretch!" Her voice was rough, ill-served by years of tantrums, thickened more by partially blocked airways. "You did that on purpose!"

He wanted to protest that he'd *never* do anything to hurt her, but part of his conscience branded that a palpable lie while another muttered darkly, *It's no less than you deserve, my girl.*

"Who are you?" she demanded. "You're not one of my servants, you're not dressed like anyone in the palace! You don't *look* like anyone I've ever known!"

He thought at first he'd somehow dropped his Cloak but

found the spell wrapped as snugly about him as when he'd left the cell. Didn't matter, she could see right through it.

She lunged, caught his arm, making sure her nails pinched.

"Captain of the guard," she cried.

"Elora, don't—" he protested, wholly in vain as she boxed an ear to shut him up. Anyone else would have received a blow in return or lesser spell to teach them manners but he couldn't bring himself to do either. Through the pouts and the plump, he still saw the child of memory, for whom he'd risked everything.

So Franjean, bless him, did it for him.

Brownie daggers weren't much longer than rose thorns, but they were much, *much* sharper, and the warriors who used them trained to find the chinks in any armor. The thickness of Elora's gown was no protection either, as Franjean's stab slipped through layers of finely woven cloth to catch the child full in the backside. She howled. A moment later Rool delivered a blow of his own to her heel. They weren't trying to hurt her; none of their pinpricks would draw much blood, they were more on the order of stings. This was the kind of play the brownies enjoyed among their own woodland barrows, against unwary, unwanted intruders, to make their targets feel as though they'd stumbled across a nest of particularly vengeful and inventive hornets.

Hands flailing, Elora tried to spin around to deal with these new attacks but was hampered by her garments. She was wrapped so tightly she had no play to her spinal column; she could bend only at the hips and that wreaked havoc with her sense of balance, especially since Franjean used the opportunity to tag her twice more, a repeat to her rear, followed up by a stab to the palm of the hand that swung blindly around to swat him. She overreached herself and down she went, bringing herself more pain with that landing by barking both knees and one elbow than all the brownie stings put together.

Thorn didn't want to leave her, but her screams had taken on a more urgent coloration—no longer her usual histrionics but howls of genuine fear—that was sure to attract attention from her minders. She clearly didn't remember who he was and instinct told him this was neither the time nor place to attempt to establish his bona fides, to her or anyone else. He considered an enchantment to put her to sleep and cast the events of the past few minutes into the semblance of a dream, but suspected it wouldn't hold on her. That was one of her Gifts; lesser spells rolled off her like water off a duck. Being who she was, of course, nobody dared experiment with any Great Enchantment to see whether her immunity applied as well to them. Finally, if the Red Lions were as good as their reputation, especially given the occasion, sorcery would be the first thing they'd examine her for.

"I'm sorry," he said softly, lamely, and then he ran.

The brownies led him around so many corners at such a breakneck, nonstop pace, that he hadn't a clue where he was being led until he burst through a doorway and into an open-air garden, a copse of trees topping a shallow slope, down which a brook babbled its cheery way to a large pool easily deep enough for both swimming and diving. He saw a rich field of grass, broken at intervals by plots of flowers, artfully arranged in terms of color and composition to delight all the primary senses. Yet there was no sense of formality to the setting, no hint of a master plan; it was more along the line of design by improvisation.

He took a step into the open, and as quickly ducked back beneath the shelter of the doorway arch as a great winged shadow swept across the scene. The Night Heron pivoted on one wing, extending its legs as it straightened to catch the topmost branches. Thorn had withdrawn as deeply into the shadows as could be managed yet was equally as sure that the heron could see him perfectly. It tossed him the barest glance, head cocked to the side at a slight angle in a manner that was disconcertingly reminiscent of a praying mantis sizing up her prey. There was intelligence in its gaze but one that was alien to human comprehension.

He sensed Elora before he saw her—from the moment of their first meeting, the old awareness, dormant for more than a decade, had reasserted itself—and knew the same held true in return. She may not understand the feeling, but it would be there just the same, growing in strength with every sight of him, as would his in return. He almost broke cover when she strode toward the tree and actually clutched his heart when the heron dropped down to her. She smiled a greeting of delight and it butted its head against her like a favored companion. It made a noise that, to him, was worse than claws scratching down a windowpane but that left her laughing. Then, both looked toward his hiding place. One hand raised to point, two mouths opened, two throats uttered an unearthly wail.

He hammered open the door behind him with his shoulder and stagger-stumbled down a flight of spiral stairs.

"Rool!" he called. "Franjean! Show me the proper way!"

They cannot help you, smalling.

The wall ahead was gone, replaced by a darkness that was beyond absolute.

"Drumheller!" Rool, beckoning from the far end of the corridor, eyes wide and white as he stared at the absolute blackness that had consumed the wall opposite. Thorn almost started a reflexive retreat to place his back against a wall all his own, until he realized that could just as easily turn phantom.

You have little time.

"What *are* you?"

Salvation? There was amusement in the reply and the sense that both word and concept were foreign to the speaker.

He blinked, vision distorting, splintering, presenting him with bodies in purposeful motion, winding their way down stairs that never seemed to end, path lit by torches that gave the scene an air of menace. With an effort, he broke the link the Other had forged between them.

"The dungeon!" he said, tremble to his body but strangely none to his voice; in all the years since his InSight manifested itself, he'd always been the one to initiate contact. Losing that control was bad enough, but the ease with which it had been taken terrified him.

They come for you, and you they must find, as you were left, else you are lost.

"Franjean," he snapped, looking around for his companions, "Rool, we have to *go!*"

Neither would budge. They kept their distance.

"Drumheller," Rool called, "the SoulEater! That's a *Demon!*"

You think I *don't know that?* he shrieked in the sanctity of his own thoughts. Its presence overwhelmed his every sense, physical and beyond, as though he stood between charnel pits, viewing both the newly dead and those aswim in their own rot, with souls all turned to sharks, their teeth eagerly rending him to the bare bones.

He sensed laughter and to his horror found that image reflected back at him.

Not so awful as once I was.

"Get away, foulness, leave me be!" His inner wards were all in place, his defenses as formidable as they ever were, yet this monstrosity made a mockery of them all.

That I cannot do. Hide you may from those who search above, but only I can deliver you from those below.

"I'll take my chances."

Are you so great a fool, then?

"Far greater, to trust the likes of you."

The corridor changed around him, and he physically flinched to behold a horde of Daikini thundering toward him. There was time to make out the captain who'd imprisoned him, and a woman all in white, who had to be the Princess Anakerie, and a much older man so tall he had to stoop his head at every doorway. At his heel, unchained and obedient as any household puppy, trotted a Death Dog. An eyeblink later they were on him, two sets of ghosts passing in the night, with only the hound aware something was amiss. It paused and looked about, uttering a whining growl that signaled its alarm. The man took no notice and brought the beast back to him with a snap of the fingers.

Decide, the Demon said, **there is not time to ask again.**

He felt a sharp sting against his thigh, looked down to find Rool beside him, his blade dark with Thorn's own blood. The brownie was visibly shaking; not even up on the Scar, when they'd faced the hunting pack of Death Dogs—not in all the years they'd traveled together—had Thorn seen his friend so afraid. Nor seen such evidence of how close the bonds of that friendship had tied them.

"It is a SoulEater, Drumheller," Rool keened, as if by words alone he could ensorcel the Nelwyn to safety. "Its every pledge is false, every word a trap! For all our sakes, *come away!*"

"For all our sakes, Rool, I don't dare."

The words came unbidden, the thought from nowhere, as though his own soul had taken momentary charge of his brain and dictated what was to come next. There wasn't a single reason to trust the Demon, a lifetime of stories telling him to do precisely the opposite.

He heard the brownie cry out as he plunged forward into the darkness . . .

. . . and then he found himself back in the cell.

His glowing stones lay before him on the floor, where he'd scattered them, with the wall and manacles just beyond.

He turned, looking back the way he came, not sure what he'd see but expecting the very worst.

Only darkness, though, as absolute and unknowable as it had been before.

Be quick, mage, he heard, and he was.

He blew on his stones to cool them and stuffed them back into his pouch. In the far distance he could hear the sound of boots on stone, the chink of mail and harness, that heralded the approach of his jailers; moreover, he could sense the sharp, conflicting emotions of the Death Dog. It had caught his scent and was eager for his blood. At the same time, though, it was aware of another presence in these ancient halls, that raised the hackles on its muscular neck and made it bare its teeth in fear.

Leg shackles closed easily. Only after that was done and he was truly locked in place did the thought manifest itself that this might be some deception, to deliver himself willingly and completely into the hands of enemies.

"Somehow," he said aloud, in part to hear a friendly voice, "I don't believe so." And snapped shut a manacle over his wrist.

Another inspiration, as unexpected and mysterious as the

impulse to trust the Demon, prompted his free hand to his waist. With swift, sure movements—no mistakes, no hesitation, because neither could be afforded—he yanked belt free from buckle and swung it, complete with his precious pouches, as far from him into the darkness as he could manage.

The Death Dog had slipped past its master, ignoring shouts of alarm and a peremptory snap of the fingers as it uttered its gobbling hunting cry and scrambled for the cell. The beasts didn't understand fear; of all emotions, this was the one guaranteed to make them most crazy. Where any other being with a smidgen of sense would tuck tail between legs and flee, Death Dogs by contrast always attacked. The greater the perceived threat, the more ferocious the charge.

Thorn hissed in frustration. His fingers were too short, he couldn't manage a decent grip even with his nails on the cuff to latch it closed. He cast all awareness of the approaching hound from his mind, and sent a small charge of energy the length of his arm and into the chain. Faint crackles of blue fire popped from one flat piece of iron across to the other. But nothing else happened. Sweat ran into his eyes, as though he'd suddenly placed himself before one of the cook hearths in the palace kitchen, blazing hot enough to shape raw steel. The crackles weren't faint anymore, and the Death Dog had almost reached him.

He heard a *snap,* and a modest roll of thunder; his eyes registered the sizzling afterimage of a bolt of lightning that had split the air between the halves of the manacle, now closed. He blinked again and saw something dark and blurry appear atop the stairs. It wouldn't stay still, swaying from side to side, then dipping down, forepaws scrabbling in frustration, as though it wanted to leap down and rend him to bloody, broken bits but didn't dare. The noises it made were nothing like any honest hound, not bark nor growl nor whine; it was a kind of burble, as though it was talking underwater, pitched higher than the shriek of boiling steam out a whistle, a tone that set his own nerves to screaming in sympathy. He set his head against the wall behind him, in the vain hope that its coolness would whirl away the sweat his exertions had drawn from his skin, and closed his eyes to shut the Death Dog away as well.

When he opened them again, he had company. The full complement of his inquisitors had arrived.

CHAPTER 6

So, PECK," THE TALL DAIKINI SAID WITH A SMILE, PREDA-
tor to prey, "what do you have to say for yourself?"

He was backlit by torches, so that most of the cut perfection of his face was defined by savage planes and hollows
and only his teeth could be clearly seen, but Thorn recognized stance and harness as the man who'd ridden beside
Anakerie on the esplanade and assumed him to be the
Maizan warlord, their Castellan.

"My lord," was Thorn's reply in desperate protest, playing
innocence with confusion and no little fear, "there's been
some mistake."

He never saw the glove, the motion was too sudden, too
fast. He barely sensed movement before feeling the sting of
leather across his cheek. Wasn't meant to hurt, this was more

the reminder given by a parent to a willful child, to pay attention and behave. Worse would come later.

"Wrong answer, Peck," the man said to him, in that same light, cultured tone.

"Forgive me, lord. What answer would my lord prefer?"

He heard a chuckle from the background, a figure blocked from view by the body of the man. At the same time he was raging furiously at himself within. Too much spirit, too openly displayed, major mistake. He wondered how much it would cost him.

The glove slapped against the other cheek, no harder than before.

"Are you going to be difficult, Peck?"

"Leave him to me, my lord Castellan—" began the captain.

"Would you like that?" A simple question, ostensibly directed at Thorn, but it was the captain who began to sweat, regretting to the pit of his soul that he'd ever opened his mouth and drawn attention to himself. Thorn said not a word, hoping silence would be interpreted as terror.

Nervously he licked his lips, casting a furtive flash of the eyes toward the Death Dog; quick as he was, the hound caught his gaze and bared teeth in a hungry snarl, jaws closing with an audible snap. The beast wouldn't stay still; he'd noted that from the start, and it wasn't due to its high-strung nature. It sensed the other presence in the cell, even if its humans did not, too faint a wisp to prompt an attack response but sufficient to put it on edge. Its claws tapped the stone like slow-rolled castanets, the rhythm broken every so often when the creature flexed them to fighting extension and scored the floor as a sword might. The captain didn't like the sounds much; the other two didn't appear to notice.

"My pet doesn't like you, Peck."

"My lord has a unique taste in pets."

"And the Peck speaks like a born diplomatist."

"What's your name?" the woman asked, speaking for the first time as she stepped around the Maizan and from his shadow. There was one other person in the room, fully armed and armored, wearing the colors of the Red Lions and the chevrons of a sergeant major. He was a seasoned campaigner, he was there in case of trouble.

"Thorn Drumheller, lady."

"Tell us of Willow."

"I"—he swallowed extravagantly—"I'm not sure what my lady means."

"Of course you don't." Her voice turned hard, its tone peremptory; she was as used to instant obedience as the warlord, yet there was as well the sense that she'd had to work far harder to earn it. She didn't have the patience of the Maizan, or perhaps the atmosphere of the cell was affecting her as it did the Death Dog. "Willow Ufgood. Slayer of the sorceress Demon Queen Bavmorda, godfather and sworn Protector of the Sacred Princess Elora Danan. The Magus. Need I say more?"

"With all you seem to know, great lady, what need have you of me?"

The warlord's glove again, sharp enough to sting. The reminders had turned pointed.

"Not a moment for wit, Peck," the Castellan noted.

"I have no wit to offer, lord, believe me. Whatever you require, I wish to provide. I mean none harm, I swear it."

"Then why are you here?"

"A question I've asked myself ever since I was dragged below. Lord, lady, I've done *nothing*," he finished hurriedly, to forestall another blow.

"We are charged," Anakerie said, and Thorn had a sudden flash of InSight that she didn't much like Elora, "with the defense of the Realm and of the Sacred Princess."

"I am no threat to either."

"This is a dangerous time. Never in history have the rulers of all the Realms Beyond gathered at a human table. Prophecy says the Sacred Princess is the salvation of the Realms, the means by which they might find their way to true and lasting peace. Which is why we will allow nothing to disrupt the ceremonies. Again I ask, why have you come to Angwyn?"

"Because I've never been. All the world knows of your city, lady, and with the Ascension and all, this seemed like the time to visit."

"The trooper says different," commented the warlord. "Says you're a Nelwyn."

"I've never denied that."

"But the Magus says *he's* the only Nelwyn."

"The Magus is mistaken."

Another slap.

"You arguing, Peck?"

"Forgive me, lord, but you are misinformed."

"You know the Magus?"

"Lord?"

"Don't be so tedious, Peck, you said you could help with the search."

"I knew him when he was a farmer, lord."

"Ah. In the days of his humble origins. A while ago, you must confess. Hardly of use today."

"I have no idea, lord, what would or would not be of use. I thought only of Elora Danan—"

There was no gentleness to this blow, the glove cracked his skin like a whip and he tasted blood at the corner of his mouth, where the skin had been gashed on a tooth.

"Forgive me, lord," he said quickly, "I mean no disrespect. I thought only to offer service to the Sacred Princess Elora, as my people had in years past. Where's the harm in that?"

"The Magus spins a different tale," Anakerie told him in her flat, cold voice, a prosecutor standing before the dock, hammering out the indictment for the jury, "of Nelwyns allied with the darkest of powers, of murder in the night, the foul betrayal of those who loved and trusted them. Because of them, Tir Asleen is no more. Did you think, because Angwyn is half a world away, none would hear the truth?"

"That is no truth, lady."

"You call the Magus a liar?"

"I know what I know."

"That's why we're here, Peck." The Maizan's smile broadened and Thorn braced himself for what was to come. "So *we* can learn what you know, learn *all* you know. You may have beguiled the boy; we're made of sterner stuff."

"Shall I order the implements of interrogation made ready, dread lord?" asked the captain.

"We require answers, dolt," snapped Anakerie, "not a blood-bath." She wasn't at all pleased with the captain for directing his every question to the warlord.

"I think," the warlord said, "this circumstance requires my lady's special talents. Consider yourself dismissed, Captain, with our thanks for a job well done. If we've need of your . . . toys, you'll be so informed."

"As my lord commands."

The captain was scrambling up the stairs as the words tumbled from his mouth, rending all sense of propriety in his haste to be away. It was only after he was actually out the door that Thorn realized the Death Dog was gone as well. The sergeant major had noted that as well and his eyes flashed from the warlord to the Princess, who responded with the merest movement of her head. Without a sound, the soldier sidestepped a few paces until his back was to the staircase wall, right beneath the entryway where the hound couldn't easily get to him. He'd loosened his scabbard, making his sword easier to draw, and held his war ax in both hands. Thorn couldn't help wondering, if the crunch came, who he'd go for first, the prisoner or the Maizan overlord.

"Looking for puppy, Peck?" The Maizan put his lips close to Thorn's ear and pitched the exchange for them alone. His manner was so elegant, his voice so richly cultured, a stranger would be forgiven for assuming he was the Royal here, and Anakerie the lifelong campaigner, more at home in the field than at Court. Thorn had never felt a voice caress before; the Castellan was a spellbinder, using it with a skill most men would devote to the sword.

"The trooper and I were attacked by a pack of those beasts in the mountains," he said.

"So he told us. A most impressive feat. Two men against a Great Hunt, I didn't think it possible."

"It's been years since I've seen any; I thought there were no more."

"Where'd you see them, Peck?"

"They attacked Nelwyn Vale, seeking the Sacred Princess when she was a baby."

"A truth. I can tell. But *the* truth?"

"The truth, lord"—words directed to the Maizan, but his gaze was fixed full on Anakerie—"is that they are evil."

"As, by extension, are those who master them?"

"Your words, lord."

"Your bad fortune, Peck, if true."

"Enough banter, Mohdri," Anakerie said, stepping close. "Let's get this done."

While the warlord and Thorn had been talking, she'd taken some jars from a carryall she'd brought with her, and mixed various substances together, taking the opportunity to focus her spirit as well for the task to come, so that Thorn doubted she'd heard a word of his exchange with her companion. Now she dipped the three middle fingers of her right hand into the bowl and turned them clockwise. When she drew them out, sparkles of tiny stars fell from them, as water would, in a glittery cascade.

Two fingers together, she drew a line across the center of his forehead, then another bisecting it, from the crown of his head to his chin. Where the two lines came together, she drew the symbol of an open eye, a magical window to his soul. Next, she outlined his lips, to prevent him from holding back any words. After that, the same to his ears, so he'd hear only her words. And to his nose, so she'd have mastery over his very breath.

At the major joints of arms and legs went more symbols, and with them the absence of any sensation. His chest was bared, and more stars were cast upon his heart.

As she worked, each marking made on his flesh was replicated on hers. They breathed as one, their hearts beat as one; in every sense, save that she could move and he could not, they became one.

He didn't try to fight, partly because he wasn't sure he could. This was an enchantment he knew and had used himself, derived as much from the essential spirit of the user as from the external powers drawn upon. In her case, surprisingly, a heart as pure as starlight itself.

"How are you called?" the Maizan asked softly.

"Thorn Drumheller," was the answer his lips shaped, but the words came from Anakerie's mouth. That was a surprise to him, betokening a bond between the two Daikini as strong and deep as the one she was forging with him.

The questions were simple: who was he, where did he come from, why was he here? He chose his answers with care, from that deepest place within him where he still held dominion. They asked of the battle, and of his friends. Of days he wished were long forgotten, and the companions he mourned. He let her feel the sense of loss, without quite revealing the reasons for it, and was rewarded by a hitch in the smooth rhythm of their breaths, as his pain struck too sharp a resonance in her own memory.

"Anakerie?" There was a surprising gentleness to the warlord's inquiry; Thorn hadn't thought the man had such kindness, or such passion, in him.

"A moment, Mohdri." Her voice was trembling and Thorn was thankful the bond between them was substantially one-way. He didn't want to know what floodgates he'd managed to open in her, to hurt her so. Instead, he used the break to shore up his own inner defenses. Hard enough to resist, but in the bargain he had to make sure she remained completely unaware that he was actively, and fiercely, opposing her. Ultimately, it came down to a battle of wills, a chess game of the soul played at snap-reaction speeds, where each move provoked a split-second counter. He couldn't have done it ten years ago. The potential was there, had been since birth, he'd known it even before he could put words to thoughts. Like a sapling not quite grown into an oak, or a length of rudely shaped steel fresh from the forge, that still needed tempering and honing before it became a proper sword. He'd been so afraid of his instincts then, because in this secret bastion of himself he'd known the true cost of embracing his heart's desire. He'd been a happier man then, in his ignorance.

The horror, of course, the awful joy, was the realization that—given a second chance, even with all he knew—he'd make the same choice. Because happy as he thought he was, he'd still been only a ghost of a man.

He had no sense of the true passage of time, save in the lines of fatigue he saw etching themselves across the Princess Royal's face. He'd built his mask properly and fastened it tight across the face of his soul; every answer had its element of truth, yet the totality of the interrogation was a lie.

At long last, she wiped the starstuff from his breast and nostrils, and the third eye from his forehead, breaking the core of the link between them. As she did, the replications on her own body vanished as well.

"Well?" prompted the warlord.

"A wanderer," she replied, after a long and thoughtful pause. "No home, no family, no more than what he says he is."

"You don't sound convinced."

"Grief."

"I beg your pardon?"

"Too much grief."

"A pretense?"

She shook her head, picking her silver clip from her braid and then threading her fingers through her hair from her forehead to pull the thick, mahogany plaits free, as though she couldn't bear it to be bound any longer.

"Hardly. His heart has been well and truly cut, by the kind of loss that mostly breaks those it does not slay. The kind I've felt myself."

"So?"

"Some come through it stronger."

"Is this Peck such a one?"

"You wouldn't think so, to look at him."

"Is he a threat, dread lady?" The Red Lion spoke for the first time. A deep voice, more suited for the battlefield than the parade ground. "Shall I kill him, then?"

She returned him the rueful smile of an old comrade in arms. "Is that your solution to everything, Jalaby?"

"It has the advantage of finality, Highness."

They'd cleared a step or three away from the wall and him, but he wasn't fooled. This exchange was as much a part of the interrogation as anything that came before. The slightest overt reaction and they'd be on him like Death Dogs. He could only act when, and if, they decided to turn words into deeds. And trust he'd have strength and skill to stop them.

Anakerie shook her head. Back and shoulders were ever so slightly bowed, with an equivalent heaviness to her carriage that betokened a hard-fought struggle. She'd put her all into the duel with Thorn, and it had cost her as much as any purely physical fight.

"It's too close to the Ascension, I want no blood spilled."

"Who's to know, Keri, who's to even notice?" Mohdri now, seemingly taking the sergeant major's part, but Thorn sensed something in voice and manner that told him different, that this was for show. He tried to focus his wits, to probe more deeply, but he still resonated too strongly with Anakerie and found his concerns blunted by her deep affection for the man. It was a brutal paradox; she knew he was dangerous, yet cared for him nonetheless.

"You ask such a thing, with the forces and personages loose within these walls?"

"That's your only reason?"

Thorn caught a glimpse of a smile from her, a wan little thing, surprisingly at odds with the tenor of the moment. She wrapped her arms about her body and held herself close, as though chilled to the bone.

"No," she mused, thinking mostly aloud. "He's isn't much to look at. Yet the Magus wants him."

"How fortunate for him the captain came to us, then, eh? Should I be flattered that you trust me, since it was I and my Thunder Riders who brought the Magus to Court? Or is this a case of holding friends close but enemies closer?"

She hardly heard the man's words; another thought entirely

was on her mind as she turned her gaze toward Thorn. For a moment Nelwyn and Daikini eyes met and Thorn blinked as InSight cast another visage across hers, a residue from the Bonding. Male to female, distaff sides of the same coin, so disconcertingly alike they might be one, separated by the span of a decade. The boy's hair was close-cropped, covering his head like a wild hedgerow, and both had the same ready, incandescent grin. She'd just lost hers since.

As she did now, with a slight shudder. And he knew she'd seen that same haunting face reflected in his own eyes. He had to be more careful, there were still too many ties binding them; no matter how hard he worked to purge them, some would always remain. She'd wrapped herself in his soul, even though he'd kept a fair chunk of it hidden. Twinned themselves in spirit, as she and her long-lost brother had been twins in flesh.

"An old rivalry perhaps," he heard the Castellan say, "a feud we know nothing about."

"Perhaps," Anakerie conceded distractedly as she struggled to recover her composure; the depth of the resonance had shaken her, as it had Thorn, yet she said nothing of it to Mohdri. "I want to be sure before I act."

"As Your Highness commands."

"Too many questions, Mohdri. If the Magus is so powerful, why his concern with this Nelwyn?"

"Ask."

"I saw no need before now."

"Would you rather learn the hard way?"

"Leave the Nelwyn as he is, Mohdri, till after the ceremony."

"That, Highness, would not be prudent."

The warlord stepped forward, one long stride taking him right to Thorn, fast as a striking cobra. Too late, Thorn saw him draw a handful of black, crystalline sand from a pouch of his own, watched it coalesce before his eyes into a slim stiletto blade of gleaming obsidian, held lightly between both palms. Then, with the faintest outrush of breath, he puffed it forward into his skull, stabbing right through the point where Anakerie had drawn forth his third eye.

Thorn convulsed, like a man dancing with lightning, lips curling back so far from his teeth he thought the flesh would tear free, thankful—in the rapidly dissolving spaces within him still capable of conscious thought—for being chained. He might dislocate every joint with his madcap twists and turns, but otherwise he'd have surely broken himself to bits. He was gabbling nonsense noises like a Death Dog and in that awful moment knew he'd been taken by the enchantment that had been used on Faron.

Then Anakerie shoved the taller man aside, with a force and fury that surprised as much as amused him, though all good humor faded in an instant when Jalaby put his body between them.

"*Damn you,* Mohdri, I gave you no such leave."

"A good commander knows when to take the initiative, my pet."

She bridled at the intentional diminutive, that was plain on her face. But Castellan Mohdri couldn't see the response; not only was his view blocked by her escort, she was too close to Thorn and there was no sense of it in her reply. She would have grabbed hold of the prisoner, but his movements were too violent and unpredictable. Of the stiletto, there was no sign; the blade and all its malefic power had been absorbed into Thorn's flesh on contact.

"He's of no use to anyone smashed to a bloody pulp!"

"Least of all himself, my intent precisely. Forgive me, Keri, you yourself said this night is too important to take the slightest risk. If anything's amiss, it's surely blocked now." He paused, allowing her a moment to reply, and when none came: "Shall we go, Princess? We've indulged ourselves enough for one evening." There was no outward alteration to voice or manner, yet he made plain precisely who was the power in the room. Thorn shook as mad testament to the fate in store for those who opposed it, and from Mohdri came the definite hope that Jalaby would be fool enough to try.

Still hidden from view, Anakerie blew on the fingertips of her right hand, then touched them to Thorn's lips, thereby passing on the ghost kiss. When she took her hand away, a scattering of faint sparkles remained on his lips, a lingering of starstuff. There was blood as well, where a tooth had broken her skin. As she rose she pulled on her gauntlet, covering the small wound.

Mohdri ushered her up the stairs, but paused himself after she'd stepped outside for a last, soft-spoken word.

"Caught you," he said with an appreciative nod at how completely the deadly trap had closed. "Just as the Magus said. Let my princess crack your shell with niceness and stab you before you can close the breach." He smiled, flashing gleaming, perfect teeth like a shark about to bite. "Poor Peck. Did you ever dream a ChangeSpell could be cast so easily? Magus thinks you'll beat it, maybe we'll toss the boy Geryn in when I come back, for First-Feast, see if he's right. However it turns out, you'll have scars across you no power can erase. Dead, broken, turned, all the same to me and mine. What matters is, you're beaten."

And Thorn was alone.

He gave voice, then, as he had over the ruins of Tir Asleen, majestic walls crumbled all to powder, with naught but dead before him and Elora's spirit long gone from the place. Everything in him that hurt, he transformed into rage and cast it out his voice. Fire exploded from his breast, lighting him from within as it followed the byways of his nervous system to the ends of his body and shot away with such fury the chains were ripped from their place in the wall. Much of the wall came with them, but his body was in such a state his spasms simply threw the hulking blocks off him, no matter that skin was broken and bones crushed beneath.

This would go on, he knew, until he was pulp and stretched to full extension between the realms of life and death, no longer one, not quite the other. It was the same enchantment that had been used on Faron, as too late he realized that Mohdri had been the leader of the dark figures he'd seen in the boy's memory. But where he was concerned, the ChangeSpell manifested itself with significant differences. It would smash his body to rubble as it would his soul and rebuild both in the image of a beast. The intellect of a man, the Power of a sorcerer, mated to the brute force of a Death Dog, all tightly leashed to the Magus who had cast the spell. To lock the Change in place, to curse the spirit as well as the flesh, required a blood sacrifice. Ideally a friend, the more innocent the better.

He fought as he never had before. He forged a sword from the substance of his soul and used it with a skill his arms would never have. Backed by a wild ferocity that danced along the edge of madness. With each swing, though, his blade shone a fraction less brightly; he took no steps forward, only back, and Shadow hemmed him in from every side. He'd seen Anakerie as the paramount threat; after the Bonding, he couldn't help but relate to her as something of a friend. His defenses *had* been down, and he was being crushed as inexorably, as completely, as Tir Asleen. The battle would have been over already had not Anakerie's farewell kiss canceled much of her remaining enchantment, which held him physically helpless, and restored a measure of his own resources.

The Magus himself was the most frightening element. Thorn had seen his share of danger; in his travels he'd honed his magical abilities as any swordsman would his blade, and learned to defend himself against all manner of assaults. Yet against this spell, his best efforts, his most wily and cunning stratagems, came to naught. The Magus seemed to know him better than he did himself; every parry had been anticipated, every counterthrust was bent harmlessly aside. The harder he fought, the more quickly he raced toward ultimate defeat.

Trust me, he heard and wished he was deaf.

You're a Demon, he shrieked in his mind, teeth so broken their jagged chunks had savaged tongue and cheeks beyond the ability to speak.

You won't die, they won't let you. They've caught you good and proper and through you, the child. Can't save yourself, Peck, how are you to save her?

You're a Demon!

Your only hope, now as before.

He didn't have long. The spell attacked the mind before the body, and he had a sudden, sickening image of his soulself, hacking away at Shadows long after everything it embodied had been consumed. Even if he survived, through some miracle, all that remained of him would be a shell.

He spat blood, and worse, but forced himself to say the words aloud.

"Help me," he asked. "Please."

All light went away; the torches left by Mohdri so Thorn could watch what was happening to himself simply winked out. The floor rose up around him, as though it had turned to tar . . .

. . . and then he *was* the floor.

In that twinkling, his InSight expanded beyond its farthest boundaries, sweeping him from one realm of perception that he had always known into another for which none of that knowledge had the slightest meaning. He was stone, every stone, from the core foundation to the highest roof point. He had no words to describe the experience, no means to catalog the overwhelming number and variety of sensations. It was like standing at the heart of a mirror room, knowing that even the most wayward glance would reveal a near-infinite number of reflections, no two quite the same.

Human instinct made him want to move, but he found himself anchored in place, the stones bound to each other by mortar, the entire edifice standing atop a plug of solid rock that was like a mountain within the earth, unaffected by the cracks and fissures that laced the surrounding substructure. At one and the same moment he beheld the dungeon where he lay, the kitchen spaces of the palace proper, and every other room as well, the entirety of Elora's Aerie, the ceremonial hall—specially constructed for the coming sacrament and, like her china and gowns, to be used this once and never again.

Everyone was moving, and he felt as though he was being pounded over every inch of his body. There was constant noise; he could no more discriminate between sounds than between sights, his brain couldn't handle the load. He was drowning in sensation, as he would in water, except the outcome wasn't death but madness.

Then, absurdly, the concept of drowning led to that of swimming. He was a rare Nelwyn, he liked the water. He wasn't very graceful; he remembered Rool muttering that he had the style of a lame frog and more than once Bastian and Anele used him for fishing practice. He stopped worrying about all that was around him and simply accepted it. This cacophony was the medium through which he moved, sanity was a matter of relegating it to the background, where it could be ignored.

Perhaps thinking of the brownies was what led him to them, for all of a sudden he was looking at them from a score of different directions and hearing their voices big as life.

"Told you! Told you! *Told you!*" Franjean had worked himself into a state. They were both still in Elora's tower and had taken refuge in the central tree of the garden there, as far from any stone surface as they could manage. "We never should have come and we of a certes *never* should have let him near this accursed place, especially when we had a clear road to freedom!"

"What do you suggest," was Rool's weary retort, "that we knock him over the head and cart him away on our backs?"

"He's been eaten by a Demon and we're *stuck!*"

The brownie had it right and wrong. He wanted to tell Franjean so, but was aware of no physicality through which concept could be translated into speech. He couldn't even throw the words into their thoughts because the consciousness he shared was wholly abhorrent to them; they would see any contact as an attack and any communication as a trick. He was as much the Demon now as he was an eagle when InSight allowed him to "ride" his soul with Anele's, and the experience was as much a wonder.

Then, as though his thought of the eagles had been a cue: "Blessed Maker," Franjean cried, "we can't even call the eagles for a pickup because of those damnable herons!"

"Keep yelling as you are, you're guaranteed to bring them back up here. Or worse."

"This is not what I would call an acceptable state of affairs."

"What do you want from me, Franjean?"

Franjean made a very nasty face. "Absolutely *nothing!*" And humped himself to the far side of the trunk to find a bole of his own to perch on.

The garden made no sense to Thorn. It was rich with growing things and was clearly tended by a loving, hardworking hand. But unlike every other aspect of the tower, it was surprisingly informal. It was a place to run barefoot and loll disreputably in the sun, in a setting where the very concept of play was anathema. He couldn't explain the herons, either. Like Death Dogs, they blighted whatever they touched, yet there was no sense of any such taint, to the garden or the tree itself, else the brownies wouldn't have taken refuge there.

He yearned to call out to his companions, reassure them that he was all right, but in truth he wasn't altogether sure that was so.

He heard Elora's name . . .

. . . and found a pair of Daikini, portly of build, powerful of carriage, dressed for success, striding along a lower gallery. There was no sense of movement, it was as if some particle of him was aware of every simultaneous moment within the confines of the castle, allowing him the ability—through the Demon—to switch from one to the other, as though he was exchanging painted illuminations in a viewer.

"You worry too much, my friend," the one said.

"I'm minister of state, it's my job," replied the other.

"The King knows his business."

"So *I* believed, until those damnable Maizan were invited within the walls."

"Their warlord is a Prince in his own right, just the man to tame Anakerie. As allies, they'd secure our southern frontiers, you can't deny that. And it's only an escort party. I doubt the Red Lions have anything to fear from a few-score men. Even Thunder Riders."

"I shall be *so* thankful when this is over."

"Heard that more'n once, I'll grant ye. Lot o' work, lot o' stress, but think o' the reward. A new balance between the Realms."

"You think?"

"I dream, ye don't? Can't go on the way they are, that's certes enow. Been playing lapdog to the Veil Folk all my born days, as my father did in his, and his father and so on back to the dawn of the world. It's our land as much as theirs, damn sinful of 'em not to share!"

"Keep your voice down, you're not making a guildhall speech."

"I'm trying to make a point, whyinhell aren't ye listening?"

"Because I've a demi-score of ambassadors in my face day in, day out, complaining that they share too much and all we Daikini want out of the bargain is more more *more*!"

"Ye've seen my plans. With engines of steam, we can haul more goods, faster! We'll gladly pay tariffs, provided," the merchant said after a hesitation, "they're reasonable."

The minister chuckled. "One man's 'reasonable' is another's tyranny. The tracks your trains run across permanently alter the face of the land. . . ."

"And roads, they don't?"

"Not as much, no. And there's trouble there, as well; why else does most heavy traffic go by water?"

"Another case—use my engines attached to paddles to drive boats."

"I can't wait till you try persuading the Wyr Clans to accept that."

"They have powers, we have our wits—only *they* won't allow us to proper *use* 'em! I tell ye, the day's coming when that has to change. Whyinhell should we suffer for their fear?"

"Because their fear could lead to our destruction."

"Mayhap that's a risk it's past time we took."

"She's only a child, my friend. You demand too much of her."

"It's that or drown, what's to lose?"

At the same time he heard a clutch of ambassadors in another part of the palace have much the same conversation, with the perspective reversed. They came to much the same conclusion, and Thorn's heart turned cold as he heard a frantic outcry, shrieked at the top of already overstressed lungs.

"I'll kill the spavined little bitch!"

Elora's dressmaker, clothes in disarray and the makings of a spectacular bruise plumping one eye where she'd evidently caught him fair with her bare heel.

Nobody liked her.

Many feared her, all were proud to have her in residence, none wanted the slightest to do with her that wasn't called for by official duties.

He opened his eyes, grateful at last for a purely physical cause and effect.

Stone beneath his cheek, but darkness began an arm's stretch from where he lay, which was where he'd fallen. He was sore all over, but when he called on limbs to stir, they did so without complaint. The aches were little more than what came after a poor night's sleep.

He pushed himself up to see that the wall was still broken and that he lay amidst a scattered jumble of stone blocks. Some were freshly stained, but he decided not to investigate further. His clothes, what remained of them, were as fouled and he began to undress.

"Well," he said.

Bargain offered, bargain kept.

"What have you done?" he asked, trying to discern a being within the darkness.

Given of myself.

"I didn't know Demons did such things."

Perhaps you don't know so much.

"Very likely. Thank you," he said simply, because that was as much formality as he could muster. "I owe you more than my life."

The Demon said nothing.

"Who are you?" Thorn wondered aloud. "What are you?"

I am, it replied, with an air of puzzlement, as though these were questions it had never put to Itself. **How I came to be, I . . . do not know. I have always been of this place.**

"I sensed that." Bound to the stones when they were freestanding, and carried with them when quarried and cut to form the first foundation. No memory of who had ensnared it, or why, or how long ago, save that it was of a time when none of the present races walked the world.

"I must go," Thorn said, but failed in his initial attempt to rise.

You cannot.

That denial got his dander up and himself to his feet, though he had to lean against a block for support.

"I'm needed."

Here more than elsewhere.

"I don't understand. What do you mean?"

There is a debt. Honor demands a settlement.

"I was wondering when we'd get around to that. If it's freedom you're after, I don't think I can. The Bindings that hold you are beyond my power to loose."

Freedom, yes. But not for me.

The darkness moved, initially revealing Thorn's belt and pouches, which he gratefully pulled to him. He fished out a canteen, and splashed precious water on his face. Fresh clothes came to hand, a fashion inspired mostly by Rool. A shirt of heavy cotton, dyed a green so dark it was almost black, as useful for camouflage in the night as in the deep woods. Trousers of wool, buckskin boots that laced to the knee, designed for hard travel over rough country. Dark sweater, woven so tightly it was virtually waterproof even without his enchantments to help. Shearling vest, built with big pockets. The sweater and vest, he let lie for the moment, warm enough in shirt alone. He scarfed some food and a flask of water from the other pouch, but what he wanted most was his carryall and, especially, his sword. He assumed they were lost to him, either in the captain's possession or the Princess's, only to discover to his amazement that both lay by his side.

"You *have* been busy," he confessed to the Demon as he buckled on his belt and pouches. There was no reply. When he looked up, a woman lay before him.

She floated at waist height, with night on every side. Tall and powerfully built, there was nothing gentle or elegant about her. Broad shoulders, long arms and legs, almost no hair to speak of, black as the darkness surrounding her, cropped close to the skull, like a day's growth on a man with a heavy beard. Tribal tattoos on biceps and thigh, plus some scars. A nose that had been broken, set between wide-set eyes and high cheekbones that defined a strong, square jaw. She had the upturned eyes and gold-touched skin of one who hailed from the Spice Lands, and the tone of her musculature, plus the calluses on her hands, spoke of a woman who earned her way with a sword.

She didn't breathe, but she wasn't dead.

He ran a finger along his lower lip, stared reflectively at the faint sparkles that glittered against his skin. There was a smudge on the center of her forehead, as he knew there was on his, where the crystal blade had been thrust home.

Same fate, same fight. And in her way, she'd won. She'd preserved her soul and her humanity, though it had cost her every other aspect of her Self.

"Who was she?"

Meat. As you are meat. Is there a difference?

"To such as you, I suppose not."

She fled from those who would enslave her. They searched, they did not find.

"You made sure of that, I suppose."

One slave to another.

It surprised him to hear the Demon express itself in such terms. He didn't think the creature could be so self-aware.

"There's an old saying, anyone fool enough to bargain with Demons is sure to be cursed as a result."

Bit late for that.

He couldn't help a chuckle.

"What is it you want?"

Freedom for my child.

"Demons can have children?"

We are what we are, it is you who name us. And define us by that name.

"I stand corrected. I think."

You know so little.

He had no counter for that, so all he did was nod silent agreement.

To come to Be in this place is to be imprisoned as I was. That, I will not permit. For your life and freedom, I require the same for my child.

His head shook of its own volition, eyes flashing from the body before him to the heart of the darkness beyond.

"No," he said. "I cannot. I will not. That is an abomination!"

Does not the one gift balance the other?

"She had a life and being all her own, you have no right to steal it!"

Both life and being are gone, wherein is the harm in using what remains?

"How can you possibly comprehend . . . ? Even if that were true, there's no way I'd be mad or desperate enough to loose a Demon from its prison. Your kind cause horror enough as it is."

Shall I then give voice then to what I know, "Peck"? Nowhere in this palace can you hide from me. I'll hound you into the very arms of those who hunt you and laugh to watch you crack the bones of those you hold most dear.

"Then do it, and be damned!"

Such I am already, wizard, why else do I require your aid? You fear the worst, Drumheller, but what of hope?

"I must be mad, to hear a Demon speak that word."

I offer you my greatest treasure, to shape and do with as you will. If there is a better way of living than we have ever known, teach it to my child.

"I've never heard of one of you talking so. Why should you care? Why should it matter?"

To Be. That is life. To be aware, that is . . . something more. I had no regard for those of your walking kind about me, until the Child came.

"Your child?"

No. The youngling in the tower. Alone, she was, and afraid, still more babe than girl, found burned and bruised and smoking in the yard whereon her aerie was built. She moved, she breathed, but in most ways she was as hollow within as this fleshform here. Only Anakerie dared touch her; the others had too much fear. She would speak to none of them. She would speak to me.

I was . . . special to her. She called me . . . friend. I knew the word but not the meaning. At first, I answered when

she called because it amused me. She spoke from the heart, she knew of no other way. Better I had not listened, better I had opened stones beneath her to drop her to the eternal fire. But she spun a spell of words and brought light where none had ever shone. It was more than I could bear; to my shame and sorrow I fled from her.

But having beheld the light, even if only for that moment, I cannot bear to keep my child in the dark.

"I should have come sooner," Thorn breathed. But his inner voice answered, without mercy, *You didn't know, did you, and you had grief enough of your own to cope with.*

Past his mind's eye cascaded a series of images—courtesy of the Demon or his own imagination, he neither knew nor cared—of a child whose spirit was as radiant as her flame-blond hair, whose nature was to reach out to everything and everyone around her. Cast in blood and fire across the face of the globe, to a land of strangers. None to answer her call, none to take her outstretched hand, no longer a needing, growing girl but an object of veneration and fear. A talisman. Abandoned first by friends of the flesh, and then by one of the spirit.

Yet, for all of that, she made a garden (he was certain it was her doing, to the bottom of his bones) of such peace that even Night Herons couldn't befoul it. And here was a Demon, speaking of hopes and dreams; a creature more inclined to eat its young, bargaining to give that offspring a better life.

The faintest of gleams on the floor caught his eye, a quick bend and reach brought Anakerie's hair clip to his hand. Reflexively, he reached back for his own, though he could feel it was long gone. Lost in the mad scramble around Elora's Aerie, or during his own seizure, he didn't know. He lightly rubbed his thumb over the oval face, its designs chased by an earnest hand whose ambition outleaped skill. Again, the twinned visage came to him, that had overlaid Anakerie's face. A last gift, on their shared birthday, before their world shattered.

The Princess loved few things more. *So how,* he wondered, *had it come to be left behind?*

Instinct, again, prompting him to action. He gathered his hair at the base of his skull, more a matter of practicality than high style, and anchored it with Anakerie's clip.

"Perhaps there's hope after all," he whispered.

Your answer, Thorn Drumheller.

"If it's within my power," he told the Demon, "I'll save your child."

CHAPTER 7

To do what was necessary required that Thorn bind himself to the Demon, in much the same way that Anakerie had bound herself to him. In the process, while his sorcerous abilities expanded exponentially, his hold on them became increasingly more tenuous. There was no light to see by in his cell, but that didn't seem to matter. Thorn couldn't see himself, couldn't see the woman he knew lay before him; all was darkness, as absolute as Creation must have been before the striking of the first celestial spark. He could hear breathing, his own, with a shiver to each intake and exhalation that had nothing to do with physical discomfort. Magic required an essential harmony of being, and hard as he worked, he couldn't find it.

With an effort that left his temples throbbing, he sharpened the focus of his InSight, closing every window he could find on the infinitely faceted world the Demon took for granted, until the darkness of the cell came alive. On one plane, darkness is simply the absence of light, but as a color black is the sum total of all the rest; the more that are combined, the darker they get.

For Thorn, it was as if he was suddenly immersed in a great ocean and able to observe all its myriad elements, currents great and small moving through the deeps like rivers, demarked not simply by force and direction but temperature, each throwing off swirls and eddies that themselves formed strata in the water the way a vein of minerals might within a mountain. In the room, Thorn saw patterns of energy, all black, but the difference now was that one was black that had once been scarlet, another black that had once been a pale rose-edged teal. Memories in the fabric of the chamber's substance of more colors, more frames of being, than he had names for. None of it was discernible straight on, of course—*Fates forfend,* he groused to himself even as he marveled at the sights, *anything should come that simple*—only as flashes at the farthest corner of his vision, like the streaks seen against the inside of his eyelids on a bright and sunlit day after he squeezed them tight shut.

His was a considerably more coherent and focused presentation, order against the Demon's natural state of chaos, and he allowed himself a silent whistle of admiration at whoever had Bound the creature prisoner. There was no stronger stone than this primordial granite; it had been formed in the earliest days of the world, cast up as the heart of the first range of mountains; time had simply weathered it down to its purest essence. By contrast, there was no more anarchic form of being—he wasn't even sure the term "life" properly applied—than Demons. They abhorred any sense of structure, be it moral or physical; their sense seemed to be that if they could thrive in a realm where no rules applied, why couldn't everyone else? Wizards feared and fought them because their own abilities were confined within a structure, the so-called natural order of things; their strength lay in their skill at weaving lesser patterns into greater ones. Demons took delight in tearing any and all such patterns to bits. The stronger the mage, the more powerful the Demons attracted to his work. They would attack, and the mage would pray his wards were sufficient to hold them at bay. Because of the forces involved, those conflicts occasionally had a spillover into the tangible world, and as with any battle, those aftereffects weren't pretty. That was how common folk came to fear Demons, to the extent that even wholly natural disasters were blamed on them. Certainly, the Cataclysm had been, though Thorn had always doubted that; any Demon capable of wreaking such havoc on a global scale wouldn't have stopped there. It would gleefully have shattered the world entire.

Still and all, Thorn told himself, *by rights and everything I've ever heard, having a Demon imprisoned in the rock should have made this the most unstable of foundations.*

Do I surprise you then, little magus?

"Damnation! Will you please stay out of my mind, I'm trying to concentrate here!"

You think too much. Action would be better.

"When I'm ready."

Your time is not your own.

"What's that supposed to mean?"

He shouldn't have spoken aloud, shouldn't have heeded the Demon in the slightest. The distraction was just enough to open the tiniest crack in the ramparts of his concentration.

He heard the sound of wings, so vast that each sweep could be mistaken for the pulse of a hurricane, beheld in his mind's eye a glory so pure it couldn't be described, that was at one and the same moment the embodiment of the Demon's chaos and the antithesis of it. He looked to his dreams, and it was there, looked to his imagination and it was there; it was at the heart of laughter, it was the radiance that eased the Shadow thrown by grief. The blood that burned beneath its breast likewise filled his own, but where he was flesh transcended by the Powers he had learned to wield, this was a creature whose essence was magic, barely restrained within a physical casement.

The dragon smiled.

The Demon spoke.

Drumheller.

Thorn felt tears, for the first time in over a decade, but no longer of sorrow. He wept from awe, and a wonder that swept across the wasteland of his soul like a spring rain, as though he were once more the farmer surveying his fields after planting, beholding not simply the fact of things but how all those disparate elements acted together to bring forth new life. He hadn't realized his wounds had gone so deep, or that he'd buried them beneath so thick a scab to mute their awful pain. The best part of him had been numb for so long; in following the path of his life he'd somehow lost his way.

My child, Drumheller.

"I know," he said, every part of him tingling, as though an electrical storm had passed by him.

You gave your word.

"I know."

He blinked, to restore himself fully to his cell and the task before him, but instead found his spirit cast once more into the wild ocean that was the Demon's Power, only now it had become a perceptual maelstrom that for all his own strength and skill he was unable to master. He knew how to swim, but only as a man; he had no sense here of how to be a fish, and so was swept helplessly away to the top of Elora's Aerie:

At precisely the stroke of midnight on the last night of Elora's twelfth year, the Vizards come for her. They are her keepers, the high priests of a religion that doesn't officially exist, charged—on peril of life and soul across the Twelve Domains—with her care and protection. One representative from each Realm, rotated each year, so that on this special day there will be twelve sets of twelve to stand by her. She never sees any one of them for more than a month; each new moon brings a new face, or so she assumes. She has no way of knowing for sure, beyond the obvious differences in their respective races; they all are masked (hence, their name), presenting her with the same unchanging visage day in, day out.

Swept helplessly away to the apartments of the Princess Anakerie:

Anakerie stands on the wraparound balcony of her rooms and stares

up at Elora's Aerie, not bothering to mask the emotions that turn her cheeks ghost pale and her eyes the color of bloody sand.

Thorn shuddered at the backwash of old and bitter hatreds, resonating off both girl and woman like stones from the bottom of a fire pit, deceptively cold to the touch but rich with the memory of what it had been like to burn, needing only a reminder and a surge of desire to bring them once more to blazing life. He sat cross-legged in the darkness of his cell and tried with fierce desperation to seal the doors and windows of his perceptions, sick with the realization that it was a lost cause. The more he used his Talent, especially while he was coupled to the Demon—and seemingly to this dragon as well—the wider and more deeply ranged his InSight, all the more acutely in the case of Elora and Anakerie because of the Bondings between them. Their feelings came together in him, the one striking resonant chords in the other, forming twisting riptides of passion that he could no more escape than control.

"It's an honor," he hears the King say, and looks around before he can stop himself, realizing too late that both voice and scene are part of Anakerie's memory. And he wonders if she is just as privy to the secrets of his own past.

A mask lies between father and daughter, on a silken pillow surrounded by a badge of office. It is a thing of beauty, a human face interpreted by the finest artisans of the Veil Folk. Perfect in every aspect, it has as little substance as gossamer yet is as expressionless and impenetrable as a statue. Anakerie will not even touch it, for within her is the certainty that once donned, the mask will leave its mark on her forever, like the harshest brand.

"I don't want it," she says, and those who watch look amongst themselves in dismay. The King has a certain tone, used when he is not to be swayed, and woe betide any who dare to cross him in such a mood. Even at thirteen, his daughter matches it.

Being a father, for all that he loves her dearly, he doesn't notice.

"This is to be worn by those who serve the Sacred Princess Elora," he explains, though his manner makes plain he would much rather simply be obeyed. "It was made for you. You will be the first to attend her."

"I don't want it," she says again in that same certain voice.

"It is an honor."

"I don't want it. I am a Princess."

"I am your king. It is my will."

"I don't care."

"I don't ask you to understand, Anakerie, nor even that you approve. I do require your obedience."

He's slain men for less. He is a throwback to a harder age, which is for-tuitous because these are bloody times. He fought a pitched battle on his wedding day, and would have perished had his fiancée not led her own troops from the altar to his rescue. She was as courageous as he, as skilled in the arts of war, and often rode beside him in the field. Her true vocation, though, was governance and they divided their roles accordingly; he de-fended the realm and she ran it. Until the Cataclysm, when the King was summoned home to discover his wife and son—Anakerie's twin—among the casualties; the one dead, the other missing. In their place, a lost soul, thrown among his household like a changeling and treated much the same. Over the decade since, he's stayed closer to home, trying to shape his hand to the quill pen instead of the sword. He masters the strategy of statecraft and the art of persuasion. But he never loses the air of the war-rior; all who deal with him know that they have but to scratch his surface, and silk will quickly give way to the steel underneath.

In these early days, however, when Elora's provenance has been es-tablished and decisions must be made about her future, the pain of loss is still too raw. He has no patience, especially with those he loves.

She is her father's daughter, a match for him in every way, but she is too young and he, determined absolutely. She will wear the mask, and at-tend Elora for her allotted month.

Instead, she flees.

The images of her lasted until she passed beyond the palace walls; they were the limits of the Demon's range. Of what tran-spired beyond, it had no interest and less care, and for that, Thorn was profoundly grateful. He was close enough to shrieking mad-ness as it was from this mad cacophony.

Elora isn't in her room.

And in that moment, resonating as he was from Anakerie's memories, Thorn was gripped by the wild fear that she had fled her fate as well.

For the palace staff, that means panic, as though a marauding army has suddenly materialized within the gates. If any among the Vizards feel the same, those feelings are safely hidden behind their masks. They don't need much of a search to find her, she isn't trying to hide. She has simply exchanged bed for garden and nestled herself in the crook of one of the oak's main branches. The Vizards surround her, spacing themselves a double arm's length apart as though this is part of the ceremony; they take great care to stay on the flagstone border; none take a step toward her, nor edge even so much as a tiptoe onto the grass. They stand, they stare; she stares back for a time and then goes back to sleep.

Thorn couldn't help a smile at the sight, and wondered how long the stalemate would last. Then his smile was gone as he beheld . . .

. . . a burgher within a public sitting room bites his thumbnail; the bluff Daikini—the same merchant Thorn saw earlier with the King's minister of state—spits it on a fire, resonances of the deed and thoughts behind it pulsing through the stones of the palace, blurring Thorn's focus like a splash of water across a windowpane.

"Has value, damn it," the Daikini says. "Her bein' here, the Sacred Princess, serves a purpose."

"Probably said the same, last place she lived," counters his companion, equally rich with drink, unable to sleep, unwilling to leave, both men falling back on the traditional means of passing the time before tomorrow's ceremony. "Look what happened there."

" 'S our land, bugger your eyes, our land!"

"Not if we say different," intrudes a new voice, as though silver bells had been turned all to blades.

The Veil Lord's proportions are all wrong, too little breadth to go with his impossible height. He is a stick figure, half again as tall as a tall man, forced to duck his head to pass beneath most doorways; only the ceremonial gates afford him an easy entry.

"We have rights," the burgher grumbles, oblivious to his companion's cautionary "shush."

"Which we honor," the lord replies, "as we expect to be honored in kind. Wherein do we hinder your commerce?"

"There are better ways, is all I'm saying."

"For you, I'm sure. How so for us? Be thankful, merchant, we accept

your trespass in our domains. As you charge for your goods and services, so do we."

"She's Daikini," the burgher says with an unsteady lunge to his feet, "she's human! B'longs with her own kind, t' stand by 'em!"

Thorn found himself torn violently away from the scene, once more bound to his own flesh, breath bouncing out of him in a single, great exhalation that doubled him over. He'd been punched to less effect.

"Are they mad?" he whispered, because that was as loud as he could manage.

They are what they are, and do what they do. It's no concern of yours.

"Elora Danan is!" This was louder, almost full voice.

When you are free. When my child is safe.

"Then help me keep these damnable visions *out of my head*!"

Ignore them.

"Easier said, Demon."

You have no need to look.

He knew that, but he was curious and there was always a sight, a scrap of conversation, to catch his interest.

"I'll do my best."

Once you begin, little mage, my offspring's life is yours alone to hold.

He knew that, too. Another reason for holding back. A mistake, the smallest hesitation, would mean the Child's death. He didn't want to think about how the Demon would react.

Again comes the sound of wings, only this time the glory manifests itself in the form of a human child, standing at the open balcony doors of a private sitting room. More than boy, less than girl, frame and age combine to confuse any onlooker as to which. Wearing clothes like a second skin, that splinter the glow of hearthfire and candles as though the fabric is spun crystal. A marvel to look upon, even as Thorn recognizes the child as the Troubador who'd spoken to him on the esplanade, but he can't help wondering how bright sun might be reflected and knows that such a terrible beauty would be the last thing his eyes ever beheld. Knows as well that his bearing witness to this conversation is no accident, that somehow this child is responsible.

"You are not what We expected, Kieron Dineer," says another voice of silver bells, this one with edges sheathed, by way of greeting. Consort to the Veil Lord, the sheer force of the woman's personality makes her chair a throne, and the suite an extension of her own otherworldly palace. She is robed for bed, and while one servant offers cider in a goblet of wrought gold, two maids comb and braid her hair. No easy task, since it is twice as long as she is tall. And, like all her race, she is very tall. The child blows a tiny puff of breath into its own cup and immediately steam rises from liquid heated almost to boiling.

"Be glad I've come at all, lady." The child's hair is a mass of unruly spikes, as though someone has taken a knife to it without any concern other than that it be short. No sleeves to the shirt, either, for what looks to be the same reason.

"I am Queen Magister of the Realms Beyond," the woman says, the frost in her voice easily overmatching the poor hearth's valiant efforts. "I stand second among the assembly to Cherlindrea herself. Do not be impertinent with me."

"And I am as my brethren would have our hosts see us, complete with Daikini name to match their features. You are but a single aspect of the Veil Folk, we are of Earth and Air and Fire and Water. Flesh and spirit conjoined, mind and passion, real and dream, transcending all boundaries, making All, One. We come to this assembly in freedom and friendship. . . ."

"You are far too trusting. Your power has made you arrogant."

"Perhaps so. But none of us shall break the peace we all of us swore upon Elora Danan's birth."

"My lord was provoked."

"Your lord should know better."

"And what of the Daikini who assaulted my lord with words and blows? Will none reprove him?"

"Your lord took care of that. I doubt any will raise their hand to you and yours again."

"Now, perhaps. But what will happen when they have that accursed brat to stand as their champion?"

The child savors its cider, and though its eyes are hooded, almost closed, Thorn feels transfixed by its gaze.

"According to Prophecy," is the infernally calm reply, "Elora Danan is

to stand champion for us all." An ever-so-slight emphasis on the last word.

The Queen Magister makes a rude comment.

"We're fools," she mutters, casting the words somewhere between a growl and a snarl, "casting everything we have, everything we are, at hazard. And for what? A promise of better times. Perhaps times are good enough the way they are? Perhaps we all should leave well enough alone?"

She sweeps to her feet and past the child onto her balcony, letting the night wind play with gown and hair and hoping it will cool her temper.

"The Cataclysm manifested itself in every Domain," Kieron tells her, holding out its cup for seconds and accepting it with a smile so charming it brings an instant response in kind from the maid. "Tir Asleen was destroyed so utterly that stone was not left on stone, and even those were ground to powder. Only Elora Danan survived. Whatever struck at her, lady, is a Power to be reckoned with."

"A Power that's not been seen since. As you yourself know, only a fool tweaks the sleeping dragon's tail."

Kieron nods its head in amused acknowledgment. "I've heard the saying," it says.

The Queen turns to face the room, leaning hands and body back against the railing, gown draped enticingly across her long, lithe form. "What will happen tonight, do you think?"

"I don't know."

"I find that hard to believe. I thought you and yours knew everything?" The mockery in her is gentle and underlain with a sense of true regret; she depends on this child more than she cares to admit.

"Allies we don't trust, a champion in whom we have no faith, a ceremony whose outcome is totally unknown . . ." Her voice trails off.

"And a Prophecy, lady, that's part and parcel of the history of every Domain. Every seer, from every Realm, had the same vision. Of one who will take the Shadow and restore its true balance with the Light."

"I know. I heard those words from our own sage's lips, as did my mother, and hers before her, and hers before that. Suppose they're wrong? Or it's a lie? Or the opposition too great? Our hopes are too high, our need too desperate."

"Have we an alternative?"

"Elora Danan?" *She makes her dismissal plain.*

"Yet you came, lady. Yet you stay."

"They're afraid," Thorn whispered, as though afraid of being overheard, understanding at last and with a rueful twist of the mouth that might have been a smile the origin of the phrase about "walls having ears." The sound of his own voice broke the cord that linked him to the Veil Queen's apartment and brought his awareness once more back to his cell.

"I'm afraid." This, a fraction louder.

The Demon said nothing; that made him angry. He wanted the contact, *needed* the focus for his anger. Through his head raced a score of arguments, like a stampede, passionate and lawyerly reasons why the planned sorcery was an abomination. Time and again he opened his mouth as though to say, *I will not do this.* But nothing emerged, not even air.

From every turret of the palace, a trumpet voluntarily burst forth, measure building upon measure until the fanfare reached out across city and Bay to the headlands beyond.

Sunrise.

Where had the night gone?

Thorn looked at his hands where they rested in the hollow formed by his crossed legs. He closed them into fists and placed them against his breast. When he reached forward, his spirit moved, his flesh remained.

She had no aura, the figure lying before him. So far as he could tell, nothing beyond the shape of her face and form remained to tie her to the woman she had been.

At that same moment InSight shatter-scattered his vision throughout the palace to show him whatever the Demon saw. He stood his spirit at the woman's head.

He stood by Elora Danan.

She wakes like a cat, wide-eyed and wary, every part of her alert from the moment she opens her eyes. The Vizards stand three rows deep, utterly still, sculptures in a stone garden forming a wall about her living one. Beyond, her maids and attendants, none of them happy to be here. She stretches, slowly, lazily, drawing out every moment, and lets them see her smile at the temptation to stay here all through the day and night to come.

There is no ceremony without her, that makes her important. But if she is truly that important, she also knows they'll find a way to get to her, probably wreck her garden in the process.

Realization and response come as one, thought prompting action as she unfolds herself with a child's glorious lack of stiffness and drops lithely to the ground. She loves to walk barefoot on the grass, and especially enjoys the way it tickles the soles of her feet, but as she craves respect today, she feels obliged to offer it in return. She kneels and brushes her palms across the earth, whispering a quick farewell. Then she's on her feet once more, making her way along the stone path she'd wound from the border to her central tree so she could stroll without disturbing fresh plantings.

The Vizards make way, with a smooth precision that looks choreographed, as though every moment—even the most inspired improvisation—has been foreseen. A year's number flank her single file on either side, twelve to the right, twelve to the left, clearing a path well ahead of her and keeping it so well behind. At a stately, almost solemn pace, they bring her to her bathing room.

It's nowhere near her rooms, of course. Built specifically for this day and this one purpose, as is every item within.

A whole new staff of attendants await her; no one she's seen before, or ever will again. Only the ones who will actually touch her are real servants, the others are nobility. They stand respectfully in the background, watching while Elora is scrubbed till her skin glows, then laid out on a padded table for a full-body massage. At the last, a soak in a pool scattered with rose petals. Her skin is rubbed and oiled until it is as soft to the touch as a newly bloomed flower. Her hair is cleaned and combed and brushed, before being drawn up into what will become after many hours' work an ornate arrangement of waves and curls, interwoven with precious gems. There is an attendant for each of her hands and feet, shaping the nails, filing them smooth, decorating them with paint. When they are done, others take their place to apply her cosmetics. Every movement, no matter how slight, to the smallest twitch, is answered by a flinch from the maids. They expect the worst, they have the wardrobe master as their example. But Elora doesn't say a word, nor does she stir, save for an occasional shift of position to make herself a bit more comfortable. It's as though she wears a mask herself.

He stood by Anakerie.

As the last echoes of the fanfare fade the Princess Royal strips to the skin and dives into her pool, alone and unattended. The water isn't much warmer than the Bay itself, her immersion raises immediate goose bumps from top to toe, but she doesn't mind as she drives herself from end to end with a methodical stroke that sends her streaking through the water like a fish. She paces herself through a dozen laps before calling a halt, lolling faceup on the surface until, with a smooth motion that appears deceptively easy, she arches her back like a drawn bow and rolls into a dive that takes her to the tiled bottom. She stays far longer than would have been thought possible for a person, then kicks herself straight up, grasping the lip of the pool as she shoots into the air and levers herself to her feet. It is a magnificent display, but she is conscious today—as she hasn't been for years—that while she enjoys the water, her brother had been one with it.

He stood by Elora Danan.

There are twelve elements to Elora's gown, brought out and laid before her with due ceremony. Stockings first, with garters to hold them in place about her thighs, and then her shoes, followed by a wrap of gossamer silk to serve as undergarment. The morning is mostly gone; the robing will take them nearly all the way to sunset.

Thorn shook his head to banish the growing sense of weight from his own shoulders, as though each layer of clothes on Elora was a weight of stones to crush the both of them.

Anakerie has no truck with the concoction brought for her; one look is enough to have it banished from her sight, along with all the functionaries sent to decorate her in the bargain. A chamberlain comes to offer protests; a glare from her makes him think better of the idea. The chancellor comes bearing her father's staff of office, with entreaties, to find her already in uniform and buckling on her sword.

"Highness," he begins. He's known her all her life and has earned her respect by treating her from the first as he would an equal.

"You cannot do this," he says.

"You cannot stop me." She finishes braiding her hair and reaches reflexively for her silver clip to anchor it, only to find that its accustomed place on her bureau is empty. After a fractional hesitation, she chooses another. "I am colonel commander of the Red Lions, Chancellor, my place is with my troops."

"With respect, your place is where your father tells you to be."

"By his side, you mean, watching him bow and scrape to rulers who, at their best, are no more than his peers? Buying favor, he believes, with that pathetic scrap of a girl."

"You have no faith in the Prophecy, Anakerie?"

"Like many of my father's guests, Philemon, I have no faith in her. And I trust none within these walls whom I do not know. Hell"—her mouth makes a wry twist—*"if history serves, I should probably trust least those I know best. If my father wants me, he must take me as I am, his finest warrior."*

"You would wear edged steel to the Ascension?" The old man is scandalized. *"For some of the Veil Folk, Princess, the merest touch of iron is fatal. Moreover, as part of the Covenant, none present for the ceremony will come armed."*

"So I'll save him the embarrassment and stay away."

"Child, you are too willful!"

"Have a care, Chancellor." Her voice goes very soft and her eyes glitter like ice crystals in a sun that offers light but not the slightest bit of warmth. *"Remember to whom you speak."*

"And you, Royal Highness, for whom I speak."

"We've played this game before, my father and I. He should have learned his lesson better."

"Please, Anakerie. The King does you the courtesy of requesting your presence."

"Were it a command, Lord Chancellor, I would refuse. My place tonight is elsewhere."

Thorn yearned to reach out for the Dragon, to recapture the sense of joy and possibility that had swept through him; he could barely recall the sensations and their loss left the taste of ash in his mouth, as though that burning within his breast had consumed him.

You wander.

There was accusation in the Demon's voice, and betrayal.

"I know," he said lamely. "I'm sorry." Then, another thought, given voice with surprising force and focus: "You see everything within the palace walls, am I right? You *are* the palace walls."

So?

"Can you find me the one they call the Magus? Elora's protector?"

Other than yourself, little mage?

"Other than myself, yes."

And if I do so?

"I gave my word. But if the leader of the Maizan is false, what does that say of the Magus he brought to Angwyn? If there's danger here for Elora Danan, I have to know. You left her alone before, Demon," he said finally. "Don't do so again, I beg you."

You gave your word, meat. Be true to it.

With the hands of his spirit form, he reached out to the woman's forehead, above the mystical third eye—as Anakerie had with him—and found the flesh cool to the touch. The glow that answered was likewise very faint; there was life in the most technical sense, or rather the potential for life, but no true *being*.

He touched fingertips to his own brow, then lips, lastly heart. He spread his hands to shoulder width, and between them left a filament of glittering silver, a spider strand of starstuff. His breathing slowed, hers remained nonexistent, as he leaned forward to run a line from her forehead to her lips, to her heart and beyond, marking all the crucial access points of power on her body. When he was done, he'd drawn a stick figure on her flesh, and his own skin was chilled.

He felt her heart, and didn't need InSight to tell the strength of it.

He placed his right hand on her temple, the other over her left breast as gently as if he was her lover, and leaned forward to touch his lips to hers. He blew a puff of air into her mouth.

Energy crackled behind his eyes, sending sizzles throughout the vast network of nerves that charged his own flesh, and he cast a portion of it through his hands and into her. It was like ladling water into a whirlpool; all that was offered was swallowed instantly, leaving neither trace nor effect behind. Another puff of breath, another cast of power. And another after that. And another.

He paused, swaying, suddenly giddy, yet never releasing his hold on her. His pulse thundered, smearing vision with monstrous swathes of scarlet, and his muscles burned so that he couldn't manage a decent breath of his own. Little spasmoid trembles skibbled the length and breadth of him, and what he wanted more than anything was to let go and walk away. He shook his head, awe mingling with stark terror, because this was the comparatively easy part; far worse was yet to come.

His heart seemed to pause, then caught itself with an exceptionally powerful beat, of such force it shook his chest from within. Hers did the same.

He panted. So did she.

He had to move his face away quickly, because what air remained in her lungs had been there quite an age and had become stale beyond endurance.

He drew a breath as deep as he could manage, and felt her chest expand to follow. From beneath his right hand, InSight showed him a growing network of glowworm tracings beneath her skin extending outward from her head. At the same time each pulse of her heart stirred blood that had been too long dormant. It moved like sludge at first, but grew more fluid with every passing beat. There was texture to her skin now, a faint roseate tint underlying its blue-white color.

Impressive.

"Meaningless." He kept his replies short to the point of rudeness; he had too much need of his strength to spare any in idle conversation.

The form lives, it breathes.

"*I* live, Demon. *I* breathe. In that, we are One. All that she has, thus far comes from me. She lives—if you can call it that—because I sustain her. What of the Magus, Demon, what of Elora Danan?"

Elora wonders if the whole point of the day is to kill her. Bad enough to wear new shoes; these arch her feet to a degree she's never found comfortable and she's had them on for what seems like an eternity. No food, either, and only the occasional sip of water that serves to intensify her thirst rather than slake it. Her clothes are too ornate, and there are simply too many of them to allow her to go to the bathroom. That has been made plain to her for as far back as she can remember, as the mechanics of the ceremony evolve; she must simply endure.

She doesn't understand, now any more than then. But she's learned

how to obey. Not that it matters. She is wrapped so tightly she can't even sit; a backing board has been provided for her to lean against, for those rare moments when she is allowed to ease the strain. She has no breasts to speak of, she's still far more girl than woman, but a corset gives her the illusion of them. Over that goes an undergown that hugs what passes for her figure all the way to her ankles, effectively hobbling her. She can no more take a decent stride than a decent breath and she wonders if the Vizards will have to carry her to her altar.

It was as though Thorn's eyes had turned to prisms, more faceted than any diamond, each window on a different scene, and the harder he willed himself *not* to see, the more irresistibly his attention was drawn.

Anakerie crosses the waryard with leonine strides, pace and manner proclaiming her mastery of both self and space. Stables and barracks are a hive of activity, as mounts are groomed and troopers hurry to finish their own equipage. The Lions are to ride today in full ceremonial regalia, as they do for a Royal coronation and other state occasions, which means every piece of tack and armor has to be polished to a mirror finish. Accoutrements are purely for show—pennant lances with blunt tips, and no shields, breastplates and helms that look mightily impressive but aren't worth much of a damn either.

She passes from light to shadow, near absolutes of both, and turns a glare on the looming column of Elora's Aerie, as though it is some hostile redoubt and she its determined conqueror.

"Jalaby," she calls, her voice topping the workaday din of the yard as it would a battlefield, to be answered as quickly by her adjutant.

"Dread lady," he calls back, on the run from the stables.

"Don't call me that, I've told you a thousand times. 'Highness' will do." It's an old joke between them; he has permission to call her by name, proprieties be damned, though he never does. "I want a change in regimental orders for today."

"Lady?"

"Even sections to ride as directed. Odd in patrol kit. Keep them neat, Jalaby, I want them looking respectable. But I also want war lances and shields."

"Has milady some special intelligence we should know about?"

"Only what I was born with, Sergeant Major. I'm as fond of theater

as anyone. If my father wants to put on a pageant to impress his people and his guests, that's his prerogative. I just want to make sure that any surprises we encounter along the way are pleasant ones. See to it, will you?"

"As Your Highness commands." And he's off, with a bellow that makes hers pale in comparison.

"Not very trusting by nature, are you?" This new voice brings a surprisingly shy smile to her lips.

"No more than you would be, Mohdri, in similar circumstances."

The Castellan casts as hard a shadow as the tower, but Anakerie doesn't seem to mind. In dress, he appears as casual as she—wool as finely woven as silk, and butter-soft leather, all in signature black—but she knows the mail shirt beneath his tunic is proof against even the sharpest points. As for weapons, the sword that hangs off his left hip is the least of what he carries.

Hers is a less overtly martial presentation, cotton and fine wool but no leather save for gloves and boots. Her trousers are snug to her ankles, with a stirrup hooked over the arch of her boot to keep their line taut. She normally wears white; not so today. Her uniform is a rich royal blue, more like deep-water ocean than sky, with a broad scarlet stripe down the outside seam of her trousers to proclaim her rank. Junior officers wear a thinner stripe and troopers none at all. The tunic covers her hips and fits as snugly, its sole ornamentation thick strands of braided frogging colored a shade darker than the tunic itself that runs from her stand-up collar straight down the button front and out the lower hem, with horizontal lines set at intervals along the way. Similar lacings—galons—are woven around her sleeve hems and up the forearm, ending just below her elbow with a representation of the Royal crest. On her collar are the only bright elements to the ensemble: the regimental insignia of a lion rampant, done in scarlet thread, together with the laurel wreath, crown, and crossed swords of her rank, in silver. She, too, wears mail under her coat and carries far more weapons than are immediately apparent. A casual observer might think her overmatched by her companion; that is a mistake, and both she and Mohdri know it.

"This is a day of celebration, Princess," he tells her, shortening his stride to match her pace as she continues her tour of the yard, *"yet I note*

you've confined my personal escort to barracks, with a full troop of your own to mind them."

"They fired at a mating pair of eagles yesterday."

"We hunt eagles."

"In your own land, perhaps. Not Angwyn."

"One of them stooped. My men feared they were under attack."

"And fired as well at a merchant vessel."

"They were challenged."

"They are guests, my lord Castellan."

"And will be reminded most forcefully to behave as such, I assure you. My dear Anakerie, I hardly think you've anything to fear from a score of them."

"I've seen them fight."

"And fought beside them." The banter leaves his tone and he takes her hand gently in his. "You should have stayed. You are one of us, too wild of heart to live a life in such a cage as this."

As gently, she disengages. "These are my people, this is my home."

"Worth your life, are they?"

His challenge is flippant, her reply is not. She fixes him with a calm and level gaze and speaks as truly as she knows how.

"Yes, Castellan, they are."

"Do they feel the same in return?"

"The one isn't contingent on the other."

"You left once."

"And came back."

They cross the aerie's shadow and the Castellan suddenly stops, staring at nothing but with his head cocked to give better reception to some sound only he can hear, as suddenly alert as he would be on a combat patrol about to engage the enemy.

"Impossible," he breathes. "The prisoner . . ."

"What of him?" Her tone grows chill.

"I could swear . . ."

"Don't keep us in suspense, Castellan, finish your sentence."

He blinks and looks at her as though for the first time.

"Why are you so angry, my pet?"

"I'm not your damn anything, Castellan, I thought that was understood from the start."

"You are unfathomable sometimes, Keri."

"Anakerie, if you please. My brother was the only one I let call me that."

"You never seemed to mind before."

"You never noticed."

"Is that why you left me? Did you truly believe I took you so for granted?"

"What was to believe, Mohdri, it was plain fact. Like horses having four legs. What about the prisoner?"

"I had this sense of being watched."

"Considering who's in residence, and the Powers they command, that's hardly a revelation."

"I know the taste of the Veil Folk; this was different."

"Legend reputes the castle is haunted."

"It wasn't a ghost."

"I didn't mean a ghost. We have Demons here, didn't you know?"

"Nor Demon neither."

"The Nelwyn's locked up tight, Castellan, and thanks to you probably broken all to bits."

"What I did was done for your protection, Princess."

"How reassuring."

"We mean you and yours no harm. The Maizan come as friends."

"And the Magus?"

"Likewise, only more so."

"Don't call me 'my pet' again. I feel like you're casting a Change-Spell."

"Would you were so easily tamed—peace, Princess, it was only said in jest!" He holds up his hands in a placating gesture, meeting Anakerie's furious gaze with the most irresistibly charming of smiles. "Forgive me."

When she says nothing, he tries a slight change of subject. "And the prisoner?"

She rounds on him. "Castellan, I have more things on my mind than that pathetic little creature you seem hell-bent on tormenting. You think he's watching us? Find me a scryer to back that up with proof and we'll proceed accordingly. Until then, I have too much else to do. And, with all due respect, you're in the way."

He takes a step to follow, but Sergeant Major Jalaby chooses that moment to hurry a section from the stables for saddling and inspection, and the yard is instantly filled with a score of men and mounts, hooves cracking sharply on cobblestones, the air alive with snorts and whinnies and the occasional neigh, commands and curses flashing back and forth with practiced enthusiasm. Everywhere the Castellan turns, he finds his pathway blocked, and with each of those turns, Anakerie puts more distance between them.

Mohdri and Jalaby lock eyes. Without breaking contact, the old campaigner tilts his head a little down and to the side and spits. And smiles.

Mohdri smiles back, and seeing what is in his eyes, the men nearest the sergeant major reach for swords and lances.

The Castellan turns on his heel and strides away.

"He knows," Thorn said with a small wail, "I'm watching."

Suspects.

"For such as him, suspicion is certainty."

All the more reason, little magus, for you to focus on the task at hand.

"Madness," he cried. "This *and* me!"

There was sweat on his face, but he couldn't break contact with either hand to wipe it off. He wanted to sleep, and remembered a day—an age past, a lifetime gone—spent hefting bags of seed corn to his barn. Each had been as big as he, and weighed more; the only way to carry them was to bend his body double and use his back as a barrow. He didn't hurt while he was working, he simply got more and more tired. His muscles recovered within a day or so, but it was the better part of a week before he came out of this eerie stupor. As though he'd walked up to the edge of the Final Abyss and leaned over to see if Death was home. Thankfully, no—but the Reaper had somehow wrapped Thorn in a piece of itself, a lingering taste of what would someday be in store as a caution about being so foolish again.

Of course, he hadn't listened. His whole life since, he sometimes thought, had become an endless and madcap reel along the edge of that chasm.

The longer he procrastinated, the weaker he became, the less able even to survive the spell, much less succeed with it.

"Can you do that to Elora Danan?" he heard himself ask.

"But, having done this," he heard himself reply, "what will she say when she sees me again? Demons are cast out of human hosts, not the other way round!"

"Can't be any worse than what she's said and done already, am I right?"

As an attempt at humor, it wasn't much—certainly not in the brownies' league—but he decided to let that pass. The discussion was academic anyway, his die had long since been cast. He would see this through to the end, whatever came.

As though that realization was a cue, the room about him grew close and heavy, oppressive in the way air can be heralding an approaching storm. There was a sour stench of burning that left a metallic tinge at the back of his tongue, the harbinger of a lightning bolt. His mouth was dry, but licking his lips brought no relief; his tongue was as raspy as sandpaper, and every part of him rapidly grew bloated and swollen. Summers were like this back home, so steamy that thought itself took an effort and movement was out of the question. Salvation then was a soak in the stream behind the house and some heartfelt prayers for an evening breeze.

The smell made him gag. He had no name for it, save that it was awful. He'd been a farmer, he knew the stench of nature. He'd been a warrior, albeit reluctantly, and knew the same of battlefields. He'd looked upon the face of Evil—at the time he'd thought *Ultimate* Evil—and gotten a taste of that foulness as well.

No comparison. This was far worse.

He tried breathing through his mouth, to no avail. He knew from long experience that the nose quickly grew accustomed to scents; it was simply a matter of waiting until he became used to this one. Only that didn't happen. If anything, it got worse. The miasma coiled about him like a lover, pressing against every part of him, soaking like water into a sponge through clothes, and then, to his horror, flesh as well.

To his OutSight, he remained unchanged.

What his InSight showed Thorn made him want to howl like one demented. His skin was boiling off his bones, great pustules bursting forth like gas bubbling from a tar pit, spreading the foulness over him. Nothing of him was anchored anymore, he felt organs slide within him as his own flesh sloughed off his bones and then the bones themselves begin to putrefy. There was rot in his mouth, in his heart, in his soul. Not the clean decay of nature but a betrayal of it, as though the component pieces of himself were there only for show, they served no other function.

And yet, as the concept of eyes melted from him, he found other means of sight. A concept of being grounded in a single, solid, *physical* form gave way to one more akin to quicksilver, where no aspect stayed stable for longer than a whim. He thought at first he was being plunged into a maelstrom, but soon realized that was wrong. In a maelstrom, the elements flow in the same general direction; there's a pattern and purpose to it that was nonexistent here.

He struggled to reassert himself, but found no self to focus on. He had a body, untouched and unharmed, reduced now to a vessel as hollow as the woman's. But the bonds that linked flesh and spirit were no more.

Too late, he wondered about a trap. Two hosts for the Demon, for the price of one.

O ye of little faith.

His voice or the Demon's, he couldn't tell.

He hated the stones about him, looked for claws with which to tear at them, laughing at the thought of the great keep above collapsing into rubble and dust, as Tir Asleen had done.

His dream or the Demon's, he didn't want to know.

He saw the thread of his soul, the one thing left him that remained untouched by his transformation. Yet even as he watched, a darker strand reached out to embrace it, winding itself around and around until the two became inextricably intertwined. The intricate knotwork twisted more tightly together until it seemed to him that a single rope had been formed, the dark and light equally balanced. In desperation, he lunged forward to grab his soul and hold it fast, forgetting he had nothing left resembling hands.

It shattered.

Like gossamer soap bubbles, like the most fragile crystal, like life itself. Blew apart before him, scattering every which way, no means to catch the bits, no means to follow.

He howled.

Elora whimpers and hunches herself forward the little distance allowed her by her robes, to the dismay of her dressers, who fear she will mar their presentation and take it out on them.

And in that same instant . . .

Anakerie hauls tight on her reins, so startling her horse that the animal dances nervously and almost bucks.

"Anakerie?" asks Jalaby, the first time she's ever heard him use her name.

"How many damned fanfares is that, Jalaby?" she asks through grit-ted teeth, projecting a calm she no longer feels in an attempt to gentle her mount.

"Ten of twelve, I think. They're almost done."

"So's the day. Procession starts at sunset, ceremony's at midnight."

"You fear treachery, Highness?"

She smiles and shakes her head. "Thankfully, no. Everyone's got too much to lose should today go wrong. I just wish I knew better what it meant should things go right."

"The people have faith."

"Probably said as much at Tir Asleen. Split off two sections, Sergeant Major, have them check the city gates. I want the watchmen at their posts."

"So ordered, Highness. I'll do the job myself."

As Jalaby leads his twenty men away at a canter, another officer joins her with a salute.

"I have the honor to report, Highness, that the Red Lions have taken up their assigned positions along the promenade, the esplanade, and the Royal mile."

She can see that, even without her field glasses. Great crowds are gathering along the seafront and the main road, with many more throng-ing the city's parks. Everyone who can walk is out tonight. A house-breaker's dream, the fire brigade's nightmare.

"The Maizan, Captain, what of them?"

"The Castellan is in the palace, together with a pair of bodyguards, to escort the Protector Magus to the ceremony. The rest of his Thunder Rid-

ers are in quarters, as you commanded, being discreetly and properly looked after."

Thorn tasted blood, not his own, coating the stone, seeping through the cracks and spaces between the massively hewn blocks, so many men, so quickly done to death, Night Herons tearing at flesh as easily as they feasted on souls. There was joy in him, a hunger for more.

Something's wrong, he thought, his gaze focusing on the barracks. The waryard was deserted, troops properly deployed throughout the city, servants going about their business within the palace, as normal a scene to the casual eye as could be expected. He saw a shimmer in the air, a faint coruscation much like a heat haze, marking the presence of what first glance told him was a minor glamour that served the same function as his Cloak; anyone crossing the yard, or looking down from the battlements, would pass over the barracks without a second thought. But he saw through the Demon's eyes and those perceptions told him this something was far more insidious, a spell of such extraordinary sophistication and subtlety that lay folk and sorcerers would be bedazzled to equal effect. All would see what they expected to see, and no more.

A pain lanced up from deep within, as if some greater Power had taken hold and snapped him in two as he might the wishbone of a turkey. The walls were blood, the air was blood, *he* was blood, awash in it, alive in it. Around him were scattered the shards of his soul, but he could no longer tell which were his and which the Demon's; there was scarlet everywhere, everything looked the same.

The second pain was greater than the first. He'd thought the ChangeSpell agony, but it was nothing compared with this.

The third spasm broke his consciousness as he himself had smashed his soul. He was no more than the *idea* of life. The concept of being. Not "I think, therefore I am," or even "I am." No "I" at all, but simply "am."

He knew there'd be a fourth spasm and a fifth; it would go on and on until the Demon's child was delivered or he ceased to be. It wasn't a tangible awareness; he lacked the coherence to string together even a single thought. More akin to fundamental knowledge, imprinted on the primal fabric of his being, like the body's understanding at birth of how to take a breath, or the heart itself to beat. Or even just the notion of thought itself.

From that nowhere, he drew back to himself a sense of self, an "I" to place before every other concept. A name to fit the pronoun.

I am

Followed by

I am Thorn Drumheller

Like waking up, only much more slowly. Begin with nothingness, a transitory oblivion—or so it seems, unless one is gifted (or cursed) enough to remember all the evening's dreams—that ends with the opening of the eyes. With sight, revelation: a rebirth of sorts. Identity, memory, awareness, answers to all the primal questions: who am I, where am I, what am I?

Shard by shard, he found himself. Accomplishing by active choice what was normally taken for granted, assuming all the scattered, disparate elements to himself, uncaring as he went which were his and which the Demon's.

He felt a vibration trickle through the fabric of the foundation stones, as though the palace itself were waking with him. New enchantments casting resonances off of Powers long dormant. Nothing would come of it, they had slept too long, were too set in their ways, to take any active part in the ceremony. But they were aware . . .

. . . as they had not been for longer than the memory of man.

Fools, he cried within his thoughts. Fools! *What are you* doing *up there!*

He wanted to hurry, that same awareness lashing him as an eager carter would a tardy mare. And the image came back to him of that day in the barn with the sacks of grain. He wanted to hurry then, too, simply to be done. Supper was waiting and a hot bath, the sweetest reward for a miserable bear of a day. Unfortunately, desire—no matter how fervent—didn't make the bags weigh any the less, or his feet plod any more nimbly. His muscles did the best they could, the task had its proper rhythm and would be done when it was done. Making himself frantic in the process wouldn't help.

He heard a final fanfare. It was precisely the moment of sunset.

At that same moment Thorn feels the doors of Elora's great hall thrown open. Within, the space is alight with a multitude of candles, casting echoes off reflective paint from the ceiling overhead to create the illusion that all are entering the vault of the rapidly darkening sky.

The room is a symmetrical oval, two aisles bisecting length and width, forming a circle where they meet. Interlaced around the chamber's circumference are the Great Seals of the Domains; the pattern is repeated along the border of the circle, with Elora's own as the centerpiece. Between each set of seals is a section of seats for the respective Domain, three for each of the four quarters. The walls describe the same arc reaching up toward the ceiling as they do from side to side, thereby preserving the room's form throughout every physical dimension.

The Vizards enter first, with solemn, stately tread, two columns of robed, masked figures, each bearing a staff of office down the central aisle, around the outer border of the central circle, and on to the end, where they turn outward to reverse direction along the perimeter of the chamber itself until they reach the entrance, filling in the lesser aisles along the way. All stand facing the dais.

Next come the representatives of the Domains. In every case but one, the rulers of each, that sole exception being Kieron Dineer. All the other seats are filled; Kieron's section, virtually empty. Sovereigns of the primal elements, Earth and Air and Fire and Water; of the primal states of being, flesh and the spirit; and of the primal mysteries. Some appear human because that is their true nature. Others do so out of courtesy. A few— proudly, defiantly—make not the slightest pretense. There is excitement, but it has a dangerous edge to it, none present are sure whether the night will end in joy or disaster, each determined to emerge triumphant regardless. Thorn thinks it like staring at a cheering crowd and wonders what it will take to turn them into a mob, their festival into a riot.

The room grows still. Two sections remain, both flanking the head of the room, opposite the doorway.

Then, to all appearances, the candle flames begin to dance. Tiny spots of light and color, buzzing wildly through the air, bouncing off each other with cries of wild delight, forming ever-more-intricate patterns with the

streamers left in their wake. Some of those watching respond in kind, others with grimaces of dour resignation at a display seen often before. The fairies take such negative responses as a personal challenge and redouble their efforts. The fiercer the frowns, the more infuriatingly radiant their smiles in return.

Until, when the chorus of light and sound reaches its crescendo, all eyes suddenly turn as one toward the doorway.

The fairies average the size of a human finger; their queen dwarfs them by comparison, though she stands smaller than a Daikini child. Cherlindrea's hair is gossamer gold, so pale it nearly matches the silver of her gown, her face and form of unhuman perfection. Every aspect of her seems to float, as though she moves through water, her gown layer upon diaphanous layer, creating the sense of what lies beneath without revealing a thing. Her wings are scarcely thicker, neither large nor substantial enough to bear her aloft—yet they do so, and without noticeable effort. As she makes her way along the aisle, Angwyn's King proudly, handsomely, by her side, all her companions rush to her; they take position behind her, their formation creating the illusion of a vast, glittering train that ripples and flows across the entire spectrum of visible light and color. It is a breathtaking display, beside which even the most magnificent fireworks display pales. When she reaches and takes her seat, it shatters, all its fairy parts spinning off like plasma from a newborn star, circling up and away to their own assigned places.

When the room quiets, and eyes grow once more accustomed to the less dramatic illumination of the candle glow, Thorn beholds Willow Ufgood standing in the doorway.

CHAPTER 8

THROUGH THE DEMON'S "EYES," THORN BEHELD THE most magnificent lie.

The figure is tall in a way Willow has never been, and handsome in a way Willow never dreamed of being. In the main, the features are his, but they've been shaped and polished to push him more toward the Daikini, what most men would consider craggy good looks. A ready smile of welcome without a hint of shyness, laughing eyes that view the assemblage with true delight, this is a man whose every move and gesture proclaims a generosity of spirit to go along with his gentle strength. There are more lines than one would expect in a face of his age, testament to the price paid for the knowledge and power that swirl from his shoulders like a greatcloak.

His colors are white and gold, the one so pure, the other so bright, it hurts to look at him. His tunic is cut to emphasize the sweep of his powerful chest, while equally snug-fitting trousers do the same for shapely legs. His boots echo the curve of his calf, one more dynamic element in an ensemble already pushing the outer edges of fashion. Gold thread is worked through the fabric of the garments, apparently for aesthetic effect, in a random display that catches the light and amplifies it so that every movement the sorcerer makes triggers a flashing cascade of micro-sunbursts, a display easily as dazzling as the fireworks prepared to celebrate the conclusion of the Ascension.

As Willow's stride eats up the distance from entrance to altar, Thorn has a suddenly absurd vision of dust motes scrambling with frantic desperation to get out of his way, lest the slightest contact mar the perfection of his costume.

Thorn can't watch, can't bear to. And yet cannot tear his eyes away. This false Willow is too splendid a glory for any living being, mortal or otherwise, to resist.

Were he himself, he would be lost. Fortunately, the Demon defines Its nature by discerning the patterns in everything and then unworking them.

The threads, *he realizes, with a thrill of horror,* the *flashes! It's how they catch the light when he moves!*

It is a variation on the spell that has been used to Cloak the barracks. Again, nothing very sinister, on the face of it. The simplest kind of glamour, used by touring conjurers to place their audience in a more receptive mood, and easily deflected by any sorcerer worth the name. One of the first lessons taught any decent practitioner of the magical arts is how to recognize and protect yourself against such manipulation; it is something done automatically. Yet the web being woven here is such a masterpiece of deception that simply to behold this deceiver—Thorn refuses to think of the impostor as Willow, deciding in that instant that Deceiver is the name he'll use from then on—is to become ensnared, and once caught, the thought of protecting themselves further nevermore enters anyone's head. It is as though the Deceiver has access to their most secret souls, that somehow he knows all present more intimately than they know themselves.

Then vision blurred, Thorn's sense of the chamber high above slipped away and he scrabbled desperately for purchase as both inner and outer reality frayed faster than the threads of that napkin the Aldwyn had showed him so long ago. He was three spirits where there should be only one and rapidly discovering that the strain of maintaining coherence between himself and Elora and Anakerie made riding the whirlwind tiger a picnic by comparison.

The Demon had no concept of structure and therefore kept trying to warp Thorn to Its way of being. No matter that what the Nelwyn beheld was illusion, a simulacrum of his mind to match the substance of flesh—namely, his body—still standing close by, his perceptions reacted as if this was real. When his trunk was stretched and twisted like molten toffee, a halting, gurgling grunt of agony was likewise wrenched with it. He felt the pain of growing wings, the bones of face and body cracking and reshaping into a myriad of wereforms, Dragon merged with Wyr, with tiny Boggarts and on toward creatures for which he neither had nor desired names. Time rolled him back to its primordial beginnings and cast him howling to its end, flashcasting through every conceivable incarnation in between. He stood at the molten heart of the world and watched it be born, basking in a heat intense enough to vaporize the strongest metal, and likewise saw it die, crumbling underfoot to ancient dust. He saw the Darkness that was at the Beginning of All Things and the Darkness to come at the End. He saw multitudes at every hand, more aspects of himself, his world, than he had numbers to count them.

But only one image of this place, this moment.

In all the countless might-have-beens, and might-yet-bes, there was no other variant on this cell and this woman.

"Why?" he whispered, unable to comprehend, refusing to accept.

Special man, special place, special moment.

"Shut up!" he screamed, terror turning his voice to a child's shriek. *Leave me alone,* he wanted to say. *I want no more part of this! I deny you, I deny myself, let me go!*

He felt something slip within him, as though from his grasp, and made a frantic scramble to regain his hold. It was the Demon's child. He was losing it.

He had two of his own. There should have been a third. But times were hard, and his wife fell ill. The women of the village pooled their resources as midwives and healers—which were considerable and normally they were well able to cope with almost all manner of ailments—but there was no improvement. A runner was sent for the High Aldwyn, in hope that his magic might succeed where herbs and potions failed, but Thorn knew with sick certainty the old wizard wouldn't arrive in time. He thought he had fallen ill himself; whenever he looked at Kiaya, his vision of her was smudged, as though she lay beneath a filthy gray veil. He'd always thought of her as a creature of passionate primary colors and wondered what she saw in as monochrome a dullard as he. Yet while he watched, those colors faded, the veil darkened, skin draping itself over too prominent bones as fever stole the flesh beneath away.

He fed her broth, even when she pushed it away, and cleaned her when she threw it up. He sat beside her most of the day and held her close at night, trying to cast warmth from his body to hers by sheer force of will. He offered what prayers he could, to any Bright Power he thought might listen. He knew he was losing her.

He was so absorbed in his battle, he had no sense of its cost on him. All his efforts, the total focus of his being, was on restoring his wife to health, and that battle in turn resolved itself down to casting off the veil that covered her. He had no idea that he was growing as gaunt as she as he stripped himself of all his strength and willingly cast it over to her. He never heard the sorrowing whispers of those who brought food and drink to his door, that the village would be mourning the loss of two instead of one.

It was the dark of the moon, on a night he'd begun to suspect would never end. The crisis had come for them both. Kiaya's fever blazed hotter than a smithy furnace, yet she couldn't stop shivering. Twice he'd placed a leather strap in her mouth so she wouldn't crack her teeth; the second time she'd near bitten it through. He'd never felt so beaten himself. He moved because he had to, each step harder than the last, to the point where he knew that if he stopped again and sat, he'd never get up.

For all the exhaustion of his body, his mind had never felt so clear. About him, all was acid-etched crystal, and he thought he was surely mad because he had the wild sensation of seeing not only the surface reality of things but the truth of them as well. The bed Kiaya lay on wasn't just a piece of furniture; he could perceive the sweat and skill it took him to carve it, and beyond that the life of the tree from whence it came. It had been an old, storm-smashed rowan, and his breath caught in wonder as he spied a resonance of the dryad who'd long made it her home.

He heard his name and turned to the bed, feeling his heart stutter-step through a handsclap of beats at the realization that it wasn't his Kiaya who called. A child, so wee and helpless a bit, hands outstretched to both of them. Not the baby as it was, for it wasn't even halfway through its term, but the Nelwyn it might have been. And Thorn felt its grip—at first so ferociously tight— slacken on his fingers. He closed his own hand, and felt Kiaya do the same, but they'd have done better trying to tackle a greased pig. The child was going, there was nothing they could do to stop it, save wish it well with a final good-bye.

There was a moment when its lifelight faded and the bedroom was plunged into a preternatural shadow, when Thorn wanted nothing more than to hurl himself into Oblivion after it. The ache of loss made a sham of the phrase "more than he could bear." Then, though, he felt a similar slippage from the figure by his side, and knew that his wife was starting to fade as well.

"No," he cried, and repeated himself with a full-voiced bellow, *"No!"*

He rounded on her, in such a state he didn't notice what was happening—good thing, actually, for the shock might have stopped his own heart right then and there—as streams of colored fire erupted from eyes and hands, twisting in and around themselves like eels as they descended on the bed to rend the veil. Fingers splayed and curled and the Power that burst from them was instantly cast as razor-edged claws. The veil tore, with

the puffed and soggy sound of rotted cloth, and from it came a
stench of unbelievable foulness. Thorn didn't care; the intensity
of the contagion only made him redouble his attack. He took her
hand in both of his and anchored himself to the floor as if he
were the tree their bed had been; come whatever may, as wild
energies ripped through the pair of them, he would not let her
go, he would not let her die.

She didn't.

That had been the night the sorceress Queen Bavmorda had
claimed the fortress of Nockmaar for her own.

The child—like many other innocents across the shires—had
sickened because it had been touched and tainted by the darkling energies of those abominable conjurations; their souls were
to merge with the mortar that bound the walls and battlements
together, to armor them against every form of mystical assault.
In Thorn's family, the spell found an especially fertile field to
take root in, for he was Power mainly ignorant of itself—exist-
ing more as untapped potential than actuality—and therefore
defenseless. His wife had none, but the baby had, in full measure. Had he not stood firm, all three of them would have been
lost. Instead, two survived and the third was blessed with a
clean passing.

That long-ago night had been a test of strength; this, he realized, was one of control, to judge whether he was master of his
passions and terrors—and through them, his powers—or their
slave.

He felt another slippage within himself, and knew he faced
another crisis, as grave and crucial as the first.

He embraced the Demon, full-hearted and with all his
strength and in that dreadful moment . . .

. . . became the Demon.

*His sight splinters, a corner of his vision revealing the Deceiver tak-
ing the hero's post at the altar, slight of stature compared with any
Daikini yet conveying the impression that he dwarfs them all. Awaiting
Elora more like a bridegroom than the celebrant, with no color whatsoever to his aura—as if he's been bleached of every human aspect—and
a disturbing hunger to his eyes.*

At the very same moment another aspect of the Demon's awareness presents Thorn with a view of the rest of the crowded chamber and the difference between what was and is becomes plain. Where Thorn the Nelwyn beheld men and women, recognizable shapes regardless of species, Thorn the Demon perceives skirling filigrees of energy, patterns of life interwoven with those of power great and small, some wholly self-contained (these mostly confined to the Daikini) while others burst forth to tangle with those around them. A common denominator binds them all, a fundamental faith in the Light.

Winding through the assemblage, however, are the delicate strands of the Deceiver's glamour, a continuous thread reaching outward from where he stands, the spider at the heart of its web, awaiting a final fly.

Thorn cast himself toward the doorway of Elora's great hall as the final fanfare sounded.

He feels Anakerie in the courtyard, pacing afoot because her horse—affected by the Princess's apprehension as she is by Thorn's—can no longer stand to have her on its back. The hackles on Anakerie's neck stand stiff as the bristles on a wire brush, the patterns of her being blazing hot with an anxiety neither logic nor action can quiet. Her focus is on the eastern horizon, already brightening with the approach of the full moon. When it rises fully into view, the Rite of Ascension will begin.

Hands-not-hands slipped again and Thorn hesitated, torn between two demands of equal weight: Elora's danger on the one hand, the Demon child's on the other.

The doors begin to open. He knows as certainly as he knows anything that Elora is doomed if she steps inside that chamber.

He knew as well that the Demon's child was doomed if he didn't act at once to complete the Spell of Resurrection.

Silence within the hall, a greater silence on the streets without, as the entire populace seems to hold its collective breath.

Silence far below, save for the hammering of Thorn's heart, beat after deliberate beat, as though some brute was urging the blood through his veins as a shipmaster would galley slaves, by beating a mallet on the drum of his chest.

It was no choice, really.

He cleaved himself, child from Demon, and then did the same again, to cast the Demon from himself.

He bent over the woman's body, his lips to hers, and let his spirit pass over to all the hollow places within her.

A final division, and with it he loosed his grip on the child. Not so easy on the child's part, he felt it hold as his own babies had, as any small thing would, desperate not to be cast aside from that which gave it life.

"It's all right," he tried to say, "you're all right, you're safe." But the words wouldn't come, because for all his efforts he wasn't yet sure they were true.

Her lips moved beneath his, a hand of flesh lifted to echo the action of the spirit and take tight hold. There were tears in his eyes, tears in hers.

"It's all right," he breathed, pulling away just enough to break the contact, their breaths still one. "You're all right, you're safe." And this time he believed it.

"Well now, Peck, look who's been having himself a righteous good time?"

His mind told him how to react, but his body lacked the co-ordination to pull it off. He was still too much the Demon, with no innate comprehension of the nature of flesh and bone and sinew, much less any sense of how to make them properly work. And so, a swift turn became a stumbling collapse that left him sprawled on hands and knees; worse, he'd given so much of himself that his weight alone was enough to set his arms immediately to trembling. He seemed to have forgotten how to breathe, he worked his lungs like a bellows, each inhalation and exhalation the result of a conscious command, desperate for air, only to find his best efforts reduced completely to naught as spiked bands tightened on chest and brain. He heard aspirate bubbles from under his breastbone and thought he might be drowning.

He couldn't lift his head to see the doorway and then didn't have to as a Death Dog—the Castellan's "puppy"—leaped from the top of the steps to send him tumbling head over heels.

Two Maizan, one with crossbow tucked underarm, the other holding an ax already scored with blood.

"The Castellan will be impressed, Peck," the Maizan continued. "Didn't think it possible for any man—or mage—to beat a ChangeSpell. Mayhap next time he'll use it on the Princess, teach Anakerie to mind her place." A rough, appreciative laugh from his fellow, a sight he looked forward to. "Pity you won't be there to see it. Whatever you are, little bit, you're too dangerous to live."

He snapped his fingers and the Death Dog charged.

Inhumanly fast as it was, the woman was that much faster, with strength to match as her arm swept round to catch the creature by its collar and hurl it at the entryway. One Maizan stumbled back through the door in a reflexive attempt to stay out of its way, as it struck the stone jamb with such force that all knew at once the beast was dead; the other lost his balance and pitched to the floor. Bad landing, left him sprawled and bleeding, ax skittering to the woman as if she'd called it to her.

She knew which end to hold it by, but that seemed about all as she struggled to her feet, body swaying with a constant series of minor adjustments as she tried to get used to standing on two feet, giving her the appearance of someone right off a boat after a long voyage. The Maizan grinned nastily as he recovered his feet and wiped his eyes clear, saber already in hand.

He lunged. She fell away before his assault, ax coming up in a twisting motion that snagged the blade at midpoint and broke it from his hold. She swept around, always giving the impression of someone on the brink of a fatal loss of balance, casting the sword out of the Maizan's reach. She had him, he knew it.

"No!"

Thorn's cry was a surprise to them all, but mostly to the woman. She staggered, the smooth progression of her spin interrupted, and her foe took immediate advantage, bringing up his knee in a brutal blow to her midsection that doubled her over, following it up with a second kick to the face that bounced her on her back. Now he had the ax.

Nothing came of it. Even as he raised the weapon Thorn stabbed his knife at the man's side, aiming for the seam where breast- and backplate joined together. There was an armored guard flap underneath and mail below that; by rights, the blade should have glanced off, with no damage done. But Thorn did his own forging, he'd spent the best part of a year underground, apprentice to the Mountain Folk—a branch of the Nelwyn tree that worked metals instead of soil—learning how to do it properly. This stiletto, he cast thin as a knitting needle, to fit between any seam and through the rings of a mail shirt. And so it went, to the hilt into the Maizan's side. Not a fatal strike, Thorn didn't have the proper angle for that, but enough to get the man's attention. Which, in turn, caught the Nelwyn a powerful thump to the side of his skull, followed by a clumsy backswing of the ax, the flat of the blade like running full tilt into a door. Down he went, while the Maizan returned to what he'd decided was the preeminent threat, the woman. As he raised his ax to finish her, though, darkness exploded upward around him. He made no outcry, it was doubtful he even knew what was happening. One instant he was there, the next he wasn't. Only Thorn's knife lay on the floor to mark his passing.

Thorn was still gawking when the woman's palm slapped his chest and knocked him aside, the sound of her hand merging with the *swish* of the other Maizan's crossbow bolt as it whizzed by. He was in the doorway, using the jamb for cover as he worked the cocking lever to recharge his bow; the archer had as clear a field of fire as any archer could wish for, and from the speed and evident efficiency of his reload, it was doubtful either Thorn or the woman would survive a rush up the stairs.

The Maizan raised his bow.

And his head separated from the rest of him.

Body and bow fell together, in a scarlet mess.

Where he'd been, stood Geryn Havilhand, double-handed broadsword shaking in his grasp. His leathers were torn, his face scored with grime and gore, soaked as much with blood as sweat.

"Bastard," he cried, and then, with face upturned as though to the whole palace above, *"Bastards!"*

He spied the Death Dog and, as though to emphasize the point, hacked at it like a logger with his blade until both stone and steel were badly chipped. He was too caught up in his frenzy to notice a pool of darkness oozing up beneath the hound; after his last stroke, when he'd exhausted himself too much to go on, the creature simply vanished, along with the remains of the other Maizan.

Thorn felt a faint taste of the Demon's satisfaction at its meal; it made him sick, but also made him hunger for more.

"They're killing the Lions," Geryn said hoarsely, tripping over his own feet as he made his way down the stairs, using the wall as a bulwark to hold himself erect. "Cut 'em down like butchers, them an' their damn birds."

"The herons!"

"Drumheller, what's happening, what does it mean?"

"Nothing good, I fear. Has anyone sounded the alarm?"

"None left of ours to try. Only reason I'm still alive is't I followed these gobshite yobbos into the Old Keep. Forgive me, Peck, I din't know this's what they did wi' yeh. I thought they'd treat'cheh better."

"Could have been worse, Pathfinder. Are you hurt?"

"Bumped an' bruised, but nowt enough t' matter. Not done well by this, though." He brandished his blade, frowning at the scars he'd left along its edge. "Done me fair service, it 'as. Deserved better in return."

"Make amends as and when you can, lad, now's not the time. See to the lady here."

The young Daikini squinted for a better look in the dim glow cast by the fallen torches and then flushed to the roots of his hair.

"Blessed Elora," he squeaked, "she's got no clothes!"

"Then find her some," Thorn told him briskly, "and quickly. Horses, too. By the Carter's Gate."

"Aren't yeh comin' with?"

"I have other responsibilities."

"How long do we wait, then?"

"As long after moonrise as seems prudent. I wish I could be more specific, but in truth, Geryn, I've no idea. Just remember to err on the side of caution."

"We can't come wi' yeh?"

"Where I'm going, and what I'm to do, it's best I'm alone. Trust me in this. And be careful."

"An' you, the same. Got'cherself a name, missy?"

Thorn hadn't expected a reply, but then he also hadn't expected any skill at arms.

"Khory," he heard, and turned to stare in dumbfounded astonishment. Her voice was deep, a husky contralto, roughened by an age of unuse, made more awkward by the necessity to resort to physical speech where Demons normally cast their thoughts directly from mind to mind. She knew what she wanted to say, that much was clear; she was finding it difficult shaping lips and larynx to form the words.

"Khory . . . Bannefin."

"Geryn Havilhand. A pleasure."

"Stay," she said haltingly to Thorn, as though finding the proper word to use was as much a challenge as the actual speech. "You."

"No," Thorn replied, as sparingly. He kept his construction direct and clear, the way he would with a child. "Stay with *him!*" He indicated Geryn and struck a tone and manner that permitted no opposition. There was a moment when he thought she'd argue, a set to the jaw, a glint to the eye, that bespoke a will as stubbornly indomitable as his own. But—this once—she let it pass and did as she was told. The two soldiers left.

He couldn't help a sigh at the prospect of another bout of parenting.

"Demon!" He made the word a Summons, as though he'd thrown a warding circle and cast all the proper invocations.

You've done well, little mage.

"I haven't bloody started, thank you very much. If the Maizan have seized the palace . . ."

Accomplished fact, that is, though none within Elora's hall know it, nor any beyond the palace walls.

"What of Elora?"

Feel the moonglow, Drumheller?

He did, as a sizzle of energy like cool fire, where its light touched the topmost towers. Throughout the great castle, trumpeters stood poised to sound the final fanfare—and Thorn sensed Maizan assassins close by to make sure the voluntary was final in every respect.

"Isn't there anything we can do?" he cried. "Can't you swallow those Maizan up as well?"

He heard the laughter of genuine amusement, not a pleasant sound at all from a Demon.

Silly little man, if my power could reach so far, in such a way, what living thing would be left to walk within these walls? Why else do you think I am bound so tight and cast so low?

"How'd you reach me then, in Elora's Tower?"

I but showed you the path. The power to walk it was yours alone.

"What?"

Speak to the stones now as you did then, they will make way for you.

He felt the weight of them, soaring skyward, their base planted firm and deep upon the earth. It was much the same as when he'd turned what he later came to know as his InSight on his bed, so many years ago. There was a resonant echo within the fabric of the stones of the mountains whence they came, old patterns broken as the raw stone was quarried and shaped, new ones formed as those massive blocks were set in place.

He thought he'd always understood the *way* of things, the form and manner of their being. Some elements were of air, some of water, some of fire, some of earth; some were solid, others not. But the Demon had shown him a different, more intense means of perception and that had profoundly shaken his faith in his own beliefs. Stone was solid, so much so that the walls of this cell helped support a building that rose hundreds of feet into the sky. Yet stone could be broken by the force of a blow, by subjecting it to too much heat or cold, or worn away by running water across it. As the outward seeming of a man belied the miraculous complexity of what lay within, so, too, was the solid frontage of a stone equally a mask. The structure was simpler than what he'd find in a more nimble, active being, but peer deeply enough and the bedrock aspects were the same.

All was energy. All was malleable.

The world he inhabited, his very body, had constancy only because he lacked the means to see it truly. Now he saw through clearer eyes . . .

. . . and wished he didn't.

At first glance, there seemed to be great voids between the core particles of the stones, as he discovered there also were within himself. A simple matter then to will himself to pass between them.

A hard-earned caution, and an innate courtesy, prompted him to look again, more closely, his perceptions a fraction wider and yet more focused. Fields of force and attraction appeared before him, reminding him of the patterns his wife cast on her loom, fragile individually yet woven into a far stronger and mutually supportive entirety. Only here the linking threads most resembled diamond dust sparkling in celestial firelight, and the motes they bound together, crystalline snowflakes. Similar in general form but each one unique unto itself.

The beauty made him weep. Not only for the glory that blazed around and within him, but also in sorrow for all those multitudes who would never see, could never comprehend.

The Demon was energy unconfined, substance without form. The world as Thorn knew it, totally the reverse. The two couldn't help but be at odds. The smallest of steps after that for one to describe the other as inimical and evil.

He reached out to the stones, presenting himself to them as a supplicant, requesting safe passage, promising to do them no harm and asking the same of them in return. It was a tedious exchange, for the stones were by nature deliberate, and made all the more so by centuries of comparative dormancy. He had power—and desire—enough to bull his way through, yet at the same time knew, however tempting and desperate the need, that would be wrong.

He never heard the fanfare or sensed the moonrise. But he felt their repercussions.

Both moments made Elora tremble. And through the double bond that made Thorn part of both Demon and castle, it was as though he stood by her side.

She stands perfectly straight, because she has no choice. Her clothes are wrapped so tight around her she can barely move, and therein lies a problem none had foreseen. A burr of memory from a time she'd deliberately cast from her, a place of shadowed cold where flames existed to steal the warmth from things instead of the other way 'round. No friends at hand in this haunted recollection, the air sharp with the tang of blood, the ring of steel, the cries of the dying. She was very small then, she hardly had names to put to things, her mind still busy fixing the connections between it and her body. In these awful dreams, there are no details to the background, only an all-consuming shadow, out of which bursts misshapen masks: faces that are overlong and narrow, like combat arrows, broad of forehead, wickedly sharp at the chin, with cheek knobs as prominent as barbs. Bad teeth and hungry eyes, she's seen more compassion in a starving wolf.

A figure in red commands them, wrapped tight head to toe beneath her scarlet robe in linen silk that has been stripped of even the memory of color. Elora is bound in black, the difference being that the woman can move; she cannot.

She feels her teeth chatter and clenches them, her fists as well, to make them stop, using that physical discomfort to put a welcome wall between her and her unwanted memory. Every Domain has its signal hue; together, they encompass the primary elements of the visual spectrum. Each their special fabric, each their singular design. The ensemble feels as though it weighs as much as she, and while the fit is perfect in every regard, she's never worn it before, has had no opportunity to get used to it.

The gown gives her figure, and cosmetics give her face, a maturity she hasn't earned and doesn't feel. All she finds herself thinking of at the doorway is how much the Vizards remind her of those mannequins from her dreams, and how much her gown resembles the binding cloths of old.

"It's your special day," she starts to tell herself aloud, before the injunctions of her dressers return to her with a vengeance. They have painted a perfect mouth on her, they don't want it spoiled by as much as a breath, much less a word.

I wish it was over, *she thinks*, why can't it end? Why can't I just end it myself? *She fantasizes a turn on her heel and a quick march back the way she came, to the sanctuary of her tree, and barely stifles a giggle, which in turn comes close to provoking a succession of strokes in the watching majordomo.*

On the other hand, once the ceremony is done, her Ascension acknowledged, she'll well and truly be the Sacred Princess. The rulers of the Twelve Domains have come to pay her homage and swear eternal fealty. After that, she reasons, no one can ever again tell her what to do. She'll be truly free. A passing discomfort is a small price to pay for such a reward.

Unless they're lying.

She's been lied to about so many things in her life, this one more won't surprise her.

The doors swing wide.

Her first instinct is to run, but the train of her gown anchors her in place, the robes further denying her any stride longer than the length of her foot, so all she can manage is a reflexive demi-step back. She knows the face that waits on the dais, though her whole life has passed since she saw it last. He appears taller than she remembers, but then so is she. The smile welcoming her is all it should be, and when his arms open wide to receive her, she remembers how warm and safe she always felt in his embrace.

He is dressed head to toe in white.

She blinks, blinks again, as the first flankers of Vizards precede her down the aisle. Of their own volition, her feet move with them, dainty hobble steps, three to their slow and stately one, which give her the delicacy of a doll. The train flows back and out behind her for twice her body length and to the edges of the aisle, forcing her to pitch her body slightly forward and push with all her strength, like an ox before a fully laden wagon. The effort makes her cant her head a little toward the floor, and she lowers her eyelids as well, to further block any sight of the altar, thankful finally for the ornate headdress that mere moments before she would cheerfully have cast from the top of her tower. She can't look at Willow standing there, the sight of him makes her head hurt, as though sand is being scattered into the orbits of her eyes. She doesn't like

him dressed up; comfortable homespun suits him better, plain attire for a plain soul.

Every eye is on her, the air of expectation within the vaulting chamber so intense she can taste it, and the thought zips through her of an elaborately decorated main course being brought before a state dinner. Some delicacies, she knows, are best eaten alive, the expertise of the chef determined by his ability to sustain that life throughout the meal. The image makes her ill; she wonders where it comes from, why it chooses this moment to show itself. She wants to scratch herself; she itches all over, as though someone has slipped a scattering of fleas into one of her robes, her skin grown unbearably sensitive to the touch.

Her mind is no longer paying attention to the tasks at hand, but that doesn't really matter. She's been trained for this moment since she was old enough to learn; if there is no consciousness at all to direct things, she knows her body can carry on regardless. With a final thunder of drums and trumpets, she takes her appointed place.

She and Willow are the same height, but he uses the dais to give himself a head's advantage over her.

"Elora Danan," she hears him say, his voice rich with all the warmth and caring that fills her dreams and memories of him. "In the name of the Twelve Domains, I bid you welcome."

She wants to scream at him, Where have you been? Why didn't you come for me sooner? But she remains silent. Instead, she turns, as she's been trained, to follow her appointed path.

A shallow ramp leads her up and around the circumference of the great, central dais, past each of the assembled Domains in turn. It isn't that the platform itself is so high; her robes are so binding she can't raise her feet enough to span the distance. Her throne as well has been specially designed so that she won't actually be sitting on it, in any normal sense, but resting at an angle.

As she makes her clockwise circuit she casts sidelong glances across the front rank of chairs for her first look at who is present. On one level is a preening satisfaction, that so many personages of note have come to pay her homage. No matter who you are, she crows with silently malicious glee, I'm your better! At the same time, though, another part of her wonders what that means. She can't wait to embrace the rank and authority they offer—and then to settle old scores (she tries to flick a dagger glance toward Angwyn's king, but the hulking brute is too thick-headed and self-absorbed to notice)—yet at the same time she wants no part of it. Those desires feel wrong, the moment itself far worse. Every physical aspect of the ceremony strikes a discordant note, the music jangles in her ears, the visual opulence twists her eyes. She is flushed and chill all at the same time, just as though she is falling ill, and has a horrified (delightful) image of herself collapsing at Willow's feet in a dead faint.

A section of seats is virtually empty and she snaps her gaze back for a second, more focused look, as always presenting (as best she can) the show that her eyes remain properly downcast and straight ahead. Only one figure, a boy—or possibly a girl, she can't really tell—sits alone in the center of the first row, resplendent in a suit of iridescent shimmer that makes it appear as though his very skin is aflame. With such a start that she loses the beat and nearly misses a step, she realizes that her stare is being returned with an intensity that beggars hers. She purses her lips, uncaring that it spoils the purity of her face painter's conception, puzzled by a curious dichotomy of vision; the boy is but a single, relatively small figure in a single row, yet he somehow seems to her to fill the entire space, to the point where she has a sense of great wings folded over a sinuously majestic body that reaches all the way to the ceiling.

"A Shaper," she breathes with a flash of recognition, as much thought as whisper, using the common term for metamorphs, and then, in awe and wonder, "By all the Blessed, a Dragon!"

Everyone else present, she notes, is joined by delicate strands of golden glitter, which leap toward her from the seats as she passes each row in turn, only to fizzle to less than dust as they come near. Likewise the boy is also untouched. The strands wind around him as if he isn't there, with a clear separation between them, while those around the others become more tangled with every moment. And the notion comes to her of cocoons growing on some monstrous web.

A stillness settles on the hall, and the quality of light begins to change. The warm and gentle radiance of torch and candle is gradually—but ever more rapidly—eclipsed by a silver splendor from above. Elora can't see; a half-dozen stacked collars lock her head in place, allowing minimal tracking from side to side, and down, but never up. Even if she can manage a look, her view will still be blocked by the brim of her head-dress. She knows what it is regardless: the full moon, Elora's moon.

The apex of the domed roof of her hall is a skylight, composed of clear and stained crystal, displaying the seals of the Twelve Domains all binding and interweaving together to form that of the fabled, long-hoped-for Thirteenth. Hers.

She wants everyone to stop looking at her, she wants to be left alone. And she has another vision, of a life to come more awful than what had come before. Year after endless year locked in her aerie, so great an object of veneration that none stop to think she might be a living, breathing, needing person as well. The looks of joy and adoration change before her eyes; they care nothing for her, only for what she can do for them. Each has their desires, and see Elora as the means of their achievement.

She shudders and watches the room turn to silver as the skylight catches and intensifies the moonglow, pitching it straight down to the dais below, where it reflects again and again off the curved walls until the chamber is lit to a fair semblance of day. But the quality of light is different and she recognizes from the first, without knowing how or why, that the difference is significant. The sun's radiance is one color among many; the moon's, none at all. Its pale radiance bleaches the brightest hues present—those of her own costume—of their glory, denying even the absolute contrast of chiaroscuro. No black, no white, but variations on what lies between. Edges lose definition, abstract highlights cast the most familiar of objects and people in disturbing new guises, so that nothing seems anymore quite what it truly is.

She never thought much about light; in truth—and this realization brings a sudden, sour taste to her mouth, the bitterness of opportunities lost—has never thought about much of anything. When light is present, she can find her way about, see what she's doing and where she's going; when it isn't, she occasionally stumbles. This isn't like that at all. The light is tangible, it has a weight, a presence that she doesn't like. She feels as though her headdress is a skylight, same as the roof overhead, only this one gives free access to her soul. As one set of glassworks lights the room, so does this other one illuminate all the secret places within her.

It hurts. No one warned her any part of the ceremony would hurt. Of course, this ceremony has never been held before, so how was anybody to know, but she isn't much interested in that line of reasoning. A throbbing in her temples, at the base of her skull, down the column of her throat. A tingling numbness in her fingertips, an ache across the front of her chest. She keeps her eyelids mostly closed, because she fears if she tries a decent look at things, her innards will flip over and take her with them. Her stomach clenches at random intervals, and more than once she chokes back the taste of bile.

She thinks she says something, is sure she hears a voice that strangely resembles her own, but only Willow is speaking, offering a wink when he sees her peeking, winsome counter to the formality of phrase the ceremony demands. Words she's heard before, but can't properly place because everywhere she rummages in her head is suffused with this damnable light. It's as if she's going blind in the vault of her own memories.

"Agthuar duatha kedthel endrai . . ."

She smells burning, opens eyes wide—the devil with protocol and procedure—but sees nothing amiss in the room about her, save that the shapes and faces of the guests have lost all distinction, fading to a nearsighted blur that paradoxically leaves the strands that bind them sharply distinct.

She looks within her mind once more, bursting through door after door in a desperate search to find the heart of the conflagration. Discovering to her horror one that opens onto nothingness, where once she knows had been memories of her earliest days.

All is silver, she is silver, her figure stiffening within as her costume imprisons her without. In her own head at least, she's always been able to run free, the form and figure of Self far leaner and stronger than the body she despises. Only that supposed strength is no longer of any use to her as flesh grows hard to the touch and more difficult to move. Earlier in the ceremony, she thought herself a statue; now she is fast becoming one in fact, and terror washes across her like a tidal race as she thinks of how helpless she'll be when the process is complete, and how easily another might reshape her image to their own designs. All her growing life, she's had no control over the fate of her flesh; she is a child, a stranger in a strange land, bereft of all who'd been her friends and *champions, and unable to find any to take their place. Her mind, though, has always and stubbornly remained her own.*

Until now.

Is *this* the ceremony? *she cries to herself in horror.* Is this what the Prophecy is all about, that I lose everything that makes me, *me?*

The reply comes with a ferocity that shakes her to the core, because she never suspected she had such defiance in her.

"No," she says, not realizing she speaks aloud, that small, simple word casting a spear into the heart of the complex construct of power Willow is building about her.

He doesn't believe his ears, he stumbles over the next phrase, has to repeat himself, and there's nothing friendly or gentle any longer in his eyes as he wills her to be silent.

In response, she clenches fists and teeth, lips stretching wide with the effort it takes to mouth that single word again.

"No!"

He slaps her.

She stares, slack-jawed. In her whole life, no one has ever struck her; she is the Sacred Princess Elora, such things simply are not done! Tears burn her eyes. Willow ignores them, ignores her, honing the focus of his chant ever more sharply, as though it alone will cut through any further resistance. She looks around as much as she is able, her manner that of a hind run to ground by dogs, but sees not even a hope of salvation. On every face is a smile, and she feels a sick sense of abandonment. They aren't going to do a thing to help; so far as she can see, they consider this the most wonderful, transcendent of moments.

All the promises, all the affirmations of love and worship, nothing but lies.

Only the dragon's face shows anything contrary. He watches the scene play out like a judge, waiting to discover if she'll stay with the role that has been cast for her or strike out on her own.

There's disappointment in his eyes; he doesn't think she will.

Streamers of argent fire swirl about the dais, cast down from skylight to floor, ringing her like the burning bars of a cage. These, too, have been stripped of color by the moon, their presence defined more by an absence of darkness than any projection of light. They begin to spin slowly about

her, as though she's become the eye of a whirlwind, each ribbon draw-ing closer together as the whole group closes on her. By the time they reach her, they'll be a solid wall of flame.

She trembles, memory coughing up an image from her backbrain, as rich in vibrant hues and textures as the present moment is absent of it. She lies in a bowl, unable to move, swathed in linen silk, bound tight with straps of leather, the air rippling with banners of fire so intense they'll consume flesh and spirit both. Someone outside her field of vision cries Words of such Power that they present themselves with physical force, like lightning and thunder, the one transcending all properties of light as the other does of sound, so that the sensations are felt as blows rather than simply seen or heard. There is an aching need to the Words, a desperate craving that reaches out through the fiery manifestations of them, like Death Dogs straining at their leash, eager for the chance to hunt and kill and feast.

"No!" she cries, in a voice so full it cracks and to her surprise makes the fire curtain shimmer, the way its cloth counterpart would when struck by a blast of wind.

More so, and this is a greater surprise to her and Willow both, the word is accompanied by an action, a hand thrown forward, palm first, to bat away the flames.

Mistake. Being of the moon, they cast a fire that's cold but inflicts no less intense a burn. With a scream that mixes startlement and pain in equal measure, Elora snatches back her hand and cradles it against her breast. The heel of her palm is black and blistered, the hand itself gripped with a terrifying numbness that reaches well past her wrist and makes her fear that her very blood has frozen in her veins.

Elora isn't sure what happens next; it certainly comes from no con-scious decision on her part. Even as she gathers her wounded hand to herself, whimpering at the thought of worse to come when the curtain sweeps over the whole of her, her body moves of its own accord, tucking her head forward and down so that the headdress will be the first of her to meet the flames. She kicks forward like a runner from the starting post, no elegance to the motion, has an awful sense of clothes burning, hair burning, a faint lash of winter down the length of her spine . . .

. . . and then she's clear, Willow before her, a moment for her to note *the shock and disbelief on his features before she plows into him and knocks him from his perch, the pair of them tumbling full-length from the dais.*

"Selfish headstrong bloody little cow," her godfather and protector squalls, again in that voice that isn't what she remembers from him yet that sounds eerily familiar nonetheless, his own hands lashing out to take her by the front of her smoldering gown and pitch her back toward the flames. "You'll ruin everything!"

"Let me go!" she screams back at him, beyond panic. "Leave me alone!"

She's made her supreme effort; it isn't enough. He has a strength that goes far beyond his frame, backed by a purpose that transcends anything remotely human. Her clothes remain her prison, they won't allow her decent movement, and even if they did, she doesn't know how to fight.

He sets her on her feet, just as he would a fallen doll, and she knows his next move will be to thrust her back into the furnace. She will burn; he will not.

"Why?" she sobs. "Please," she begs.

"For a world that must never be" is his reply. "The sacrifice of One, for the salvation of All."

"You heard Elora Danan, Deceiver," says a new voice, seemingly from nowhere. "Leave her alone!"

In an eyeblink, the two on the dais became three. To Elora, Thorn seemed to pop up from solid stone; events moved with such speed there simply wasn't time for her to notice the black blotch that blossomed against the silver-suffused floor (and, to be fair, she had other concerns to occupy her). Thorn struck Willow behind the knee and, when the taller figure staggered, boxed both his ears to force him to release the girl. A quick grab for her, to pull her past him and out of harm's way. Then, at the last, a matter of giving the fiend a taste of his own medicine, by grabbing the scruff of his neck in one hand, his belt in the other, and heaving him forward into the flames.

He went in, he didn't come out the other side.

Thorn's eyes were bright, both from the excitement of the

moment and the effort of sliding himself through the body of the castle, and he sensed he must look more than a little mad himself as he stood before the girl.

"Elora Danan," he said.

"I *know* you," she replied, but the confusion in her voice meant she hadn't fully put together the particulars of that realization.

"I'm a friend, I'm here to help."

"Little Nelwyn fool," cried the voice of a God announcing Armageddon, "you've done more harm than you can know."

The column of fire was gone, and with it all semblance of Willow Ufgood's humanity. The face and the form hadn't changed, at least in basic shape, but flame had taken the place of flesh, and Thorn thought—to both horror and fascination—that he'd come face-to-face with yet another Demon.

"And now," the Deceiver told him, with a smile that was terrible to behold for all the torments it promised, "you'll pay the price."

CHAPTER 9

I WON'T LET YOU HARM HER," THORN SAID, PROJECTING an implacable determination he didn't truly feel. His adversary seemed to sense that lack of resolution, for the Deceiver's next words . . .

"As if your desires matter, Peck."

. . . were followed by a bolt of withering flame that corroded stone to powder where it struck and would have done the same to Thorn himself had he not dived aside, and yanked Elora with him. Thorn looked for the portal through which he'd arrived but saw it gone as well, sealed by the same attack.

The Deceiver didn't give them any respite. A sequence of bolts this time, one for Thorn, the other Elora. His, Thorn allowed to tumble him backward over Elora's prone body, in such a way as to entangle the pair of them in her massive train. Which in turn prevented him from blocking the second bolt as it sizzled the Princess from end to end until the outermost robe collapsed on emptiness, all within it utterly consumed.

The Deceiver seemed genuinely amused, a delight echoed by the watching crowd, who raised their voices in a cheer.

"Don't mind them, Peck," he said with a dismissive wave that left a trail of cast-off flicker flames behind it. "They see only what they believe is Elora Ascendant."

"You've a rare gift for lies."

"Look who's talking! I've seen the disappearing pig trick before, old friend, it's long lost its power to fool me. That blast was meant to capture, not destroy. So make it easy on yourself and show me where you've hidden her."

Thorn skibbled on fingers and toes, like a cat ready for a fight, a sideways crab scuttle that put a little more distance between him and the Deceiver and brought him farther around the circle. His thoughts were racing, gathering data the way the brownies did souvenirs, building a picture of his adversary as quickly and comprehensively as could be managed. He was at a disadvantage from the start, because the Deceiver was evidently familiar with him, enough to call him a "friend." He knew of Thorn's skill at sleight of hand, but not where the girl had gone. That meant limits. Most disturbing, though, was what he'd said just as Thorn had arrived, about sacrifice and salvation; not simply the words themselves but the tone he'd used, as though this was a positive act, a *necessary* death.

The air had grown increasingly chill, so much so that Thorn could see his breath and feel goose bumps raising from every quarter of his flesh; the more intensely burned the Deceiver's flames, the more they drew every scrap of warmth from the room. Almost as though he was re-creating this chamber in the moon's literal image, transforming it into a desolate, frigid wasteland decorated with the semblance of life, but not life itself.

"I have no time, Peck, and less patience. Return the child. Her destiny was ordained before the world itself was born; give her leave to embrace it."

"No."

"I'm her protector, Nelwyn."

"Another lie! I know the enchantments you work here, Deceiver, you want her life and soul!"

"And if I do? Are they not the smallest sacrifice for the future? There is more at stake than you could possibly comprehend; your interference is the *cause* of eternal desolation, not its end."

Thorn rounded on the guests, to face Angwyn's king and Cherlindrea.

"Majesties of Earth and Air," he cried. "It's not supposed to be this way!"

"Says who?" challenged the Deceiver. "Have you some special insight into Prophecy?"

"I know what's right," Thorn snarled, taken aback by his vehemence, "and this is *not*! You are deceived." He addressed the crowd once more, deliberately turning his back on the blazing figure on the dais. "Elora is betrayed!"

"A wasted effort, Peck. They no more hear you than the child. *I* am Salvation, not her."

Despite himself, he had to look, drawn by a force of command such as he'd never before heard, as inexorable and irresistible an attraction as those that held the world together. The voice was honey, water to a thirsty man, love to one who'd never known it. The flames were indeed all-consuming, but from their ashes would come the rebirth of something better. The old hatreds, rivalries, conflicts would be burned pure, even the most primal concepts reduced to their essence, shapeless clay awaiting a Maker's fingers to give them proper form. To eyes and ears, it made perfect sense; to heart and soul, a dream worth dying for.

He saw a dazzling smile that had nothing whatsoever to do with the face around it and couldn't help answering in kind. When he'd first entered the room, his colors were his own, a stark and earthen contrast to the argent majesty that had subsumed the rest. Now he'd grown more pale than not and found his strength of purpose fading as well. He knew that was important, but it didn't seem to matter.

Step-by-step he made his way toward the embrace of oblivion, eyes only for the glory before him, as the Deceiver had eyes only for him. As a consequence, neither was aware of any other presence until Elora blindsided Thorn like a charging ram and sent the pair of them crashing off the dais and over the lip of the first pew, to the feet of Kieron Dineer.

"There's hope for you yet," he said with a shy, slight grin that encompassed them both.

"Who?" gabbled Thorn, shaken by how easily he'd been snared, at the same time placing where he'd seen the lad's face before, in the Faery Queen's apartments. "What? Where?"

"You'd better go," was the reply. "Things here, I suspect, are about to turn very nasty. The city won't be safe."

"Who *are* you?" Elora demanded.

"One who wishes you well. You saw, and named, me truly before; it's one of your Gifts, no falsehood can for long beguile you. Now do as I say, and quickly."

He stood, catching the Deceiver's next attack full in the chest, and both Thorn and Elora quailed beneath him, instinctively trying to make themselves as small as possible, while human guise peeled way before the burning onslaught like the layers of an onion. Kieron's flesh stretched high and wide, clawed forelimbs gouging parallel scars in the pristine stone as the crest of its towering head brushed the ceiling. Sinuous neck, leading to a body of such strength that a single sweep of its wings could generate a wind capable of tearing full-grown oaks from the ground. What they'd thought was costume now stood revealed as the magnificent creature's skin, which glittered with an iridescent life of its own, a cascading riot of brilliance that left not one color true to itself but ran them all together in a never-ending exercise of pure creation. Thorn thought of a field of grass, rippling in the wind, the shape and texture of the stalks changing with the breeze; this was much the same, only instead of variations on a single color theme, this embraced them all, from those common in life to others that existed only in dreams. He'd never seen such beauty.

Beside him, sharing both thought and imagery through the link they shared, Elora smiled in wonder and delight.

That was the only moment they had to enjoy it, for with the manifestation of the dragon came the realization that it was in as desperate a fight for life as they were, with an outcome just as much in doubt.

Down every aisle came the Vizards, halberds leveled, and Thorn covered Elora's body with his own as the dragon struck out with head and tail and dashed a double score of masked figures aside, clearing a path for them to the main entrance. Thorn didn't wait for urging, he was on his feet—Elora tightly in hand—and scrambling for the exit before the last bodies fell.

Unfortunately, the Deceiver wasn't about to let them go quite that easily. Thorn heard a volley of Words flung after them, and his heart stutter-stepped as he registered the implications of the spell. Each element was potent unto itself; combined, they formed an enchantment whose power was equaled only by its unspeakable foulness. With sick desperation, because he knew he was too late, he pivoted Elora behind him, placing his body between her and the dais and summoned a shielding spell to protect them.

As much use as raising a piece of paper to stop a charging knight's lance.

Ice slapped him in the face, the flames freezing every bit of moisture in the air, and casting them about in a hurricane vortex that made them as vicious as tiny blades. This fortunately was something he could defend himself against, but their force was such that they were still able to draw blood before he could fully block them. The Deceiver extended a hand and Thorn braced himself for what was to come.

It was Elora, though, who screamed.

Her eyes blazed with the same awful fire as the figure on the dais, her arms outstretched, back arching to full extension, so much so that her body was drawn up on tiptoe. Thorn knew at once what was happening: the Deceiver had summoned the Powers with his spell, but—for no reason the Nelwyn could fathom—was channeling them through Elora. Energy so raw and primal it burned his eyes to behold it, exploded from her. Instinct made him hurl snares of his own to catch them, but they avoided his grasp with infernal ease; the couple of times he was successful, his own enchantments were shredded in a twinkling. Not so much that the power was greater than his, but the sheer knowledge, the skill, of the creature on the dais beggared his own; the Deceiver operated on a level he never imagined even existed until he met the Demon, much less one he hoped to attain.

"Forgive me for this, Peck," he heard from his foe in a voice deeply colored with sorrow and regret, and he knew in that instant he was dead. "But know at least this is for the best of causes."

Elora screamed again, and with that cry gave voice to even more bursts of energy. Thorn knew the touch of one would be the doom of him, racked his wits for some means of turning the attack away as the contrails of flame rose over him like serpents poised to strike, refusing to acknowledge even a hint of despair, much less yield to it.

But the blow never fell, at least against him. While Thorn watched, aghast, every element of the Deceiver's attack was turned from him to the dragon, who made no effort to deflect them as they ripped into him, each plunging deep as a spear and, he knew, with as deadly an effect. As fast as the Deceiver poured his infernal energies into Elora, Kieron drew them to himself.

Thorn made a desperate grab for the girl, only to reel away in flames himself, sacrificing the last of his own circle of protection to douse the fire before it could consume him.

"What have you done to her?" Thorn screamed, a shipmaster into the teeth of the gale that means to sink him. *This is no good,* he raged to himself, *she and the Deceiver, they burn with the same fire, they're each as deadly to the touch as the other, how in the blessed, bleeding hells can that be? The dragon's keeping her from being consumed—I'll owe him and his beyond death for that—but there's still more Power coursing through her than I can safely cope with.*

"Shown her, as I will you, Peck, the true path of Destiny," came the self-satisfied reply. The battle was taking more effort than the Deceiver had anticipated, but he had no doubt any longer of the eventual outcome.

The dragon's sparkle was fading, turning silver like everyone else within the hall. Yet when Kieron looked a last time at Thorn, a glance that took in Elora as well, there was a frightening smile in its eyes, a twitch of genuine humor to the back curve of its mouth. A sureness that all was far from lost, that hope still remained.

Its great head snapped forward, and honest flame leaped forth to counter the lunar cold, a gout of raw heat sufficient to put the molten heart of the world to shame, as though every scrap of what it had absorbed from Elora had been transformed within itself. Now, at long last, it was the Deceiver who was put on the defensive, as scarlet streamers danced around silver ones. He didn't seem to mind; indeed, it was as if he relished this test of his abilities, measuring his true worth by that of his foe. For the briefest of moments he was wholly enveloped, the glare of the dragon's breath tinting the skylight above so that the moon itself shone scarlet. But its effort was like a candle, shining most brightly the instant before going out, as a lance of incandescence burned the air between the Deceiver's outstretched arms and the dragon's breast. A great light burst within the huge creature, its head snapping upward as though some force had cracked its neck like a bullwhip; flame scored the ceiling, marring the designs of every seal, turning from scarlet to silver, from absolutes of heat to those of cold with such force and intensity that the core crystal of the skylight broke with a terrible *crack,* worse than the sound of any bone giving way. Then, almost all turned to silver, save for the color of its eyes, Kieron turned its gaze on the Deceiver, with a look as full of compassion as of sorrow. Not for its own passing, but for the soul of its slayer.

It fell, with a crash that shook the tower to its foundations and made those watching and waiting below wonder nervously of earthquakes. As the dragon collapsed it took with it whatever remained of the power that had manifested through Elora, so that she collapsed as well, into a boneless heap that Thorn caught before she struck the floor.

At first, the Deceiver was too flush with its own triumph to realize what had actually happened. Thorn, however, saw at once. The crest of the Kieron's head stood far higher than the Deceiver's, cutting off his view of them.

He had at best a few seconds to act.

He settled Elora in his arms as best he could and placed his right hand flat on the flagstone floor, casting forth a charge of warmth to remind the stone of what it had been, his undertaking rewarded by a change in color and aspect.

He spoke quickly, hoping the stone would understand his need for haste. The fabric of the floor changed, and he knew his gateway had opened. He didn't look back, didn't hesitate in the slightest—do so and he and Elora would both be lost—he simply dove in, as though it were a pool of water.

Nicely done.

"Where are you leading me?" he demanded of the Demon, sensing from the first this wasn't the route he'd come. They were moving far faster than before and not because the stony bulwarks of the castle were being any more accommodating.

Think you that your adversary can't spy your trail? Maybe not the way you're going, but of a certainty the way you've been.

"You're not so helpless as you let on."

Why rattle chains when all that'll do is bring on heavier ones, more tightly fastened? The less they knew, the more I could do.

"But now they'll know."

That they will.

"I can't leave," he said hurriedly, "not without my friends."

A terrible risk for so small a reward.

"I'll be the judge of that. Do you know where they are?"

This is a mistake.

"Take me to them," he snapped. And then: "Please."

We are there.

It was Elora's garden. The transition was instantaneous—first there was darkness, combined with the sensation of being covered all over with down cushions, with pressure applied to every inch of his body and resistance to every movement. Then, suddenly, freedom, the medium of stone exchanged for that of air, so stark a difference that he emerged like one shot from a catapult, almost pratfalling before regaining his balance and bringing himself to a stop.

"Franjean," he called, aloud and with his thoughts. "Rool!"

"By all the Powers," came Franjean's reply from around the corner, "what have you been playing at?"

"About given up on you, Drumheller," said Rool.

They came into view. They stopped. They stared.

"Come *on*," he whispered, without daring a backward glance toward Elora's hall, as though not looking meant nothing was happening. "There's no time, we've got to *go*!"

Franjean's face twisted ugly with hatred and when he spoke; he made his words as harsh and cutting as any weapon.

"Demon!" he cried.

"No," Thorn protested, and tried to reach them with his In-Sight.

Rool said nothing. The weapons he used were the real thing, Thorn using his Power to bat aside a thorn arrow that was aimed at his heart. He lunged forward, but Rool leaped clear, slashing at his grasping hand with one of his bone swords, the pair of them disappearing from sight into the nearest of Elora's flower beds.

"What are you doing?" he shouted. "It's me, Thorn!"

He wanted to search, but the Demon wouldn't let him by opening a portal in the ground beneath his feet and dropping him back into the embrace of the tower stones.

"They didn't know me," he stammered as he felt himself being rushed along.

Knew you only too well, meat.

"Damn you, monster, what have you done to me?"

Change in states of being, one of the things that makes existence interesting.

"That's no answer!"

Done, little mage? Nothing. You freely took what was

freely offered, both Power and price. **There is Demon in your soul, Drumheller, for now and ever . . .**

The Demon paused a moment and when it spoke next Thorn sensed the smallest smile in its voice.

. . . as there is Nelwyn in mine. Which of us got the better of the barter, do you wonder?

"There has to be a way to get them free of here!"

Their choice, their fate. Worry more about your own.

"What about yours? Will the Deceiver do you harm?"

Does it matter?

Thorn wasn't surprised to discover that he did.

So long as my child is safe, I am content.

"I wish that was a promise I could keep, but I couldn't even protect Elora Danan."

Bitterness ill becomes you, mage.

"I don't like being beaten. I don't like being forced to run."

Thought Daikinis were built to stand and fight. Nelwyns made of smarter stuff.

"This isn't a moment for epigrams, I'm sorry."

You have life and freedom and Elora. Could be worse. Build on that, try again. Fin Raziel wasn't reborn in a day, remember.

"For all the good that ultimately did. No matter how hard we strived, no matter how many victories we won, Evil abides."

Silly little mage—does not Good?

Thorn's next movement pushed him into open air, and a bracing chill painfully close to that of Elora's hall. His foot skidded on cobblestones, and breath hissed from the pain of a twisted ankle, forcing him to set Elora on her feet to keep them both from falling.

Hands caught them on either side, and for that first flash, he thought they'd been recaptured.

"Blessed Bride," said Geryn, "where'd *you* come from? Not to worry," he continued in a rush, taking most of Elora's weight, "I've got the lass."

Thorn saw frost on every exhalation; eyes followed the hand on his arm upward past a shoulder to a woman's face. Geryn had been true to his word, and found Khory a decent set of clothes: knee-high riding boots and buckskin breeches, cotton shirt, leather tunic, and a sheepskin-lined vest, all belted at the waist. There was a tattoo over her left eye, so intense and colorful he didn't understand why he'd missed it earlier, that filled in the whole of the brow ridge of her eye socket and then flared up and out along the flank of her skull until it met the hairline. To Thorn, it most closely resembled the feathering of a raptor's face, as if that eye had been transposed from some great hunting bird.

"Thank you," he told her; and gentled free of her grasp. She answered him with a quick and ready smile that was a disconcerting reminder of his own.

"Why's it so cold?" he asked as they moved along the passage to where a clutch of horses stamped their hooves nervously.

Khory tapped his arm, pointed with her chin, but in truth he'd intuited the answer the moment he'd framed the question. The direction she indicated was simply confirmation.

Elora's Aerie *burned*. As though the Deceiver had set it alight with the same witchflames that had ensheathed it. The magical blaze extended down the column for possibly a quarter of its length, but already the flames were having a perceptible effect on the surrounding city. It wouldn't stop when it reached the bottom, either, he knew. As within her hall, these eldritch flames didn't give off warmth, they absorbed it, sending the air temperature in the vicinity of the palace plunging.

"We have to go," he said.

"Suits me," replied Geryn. "But where?"

"As far and as fast as we can manage."

Admirable goal; achieving it wasn't so easy. Geryn had a quartet of Daikini warhorses standing nervously at hand, their eyes wide and ears back flat against their skulls, more than ready to run. Problem was, the Pathfinder was the only one among them who could properly ride. Thorn was most comfortable on a pony; with proper adjustments to the saddle, he could manage a full-sized horse, but these animals were so big he could walk upright beneath their bellies and still have room to spare. Khory hadn't a clue of what was required.

He gave Elora—thankfully, still unconscious—to Geryn's charge, the young man setting her before him on his saddle, looping the reins of the other horse about his pommel. Thorn had Khory set him in place and used InSight to *reach* into the animal's mind, immediately feeling a thrill from its nerves to his, as he'd feel in the midst of a lightning storm when the sky was as super-saturated with energy as rain.

Small wonder the animals are so upset, he thought, *if this is what the night feels to them.*

He cast an image back to Khory of what was required of her, and to his delight, she swung herself with lithe abandon into the saddle. She tried her best to fit feet to stirrups and use her legs to anchor her in place, but they both quickly found a limit to her expertise. Thorn held tight to the reins, Khory to both him and the pommel.

It was Geryn got them going, with a tap of the heels that sent his mount on its way as though shot from a spring cannon. Thorn's charger needed no urging to follow; indeed, he had to haul tight on the reins, adding to it a fair measure of calming thoughts, to keep the animal from running away in blind panic. The two riderless horses followed, happy to be led from this awful place.

The city was chaos. Whatever people had expected from Elora's Ascension, this wasn't it and they weren't taking it well. The main thoroughfares were blocked, and from the sights and sounds of the downtown mercantile district, more than a few were using the opportunity to enrich themselves. One of the warehouses was ablaze, but its flames were no match, in color or intensity, for the silver conflagration engulfing the tower. Geryn found them a roundabout route away from the heart of the disturbances, holding mostly to residential side streets and keeping their pace at a steady walk.

"No sense in headlong flight until we've a proper clear road ahead," he told them over his shoulder. "Don't want to push too hard, too soon; we want these horses to last. Don't want 'em panicked, neither. Nor hurt, they take a misstep on cobbles."

Thorn didn't look back, didn't want to think about what was

happening behind him, grateful that most of his focus and energies were needed simply to keep himself and his companion mounted. He heard a moan from Elora, a hurried reassurance from Geryn.

"Looks all right t'me, Thorn," the trooper said. "More she's havin' a nightmare, like."

Thorn knew the cause, felt a resonance from her as the Deceiver's flames claimed her garden. There was a pricking behind his own eyes that had nothing to do with her, as he thought of the two brownies. Good friends, boon companions, they had kept company for years when his own family had been lost from him. What a shame to lose them when he had finally regained Elora.

The whole of Castle Mount was alight, illuminating the city with such intensity that it seemed as though the moon itself had landed among them. Thorn had never seen so pure a radiance; it painted the night in absolutes, defining objects wholly by the shadows they cast. Around them, the world appeared to lose substance and become nothing but increasingly abstract silhouettes.

He thought the streets would be thick with people fleeing the fire, but while they encountered a fair number, it was nowhere near what he'd expected—no more in fact than they'd find on a normal workday—and they negotiated their passage without much trouble. Even those who ran didn't appear to have the stomach for it, and Thorn knew with heartsick certainty that none would escape. It was as if the whole city understood that it was doomed and people were merely going through the motions, a purely backbrain response, no different than the primal, mindless urge for survival felt by the riders' horses.

And every other animal in the city. Thorn saw cats and dogs, household pets and beasts of burden, vermin of every description, horses and mules, sheep and cattle. A veritable stampede from the stockyards as an entire herd burst forth from the slaughterhouse. They came through the streets like a flash flood, with as little concern for whatever lay in their path. The Evil that sapped strength from every human resident acted in their stead to galvanize their collective will. Death was preferable to those icy flames, and since they knew a head-on fight was useless, they showed resistance and defiance with the only means left them: flight.

The rats were first to reach the gates, swarming in a furry tide over the bodies of the freshly slain, ignoring what only hours before they happily would have feasted on. The gates themselves were closed tight, but that didn't even slow them down as they rushed up and over the wall. Those able to follow, did so; the rest were left to fill the plazas that backed every entry to Angwyn, milling about in ever-greater agitation, giving passionate voice to their distress.

Angwyn was built on hills, and they in turn grew from land that gradually rose from the shore toward higher ground inland. From where his horse stood, Thorn had a commanding view of the entire city; only the King's Castle Mount stood higher. He could just bear the sight for a span of heartbeats, but even that brief glance showed that the conflagration was spreading, and more rapidly with every passing moment. A fair distance still separated them, but that wouldn't last long.

"We'll have to find another way!" yelled Geryn, in a mostly vain attempt to make himself heard over the din.

"The other gates'll be no better," was Thorn's reply. "You'll find animals everywhere you turn; this is as good as it gets! And the more time we waste trying, the greater the risk of being caught by the fire."

"No offense, Peck, but tha's of damn-all use."

Thorn didn't answer. Instead, he took tighter hold of the reins and gave his horse a silent nudge. The challenge wasn't getting her going, it was keeping her from trampling anyone along the way, not to mention keeping her two riders safely in place on her back.

The mare's nostrils flared wide with every breath as she picked her way delicately through the crowd of beasts. She drew in air with such force Thorn could hear her, even over the frightful, wailing hullabaloo that filled the square. Sweat was likewise caked thick across her chest, as though she'd been running full tilt, and his arms ached well past his shoulders from the strength needed to hold her in check. He was breathing just as hard, in sync with her, and was sodden with his own sweat. In addition, he felt as though a barbed, iron spike was being driven with exquisite deliberation right between his eyes and through to the back of his skull. He was beyond nausea but, fortunately, also beyond the capacity to imagine what he'd feel like when this was done.

"Khory," he called to his companion, "are you all right?"

There was no reply.

Newborn, remember, he told himself acidly, *and Demon to boot. Why in the blessed, bloody hell should she have the slightest clue what I'm talking about? Especially when I'm not altogether sure myself!*

"Is this fear, Drumheller, what they are feeling?"

He craned about for a look at her, but she was between him and the awful majesty atop Castle Mount; it took away her every feature and turned her into a cutout silhouette, a shape without identity. If she moved aside, the glare would do the same to him, only in reverse.

"Your speech has improved."

She shrugged. "The words come naturally."

"The people are afraid," he told her. "The animals are mainly angry. They want to fight, their every instinct tells them that's the right response. But at the same time those instincts tell them just as strongly that fight is hopeless. This isn't a foe to be brought down with tooth or claw; best simply to get out of its way until the threat is past, then take up your lives again. One force of nature speaking to another."

"Drumheller?"

"Yes?"

"The warrior in the cell sought our lives. Why did you keep me from taking his instead?"

"Some say the moment and manner of a person's birth sets the tone for the rest of their life. I didn't want yours stained with blood. It's a hard thing, killing. Not a thing you should rush to learn. Or that should ever come easily. Help me down, please."

They found their first body just inside the gatehouse, nicely done to death with a slit throat. Only Sergeant Major Jalaby had managed to draw his sword, and from the state of the blades he'd given a fair account of himself before the Maizan took him down.

"Damn," Thorn muttered sadly at the sight, and repeated himself much more emphatically when he saw the locking assembly.

The Thunder Riders hadn't stopped with the massacre of the guards; they'd jammed the door mechanism as well, beyond any hope Thorn might entertain of setting things aright in the time left him.

"Damn!"

He strode back to the common room, his purposeful traverse shaken at the start by a startled squeak and a frantic set of staccato jiggle hops as he struggled to avoid stepping on any more critters underfoot. A fair struggle, considering they covered the floor like a thick-pile carpet.

He went to one knee before Jalaby and looked past his sightless eyes, wishing there was a way to wipe the shame of failure that was the last image imprinted on the old soldier's soul. He looked for the man's sword, turned his head when he heard the hiss of steel slicing air to find it in Khory's hand as though each had been made for the other. With a shallow nod, he accepted the decision and took a lesser blade from the dead man's other hand.

"With your blessing, old campaigner," he said, "I ask this boon: a chance to set things right, to throw defiance in the face of treachery and perhaps plant the smallest seeds of a victory to come."

"Do you believe that, what you say?" asked the DemonChild.

"Of course. It's hope."

He started for the door, then stopped when he heard Khory's husky, resonant voice behind him.

"I ask a boon as well, old campaigner," she said, expanding on his words but speaking them with the same intonations and accents, as though she possessed the raw knowledge but needed him as a template for how to put it all to proper use. "These weapons, and with them, a chance to set things right."

"Why did you ask," he queried with genuine curiosity when she was done. "He's dead; it doesn't matter what you do, he certainly can't stop you."

"Why did you?"

"It's not the Demon way."

"Am I a Demon?"

He opened his mouth to reply, then closed it with the *clack* of teeth brought smartly, sharply together, because he had no true answer for her.

There was an eerie stillness about the gate, and he realized it flowed outward from the guard post, as countless tens of thousands of eyes—none of them human—turned to him in mute expectation. Within the room, "hope" had simply been a word; here, it was a person.

"Neat trick, Peck," called Havilhand.

"To say the least," Thorn replied, watching the animals scuttle aside to clear a path for him. "How's the child?"

"Still asleep, bless 'er. She'll need clothes, an' we ever get clear o' this. What she's wearin', it's mostly tatters. Damnedest thing, I tell yeh, cloth looks like it got scorched an' froze, all inna same breath."

"Something like that. Be ready to ride."

"I'm a Pathfinder, little friend. We're s'posed t' be *born* that way. 'Course, it's always better, havin' somewheres t' ride *to,* an' yeh catch my meaning."

"Be patient."

"Be quick."

"Drumheller!" Khory, from atop the wall, which made him stare in dumbfounded astonishment: *How did she get herself all the way up there!*

He would have said the same aloud, but she didn't give him the chance.

"Riders, from the land, coming fast."

"How many?" demanded Geryn.

"More than we can handle or afford," Thorn replied for her, using InSight for a quick glance through her eyes, and waved her down, while he made his way to the gate.

There were no niceties to manner, word, or gesture; he was as focused as he was sure the old warrior had been. He slashed the blade across his palm, coating its edge with blood, then slapped the locking crossbar that held the great, looming double doors closed, leaving a blotch of darkness against wood that—like the people in the Elora's hall—had been bleached by the Deceiver's radiance of all color. A link established between the three key elements—himself, the blade, the target—he quickly marshaled his will, letting the grief and fury that had raged in him all evening crest unchallenged, unchecked. A tidal wave of force burst out from the heart of his being. Part of him thrust anchors deep into the good earth beneath his feet, so the power he was manifesting wouldn't destroy him when he put it to use; simultaneously, another, far vaster aspect reached out across the plaza, drawing strength from the assemblage and using it to add to the force he was bringing to bear.

To Geryn, turning his head continuously from Thorn to the no-longer-distant flames and back again, the scene appeared to be the height of silliness. A modest little manform, whose head barely reached the Pathfinder's waist, waving his arms against a pair of gates that dwarfed the average town house in width and height and were said in the bargain to be proof against any assault, whether from battering rams or the forbidden black powder explosive. He had no idea what Thorn intended with his knife, and even less hope for any success. He knew from his own experience how impervious ironwood could be, had seen crossbow shots that had punched through proper armor with ease bounce off a plank. These doors were thicker than a stout man's body. Couldn't be burned, couldn't be broken.

Force and fury came together in a rush as Thorn brought his blade up and around in a grand, sweeping gesture of uncharacteristic flamboyance, to bury it most of the way to its hilt in the center of his bloodstain. As it struck he unleashed a huge shout that to Geryn sounded like a formless bellow. Khory could tell the difference, her nostrils flared, her teeth baring ever so slightly in reflexive acknowledgment of the energies the Nelwyn was manifesting.

The sound of Thorn's voice echoed across the plaza, and the scene was suddenly gripped by a silence that was as profound and all-encompassing as it was sudden. Not just the absence of sound, but of even the *concept*. Geryn hunkered his head as low as possible between his shoulders and hunched his body in turn protectively over Elora's, against the shock blind instinct told him was to come.

It was a wonder.

The doors blew off their mountings, shattering under the impact of some monstrous and invisible wrecking ball that sent them flying outward from the plaza. This was a blast whose sound matched its fury, yet the noise was so far beyond human comprehension that Geryn had no true sense of what it was. Asked, he could never describe it. He might as well have been deaf.

Beyond, the Maizan riders were thrown and scattered by the titanic shock wave. Horses fell, others cast off their riders, while still others fled in total panic. Only Anakerie remained the mistress of her mount, but it did her no good, that skill and determination, as the animals that thronged the inner plaza took full advantage of the open way to freedom.

So, too, did Thorn and his companions. Khory needed no instruction; she scooped him into the saddle before the blast had begun to fade; he in turn urged his horse on its way the moment he was in place, with a silent command to Geryn's animal to follow.

They were seen, but the Maizan hadn't a prayer of stopping them. They simply couldn't be reached through that awesome stampede; it wasn't even worth making the attempt. The riders watched them go, and resolved to catch them later.

Anakerie, however, wasn't interested in the fugitives. She leaped from her own horse, once it recovered a semblance of composure, and forged her way along the wall to the gate, plowing across the flood of wildlife with grim, implacable determination. She might be slowed, but never stopped.

She was exhausted by the time she reached the guardhouse steps. While she caught her breath, back to the wall, hands at her sides, gulping air through a mouth as gaping as a fish's, she surveyed the torrent before her. She didn't believe her eyes; there seemed to be no end to it. More animals than she could count, of every shape and description, anything of any size that could walk or crawl or fly, but not a person among them. Beyond raged the fire that drove them, ranging beyond her frame of vision in every direction, from side to side and up into the sky.

She stumbled through the door, as much to put a solid wall between her and that awful sight, casting off the fatigue that turned her limbs to lead and restoring their suppleness by sheer force of will. In its own way, inside was no better. She took in the entire setting with a glance, but truly had eyes only for Jalaby. His mail shirt was gone, his leather tunic as well, and all his weapons. He looked strangely small to her, crumpled against the wall with hands and feet splayed, and sadly old. That was the aspect she found most upsetting; she thought it obscene. He'd taught her everything, was more a father to her than the King, and she expected him to remain as eternal and unchanging as the walls themselves. Now he looked like any other man, done suddenly and violently to death.

Training made her sheathe her knife, grief pushed her forward, body sinking toward the floor, so that she reached him on her knees. She meant to gather him into her arms, as though her tears would wash away his wounds. But gloved hands closed on her shoulders and pulled her to her feet.

She knew Mohdri's touch and tried to shake him free, determined to finish what she'd started. He had other ideas.

"Damn it, Keri," he cried, presenting a passion that matched her own, "there's nothing you can do here!"

"Leave me be!"

"There's no time, woman. The flames are in the plaza, we have to *go!*"

She wasn't in the mood to argue, so she hit him, a blow that would have dropped most men. He hit her harder, a pair of punches that took her wind away and left her hanging on to consciousness by her fingernails. He pitched her over his shoulder, none too gently, and took hold tight enough to leave a bruise. He cleared the doorway at a run.

Anakerie had fought her share of winter campaigns, and roamed the highlands of World's End for as late into the season as she could make a trail, but nothing in her memory prepared her for such a cold as this. She felt the mucus freeze in her nostrils and fumbled a scarf across her face to keep from burning her lungs. The skin of her face stiffened almost immediately and she knew only a few minutes' exposure would guarantee her frostbite and probable disfigurement. She buried her face into Mohdri's cloak and prayed he didn't miss a step, for at the speed the flames were coming, a fall would finish them both. Yet somehow even then the unbearable light flooded her perceptions, as though the whole of her skull had been transformed to clearest glass, affording her not the slightest protection.

She heard the sound of horses, close and coming fast, and marveled at Maizan discipline—for warriors *and* their mounts—that allowed them to race to the maw of hell to save their Castellan. Mohdri flipped her onto one's back, Anakerie scrambling with clumsy desperation to right herself, wondering sickly as she did what was the point. How could they possibly outrun so fearsome and impossible a fire?

"By the Abyss," she heard in hushed wonderment, and tried to collect herself as the troop reined in their headlong flight almost before they'd properly begun.

"Mohdri?"

She didn't want to look back; bad enough the landscape before her was lit bright as day yet transformed beyond recognition by the *quality* of that light.

"It stopped," he said in a ghost voice, a man beholding a miracle.

"What?"

"See for yourself, Highness. The flames reached the city walls and stopped. They've gone no further."

She didn't try to turn her mount, but held its reins pulled tight to keep the animal from bolting as she lifted herself on her stirrups and pivoted at the waist.

There were no more flames, save for stray, residual flickers here and there, yet everything before her *glowed*, like a campfire that had burned down to coals. She thought of ice and diamonds, of every image that came to mind associated with winter and desolation, and found them all wanting.

"You should have left the Peck to me," Mohdri said.

She had a host of replies, but didn't trust herself to give voice to a single one of them. Instead, she sat silent and still, staring. The radiance was easier to take, provided she closed her eyes to slits, as she would under the full desert sun or on a snowfield, but the cold was borderline unendurable. She could see pools of ice forming in the ruts and hollows; it wouldn't be long before the ground itself turned hard as stone.

"We'll need patrols, at the other gates, to see if anyone got out," she said in a tone as unreal in its way as the night's events.

"If you hadn't joined me for an inspection of my encampment beyond the walls . . ."

At his words, Anakerie seemed to shrink in a little on herself, as though this was the moment of realization that if her worst fears came to pass and the other gates were closed, she was all alone. No family, no people, no home.

"Do you think this was Elora's Ascension, then?"

She responded with a humorless chuckle. "Whether it is or no, Mohdri, there'll be hell to pay. The Domains were at each other's throats before; this won't make things better. Like Tir Asleen, save that only one King and Court was consumed there; tonight claimed them all. The whole world's just been turned upside down."

"Forgive my presumption, Highness," Mohdri told her gently, out of respect for her loss, "but I would remind you that you earned your place among the Maizan long ago. As you have in my own heart." She swung a heavy head to face him. "Command us as you would your own, it is our pleasure to obey."

"Let's away from here first, my lord," she replied formally, keeping as firm a grip on her emotions as on her reins. For all his seeming generosity, she had lost everything and both knew it. "We'll wait for the sun; perhaps then we'll be able to see what's been done to my city."

"And those others we saw, Keri?"

"Three horses," she recalled aloud, "four riders: two men, two women. One man in Royal Angwyn colors. One Nelwyn."

"Keen eyes."

"I don't know the man, I don't know the woman—but before her on her saddle rode the one who called himself Drumheller. She carried Jalaby's sword. The girl was Elora Danan."

"Abducted, do you think?"

"Or a party to this holocaust. I want them, Mohdri."

"I thought you might."

"Alive." It was a pointed command, not what was expected from someone whose city had just been consumed by magical flames. Some of the Maizan appeared visibly offended and even their Castellan stiffened under the lash of her tongue.

"As my lady commands," he acknowledged in a neutral tone.

"Find a printer. There should be one in Bocamel, the village near where you're bivouacked. I want flyers at every crossroads, posted at every inn and way station, heralds as well the length of the peninsula, with a shipment to go out to all the East Bay cities."

"Reward?"

"One hundred thousand crowns." That got everyone's attention; it was literally a King's ransom. "But only if they're alive and substantially unharmed. They're of no use dead."

"You've seen what that damned sorcerer can do, Anakerie!"

"And I pray to see him *un*do it, Mohdri. They may not be slain within the walls, my father, the other Royals, the people; until I know better, I choose to hold to that hope. I need a place to work and one of your household sorcerers; I'll also be sending word to the Realms Beyond. Whoever he is, that cunning little man, whatever he's about, by morning I want him to find every hand turned against him. Wherever he runs or tries to hide, every door and pathway will be closed. Whatever the cost, Lord Castellan, I want Thorn Drumheller found."

CHAPTER 10

"NOBODY FOLLOWIN'!" GERYN CALLED AS HIS WEARY horse labored the last stretch to the crest of the ridgeline.

"You don't sound happy," Thorn told him, from where he was hunkered down by Elora. She was still dead to the world and that was starting to worry him. It wasn't a coma, nor injury of any kind that InSight could tell, but nothing like a normal sleep either. The best image he could find to describe her condition was a state of nonbeing that was too uncomfortably reminiscent of how he'd found Khory. The DemonChild was tending to the other horses, and that, too, was something of a surprise to him. By rights, the animals should have been in a sweat, responding to those elements of Self that made her native kind anathema to more stable physical forms. Yet they accepted her as they would any ordinary person.

He fished another carrot stick from his pouch and crunched absently.

"Plenty reasons for't, I s'pose," the Pathfinder grumped, taking a towel from under his saddlebags and using it to wipe the sweat from his horse's neck and breast. "Prob'ly in a mess o' their own, 'cause a' what hap'n'd."

"It's all right, I don't believe that either." Thorn rose and stretched, his sore thigh muscles and backside provoking an exaggerated wince and reminding him why he preferred to walk. "If they're not coming after us, it's because they believe they don't have to."

"Can yeh not magic us on our way, then? We've pushed these poor bits hard as we dare for t'night. Fear ate 'em up as much as true runnin'."

"Not that simple, my friend, I'm afraid. For one thing, we need to have a place to go."

"Far from Angwyn, I'll settle for that."

They both turned heads to the north, and a glow that drowned the starshine overhead. It was a crisp, clear, lovely night, without a hint of haze or fog, and stars should have filled the sky, constellations readily marked and the majestic sweep of the nebular cloud spectacularly visible. But only the brightest now could be seen, even toward the far horizon.

"Never seen any forest fire cast up such a shine," Geryn said, ending with a deep and breathy sigh. "Don't seem so bright as it was, though. Maybe it's run its course, d'yeh think?"

"Anything's possible."

"S'pose I don't believe it either. Damnation, Peck, what the hell *happened?*"

"I don't know."

"Are they all dead in Angwyn, d'yeh think?"

"I don't know."

"Don't know much, do yeh?" Geryn didn't wait for any answer. "I seen the pennants, weren't only monarchs in attendance, but pretty much all the nobility as well. Not simply of Angwyn alone, neither, but the Realms Beyond. Heard talk in the bar-racks"—he sounded like he didn't want to believe what he'd heard, the enormity was too great to comprehend, like trying to envision the world—"that the population of the city had doubled an' more this Festival Week. Blessed Bride, both head and heart have been cut from the Kingdom."

"Anakerie's free," Thorn noted in passing, rolling her hair clip between his fingers before putting it once more to use. He'd de-liberately muted any awareness of her; the bond between them was mutual, and even if she wasn't sensitive enough to follow it to him by herself, any wizard could do it for her.

Geryn nodded. "Aye. Saw her standard among tha' troop o' Maizan when we rode out from the city. D'yeh think she was party t' what they did?"

"No."

"Yet she rides with 'em."

"You don't need chains to be a prisoner. Circumstance can im-prison you as easily. As cruelly."

"Who are you?" challenged a girl's voice, and the two men turned their eyes to the bedroll where Elora Danan lay. "This isn't my tower, what have you done?" She wasn't at all fright-ened, the dominant tone to her voice was outrage.

"You're safe with us, Elora—" Thorn began, but she didn't let him get any farther.

"I *know* you!"

He smiled, thinking of the way she burbled happily as a baby when he held her.

"You're the Peck who bloodied my nose! Guard! *Vizards!*" Her cry was shrill and demanding, cutting the night and their hearing like a knife, so keen the sheer noise of it was a right royal pain.

"There's none about but us, girl," said Geryn, who hadn't yet twigged to her true identity.

"I am no girl, wretch." She sneered with a haughtiness honed by a lifetime's practice. "I am the Sacred Princess Elora Danan, and the proper way to address me is on your knees."

"Bless my soul," Geryn muttered in pure and absolute wonderment, something in the way she spoke making him take her words at face value, without the slightest question or doubt. He was on his knees before he finished speaking, dropping as though the locking pins had been summarily yanked from his joints, folding more neatly than an articulated puppet.

"The proper form," she continued, "is 'Your Most Serene Highness.' And I'll bless your soul when you've earned it. As for *you*"—and with that, she confronted Thorn, who didn't appear anywhere near so impressed—"not a chance, not ever. Find me a gateway to hell, I'll gladly push you in."

Actually, Thorn was asking himself if he wasn't already there.

"Don't you remember?" he demanded of her.

"Yeh never told me, Peck," from Geryn, with a sullen and resentful undertone.

"The Rite of Ascension? The Deceiver's spells?"

"The only 'Deceiver' I know is the one I see before me."

"Stealing the Sacred Princess, are yeh mad?"

"Your precious aerie's gone, Elora," Thorn said with flat brutality. "And the King's city with it. *And* the Rulers of the Twelve Domains."

"Blessed Bride, they'll be hunting us t' the ends o' the earth an' time t'gether."

He rounded on Geryn. "Will you please *be silent*!"

"Only speakin' my piece, is all."

"Well, save it till later! And in the meanwhile, Geryn, consider, if you will, Elora's fate if we *hadn't* taken her!"

"Liar!" she cried, and caught Thorn across the face with her fist to send him sprawling. She was already in motion to leap atop him when the point of Khory's sword persuaded her otherwise. The DemonChild straddled Thorn, features mostly shrouded in darkness, the blade held so steady she might have been cast from steel herself.

"Stop it," Thorn cried, appalled as he heard the beginnings of a stammer he thought he'd lost years ago. "The *both* of you, I *mean* it, right this instant!"

He glared at Khory until she backed away, which she did with a sniff that told him he deserved whatever was coming. Thorn then climbed to his feet and right into Elora's face, she surprising him by standing her ground.

"You don't know me?" he challenged.

"From the tower," she replied, with a slight stammer of her own, shaken by the intensity of his focus but starting to feel the cold as well. "You and those two awful little"—her mouth twisted in disgust, which didn't do wonders for her appearance—"*bug* men."

She wasn't concentrating, and even if she was, her defenses were no match for him as he used InSight to peer within her memory.

"Bastard," he said with a feral snarl that would have done justice to the most fearsome predator. It made Elora jump with self-conscious fright, as though she was expecting to be struck, which only made him all the more angry. He turned to the north and the horizon's distant glow, to cry again, much more loudly, *"Bastard!"*

Her memory was a mess. Like a chalk pattern on a blackboard that some prankster had attacked with capricious abandon, erasing random swathes, so that while the structure as a whole remained substantially intact, there were arbitrary gaps among the connecting elements. Even if an image existed, the context was lost, as well as any means to properly access it. She might know his face of old, but have no idea where it came from. Remember an incident, but not who was involved.

"The Spell of Assumption," he said, more calmly in voice if not in feeling.

"What?" from Elora, dismissively.

"Do you remember the flames?"

A breeze skirled across the ridge, with a bite all out of proportion to the season and its velocity, and Elora reflexively clutched her arms, finding bare skin where she expected layers of ornate cloth. She looked down at herself, and the ruin of her gown, and her face twisted into something ugly.

"You are in such trouble," she announced, a judge passing final sentence.

"What I bin sayin' all along, Most Serene Highness," offered Geryn.

"Look at your hand," Thorn said.

He'd bandaged the wound, the first time they rested their horses, pulling some medicinal herbs and powder from his pouch along with the pristine dressing.

"You did this!" Accusation, not question, and he knew she meant caused the wound in the first place.

"The Deceiver—" he began.

"What 'Deceiver,' Peck?"

"The creature who pretended to be Willow—"

"You lie and you lie and you lie and I won't hear *any* of it! Willow Ufgood is my protector! My godfather! My *friend*!"

"The Spell of Assumption," he told her harshly, "guts a person's soul as a fisherman would his catch. It *burns* from you all that you were—every memory, every aspect of Self—leaving you a hollow and wholly empty vessel." Of their own accord, his eyes sought Khory's, to find her sitting apart from the others on an outcropping of rock, running a whetstone the length of her blade with a practiced hand.

"I don't believe you. I don't remember anything like that." She spoke bravely, but her lower undertones broadcast the dissonances of a growing apprehension as she encountered more of the gaps in memory Thorn had spoken of.

"The Deceiver's doing." His tone moderated, he was thinking aloud. "He needs a host to anchor him to this world. Which means he isn't at all what he appears; he was casting a glamour from the start. No grand revelation there, that was obvious the moment I saw him. But to ensnare everyone there . . . that doesn't just betoken power, but skill. And knowledge, intimate knowledge, of how to beguile each in turn."

"I've had enough of this," Elora announced.

He faced her without really seeing, still enwrapped in his musings. "That has to be why he kept out of sight until the very end, when he was ready to strike. He had to know of your ability to see through falsehoods. But the same supposedly holds for spells. How could he know so much yet make such an obvious mistake?"

"You're taking me back."

The force of her demand broke his train of thought, which made his response more than a bit curt. "There's nothing to go back to."

"So *you* say. And I'm supposed to take your word for it?"

"Doesn't really matter, one way or the other, truth is truth."

She stuck out her tongue and turned to Geryn.

"You," she announced. He straightened to attention. "I want to go home. You take me."

The Pathfinder took on the air of someone offered a choice between impalement and being drawn and quartered.

" 'S awful late, Highness."

"Most Serene Highness!"

"Pardon, beg pardon, Most Serene Highness. But I gotta tell yeh, the horses can't handle that ride, 'specially this late a' night. There's no track t' speak of, they need their rest same as us an' we need daylight."

"I heard you ride, that's what woke me."

"I was born to it," he told her with a shy, proud smile. "Were you?" He gathered strength from deep inside, and stood plain fact against her desire. "Yeh've not sat a saddle a day in your life, before t'night. Yeh haven't the stamina yourself for a long ride, nor the muscles to stay mounted, much less properly control your animal. You're sure to do yourself an injury before we go a league, or worse do one t' your horse. Forgive me, Most Serene Highness, tomorrow may prove different, but yeh'll go nowhere in the dark. It's not safe."

It was the longest speech Thorn had ever heard the young man make, possibly the longest ever attempted in Geryn's life, the words planted like bricks on a foundation, one after the other to form a neat, solid, unassailable wall.

"B'sides," he finished, "the Peck's right. Angwyn's cursed."

"You hateful creature," she snarled, as if her words had the power to strike him down. "I hate you both!" Then, in an upspiraling shriek, *"I hate you!"* And she collapsed to her bedroll in tears.

"Good thing we weren't followed," Geryn noted as he shifted himself closer to Thorn, as uncomfortable in speech as posture by what was happening. "Way sound carries in the night, they'd be finding us for sure."

"What have you done to me?"

Thorn barely registered the shriek of almost incoherent rage before the child was on him, flailing away with every limb and voice besides, smashing smashing smashing without the slightest sense of purpose other than to do him harm. He tried to defend himself, but that proved next to useless without the wits necessary to tell his body how to act. His mind was vaguely aware of what was happening, but all the wake-up connections hadn't been made; the horses were hitched to the wagon, but he lacked the reins to direct them. Elora's emotions didn't make the task any easier. They pummeled him like mallets against a kettledrum, beating a fast-paced tattoo, adding bruises galore to the aches and pains left over from last night's flight.

He knew what to do on a horse; he simply didn't have the body for it. Sitting astride made him feel like a wishbone at the Solstice Feast, bowed near to breaking, and he was never sure which part of him would crack first, tailbone or hips. He couldn't reach the stirrups, which meant he couldn't adapt himself to the movement of the beast, which meant a merciless pounding. Normally, a healing cast would have taken good care of it, and left him reasonably recovered when he woke. But Power exacted a physical toll, same as any other kind of exertion; he'd done too much, he didn't have the energy to spare at the last for his own needs. The thought had occurred to him, accompanied by a wisp of desire, but only in the final, fleeting moment before sleep claimed him.

He pushed Elora away, hard as he could; she bounced back before he could recover. This time, though, he was a little more ready, and when she crashed against him, he took hold of the front of her gown and pulled as hard as he was able, rolling his own body at the same time in hopes of ending up on top.

He felt a smear of icy wetness across his face and, while he planted his knees on her shoulders to pin Elora in place, took a look around to see what had changed.

The escarpment was dusted with a mix of soggy snow that was melting as it touched down—hence, the sodden nature of the ground—but was falling steadily. Clouds had crept in while they slept; the sky was a mantle of sullen gray from end to end, as though some giant had spread his dirty eiderdown across the world. The air was chill, borderline freezing, but Thorn knew at that glance it would get no warmer during the day, and tomorrow would be worse.

When he looked down at the still-struggling firebrand beneath him, he thought at first she'd managed to knock his sight silly. Or that the Deceiver had reached out to bleach the day of color as he had the night.

"Stop," he told her, and she spat up at his face, shrieking incoherently at him as she had her servants. He'd never seen a baby so out of control, couldn't imagine it in a Royal Princess—or any decently raised child—much less Elora, who'd been the soul of joy, even when circumstances were most dire.

"*Stop,*" he repeated, using nothing of his Power as a sorcerer but drawing instead on the skills of a father.

She gulped, then hiccuped, the chain of her frenzy abruptly broken. The quality of her tears changed as markedly, as quickly, pouring now from her eyes in a desolate stream, while she gulped bellows' breaths whose trembles had nothing to do with the unseasonable onset of winter.

"What have you done to me?" she demanded again, in a voice from her belly, eloquent testimony to the depth of her heartbreak.

He reached down, and felt a twinge in his own heart to see her flinch at his approach, as though his fingertips held knives to cut her to the bone. Gently, he brushed aside a scattering of snowflakes from her silver skin.

She was warm to the touch, and her flesh felt as it should. Only its color had altered. He levered himself clear of her, casting a glance across the whole of her body that could be seen through her gown to confirm what he already suspected, that the transformation was all-encompassing.

She gleamed, like she'd just come from the jewelsmith, more pure than the metal itself had any right to be. All the gold was gone from her hair as well; if anything, it had turned more pale than her skin, shot through with blue highlights, like the after-image flashes reflected off an ice field. Only her eyes retained their color, a blue grown so intense it was mostly black. They were the wrong eyes for her face, no longer any good for hiding the pain that racked her soul.

The Deceiver's doing, but there was no way she'd believe that. A side effect, he assumed, of the Spell of Assumption. Or possibly some interaction of Elora's own Powers with the energies the Deceiver routed through her when he attacked the dragon.

But that shouldn't be, he thought. *How could he have gained such complete access, such complete control? And if he held such sway, how then was Elora able to cast him off? The false face spoke of knowing me, as though we were friends. Except I have no sorcerous friends, who also know Elora. Certainly none of such Power and malevolence. The Deceiver's talisman seems to be the moon; both the light and the fire he casts are cold. Perhaps, since his intent was to displace Elora's soul with his own, this was his way of remaking her psychically in his own image.*

He shook his head in dismay, because he could see where his logic loop was leading. *Except,* he finished in frustration, *spells aren't supposed to work on her, not to any lasting, permanent effect; I thought Fin Raziel and I made sure of that.*

She was awkward getting up, too much belly, no reserves of strength, and Thorn thought of how right Geryn had been last night. She was less able to sit a horse than he.

"You'll pay for this," she told him raggedly. "For what you've done to me."

He had no answer for her, certainly not one she'd accept, and avoided the moment by casting a look about for Geryn Havilhand. No sign of the Pathfinder; only Khory, huddled snug under the lee of the ridgeline, where an umbrella of rock provided a sort of refuge against the snow.

"Khory," he called, annoyed that the DemonChild had left him to struggle alone. She'd been ferociously quick to protect him the night before; now it appeared she couldn't care less. His next thought, which turned him quickstep all the way toward her, was that something had gone wrong. Body and soul had proved incompatible, his spell hadn't forged a permanent bond.

He managed a half-dozen steps before the thump of hooves, the jingle of a bridle, announced the Pathfinder's return.

Turned out that was true, only not quite the way Thorn assumed—as the young man's bound and battered body was pitched over the crest, to skid downslope to Thorn's feet.

A stranger rode his horse, but he hadn't come alone. A half-score bravos lined the ridge, hefting whatever weapons had come most immediately to hand. Salty lot, a veritable hodge-podge of men and gear, which Thorn recognized as whoever must have happened to be in the tavern when Geryn rode in.

"Fortunes made, boys," the rider announced, to the rumbled approval of his fellows. "We're all rich men, sure!"

The air inside the roadside ale house was so thick with smoke and the stench of unwashed bodies that breathing was sheer torture, but Thorn had learned the hard way the price of complaining. He was struck more in reflex than by intent; these were men to whom violence came as naturally as a heartbeat, the kind ever eager to demonstrate their courage and prowess against those weaker than themselves. The only reason they'd made a move against Geryn, it turned out, was that the Pathfinder was too weary from his own travails to realize his danger until the bung starter clapped him upside his head.

Geryn was the one most physically like themselves, which in their eyes made him the only credible threat. Thorn was too small of stature, useful mainly as the butt of increasingly crude gibes, and Khory, a woman. She hadn't said a word since well before their capture; her basic expression hadn't altered a whit. If prodded, she'd move and keep going until stopped, or she ran into an obstacle; that provoked a round of cruel merriment as she was pointed toward a wall and sent on her way. She'd walk forward, an idiot's expression on her face, eyes wide and unfocused, seeing without comprehension, right into the wall, and then she'd stand there, face and body pressed against the rough-hewn timbers, without the slightest notion of what to do next.

That fun quickly paled and one of the bravos shoved her into a corner, where she sank to a loose-limbed seat on the floor. Thorn yearned to reach her with InSight, but he didn't want to risk giving her away if she was shamming and wasn't prepared to deal with the pain of discovering that she wasn't.

Elora they gave a wide berth to. None present would touch her; most weren't willing to even approach. They took her from the escarpment in a pole harness—essentially a lariat loop at the end of a ten-foot quarterstaff, intended to both secure and restrain an animal.

She, of course, was outraged and told the men so in no uncertain terms. They turned out to be less patient than Thorn. Before the child knew what was about, their captors had slapped in place a leather mask that covered the whole of her head, leaving Elora able to breathe but not to speak or see. A broad belt went around her waist, with buckles to secure her wrists behind her back, and once they'd reached the tavern, she was shackled to a ringbolt on the wall, with a set of hobbles at the ankles as insurance. Geryn they hog-tied with two stout lads poised to kick him back to unconsciousness whenever he so much as stirred. As for Thorn himself, a neck collar was fastened to yet another ringbolt, and his hands tied behind his back by leather cords.

Much was made on their arrival of a flyer that a post rider had brought during the night, so fresh from the printer that the ink had partially smudged in transit but amazingly comprehensive in its descriptions of the fugitives: a girl, a Nelwyn, a renegade Pathfinder, and an unknown woman. The reward was very impressive; more money, Thorn knew, than this entire village would see in a score of lifetimes. That was why the prisoners had been humiliated but not substantially harmed, save perhaps for Geryn; none present wanted to jeopardize their windfall.

Still, when one of the men wanted to take Geryn's horse, to take word of their capture to the Princess Royal, the leader sent him off on shank's mare, as a runner. Even with a fortune in the balance, he wasn't prepared to give up the horse.

"Mebbe she's a Magick," posed one of the men, tossing a thumb to where Elora sat in an awkward huddle, legs together, knees bent to the side. "Not just silver t' look at, I'm sayin', but the real thing through an' through."

"So what if she is?" asked another, burping the foam off his rotgut beer.

"Worth a lot more then, I'm thinkin', than what's been offered."

"Yer a daft bugger, Mallow," said the leader, with a cautionary shading to his laugh.

Mallow got the message. "Jus' thinkin' aloud, is all, Simya, meant no harm."

"I'm as greedyguts as the next, Mallow, but I also wanner be around t' spend the coin, once it's mine. Y'heard the herald, di'ntcha? Warrant bears the seal of Royal Angwyn, an' the Princess wants 'em *all* breathin'." He sucked thick foam from his upper lip and made a great show of waggling Khory's sword, making clear by the demonstration that he had no training and less innate ability. "B'sides, where'dja go t' get tha' kind of price for her? You think the corsairs carry that much cash in their strongbox? An' what's to stop *them* takin' her from us? Law wants her, law's willin' t' pay, let the law have her. It's our civic duty, am I right?"

Gruff round of agreement from the others, thick with amusement at finding themselves on the proverbial side of the angels. Mallow hunched farther over his own stein, projecting a disposition as sour as its taste, while Thorn busied himself persuading his bonds they'd be much more fulfilled undone. That was the advantage of working with materials that had once been alive, rope as opposed to iron, for example; they had an inherent memory of animation, which made them that much more open to the right suggestion. Steel had to be reshaped, same as it would in a forge, using the power of will rather than strength of arm; leather moved of its own accord.

Unfortunately, personal freedom meant nothing unless he

could come up with a means to help the others. He was still tired; that was the main reason he'd been taken unawares; not only were his senses dulled, he hadn't the discernment to pay them proper heed. Moreover, power used here might not be available later on, when truly needed.

He felt a pang like a knife slash as he thought of the brownies. This was the kind of situation they excelled in; turn them loose, they'd have this place in such an uproar, he and the others could *walk* out unnoticed.

Mallow was sidling glances toward Khory and not bothering to mask at all the thoughts behind them.

"If'n I don't harm the bitch, Simya," he announced, swiveling on his stool to put his back to the bar, resting insolently on his elbows, "who's to object t' my havin' a bitta fun with her, eh?"

Simya didn't think the question worth open comment; he simply waved a hand in acquiescence. Thorn said nothing; there was no purpose to it since none would listen, and he couldn't afford another thump to the head or worse.

Mallow had other ideas, reaching down to scoop him up by a handful of tunic till they were face-to-face. The movement yanked Thorn to the limit of his throat chain, which in turn left him strangling.

"Got no objections, do ya, Peck?" The man's teeth were rotten, his breath enough to kill. Thorn put every aspect of defiance and fury under lock and key, presenting as innocuous a front as possible, letting the men continue to believe he was a lamb among lions.

"Please, sir, we mean none harm. You don't want to mess with the lass, her wits are gone, she won't know what's happening, you'll get no pleasure from the act." He was gabbling, running one word over the next, like clerks in such a scurrying rush they clipped each other's heels.

Mallow's smile was a view that put some sties to shame, the man as filthy within as without.

"Wrong there, Peck. I'll be havin' myself a *fine* old time."

He let Thorn fall, to a landing that sent a flash of pain across an ankle and brought forth a snarl he had to duck his head to hide. The Daikini hitched up his pants and swaggered the length of the bar to the cheers and applause of his fellows, even Simya joining in by hauling Khory to her feet. Mallow raised his hands in a triumphal gesture and spun all the way around, before he put a hand under her shirt, the other under her trousers, and his lips on hers.

It was a long kiss, and when he was done, she looked the worse for it. Through it all, Khory reacted not a bit. Her eyes didn't blink, nor did her expression change; if he gave her pleasure, or as was far more likely, pain, she didn't appear to notice.

There was more laughter, but the humor was directed at Mallow rather than the circumstance. The Daikini himself looked a bit confused and almost embarrassed. He was almost ready to step away when Geryn's hoarse voice broke through the din.

"Leave her be, damn yeh!"

One eye was swollen completely shut, the other marginally better, with bloody bubbles on every breath from a rib too badly broken. His minder didn't kick him silent; why bother when a solid nudge would do as well? He poked Geryn's side and the Pathfinder twisted in agony, locking his cry away behind teeth clenched so tight that by rights they should have shattered.

His charge was all the motivation Mallow needed. He gave the trooper a leer in return, yanking Khory's shirt open to bare a breast as he hustled her past the bar to the cubicles beyond.

Simya dropped down on his heels before Geryn and pulled the young man's head up by the hair, waggling a finger before him and making clicking noises.

"Shoulda kept'cher mouth shut, laddie," he said chidingly. "Mallow woulda been content with what he had; prob'ly have more fun playin' with hisself than the likes of her, daft little bint. But you had to go an' call him on it. Comes a point a' pride then, y'see. He backs down, it's 'cuzza you; he won't stand for that. Hadda spit in your eye. Too bad for her."

"And suppose"—Geryn coughed, spat froth and blood to the floor; his broken rib made it hard to draw a decent breath, and the way his head was held made it worse—"suppose . . . the Princess wants her . . . untouched."

Simya hadn't thought of that and clearly didn't like the implication.

He dropped Geryn like a stone—Thorn had to wince at the clunk the Pathfinder's head made when it hit the floor—and bulled his way to the back of the tavern, bellowing Mallow's name as he went, together with the injunction that he stop what he was doing, right straightaway, or suffer the consequences.

He managed a step around the corner to the cubicles before Khory's booted foot took him in a splendid high kick right across the bridge of the nose. He stumble-staggered backward as if he'd been poleaxed by a battering ram, features splashed with blood, face broken beyond easy repair. Khory herself stepped immediately into view, a wriggling, terrified Mallow in her grasp for the few moments it took to pitch him into the crowd closest to her. As they collapsed in a jumbled mess she hopped with feline grace over the bar and grabbed up the bung starter, essentially a broad-headed mallet on a double-handed haft, used to hammer spigots into beer barrels. The first man to follow caught a short jab to the head, the next a full-fledged swing that doubled him all the way over and was sure to leave him with a wicked ache in the belly for a fair while to come.

Thorn yanked his hands free the moment Khory made her move, tearing open the buckle of his collar and dropping flat to the floor as the nearest thug made a lunge for him. For the instant the man was off balance, Thorn shifted into a sideways roll that tripped him up quite nicely. As he landed Thorn scrambled onto his back and clamped the collar around the Daikini's neck. One down, but so many more to go.

He scooped some powder from his other pouch—where he kept his working tools and materials, as opposed to the necessities of life—and puffed it toward the men watching Geryn. Each tiny dust mote was instantly imbued with a manic life of its own and the combined properties of a burr and a very hot coal. Compared with these, hornets were a blessing; by the time Thorn reached Geryn, the Daikini were yelping and hopping like madmen, slapping at itching little horrors they could barely see, but who gleefully inflicted torments far out of proportion to their size. Thorn saw one man clutch his groin, heard another utter a *rowlowlowl* ululation as a swarm attacked his backside.

"I can't lift you, Pathfinder," he told Geryn. "I sure can't carry you. I'm sorry, but you'll have to get out of here on your own."

"Not without my weapons," hissed the young man.

"The hell with them, it's Elora Danan who's important!"

Khory was a marvel. She'd watched the men roughhouse all through the night while they manhandled her, and somehow managed to gather their rude skill unto herself. More importantly, Thorn could see her improving with every exchange of blows. She was learning as she went, drawing raw knowledge from the world around her as a sponge would water.

Good as she was, though, better as she got, she was still alone. When she aimed a swing at one man, Simya stepped in with surprising speed for so bulky a form, especially considering the blow he'd already taken, and put a ham-sized fist into her side beneath her ribs. The force of the blow would have killed any ordinary person, turned kidneys to pulp; it doubled Khory over, mouth forming an "O" of shock as she struggled for a next breath that refused to come. Thorn was out of time and out of alternatives. He pulled an acorn from his pouch, that would turn the floor and every unprotected thing on it to eternal stone, and made ready to throw it.

Then, the ceiling fell in and Ryn Taksemanyin crashed among them, in a hail of broken wood and thatch. The Wyr landed beside Simya in a crouch and, before the big man could react, scooped his legs out from under him and dropped him with force enough to shake the floor. Ryn had claws, but he preferred knives, three in each hand, held between clenched and folded fingers, and used them with wild, madcap abandon. Never to draw blood, Thorn saw that from the start; most of the wounds that followed came from one thug striking another by mistake. Their rescuer never stayed in any one place long enough to be seen, much less struck. By the time his foes reacted, the damage was done, their laces slashed, pants about their ankles, cloaks pitched over heads. Clodhoppers against quicksilver, no contest start to finish, in so dazzling a display of agility and charm that Thorn couldn't help a smile.

He called Khory to help with Geryn and hurried to Elora, wincing in startlement as something hot flicked the back of his neck. At first, he thought he'd run into one of his own mites, but a glance upward told him the situation was far more serious. A torch had ignited the roof, and even though the outside air was damp and thick with falling snow, the bulk of the thatch was tinder dry. It burned hot and it burned fast and Thorn knew they had precious little time before the whole building was engulfed.

He didn't waste time with niceties; he freed Elora from the wall, but that was all as he cast about for an exit. Ryn popped up then to point the way.

It was only when he was well clear of the tavern that Thorn realized he and Elora were alone.

"Khory," he cried, and started back the way he came.

There was no saving the place; the whole of the roof was involved, flames giving a deceptively rosy cast to the snow-carpeted roadside clearing as they worked their way into the walls. Bodies tumbled frantically from every opening, sounding cries of alarm and fright as most hurried to save themselves and only a few whatever was of value within.

Among the latter were Khory and Geryn Havilhand, hustled out the door by their Wyr deliverer just as the lodgepole collapsed, pulling the bulk of a wall along with it.

"Horses!" Thorn called, but had little hope of regaining them. The stables were on the far side of the tavern, with too many folk in between for a successful sally.

"Already taken care of," said Ryn with a smile to his voice to make up for the one the shape of his mouth couldn't seem to manage. "Saddled, ready, and waiting. With as much of your belongings as I could find."

There wasn't much point in riding, Geryn was too badly hurt, so Thorn grabbed one set of reins and motioned to Khory to take the other two. He was turning toward Elora to remove her mask when he discovered that their rescuer had beaten him to it, snapping the buckles and unthreading the laces with the uncanny dexterity of a born sneak thief.

They were well into the trees, along a sidebar trail used mostly by woodland creatures, but still too close to the tavern for Thorn's comfort; though, from the glow they could still make out through the mist and snow, and the harried cries echoing through the night, they didn't have to worry much about pursuit. For the moment. That would change the minute the messenger from the tavern reached the Princess and her Maizan allies, and Thorn wanted to be long gone when they arrived.

Elora coughed as the gag was gently pulled free, then her eyes went wide as could be as Ryn placed a hand over her lower face to silence her, a finger bisecting his own lips for emphasis. Thorn expected a tantrum, but she surprised him with a twitch at the corner of her mouth that might have been the beginnings of a legitimate smile. An expression he'd seen before, when a fairy had danced on the baby Elora's nose.

So, he thought, *the world's still a wonder to you, child, no matter how hard you try to deny it. Might be some hope for you yet.*

"I'm a friend," Ryn told Elora, looking her straight in the eyes, although his words were for them all.

"And we're thankful for it. . . ." Thorn replied, ending the phrase with an interrogatory uplift of tone.

"I *know* you," exclaimed Geryn, to Ryn, "from the riverboat."

The Wyr nodded, and answered Thorn's unspoken query.

"Morag put me ashore, a cove a small ways along the coast."

"Why?"

"Had a dream, cast a Looker"—a prescient trance—"to see what's what. Best we go, Drumheller."

"Geryn needs healing," Thorn told him.

"I can manage," protested the Pathfinder, proving the point by hauling himself into his saddle. "Wizard," he added to Thorn, "can't yeh magic our trail?"

Thorn shook his head. "That'll be the first thing the Maizan'll look for. And I'll wager any odds their trackers are Warded so they can see past any glamours. Speed is our best hope, but we won't make any until I make you well."

"If you can hold till daylight," Ryn said, "we'll call a halt then. At least the snowfall's heavy enough to fill in our tracks; if they want to find us, they'll have to look very hard."

"They do," Thorn told him grimly, "and they will."

They made fair time. Ryn had a knack for finding the easiest, quickest pathways through the forest, but that didn't always mean he'd follow it. If a trail was natural to him, it could be the same for any pursuit, which meant that every so often they'd follow a harder route. The best they managed was a brisk walk, fair progress considering Geryn's condition and the comparative ignorance of the two women. Ryn led the way, while Thorn brought up the rear, senses cast wide for the first hint of anyone following. Thus far, he'd had not the slightest contact, but the strain was telling on him. Being that *aware,* especially while making sure not to be noticed in the process, was as wearing as any physical exertion and he was nearing the bottom of his reserves. The snow wasn't helping. Pretty to look at, sheer hell to plow through. Even Ryn, stumpy as he looked, had longer legs to serve him.

Along the whole of the peninsula—from Angwyn to where it broadened into the mainland proper—the ground was split lengthwise by a series of ridgelines, serrations that rose and fell from a central range of hills that defined the landscape like a spine. Depending on the formations of the slopes, the countryside alternated between forest and open meadow. The trade-off was obvious—speed for cover. Problem was, Thorn had no idea which would be the better choice.

Ryn found them a small defile just within the tree line, where a jumbled rockfall created a fair shelter about a pool of water that turned out to be unexpectedly warm to the touch.

"Hot spring," he told them, which also explained the lack of snow and the richness of the vegetation in the vicinity. Regardless of the air temperature, the ground would never even grow chill, much less freeze.

"This is new," Thorn observed.

"Hot springs in general," Ryn offered with a burble in his voice to match that of the water coursing merrily through the fallen stones, "or this one in particular."

"Both. This was never the country for them."

"Land's been lively lately. Maybe wanting to be part of Elora's Ascension itself."

"There speaks someone who's never felt the earth dance beneath his feet."

"Truth, Wyrrn have precious little sense of the earth at all."

But even as Ryn spoke, his words struck a discordant note in Thorn, and for the most obvious and glaring of reasons: because, for a being far more at home at sea than on the land, this particular Wyr was leading them through the forest like a born woodsman. Still and all, he hadn't lied; he might be the sole exception that proved the rule, that rare sport who walked between both domains. Something else about him was familiar; the pattern of his speech, the way he carried himself. Try as he might, however, Thorn couldn't make the proper connections to solve the mystery. Since no element of what he saw or heard with any of his senses, physical and otherwise, suggested the slightest threat or danger to their party, he decided to honor Ryn's privacy and leave well enough alone.

Khory lifted Geryn from saddle to ground while Ryn stripped the animals of their gear, rummaging in their packs for something to feed them. They combined the horse blankets to make a lean-to that would give the Pathfinder a dry and fractionally comfortable place to lie, and Thorn took advantage of the steaming mineral water to mix both soup and poultice. The latter was exclusively for Geryn; the former, he made sufficient for all.

Khory pursed her lips, savoring the feel and heat of the rich broth as well as its taste.

"Good," she said.

"I had a good teacher." His words were gentle, the emotions behind them far less so as his mind rolled back to those first weeks on the road. He'd shared the cooking chores at home and considered himself a fairly decent cook—until he met the brownies. Franjean was the worst; a self-styled gourmet of the highest discernment, he never let an opportunity pass to revel in the abyssal depths of Thorn's ignorance of the culinary arts. There was nothing Thorn could attempt that Franjean and Rool hadn't tasted better. The hell of it was, when Thorn attempted a turnabout and challenged his diminutive companions to try their own hands at a meal, they turned out to be right, that first dinner a wonder he still remembered. They proved to be foul taskmasters and worse teachers, but he persevered, watching, listening, learning from them as he did from the Powers he was slowly mastering. He knew they'd never consider him their peer, an honor they conferred on no one, but that mattered less with every passing year. It wasn't the goal that mattered to him, he gradually discovered, but the joy of making the attempt.

He felt a thumb wipe across the crest curve of his cheekbone and looked up to behold Khory.

"My friends," he said, not sure, not really caring, if she understood, "I miss them."

"Your friends," she said pointedly, "need you."

Two of Geryn's ribs were broken; that was a matter of gentling them back into place and reminding them of how they, and the lung they'd butted against, felt when they were whole and healthy. For the rest of the Pathfinder, the damage was mainly cosmetic, bruises and abrasions, the detritus of a determined thumping. Thorn spread the poultice across the whole of Geryn's chest, to buttress the body's natural defenses against any opportunistic infections. With the bulk of Geryn's strength devoted to the active healing of his wounds, he was especially vulnerable to any wayward strands of disease that might be lurking about. Thorn had seen it happen before, in his early days before he knew better, save a body from the slash of a blade only to lose him after the fact from a bout with ague.

The sun was near zenith before he was done, though none could tell from such a gray and formless sky. There was no discrimination between earth and air, they blended seamlessly in the distance as though the world had been resolved down to a globe of fluff. The only way to tell day from night was that during the day a body could more easily see.

Thorn stretched until he heard his joints pop, then rubbed his face in his hands before moving fingers up to scourge the crown of his head. Geryn was asleep and Thorn wanted to join him.

But a prickling sensation deep inside his skull brought his gaze around to Elora, sitting as far from the others as she could manage and not be under the snow, refusing to respond even to Ryn's most charming approaches. She held her elbows tight to her body, and her legs were so close together they might have been a single limb.

He didn't ask "What's wrong?"; the list of her answers would break his heart.

"May I help?" was what he tried instead.

"I . . ." she began, after a number of silent false starts. She held her mug of soud as tightly as she did herself; she hadn't tasted a drop. He wondered what she made of this, probably the first night since infancy she'd spent outdoors.

He held out a hand to lead her, used the other to set her soup aside for later.

"Where are you taking me?" she demanded, balking as they reached the lip of the overhang that sheltered them.

"Trust me," he told her, praying she'd believe him this time.

"It's cold, and wet."

He swung his cloak off his own shoulders and onto hers, raising its hood to cover her head.

"That better?"

"I still want to know where I'm going." Her voice took on a pouty quality that was ferociously unattractive. Probably made her minders want to slap her silly.

"I assume you desire privacy. It's more practical, and more polite, for us to move than to require everyone else to."

From the look she gave him, Thorn understood that was a concept as revolutionary as she found it unacceptable. She was the Sacred Princess Elora, after all; people were *supposed* to defer to her. Part of the natural order of things.

Except that the natural order of snow was to fall in winter.

There was a little niche below the pool, protected by a shelf of its own. He twisted the air slightly to waft a steady stream of warmth inside from the steam rising off the pool. Not an ideal toilet, but far better than they had any right to expect on the run.

Elora simply stood there, almost at attention, even the straight parts of her clutched as tightly as her fists, the need to speak as absolute as the determination not to. He wondered suddenly if she knew what to do—*Mark of the Maker,* he thought in horror, *she can't have led* that *sheltered a life!*

"My gown," she said at last, as if those words alone were sufficient explanation.

When no response came, she fixed him with a basilisk glare. "My *gown!*"

He approached, and with that closer look came comprehension. In some cases, the child had actually been sewn into her costume, far beyond the capacity of any person to dress or undress themselves unaided.

It was a struggle, and more than once he almost called to Ryn for assistance, certain the Wyr's fingers were far better suited to the task. He'd thought himself dexterous, prided himself on his needlework in fact, but as far as this job was concerned, he'd do better wearing steel mittens.

There was another reason he wished himself away. This close to Elora, his InSight was keenly aware, and with each touch of her gown came wave after wave of imagery. To the girl, this costume had been a torment—and he caught recurrent flashes of physical memory from her through their bond, on levels far beneath those of active thought, of that awful night on the sacrificial altar at Nockmaar, his lips tightening at how her body blended Bavmorda's attempted sacrifice with Elora's own Ascension. Not so, to the crafters who built it. Into every scrap of fabric, every cut, every stitch went the love and prayers of a generation. There was as much art as skill in the making of the gown, all offered with hopeful hearts by folk who saw in Elora the end to suffering.

To Thorn, they all had faces, and the longer he worked, the more real they became.

Elora knew none of this and cared less. This was simply a

dress, one more ordeal to endure in a life that was nothing else but.

Her shift was just a pullover; he decided to let her manage that herself.

"Well," he heard when she finished her toilet, in that same infuriatingly imperious tone.

He hazarded a look. She wore the shift. The rest of her gown was where he'd placed it.

"Well?" he repeated back to her. She stared at him as if he was too dumb to live. And when that didn't work, said, "I've worn these." She brandished the gown. "I don't wear clothes twice."

Ah, he thought.

"You do now," he said, and made the mistake of turning his back once more.

She threw her clothes at him and screeched, "You should be flogged."

"You should be better behaved." He picked them up as quickly as he could, before they became too sodden to carry—since some had landed in snow and others in the stream—and wished for a way of presenting Elora with the visions he had seen, the emotions felt. But all her barriers were closed tight, the bond operating substantially one-way, and he didn't need InSight to tell him forcing the issue would be fatally wrong.

He fished in his pouch, pulling free a spare set of clothes and offering them to her.

"Under the circumstances, this is the best we can do for you, Elora Danan."

"You will address me—"

"By your name, as I always have," he finished, cutting her off more sharply than he'd meant to. The tone of her voice was getting to him.

"They're ugly," and to emphasize the point, she made a supremely ugly face. The joke on her, of course, was that it wasn't a whole lot different from the expression she usually wore.

"Actually, they're mine. But we're close to the same size still—"

Now it was her turn to cut him off, not with words but by thrusting the offered garments back at him with such force that she sent him stumbling off balance; he had to scramble something fierce to keep from a nasty slip to the rocks.

"I want nothing," she snarled, "except to be rid of you forever!"

She grabbed up her own clothing and made her way up the channel to the main cave. Thorn bit back a rejoinder and tried to do the same with the rage that gave it birth. Suddenly, as he was struggling to his own feet, a charge of energy set his fingertips tingling. He stayed on his knees, splaying both hands to their fullest extension, touching the stone more delicately than he would the most fragile sheet of rice paper that would shatter with a harsh breath. There was a sheen of water between them, formed by a slight hollow in the surface of the rock, and he willed it to be still, the surface growing flat and pristine as a piece of new-hardened glass.

There was a constant trembling to the ground, not a movement within the earth—some minor temblor or other as the tectonic plates snugged themselves together, like a body shifting on its bed in a never-ending quest for the most comfortable spot to rest—but *upon* it. A puff of his power made the tiny puddle a scrying pool, a window through which InSight could show him virtually anyplace in the Realms, and he cast his vision outward to find the cause.

The sight made him gasp aloud; that was sufficient to break his spell. Probably for the best. He saw what was needed; any lingering might lead to discovery by the horde's own enchanters, and a duel was the last thing he could afford.

"Geryn, up," he announced as he reentered the main cave, the command in his voice snapping the Pathfinder instantly and completely awake. For the young man, it was like discovering that he was asleep inside a sleeping bag of spikes that were somehow simultaneously poking him both from without and within. It wasn't pleasant and he said so in his most profane manner. Then, realizing Elora was close at hand, he flushed violently and stammered an apology.

She took no notice.

Thorn had no time for this, and less patience, the urgency of his manner so marked that the others almost immediately fell silent.

"Morag," he demanded of Ryn, "she's waiting to pick you up again?"

"Yes, why?"

"Will they take us as well?"

"Wha'thehell?" protested Geryn. "I'm a Pathfinder, Drum-heller, I don't do boats. 'Specially when we've sound horses to carry us."

"Splendid, Havilhand, only we've nowhere on land to go."

"What'cher worried about, them yobs from the city? The Princess is a lone rider, mate, and I'll stack my skill against them cursed Maizan any day. They'll never find us, yeh've my oath on that."

"Save your breath, Pathfinder, you'd be forsworn from the start." The young man looked perplexed, until Thorn explained. "They don't have to find us, when they have the whole of the Thunder Riders to help. I felt the ground tremble, saw my proof in a Vision Pool. They're coming from the south, sweeping the peninsula from shore to shore. Not just with men and hounds, Geryn, I could taste the forces bound to them. Seekers from among the Veil Folk. We have to find another way. Run or hide, or fight, it makes no difference. If we stay on land, we're done."

CHAPTER 11

MORAG WASN'T HAPPY, AND SHE WASN'T SHY ABOUT proclaiming it.

"Damn well shoulda known better," she said, accent as broad as her shoulders, eyes narrowed to slits against the wind slicing off the cove.

There'd been no wind on the Bay side of the peninsula's central spine; that began to change as soon as they began their descent to the seaward shore. It was cold and it was hard, as though it came straight off an ice cap. Cloaks were of little use; all of them were shivering by the time they reached the shore. There was no snow, the water in the air turned straight to ice and the spicules struck at exposed flesh like vicious little blades, leaving the skin unbroken but casting forth all the sensations of drawing blood.

The cove was surprisingly calm, thanks mostly to a curving tail of earth and rocks that acted as a breakwater, the storm manifesting itself through the rolling thunder of the surf, with an occasional splash of spray over the top for emphasis. There was no cheer to the scene; even the still water had an angry slate quality to it that was a disturbing complement to the darkly clouded sky. Thorn knew where the sun was; by rights, they should have been in the warm lag end of the afternoon, building toward a lazy summer twilight. But lanterns were needed now, not merely for illumination or to provide benchmarks for people trying to get their bearings, but for the simple comfort of something warm against the overarching gloom.

"How bad," Thorn asked her, "is it?"

Morag snorted, dismay and disgust leavened with black humor.

"Got a fair lie here, Drumheller, good cover from both sea an' sky. Only a fool sets sail in weather like this when she don't have to. Better t' ride it out, wait f'r a better day."

"And if that day isn't coming?"

"Damn, y' talk bleak as Maulroon. Tell y' true, y'r better on shore."

"We're dead on shore, shipmaster."

" 'Fore we're through"—she grinned without humor—"that may be the more desirable fate. Y'r set on this, Drumheller."

"Believe me, if there was an alternative . . ." His eyes turned north, as though he could see through the lowering cloud base and perhaps even through the fabric of the land itself to the argent glow of cursed Angwyn. "But there's intent behind all this and cold calculation." He gave a rueful chuckle at the unwitting pun. "Think—since the destruction of Tir Asleen, Angwyn's been the acknowledged seat of Daikini power. Now it's gone, and with it the ruling caste of all the Veil Folk in the bargain. The whole world as we know it, Morag, is up for grabs; we've seen how, we don't know why, nor even who's responsible." Eyes and voice turned bleak as the sea. "Our only hope in this enterprise, shipmaster, is Elora."

"Y' know how much faith Maulroon has in her."

"Doesn't matter anymore, she's all we have. We have to buy time, to learn about our adversary, to prepare ourselves for the day when we can face him on fair and equal terms."

"Y'r damn daft, is what y'are, Drumheller. As am I, f'r doin' as y'ask. Shando!" She was yelling into the teeth of the wind; it took two tries for her mate to hear. "Get our passengers properly kitted out. Skins an' harnesses, the lot."

"Do we wait for the tide, Morag?" was his shouted reply.

"Damn, no, man, y're talkin' daft as the Nelwyn! Storm surge's pushed up the tide, we should have no trouble wi' draft. Better that risk, I'm thinkin', than trying to tack past the break-water after dark."

Shando dropped ashore beside her, sweaters and waterproof oilskins transforming him into a bear of a man, with the bellows' breath of someone pushed close to his personal limits. When he spoke, his teeth bared unconsciously into a silent snarl, as though he was facing a battle, the outcome no more than a toss-up.

"Hatches triple-battened, Morag," he reported. "Breakables locked away. Lifelines rigged, crew fed. We're as ready as we'll ever be."

"I'm sorry," Thorn said lamely.

"Ha!" Morag laughed. "Damn Taksemanyin, the fault's his alone f'r talkin' us t' shore, that bastardly charmer. We'll run y' down the coast, if we can, move south as they move north, try t' put some decent distance 'tween you an' the Maizan. But I of-fer no guarantees, Drumheller, not on a day like this, wi' storms blowin' out o' nowheres the like I've *never* seen."

"I understand."

She fixed him square in her gaze. "No," she said, "y' don't. But y' will. Get y'r folk aboard, we'll be off."

"Morag." A panicked cry from the masthead, face and out-stretched arm pointing up and away toward the cliff trail they'd descended along.

Eyes followed, narrowing in a mostly vain attempt to discern coherence from shapes that were little better than dark black blobs against a leaden sky. All Thorn could distinguish with the naked eye was a sense of movement, but he didn't need Out-Sight to tell him what that meant.

For a fateful moment everyone froze as both crew and fugitives assimilated the realization that they'd been found. In that moment Elora Danan hammered her heels into the ribs of her horse. The animal reared and bugled, bridle jerking from Ryn's hands, and was running before its forefeet struck the ground again. The girl couldn't ride, but that wasn't necessary; there was only the single path, the horse experienced enough to negotiate it safely. All that was required from Elora was that she hold on.

The Wyr was on her heels that selfsame instant, dropping flat to the ground, casting off his human stance in favor of a four-footed scramble that sent him up the sheer face of the cliff with frightening speed. Geryn was barely a heartbeat slower off the mark, ignoring stabs of pain from his still-healing body as he leaped into the saddle and kicked his own mount into pursuit. Elora had the edge on raw speed; she'd so startled her horse and was projecting such fear of her own that the poor animal couldn't help but respond, panic flooding its system with adrenaline and giving it supernatural strength. But Geryn's skill more than struck the balance; he knew how to take every turn without losing stride, when to gallop, when to rein in, making it clear to those watching below that he would quickly close the gap between them. Unfortunately, the Maizan were descending at a similar headlong pace. He would catch her, that was certain, but there was every chance they themselves would both be caught in turn.

That assumption reckoned without the Wyr. Ryn sprang up before Elora's horse well below the Maizan, her animal going up on its hind legs so high, so fast, that Elora lost her grip and was shot from her saddle as though from a catapult. Thorn's heart surged to his throat as he watched and only began to beat sensibly again when Geryn charged up from behind in time to catch her before she struck the rocks. It was an incredible stunt; the Pathfinder literally plucked her from the air by a hefty clutch of her clothes; without breaking stride, he threw her facedown across the front of his saddle—he had to be counting on the impact to shock the breath from her body and keep her quiescent for those first critical moments—and immediately wheeled his mount back the way he came. Thorn lost sight of Ryn, thought in horror that the Wyr had continued up the escarpment to try to delay the pursuing Maizan, certain both men and animals knew full well how to deal with such foolishness. At the same time Morag was calling the last of her people aboard, slipping all her mooring lines but one. Thorn knelt to the ground, reaching out a hand in preparation for calling down a minor mud slide to throw a roadblock in the Maizan's path . . . but some instinct made him pause and look again, with InSight, to see if his deceiver was riding with them.

Geryn could ride, of that there was no question, as he tore off the trail and along the shore at a breakneck gallop, reaching the ship at roughly the same time as his Wyr companion.

"Bloody foolishness, that was," he stormed, yanking Elora to her feet without the slightest deference or ceremony, too upset to notice or care.

"I'm not going with you," she screamed, mostly at Thorn. "I want to go home!"

"Bad as you think we are, Elora," he told her flatly, "that way lies far worse."

"*Liar!* I'm the Sacred Princess. You stole me from my palace. They're riding to my rescue."

A sudden shriek from above, as a horse put hooves fatally wrong on the slippery track, pitching beast and rider to the rocks below. The wind stole away the sound of their impact and distance made it hard to see, but Elora stared as though the scene were lit by brightest daylight.

"Drumheller," from Morag, by her wheel, a voice of such command she turned all their heads. "It's *now* or never!"

"Bring her," he said with an inward sigh, because however necessary the decision was, he knew it was wrong. He was taking what should be freely offered, and probably losing her forever as a result.

Elora struggled in Geryn's grasp, the Pathfinder looking genuinely torn. It was a doubt Thorn couldn't afford.

"Bring her!" he snapped, his manner a match and more for the shipmaster, and Geryn frog-marched the girl over the gunwale. Ryn followed, Thorn came last, with a measured look at their pursuers. He slipped the final mooring and sprang for the rail as the swell pushed the ship clear.

He didn't move at first, but made himself as inconspicuous as possible by the counter as the crew busied themselves setting sails. This ship lacked the size of the dromond; paradoxically, there was an air about it of much more inner strength and solidity. The one built for cargo, this for sheer travel, like the difference between dray horses and Thoroughbred hunters. Long, sleek hull, two tall masts, nothing like the larger vessel's massive freeboard. The sails were different as well, a gaff rig for this schooner as opposed to the dromond's lateen.

Thorn hazarded a look toward the shore, conscious that the low railing afforded little protection even to him, but the Maizan there weren't shooting. Movement off to the side caught his attention, and he narrowed his gaze at the sight of a splinter group of riders racing pell-mell for the breakwater. They were led by a strongly built figure that Thorn recognized even from this distance; Anakerie quickly outstripped her fellows, refusing to slow her pace even when the others fell back and finally called a halt in the teeth of the surf. Her horse was equally fearless, plunging ahead regardless of wind, regardless of wave.

"Total nutter," noted Morag, eyes ranging from the course ahead to the sails above, fingers light on the wheel as she matched her course to wind and water.

"Mad she may be," he conceded, and pulled the silver hair clip from his sodden hair, "but magnificent." He wished there was a way to return it to her, yet found himself strangely reluctant to part with it.

"Anakerie, is it?" He nodded, but she didn't see, so he answered again, aloud.

"The Princess Royal, yes." And then, "Shame we can't bring her with us."

"Don't talk daft," Morag scoffed. "We let her aboard, we're all ghosts. Even my best swords'd be no match for her."

"It's wrong to leave her with the Maizan."

"Weather's wrong. Whole face of the world's gone wrong. Why should she choose different?"

"You think I'm making a mistake, with Elora?"

"Dunno y' well enough to judge, nor her neither. Maulroon, he trusts y', asks me to do the same, there's the end of that. But that wee bit, she don't seem the kind of lever t' move mountains. Don't seem much of anything, t' tell y' true."

"That's the problem. We're walking a fresh trail, mainly blind-folded. No true notion where it leads, or what we'll face along the way. Only hope. And the certain knowledge that the journey *must* be made."

"Daft. Not f'r you, Drumheller, wouldn't have the brat as pas-senger." There was a cry of outrage from the cabin below; Elora wasn't going quietly. "*Damn* sure wouldn't have her f'r crew— *tacking!*"

Morag was all business again, reflections shunted aside by their turn toward the breakwater. There were crashes and groans all about as massive booms swung across the deck from one side to the other, Shando and the two sailors hauling on lines to pull the sails once more taut, water hissing alongside as the ship set-tled on the new tack.

The shipmaster held out an arrangement of straps and buck-les.

"We've foul-weather gear f'r the rest," she told him apologet-ically, "but nowt y'r size."

"Not to worry," he told her. "My clothes are proofed against water." *And snow,* he thought, *and sleet, and hail, and grit, and even normal wear and tear. Being a mage,* he conceded to himself with an inward smile, *occasionally* does *have its practical uses.*

"Y'll wear the harness nonetheless. Unless y'r as much a'home i' the water as tha' bloody muskrat!"

"No fear, shipmaster," Ryn said with his infernal good cheer, already wearing his. "On a day like this, I'd much prefer the ride. And, of course, the company."

Thorn pulled the contraption across his shoulders, settling the harness into place much as he would a backpack. A larger strap went straight across his front, locking into place directly over his breastbone. Attached to the lock was a wide-diameter shackle, through which would be threaded any safety lines.

"Once we clear the breakwater," Morag told him, spacing her words, careful with pronunciation, to make absolutely sure he understood. He was the last to hear the speech, it had lost not the slightest intensity in the retelling. "Y' make *sure* y're on a line. Use another shackle, or tie yourself a bowline, so long as y're on deck y' must be anchored. Go over the side, there's not a chance in hell y'll be saved without it."

"I understand."

"Can y' moderate wind or water, cast us a fair path through t' where it's clear?"

"I'll try."

"Bugger me wi' a marlinespike else," she fumed in exasperation, "why's it the likes o' you're never sure o' what y' c'n do, while the opposition has itself a fine old dance?"

"No regard for the consequences, generally."

"No bloody balls, is more my thinkin'."

"Morag," came the call from her mate, "come up a few points, we're passin' too close to the rocks!"

"At least we'll miss 'em, Shando," was her reply. "Another tack'll put us more broadside t' the main swell wi' too little room t' beat free o' the opposite shore. We'll ha' too little headway t' thread our way through the reefs."

"Look!"

Thorn followed Ryn's cry and outstretched arm, and wasn't surprised to see Anakerie right at the end of the breakwater. Her horse stood right behind her, both as still as statues, as though the rocks had claimed them for their own. In the short time it had taken to cross the anchorage, the storm had visibly worsened, surfspray exploding constantly over the breakwater, presenting clear evidence that it was only a matter of time, and the still-rising tide, before the mole was wholly overwhelmed. The Princess seemed lit by an inner light, her own variant on the spectral silver that had claimed Elora. To Thorn, the contrast couldn't be more marked, or more sad. The child appeared to have been claimed by the otherworldly aspect of her heritage; she had been stripped of the outward portions of her being that marked her as human. Anakerie was like looking at a ghost, someone with the facade of humanity, who had cast aside all within herself that gave it substance. Each was at a crossroads. The Princess Royal had freely chosen her path; the Sacred Princess was being dragged kicking and screaming down hers.

Thorn knew she'd seen him, had eyes for no other aboard, and had a presentiment that whenever they met again—in skirmish or full battle, alone or in the clash of armies—that would always be the case. It was almost as though he was daring her to try her worst, as he stood stock-still at his full height, admittedly even then not so great a target, while she nocked arrow to bow, pulled it to its full extension, and let fly in a single motion that was as smooth as it was deadly.

Wind and rain, distance and difficulty notwithstanding, Thorn knew the moment she fired that her shaft was destined for his heart. She believed him responsible for the ensorcellment of her city, the loss of her father, the death of all their dreams of peace; she would have those scales balanced (even if only a little) with his life. And he, poor noble clown, thanks to the link forged between them in the dungeon, felt enough empathy to allow her a decent chance to try.

The arrow crossed the rail . . .

. . . and Khory's hand plucked it from the air.

Thorn blinked. He hadn't been aware of her approach, nor seen her hand make its move. Ryn was impressed as well; the DemonChild's speed and accuracy outstripped his, which he didn't think possible.

"Are you daft?" Khory demanded of him, in uncanny mimicry of the shipmaster.

"Shouldn't we seek cover," Ryn suggested, "before she tries again? We're still well within range."

Another had joined the Princess on the point and it was immediately obvious that neither man nor mount was particularly pleased to be there. The Maizan Castellan grabbed Anakerie by the arm and yanked her from her stance, batting aside her reflexive slap in such a way that the attacking arm was pinned in a painful twist behind her back. Thorn found himself wishing for a bow of his own, to teach the Thunder Lord better manners.

"Get below," Morag said, as implacable in her own way as the seas, "the lot o' y's. If y've any favors owed by the Powers Beyond, or better yet any Gods who'll answer when y' call, we could use the help."

The cabins were far more spacious than Thorn would have believed from an outward examination of the hull. The largest was devoted to a communal living and dining area, with separate sleeping compartments farther forward. Storage lockers were at the very bow and stern of the boat and beneath the deck.

Thorn was the last down the companionway steps when they fully cleared the breakwater and got their first taste of what lay beyond. The lead swells struck the hull as though they were solid objects more than liquid, shaking the schooner along its whole length with such force that Thorn lost his footing and had to make a desperate grab to keep from falling. He ended up dangling like a monkey before finding his purchase once more and lowering himself to the marginal solidity of the deck itself. Only a wrenched shoulder for his troubles, which he had to figure was better than a twisted knee or back, or a possibly broken bone, the price he'd have paid for a nasty landing. He couldn't stand erect, couldn't stand at all without bracing himself against another object that was bolted to the deck or bulkheads (he couldn't reach the ceiling); the boat's movement had become far too lively.

Each wave they encountered hurled itself at the prow like a suicide charge, determined to be the one to smash the boat to bits. The contact threw their bodies forward, as any collision would on land, the shock most keenly felt from the shoulders up, their heads being the one part of their bodies most difficult to restrain. They suffered from getting bounced every which way; they suffered as keenly from the stress of keeping muscles tensed against the continual series of hard knocks. Bad as it was for the passengers, Thorn wondered how much worse for the ship herself, at what point would the stout wood of her hull give way against the merciless battering? They could hear water sluice across the deck, with the same angry sound it would make cast upon a hot griddle. There was a constant groan from the timbers as the hull flexed and warped from the pressure of the seas. The tumult was just as wild overhead, as every tack sent the booms from one side of the ship to the other with a tremendous crash, followed by the sound of lines being hauled through blocks and chains pulled speedily taut. The wind didn't howl, it roared, which in turn drew wild laments from the rigging which to some sounded like defiance, to others sheerest agony.

There was no light, the boat's movement was too violent and unpredictable to risk even a shielded lantern and the air quickly grew too damp to support most flames. There was sufficient ambient light to see up top, though that would change with sunset, but the cabin was little better than a cave. Elora and Geryn sat together, the Pathfinder doing his best to shield her, and master his own terror at the same time. Of them all, only Khory seemed unaffected by their ordeal; she appeared far more fascinated than upset by what was happening, as she was with everything. Stood to reason, Thorn conceded, using analytical thought to keep his fears at bay; a creature born of chaos would be right at home in the middle of such riotous pandemonium. Elora, poor thing, was shivering and sobbing; they were all bitterly cold, the air dank from seepage through the portholes and the seams of the hatches.

"Not good," Thorn heard from Ryn.

"Is that a general observation, my friend, or a reference to something specific?"

The Wyr's response was a coughlike bark, offered with a lively bob of the head that Thorn interpreted as a laugh, which was good because Thorn had attempted a joke.

Ryn clambered carefully from his perch at the forward end of the cabin, the attention he paid to every movement eloquent proof of how serious and dangerous their situation was. His steps were accompanied by a shallow sloshing sound, which in turn prompted Thorn to lean forward to confirm what that had to mean. The ship chose that moment to go through a wicked corkscrew motion that pitched him forward and down as the bow dropped into a trough, then sharply up again as the wave beyond shoved it skyward. For a frightening moment he found himself airborne, until Khory snatched him to her with a sure-sighted grab of his safety harness.

"Water," he squawked, mostly concerned with regaining both physical and mental equilibrium as both mind and belly did flip-flops. His stomach heaved and he tasted bile, barely managing to choke back anything more. Elora wasn't so fortunate. She doubled over, vomiting miserably onto a deck awash to the depth of an inch. It was an awful sight—Thorn didn't want to imagine how much worse to experience—as the child coughed and sobbed and retched some more, long past the point her stomach was empty. The sudden, gusting stench was indescribable; it proved more than Geryn could bear either and he was just as sick.

Air swept down the hatchway with a squeaking clump of rubber-soled sea boots as Morag dropped among them. Her face twisted at the sight, but more from the presence of the water itself than the fetid waste floating on it. A glance evaluated both the situation and the state of the passengers.

"You"—she jabbed a thumb at Taksemanyin, then at Khory—"time y' made y'rselves useful. One pump for'ard, the other behind this panel. Clear the bilges hard as y' can, till y'r hearts split or I say dif'rent. Ryn, show her how."

Then she rounded on Thorn.

"We can't go on, Drumheller," she told him flat, and behind her words was a string of profanities strong enough to make him blush, had he the color to spare.

"Perhaps I can—" he began, but she waved him silent.

"Welcome to look, even t' try, wizard, but y'll pardon me, I don't hold my breath. See what I mean on deck."

"The others?"

She looked actually sorry.

"Stay where they are. Safer, believe me."

"Geryn . . . ?"

"Guard her with my life!" the trooper pledged. "Damn yer soul, Drumheller, for puttin' her at such risk!"

He had no words for Elora, and she offered only sobs in return as she huddled herself tight as a drenched kitten in Geryn's arms.

Khory hooked his arm.

"Look after *you,*" she said.

"I'll take care of myself," he snapped. "Elora's the important one." Then he caught himself and moderated his voice. "Do as Morag says, Khory. The boat sinks, we're all lost."

"Trust me," Morag assured her. "He'll be well."

For years Thorn had lived with spells that blunted the effect of weather. He kept himself dry in monsoons, cool in deserts, surviving the worst nature had to throw against him. But he'd never seen a storm like this.

The wind was more fierce than he could ever remember, lashing at him with such force that he could only moderate its direct effect on him; there was no way to spare the others or the boat. They looked as though they'd been in battle. Cuts and bruises abounded, one of the crew clutching a hand to his chest where a runaway line had sliced it bloody, almost to the breastbone. There were no crests to the waves, the wind blew them flat, sending the tops slicing through the air as spume, the water like oil, blacker even than the sky. Loud as the storm had seemed below, it was no comparison to what assaulted him in the open. He thought of all the dragons that ever were, compressed into a single awful beast and that monster roaring with force enough to crack the world to its core.

"Can. You. Help?" Morag put her lips to his ear and bellowed in a voice already savagely torn.

He cast his InSight free, to gain a sense of the tempest. Didn't take long, wasn't a happy answer.

"It's wind and sea," he said. "Wholly natural forces, nothing magical. I can't see the end of it."

"What I feared." Morag nodded in harsh agreement. "Wind's against us, water's against us. Not only the wave fronts pushed by the wind, but the ocean current as well. We push into the teeth of it, we'll lose the hull, sure. Seams are flexing by the bow, Drumheller, working themselves more loose with every hit. She's well made, my ship, but it's like being hit again and again by a bat'ring ram. One of us'll have t' give, an' it won't be the waves. We can't cut across the face o' the storm, neither, we're sure to broach. Our only hope's to run before it."

"And that isn't much, is it?" Worse, that would take them back the way they'd come, toward Angwyn, but he didn't need to speak that realization aloud; Morag was as aware of it as he.

"I told you, wizard, we're safer on the land. Won't lie, wind like this, we'll have t' reef the sails tight as they'll go, then add a sea anchor t' hold us steady."

"I'll do what I can."

"Coming about's the bitch. Keep us afloat through that, we'll maybe have a chance. Whate'er hap'ns, y' canna let us broach, swell'll capsize us easier'n flippin' a coin."

They maintained their course until all was ready, enduring the relentless pounding while Thorn struggled to hold the wheel and Morag and Shando hauled a sail from its locker and threaded an anchor chain through its gromets. The chain, in turn, was bound to the stoutest hawser aboard, a rope only marginally less thick than Thorn's wrist, and finally secured to a pair of bollards by the stern.

" 'Nother reason not to get this wrong," Shando told Thorn, as he took the Nelwyn's place at the wheel. "Don't want to yank the transom off the stern."

The deck was perpetually awash, often to his knees, no problem for the much taller Daikini but a serious one for him as he struggled to establish the focus needed for his spell and keep his footing. The harness might keep him from being washed overboard, but a misstep could still leave him badly hammered. Worse, with all the activity centered about the cockpit, he couldn't help but be in the way. He thought of returning to the cabin, and from his feet below felt as much as heard the rhythmic *kalumpa kalumpa* of the pumps. He shook his head; he couldn't go back into that hole.

The hell with pride; he was about to demand some help when

a pair of sodden arms pulled him from his seat and guided him over the cabin roof toward the mainmast.

"Thank you, Morag," he gasped, as breathless from his preparations as if he'd run up a mountainside. The actual spell would be far worse, a reality the woman readily appreciated.

"Gave your lady friend my word," she said as she shackled him in place. "Don't y' talk, don't y' worry. Long as there's a mast, y'll stay put. Just make sure we keep the mast, hey?"

"If there's a way to bring us through, I'll find it."

"Damn well better. But I gotta ask, Drumheller, is she worth it? Seems t' me, world did fine before Elora Danan took the stage."

"Bavmorda—"

"Whole damn world between Nockmaar an' Angwyn, she was nowt t' me."

"Whole damn world, Morag, but still only *one* world. It's a long way from your foot to your heart. Get gangrene in your toe, how long before it kills you? We can't stay apart any longer; we have to find a way to live *together* or some of us won't live at all."

"Y' think *she* c'n do that?"

"I've seen Tir Asleen, Morag. I've cataloged all the broken places of the world." He waved an arm to encompass the storm. "This is the alternative. Chaos and war and shadows on the land and soul."

"Morag!" from Shando. "We're *ready!*"

For all his brave talk, for all the heartfelt beliefs that bulwarked his courage, there was a moment, right at the start, of a doubt so fundamental it nearly destroyed them all.

He was a Nelwyn, the smallest of those races not bound to the Veil Folk (as the brownies were), with ambition to match their stature. The essence of Nelwyn life was simplicity in thought and deed. Work in harmony with the world and all its beings. Hard to be arrogant, especially in the ways that came so naturally to Daikini, when you're the size of every predator's favorite prey. Do None Harm, was the rule, Think None Harm. And with that came the codicil, unwritten in any codex of law but passed down from generation to generation with the inexorable force of a glacier moving to the sea: Above All, Never Be Noticed.

He'd chosen to involve himself in the larger world, to take action when any sane, self-respecting Nelwyn would have walked away. As indeed, all of them had, which he discovered when he returned from the ruins of Tir Asleen to find valley and village deserted, family, friends, neighbors spirited away to a safer, secret place. Leaving him alone among his kind in all the waking world. He didn't understand why. The urges, the dreams, the desires that drove him then, drove him still, and remained mostly mystery. Each time he took a step, he yearned that it would return him to the life he was born to, the joys he feared were forever lost. Every moment he thought of Elora Danan, the love he felt for her was twisted by a resentment at what that love, that dedication, had cost.

He wanted it to end.

In this instant it almost did.

He became wind and sea, his sense of self expanding exponentially to encompass the forces plunging through him. He stood on the floor of the ocean, in such deeps that nothing swam there remotely resembling any fish he'd ever seen, whose denizens generated their own light because here was a darkness no sun could possibly illuminate. He reared to the top of the sky, a place of extremes, where night turned as cold as day blazed hot, beyond the layer of air that sustained all life below, and into a realm as vast as the stars were numberless. Awareness reeled and he felt a choking gust of terror that he'd somehow been returned to the Demon's domain as he beheld the world as a great globe, curving down and away on every side, spinning through an endless void.

There was a piece of the Demon in this, as there was likewise a foulness to the weather, a taint that told him that while the storm was natural, its genesis was anything but. A glance showed him the facade of the world—clouds, wind, rain, sea, land—but a blink of the eye transformed his perceptions to reveal the elemental forces that generated those effects. Patterns of heat and cold and pressure, affecting the water and the air above.

In that flash of terrible transcendence, he understood the way the physical world worked, saw how the energies of the storm could be diverted and moderated. The power was his for the taking, had he the courage to seize it.

He hesitated, heard sudden laughter, the Deceiver's voice, mockery leavened by true regret. Recognition that he was unworthy colored by sorrow that he should come to such a moment.

"Who are you?" he screamed, in the voice of the wind. *"Why are you doing this?"* With the power of the wave.

Morag threw the wheel hard over, her ship spinning as though mounted on a pole. Shando and the crewmen hurled the sea anchor over the stern, pulling frantically on the lines in order to open the mouth of the sail wide. From on high, Thorn's spirit form saw at once that the maneuver wasn't fast enough, the waves came too close together, the schooner cresting one rank at the head of the turnabout but not completing the maneuver before she dropped fully into the trough. She was still mostly broadside when the following wave swept the hull upward, everyone on deck grabbing frantically for handholds as it heeled close to vertical. Ears presented him with crashes from below as cupboards popped from mountings, a scream that had to be Elora.

His moment of supremacy had passed, he knew that. His own hesitation, the ridicule of the Deceiver, had cost him a chance to do the greatest good by moderating the storm as a whole. His poor alternative was to act here, to save Morag's ship, which he did by slapping the waves briefly flat, gentling the swells enough for the shipmaster to regain a measure of control and put her stern square in the face of the sea.

He was thankful for the spray and rain; they hid his tears.

"Did well," the crewman congratulated him, in ignorance, as he released Thorn from the mast.

"Did *nothing*," was the savage retort, and he saw when he caught Morag's eyes that she knew it, too. For all that, there was no condemnation in her gaze. He'd done his best, and that was all she asked from anyone.

He collapsed to knees, to his rump, a forlorn figure at the base of the mast, presence almost wholly forgotten as Shando and the crewman hauled down the sails and lashed the booms tight. The mainmast was bare, its sail fully stowed. Only the barest slivers of canvas showed from foremast and jib, sufficient to maintain headway and no more.

"Y' ride a horse up a hill, y' give him his head, don'tcha know," Morag explained when he crawled to the cockpit and asked what they were doing. Shando watched the lines and sails while she held the wheel. The crewman had gone below, to tend his friend. "Can go as fast as he's able 'cause he's pushin' against the trail, against the weight o' things. Turn around, though, start a descent, it's way dif'rent."

They crested a line of swells, the hull rearing so high that the curve of bow to keel could be seen by anyone fool enough to stick a head over the side to look. Morag pushed the wheel, playing with the ship's heading, and Thorn gasped as they seemed to skate down a vertical wall of water. A moment before, he'd been staring at air; now there was nothing off the side but black ocean, close enough to touch. Morag caught him by the collar, giving him the chance to wrap his hands tight about the rail before she snapped a quick-release shackle through his harness ring. She looked as though she sailed these monster seas all the time, but Thorn needed no InSight to see how concerned she was. There were lines gouged deep in the skin of her face, slashes reaching back from the corner of her eyes to her hairline, and others plunging past her nose and mouth, demarking the toll this ordeal took of her.

"Go too fast," she continued, as though this was a casual evening's conversation in some comfy seafront tavern, "y' can't negotiate any turns, pitch y'rself straight off the road. Much the same here. Go into the wind, we have lots of control but no hope o' lastin' through the poundin'. Run before it, we're not hit so hard, tha' pressure's gone. But we have t' work t' stay with the sea, t' control the way we cross the swells, else we broach or worse. Anchor's like a brake, keeps us from goin' too fast, gives me the chance t' ride the surge."

"For how long?"

"Long as it takes, what'cher think?"

"Or as long as we last," said Shando.

Thorn thought to go below, but there was more water than before despite the efforts of the pumps, and the stench was worse than any privy. The motion of the schooner wasn't as harsh; she moved through the swells in long, sloping curves rather than the continual series of sharp buffets, but the wind had lost none of its force. Quite the contrary. It put a constant pressure on every component of the vessel, testing them all to the utmost.

He heard a *snap,* akin to the breaking of a frozen branch, and Shando swept him down as a wire stay whipped past his head. Morag wasn't so fortunate as the frayed end cut through coats and sweaters with the sinister ease of a multibladed razor. She went down with a cry, taking the wheel with her through a half turn that spun them toward the following sea. Shando placed his hand against Thorn's back and literally threw the Nelwyn the length of the cockpit, to collide with the steering assembly.

Thorn didn't need to be told what was required. He grabbed for the spokes, hissing a curse as he barked a set of fingers on the ice-slick wood, pulling toward himself in a desperate attempt to restore their heading.

It was a wild descent down the face of the wave, an even more lunatic climb, water crashing over the gunwale to fill the cockpit to his waist before draining out the scuppers. Shando ignored the flood, bracing his wife in place and tearing her oilskin jacket open to see how badly she was hurt.

When he turned back to Thorn, he looked like a butcher, with blood on hands and arms, smeared wetly across his front. Thorn thought the worst.

"No bones broke, thank the fates," Shando told him. "But she's sliced t'hell'n' gone. Not a hope o' patchin' her wi' any kind'a dressing; be there nowt y' can do, mebbe?"

They exchanged places, Thorn locking his harness to the side rail and straddling Morag as best he could. Her skin was as icy to the touch as the water, eyes disfocused, lips and fingertips blue with a mix of cold and shock. She tried to fix on him, but it was more effort than she could manage right then as he reached through the open coat to the ruin of fabric and flesh beneath. There wasn't time to be pretty and he hoped she'd forgive him the scars he'd leave her with. He sent a charge of energy out his arms, so intense a burst that she spasmed up from where she lay, letting loose a scream that would put any banshee to shame.

"Bride's Gift, Nelwyn," she said when he was done, tables turned between them so that he was the one bereft of strength and she holding him close, "y're a useful bod t'have about."

"Don't leave port," he returned in like humor, "without one. My ears hurt, Morag."

"Swallow. Pressure within is greater than that without."

"Like being on a mountaintop, you mean?"

"Aye, if y' say so. Not much f'r climbin', me, anythin' but a masthead. Storm's doin'. See the glass there," and she indicated a barometer fixed in plain view next to the companionway. "Lower it goes, worse the storm."

"It's very low."

"Tell me about it."

"Morag." Shando, pointing from the wheel, while Burys—the less injured crewman—did his best to resecure the torn halyard. "See there, tha' glow? Too big f'r a lighthouse."

Thorn wanted to stand for a better look, but he had trouble enough simply holding on, and knew as well that he'd have to clamber a goodly way up the mast to get a really decent sight. Even Morag's view was limited to the moments when the stern popped over the crest of a swell. An occasion when he wished fervently for the eagles, and he felt a pang of longing for their God-like outlook on the world, the ease with which they bent the wind to their needs. At the same time he also knew they'd be far smarter than to venture into such a storm; this was a night to snuggle deep into their nest and wait for a decent dawn.

"Angwyn, I'm thinkin', Drumheller," said Morag.

"Aye." In tone and taciturn manner, a match for her.

"Fair protection, once we're past the King's Gate, from wind and water."

"We don't want to go there, Morag."

"Thinkin' aloud, is all. North coast's a mess for two, three days' sail at least." Unspoken between them was the truth that, unless the storm moderated about them, they wouldn't last so long. They'd been battling barely a night and they were already exhausted. The schooner might survive the pressures, their bodies would not.

"No fair harbor," she went on, "wi' the force o' the storm shovin' us ever inward. Many's a rover's cracked on those rocks in decent weather—by the *Gods*." Her voice dropped to a whisper, forcing Thorn to pluck the words as much from her thoughts as the air. He understood how she felt; his response was much the same.

The bulk of the city was hidden by a headland that formed a natural barrier wall for the last stretch of shore before the Gate, as though there'd been a solid phalanx of mountains running all the way along the coast except for this one gap where some giant or other had seen fit to carve out an opening. Estates and housing tracts had gradually made their way toward the water, but they remained minor encroachments in what was still mostly undeveloped land. On a clear day, the tops of the major palaces could be seen from a seaward approach, and of course, Elora's tower; the true glory of Angwyn, however, was saved until vessels actually entered the Bay.

That had all changed. Imagine a city dipped in silver, or swept by the mythical Winter Queen until every surface was covered by layer upon delicate layer of glittering snowflakes that glistened and sparkled with a life of their own. The buildings were ablaze still, glowing from within like coals on a fire, except that these cast off no heat but instead absorbed it. Ice had been spun into gossamer spiderweb strands that linked every structure and, Thorn suspected, every being within the city walls, transforming the metropolis into a confection so delicate the slightest tap with a hammer would seemingly shatter it all to dust.

Yet the appearance was deceiving. Thorn could feel the cold from here, not so much on his flesh but in the marrow of his bones and, deeper still, in that part of himself he knew to be his

Soul. A man might well be able to destroy the entire city with a single blow, but he'd be frozen solid himself long before approaching close enough to try. Sapped of purpose and will first, until what remained was an empty automaton plunging forward on sheer momentum. Sapped lastly of life, but more likely turned inside out and filled with whatever malevolent purpose now made its home within those great walls.

"Never beheld *evil* before," Morag said, as hushed and reverent in thought as in speech, as though any louder a voice might attract the attention of whatever force had struck down Angwyn.

"We can't go in there, Morag."

"Damn straight!"

Taksemanyin's head popped up the companionway steps.

"Drumheller," he cried, "Elora Danan is gone!"

"There!" Another cry, another point, from Shando, to a figure clambering awkwardly up the forward companionway, making her way around the foremast until she was in front, with her back plastered to it.

"Bleeding, bloody *hell.*" A snarl from Morag, that broke into a cry of agony as reflexes sent her after the girl, only to hurl her against the inescapable fact that her healing was far from complete. Pinned where he was by Morag's body, and his own harness, there was no way Thorn could reach Elora, which left it up to the Wyr as Ryn levered himself fully into view and plunged ahead with wildly reckless abandon. Burys was closer than any of them, but he had his hands full with rigging as Shando guided the ship up the slope of the next series of waves. There was a different feel to these, broader and higher than what had come before, that made Thorn pause in his struggle to release his shackles and take a closer look around. A glance over his shoulder showed him that Morag had a similar realization, as stark on her face as the lines carved by hours of constant exertion and stress.

"I am Elora Danan," the child called, thin-voiced against the gale, with something to the way she spoke that brought Thorn back to her with a start, his own heart pounding fit to break his breast.

"A *Summoning!*" he cried, mostly to himself because none of the others would understand. Without a clue to what she was doing, she was hurling her innate strength and power into the storm as a fisherman would a net.

"Elora, no!" A desperation tactic, a command of mind as well as body, a net of his own to entangle her to silence before she went too far. But she was quicksilver in his grasp, as she had been in the Deceiver's. Her power was wholly her own, answerable to none.

"I am the Sacred Princess Elora Danan," she said. "It is my destiny to rule the Thirteen Realms. It is your duty to obey! Wind and waves, hear me, I command you to be still!"

She was hardly wider than the mast itself, a plump scarecrow in tattered finery, hair blown to hell, stinking of her own vomit, so weak she trembled where she stood. Yet she called the storm to silence, and for that first, wondrous moment Thorn thought that the girl—by sheer gall—had pulled it off.

Suddenly the scene was gripped by an active *silence.* Thorn thought of the Scar, in those moments before the mountain powers came for him, and of the confrontation with the Deceiver, when even the concept of sound had been stolen away from the world.

They reached the crest of the wave.

And the mystery was broken by a hollow wail from Shando. "Oh, my *God!*"

CHAPTER 12

THE MOMENT WAS FROZEN, AS THOUGH THE WORLD IT-self had been crystallized, just like Angwyn, every component element etching itself on Thorn's brain with the terrible clarity found only at the height of a midwinter day. Before him, Elora stood like a ghost made flesh, her skin more pure even than alabaster, the same spectral silver as the moon. He couldn't see her face, didn't really need to, he thought he knew her well enough to picture the features in his mind's eye. She was gripped by the strength of manic desperation; she had gone beyond her terror to embrace that special courage of the mad, where there was no thought of risk, less of consequences. Action was required; that was all that mattered.

Everyone had forgotten how to breathe, the world included, and their collective hearts how to beat. His mind was racing faster than he could have imagined possible, yet paradoxically his body had totally lost the capacity to execute its will. He could no more cry out to the child than move to stop her. Wouldn't matter anyway; their fate was sealed the moment she opened her mouth.

They crested the wave, a higher, steeper climb than any previous. Only this time there was no slope to negotiate on the far side. Instead, a sheer drop, as though they'd come to the edge of a cliff. As they reached the top the wave itself began to break, the shoulder withdrawing into a curl, leaving nothing but air between them and the trough, better than a ship length below.

Shando was the first to break the spell, spinning the wheel hard over in a reflexive, last-ditch attempt to reverse their course, hoping to ride the scend of the wave to a saner patch of water. But he found no resistance under his hands, the crest had fallen away beneath them, leaving the rudder hanging uselessly in the open. The bow pitched forward, and Thorn heard a last cry from Morag—raging defiance against an onrushing doom—before they struck.

"Hold on!"

Thorn had known boats that rolled from side to side, had been aboard some that came within a hair of truly capsizing, but he'd never seen one pitch end over end. The most striking image to come to him as they fell was the utter lack of sound. He knew there had to be noise, they'd been bludgeoned by all manner of it since setting sail, a perpetual crescendo of howls and roars and crashes, wails, creaks, groans, thunder in the air and thunder from the sea, more kinds than he had names for, each determined to supplant the others. Perhaps that was the answer, the storm had simply beaten him deaf.

He grabbed for the nearest handhold as the deck tilted vertical, saw water on every side as the bow plunged into the trough, like plunging into a black well, or the maw of some impossibly rapacious oceanic predator. In that flash, the spindrift took on the aspects of teeth, the gusting stench of salt spray became the creature's breath.

He saw the foremast break, the shock of impact tearing him loose from the stanchion he was holding and dropping him to the limit of his lifeline with such force that it felt worse than being poleaxed by a sledgehammer. The deck kept turning, and with it came the realization that the ship was being pitched over onto its back. He had a hand on the railing, and he dragged his head out for a clear view behind; for some lunatic reason he had to see what was happening. The wave reared above them like a mountain, only this one was falling after them, like taking a sheet and sweeping it up and over a set of pillows. Only mass and momentum had given this avalanche of water the consistency of solid rock, and when it struck it would smash all before it. He had no thoughts for Elora—indeed, for anyone else aboard. The moment refined his awareness down to the sense of single self. *I am,* about to become, *I am not.*

Arms gathered about him, Morag using her body to shield his as best she could. He held the deck, eyes tight shut, achingly conscious of how naked and exposed he lay, how weak and insignificant his vaunted "Power" seemed in the face of such elemental fury. He felt overwhelmed by the enormity of the disaster; within his head, thoughts flashed and crackled like wildfire, but when he tried to translate them into action it was as though he'd plunged himself headlong into a tar pit. No amount of effort seemed able to produce an effective response; he needed to be quicksilver and instead was molasses. He thought there would be a final shock to herald his oblivion, but it wasn't like that at all.

Multiple impacts set the hull to trembling, InSight filling in the gaps in his perception—no matter that such awareness was the last thing he wanted—as the mainmast snapped like a twig, wrapping the hull in a tangle of massive splinters, tearing sails and cordage. The wreckage struck at the ship like catapult balls and Thorn bit back an outcry as something jagged stabbed him through the leg. In another instant they were underwater, the world still rolling all about him, as the riptides within the wave tried to yank him free and the schooner continued through the whole of its somersault. He felt Morag slip, lunged for her harness, but couldn't find any decent purchase; the motion of the vessel, the force of the water pulled him in different directions, all of them apart. He cried a protest as fingers were bent free and Morag torn away, one of her buckles—its tongue bent into a wickedly curved hook—scoring the curve of his scalp right to the bone. She was hurled against the coaming of the aft companionway hard enough to bend her double, then dropped below from one end of the cabin to the other like a broken rag doll, one leg twisted back on itself in that awful way that meant her hip was broken.

He couldn't see anymore with eyes, didn't need to, howled because of it, as InSight danced from mind to mind, tantalizing him with flashes from everyone save Elora. Hatches and portholes gave way under the tremendous impact, water bursting into the cabin with the force of fire hoses, solid wood visibly flexing like sheets of tin, so that even cubbies thought stoutly secured were sent flying. There was no sign of Burys; Thorn had a faint residual flash of him being swept away with the masts. There was little sense to be made of the images from below; the thoughts of Morag and Geryn were as knotted and shredded as the equipment above, dominated by ever more intense spikes of fright and pain. The cabin itself was like a bowl filled partway with water being fiercely sloshed about. There was air to breathe still, but each attempt to reach it put the body at risk of being slammed against some bulkhead or other. Taksemanyin held on like grim death, eyes fixed on Elora, the Wyr's anguish plain as hot steel at not being able to reach her. Of them all, only Khory viewed the disaster with any equanimity, the Demon-Child too unused to the life she'd assumed to fear the loss of it. Like any newborn, the wonder of being transcended all other concerns; and since her heritage was purest chaos, the concept of death had even less meaning.

He didn't know how he survived, knew even less how the ship managed, but that was what happened. His lungs lost their breath with that first shock, and he was certain he'd never draw another when a blast of wind slapped his bloody scalp, the salt in the spindrift making him hiss with pain.

"We're alive," he said aloud, as though the act of speech, and the hearing of it, made it real.

The schooner was a shambles. Even to his untutored eye, its survival was the most extreme of miracles; by rights, the boat should have gone straight to the bottom. The masts had been shorn away at less than a man's height above the deck, and with them pretty much every piece of gear on that deck, no matter how thoroughly tied. Jagged holes in the planking, along the gunwale, marked where lashings may have held but the ship itself, not. Inexplicably, the sea anchor hadn't given way. It alone gave a semblance of order to their bedlam universe. But that was only a transitory respite. The waves were as monstrous as ever, and the transom had developed a nasty crack that made its ragged, uneven way past the waterline. It wouldn't be long before a combination of wave motion and the drag of the anchor itself tore the whole stern loose; then, even Thorn knew they'd sink in a matter of racing heartbeats.

The deck was mostly awash, the schooner reduced to a few handspans' worth of freeboard that no amount of work on the pumps would improve. Thorn coughed salt water, coughed blood, choked, and finally heaved forth the roiling nothing that remained in his belly, with spasms so brutal it was like someone had hooked a fishing line through his middle and then bounced him continuously from a height. A stretching cat couldn't bend its spine through so extreme an arch.

Shando was yelling, but to Thorn the man sounded very far away, with hardly any voice to him. He wanted to help as the Daikini struggled forward to the companionway, but the best he could manage was a roll onto his backside, with his shoulders propped high enough along the rail to keep from drowning.

It was Geryn who pulled Morag free, both their faces pale as sheets of new-pressed parchment, only his was from lack of warmth and hers, lack of life. The men had to hurt her, bringing her onto the deck, she was broken in too many places for them not to, but she didn't make a sound or even a twitch to show that she'd noticed.

Shando loomed, managing to hold himself erect despite the logy, wild-ass motion of the ship.

"My wife needs you, wizard," he said in a flat-toned demand that allowed for but a single outcome.

Thorn didn't respond quickly enough to suit the mate, so Shando scooped him up by the harness and deposited him beside the locker where Morag lay. The Nelwyn collapsed where he was dropped, which brought Shando a glare of preternatural rage from Khory, so intense it made the man back off a step and once more take his post at the wheel.

"We're a pair, Peck," the shipmaster offered with wry humor, in a voice as deathly as her appearance.

"We really must stop meeting like this," was his retort.

"No more worries on tha' score, I'll wager."

"Save your strength, Morag," he told her, scrabbling for balance as a sudden lurch sent the deck into a steep upward tilt. He didn't believe it possible to feel colder than he was, but when the boat began to move, his first thought was that they were going to roll again; it was as though a specter had taken lodging within him, coating every organ with hoarfrost.

" 'S all right, m' wee friend." She smiled, setting a finger trembling in cruel mockery of the intended pat on his hand. "Tha's a wave we can ride."

"Don't try to talk."

" 'S all I've left me. Canna feel anything, 'cept bein' so cold. S'pose I should be thankful . . . small favors, eh?"

He wiped her face clear of blood, feeling the crack to the skull just beyond her hairline.

"Toren?" She meant the other crewman below. Thorn looked to Geryn, caught an image from the young man's memory that he thrust as quickly from his own thoughts. Morag caught the flash behind his own eyes and her lips tightened in sorrow.

"Burys, too," she said. "Saw the rigging take him."

"Hush, Morag," Thorn implored. "Please."

"Hush, y'rself, Drumheller." She spoke with a pinch of her normal asperity. "Whereaway are we?"

He didn't need to look; he could feel Angwyn's infernal chill burning into his back more intensely than the sun. She gripped his hand, with more strength than he thought left her, tight enough to make him wince as she gave him entry to her knowledge of the sea. To his mind came a vision of the scene in large, as though he'd once more assumed his God-like perspective to gaze down on the world from among the stars. He beheld the storm as an enormous swirl of clouds, racing toward and around Angwyn as though the city had become an open drain, sucking in the air; and, as with any such circle, the closer one came to the center, the faster one spun. A stationary cyclone, brought into being by the cold flames that had claimed Angwyn, with the city itself paradoxically safe in its eye. He looked more closely, his perceptions sharpening accordingly as he incorporated the ocean currents into the view. He saw a great river of water sweeping along the coast from south to north, casting off lesser tributaries just as its landlocked counterparts did. One such curled through the King's Gate.

At the last, he saw their schooner, mostly adrift, its base course defined by the joint movement of wind and wave. They were fast approaching a junction in the stream, that would either take them on up the coast or sharply east and into the Bay. Already, eddies were snaking about the keel, drawing the hulk ever farther to the side, making it that much easier to be ensnared.

With a start, he found himself back in himself, his bright-eyed stare of wonderment and dismay mirrored by Morag's.

He thrust himself to his feet, floundered a few steps forward to brace himself on the stove-in roof of the cabin, eyes slitted as narrowly as possible as he strained to see what lay ahead, beyond the next wave. Khory took him by the arm, a relaxed grip but also one that left no doubt that the arm itself would be torn from her body before she let him go. There was a tremendous reservoir of strength in her and he partook of it with the care of a man dying of thirst, desperate for succor yet painfully aware that too much of a good thing would be as damaging as too little.

"Duatha Headland," he said when he once more crouched beside Morag. Her nod was even more tremulously weak than the earlier twitch of her hand. There was no pulse that he could feel; life was pouring from her faster than warmth from the world.

"It's like a breakwater," he went on, mixing her certainty with his own inspiration, "acting on both sea and sky, splitting the force of the storm. Part goes up the coast, the rest into the Bay."

Another nod, the brightness of her eyes belying the ongoing fragility of her flesh.

"The main current stays without, the wind pushes us in. We have to stay with the current." He saw what had to be done and shook his head. "There must be another way. The schooner won't hold together."

"Long enough, with your strength."

"My strength is a shadow of what's needed. And casting an active spell is as good as raising a flare to tell the Deceiver precisely where we are."

"An' he's sure t' come f'r us, hey?"

"With all the Powers at his command. I'm not sure I can match him."

"Damn you, then!" She took a hard breath, as deep and forceful as she could manage, to restore a semblance of normal vigor to her voice. Her breast hardly stirred. "Damn him more! That infernal city makes shadows of us all. Burns out of us what's true, leaves only the shade, form without substance. Elora's the best of us, y' say; look what it's done to her."

"Morag . . ." he began, but she willed him to silence.

"What, Thorn?" she muttered in a rushing outbreath of impatience. "Canna save my boat and save me? Y' wee damn, daft bugger, don't save the boat, there's no point what y' try wi' me? Make some sense, will y'?"

"I brought you to this. I made you sail."

"Y're worth it." She jutted her chin weakly, vaguely in the direction of Angwyn. "If tha's wha's ahead f'r us, wizard, she sure as hell better be."

"Khory," he called, marveling that his voice could still make itself felt over the surrounding violence. "You stay by Morag, understand? Whatever comes, you're to save her. My wish, my orders." The DemonChild flashed defiance, as though his was the only life that would ever matter. "Please."

"Damn you, Peck," said Shando, "what's happening?"

He couldn't look at the man. He ached enough already, lives pouring away like sand through his fingers, friends he couldn't save. His mouth twisted as desire swept over him like the great wave that had smashed their boat, not for an ending, because he was sure that would come soon enough, but for there never to have been a beginning. "The Great Mystery," he'd heard the High Aldwyn announce in days that came as rarely to him in memory as in dream, "is the bloodstream of Creation. And the way we divine that mystery, the path by which we become One with All, is called sorcery." Being a Nelwyn, the challenge Thorn faced had been to dip his finger into that mythic "bloodstream." Now he felt like he was drowning in it.

He looked at his hands, and saw them bleached of all color. There was no light to their world, this small patch of existence, as lost on the wild sea as the globe seemed amidst the stars.

The cry was a wonder. It boiled out of some deep and hidden place within, that he had never before encountered, transcending the limits of flesh and even imagination, casting itself up and out as though by sheer volume it could cow the storm. The image came to him once more of that frightful wave, only this time he stood alone atop its crest, giddy with delight, terror mixed in equal measure, as the trough dropped away before him, far beyond the depth of any abyssal canyon. He danced along the edge of disaster, flush with Power he no more truly understood than desired. He didn't know how to hold on, he didn't dare let go.

Khory had seen a danger the others had missed. The transom had developed a nasty crack that made its ragged, uneven way past the waterline. It wouldn't be long before the combination of wave motion and the drag of the sea anchor tore the whole stern loose; then, even Thorn knew they'd sink in a matter of racing heartbeats.

Unbidden, the demon child sprang to the stern, to release the anchor the only way she knew how, her booted foot lashing out against the broken transom before Shando or any of the others were even aware she'd moved. With a sickly *pop*, the top of the weakened panel gave way, which in turn placed far more pressure on the remaining coupling than either wood or iron could endure. After a moment's resistance, the cleat exploded free.

The schooner shot forward like a bolt from a crossbow, Shando screaming the foulest of curses as he struggled to keep control of the wheel, bracing himself in place with spread-eagled feet as the hull hissed diagonally down the face of the swell. The wave began to form a curl overhead, threatening to overwhelm the boat, but they had too much speed to be caught, making an easy transition from trough to scend. Thorn knew they wouldn't be so fortunate much longer, but took the opportunity to shunt them squarely into the heart of the primary current. He couldn't overmaster the storm; these were primal forces, they didn't much care for *dictats,* as Elora had discovered. The trick was to manipulate the elements, to do with bands of energy what Shando was attempting with wheel and rudder. The danger was that Thorn's display of power would mark their position as surely as any beacon. He had no idea of what else the Deceiver was capable of, and no desire to learn, but they likewise had no alternative. The risk had to be taken.

The hull broke clear of the wave for better than a third of its length, crashing down with a spectacular burst of spray. It was a magnificent sight, as impressive a ride, though Thorn would rather have a Death Dog by the tail as he cast ahead for the course that would carry them past the Gate.

"Doing well, little wizard," Morag said, lips unmoving, sound barely stirring the chords of her larynx. He marveled at her tenacity, the will that continued to bind spirit to flesh long past the point when flesh could do no more. He started to offer some of his strength, telling himself it wasn't too late, there was still a chance to save her, but she spoke before the desire was even fully formed, as though their thoughts were twinned.

"No." There was no force to her voice, that didn't matter. She spoke to him with all the authority of a shipmaster and expected to be obeyed.

"I can manage," he protested.

"No," she said again, and there wasn't a hint of weakness to the glare in her eyes or the set of her features. "Trust me, Drumheller. I know my ship. I feel how she moves. Y' have precious little strength left y' as 'tis, none at all to spare for me."

"I'm the best judge of that, Morag."

"Not on *my* deck."

"We have a problem." This from Taksemanyin, fur so plastered to his skin that it gave him gleaming, sculpted lines, as though he were some polished statue come to life. His proximity was to Thorn and Morag, but his words were meant for them all. He'd brought Elora with him, the child apparently unhurt, her face slack with shock. Ryn had tethered their harnesses together, on a short enough lead so that she was always within reach; she wasn't giving him any trouble, initiating no action, moving when bidden, staying where put. Thorn had seen more animated sleepwalkers.

"I couldn't go below to be sure," continued the Wyr hurriedly, "but I think the water's rising. Each time the bow goes under, when we cross a swell, it doesn't come up as high or as quickly as before."

"Told y'." Morag smiled at Thorn.

"Prob'ly cracked the keel when we flipped," Shando offered from the wheel. "Not an outright hole, thank the Makers, else we'd be swimmin' a'ready."

"Pumps?"

Morag's head twitched fractionally from side to side, the pain of that acknowledgment far worse than any of her body. Her love for the boat was a tangible thing, as intense as any Thorn had known, colored with an undertone of true regret because it was more than Morag's love for her husband. She would miss him, but miss her schooner more.

"No more subtleties, then," Thorn said. "I'll push us to the shallows as hard and fast as I can and hope both hull and luck hold."

"What's that supposed to mean?" demanded Shando.

Thorn took a last sight of where they wanted to go and where they feared, then reeled in momentary shock as Morag's hand grasped his—in a grip as firm as ever he'd felt from her—and a charge of energy swept through him as she cast over the last of her life. She gave him no chance to protest or refuse; by the time he turned about her eyes were glassy. His suddenly burned with tears, his heart wrapped tight with hot wire, branding another scar alongside all the rest, his own private memorial for those he'd loved and lost.

He gripped his chest, unable to speak, hardly to breathe, mutely waving aside any offers of concern or assistance, conscious of Khory's eyes on him. She alone kept her distance, respecting his need for momentary solitude. She had strength to spare, that he knew, but he couldn't bring himself to ask for it. He felt tainted enough by the process of her birth; he thought of her like a vampire or a were, and feared what repeated contact would do.

Without straightening, he clenched one hand into a fist and punched down at the air before him, his face twisting darkly as emotions manifested themselves in concert with the blow. About them, the storm reacted as if *it* had been physically struck. The wind seemed to hiccup—had they been under sail, they'd have been in real trouble, as gusts roamed the compass, whirling in on them from every direction and every intensity, from breeze to gale. The sea was no less outraged, but it was a denser medium and thereby far more ponderous in its response. Swells grew visibly in size and number, with less time between for a recovery, which quickly taxed Shando's abilities to their limit and beyond as he struggled to maintain proper headway. Before, they'd simply been running ahead of the storm, wherever wind and current would take them. Now they had a goal, and as the helmsman played with his wheel to keep them from being overwhelmed, so, too, did Thorn shape each wave in turn, smoothing the best slope for ascent and recovery.

It was the hardest thing he'd ever done.

It was magical.

It didn't last.

His last coherent recollection was a sullen mutter from Shando. The headland was marginally visible, a more solid darkness against the murk of the sky, and he was wondering where they were going to come ashore, a fairly relevant concern along a coast mostly noted for the ships that ended up smashed on its rocky, inhospitable shore. He felt a surge up the length of his back, as if someone had reached within to twist his spinal cord into a corkscrew. He tried to cry a warning, but the moment between thought and execution was too long. Doom was upon them all before the words were spoken.

It was a Spell of Dissolution. Not the one that attacked Elora's soul, but a purely physical assault, a savage attempt to reduce them all to their component atoms. In sensation, the image came to him of an infinite number of fishhooks, all cruelly barbed, sunk deep into every particle of his being, tugging outward with the kind of strength necessary to topple mountains. His response was as quick, matching strength for strength, countering by wrapping everybody in swaddling cloth that snugged them back together while also muting the worst of the pain. For this assault wasn't simply meant to kill, but hurt them as much as possible in the process. He wanted to protect Morag as well, but there wasn't enough of him to stretch that far, not if he was to do a proper job of protecting the living. Her flesh spiked outward, until gaps began to appear, not because the skin had been torn; it was like a piece of fabric expanded to the point where one could see between the constituent threads of even the finest weave. From Shando came a hoarse wail that mingled measures of grief and rage, but above all, the shame of utter helplessness, at this desecration of his wife's body, and Thorn realized with horror that the mate didn't know she was already dead. He thought he was witnessing her murder.

Exposed to view, Morag's internal organs became subject to attack. Blood sprayed them all, immune to the action of wind or wave, turning the cockpit into an abattoir as separate strands of muscle, tendon, ligament, and ultimately nerves were torn from her. Thorn watched them braided into a foul rope, a barbed strand for every life aboard, and then the whip used to lash him across the face and body. In sensation, it was like being flayed to the bone, but while the vision was true, the feelings were not. The Deceiver, true to its name, was trying to break his concentration and thereby allow the spell to attack them as it had Morag. Thorn heard retching from beyond the frame of his vision, wished he could indulge in the same, as a joking semblance of the shipmaster took form in the air. She was being stripped to nothingness and then rebuilt.

The cry burst from him again, without warning, throwing him forward in a galvanic movement to send his clenched fists hammering down on gleaming skeleton that was all that remained of Morag. He struck her on the breast, but it was as though he'd struck every inch of her, so completely did she shatter. In less than an eyeblink, clean bone was powder, and that, Thorn made sure, whirled far and away on the harshest gust of wind he could manifest, scattered across her beloved ocean beyond the Deceiver's power to resurrect.

But the bastard had a final card to play, as Morag's skin popped back together before him, a dangling pennant of flesh until air puffed it full as life and gave it a coarse form of animation. She took the whip made of herself in one hand, beckoned with the other in a crude parody of sexual invitation, lips stretching into a smile that Morag never made, lids opening to reveal Shadow where eyes and soul had been.

Thorn felt something hard, sharp-edged in his hand, realized without looking that he held an acorn, couldn't help a smile of remembrance as he recognized the High Aldwyn's gift to him, when he left on that first, fateful adventure.

He charged the seed with power and tossed it, all in the same motion, to strike Morag fair, right over where her heart had been. In that twinkling contact, she was both transformed and condemned. Flesh became stone, of far more weight than any wind could support. And down she went, beneath the surface without a splash to mark her passing.

A small victory, in the scheme of things, and all the Deceiver was in a mood to allow, as the same force that attacked them now turned on their vessel. In its way, the schooner was as near the end as its mistress had been; when the Deceiver struck, there was too little left for Thorn to save.

Nails flew from planks, another assault to shield against, and then the wood itself tore, one piece from the next, as the glue that bound them—and the enchantments and blessings that reinforced the physical connections—were torn asunder. None of them went easily, the ship had far stronger wards binding it than those who sailed her, and the stresses quickly found release in a ferocious burst of energy, an explosion that created a false sunrise through a globe of light that reached all the way to the ocean floor.

When it faded, the storm rushing with renewed, almost manic, fury to fill the space where it had briefly reigned, there wasn't the slightest sign of the schooner. It was as if ship, crew, passengers had never been.

He knew it was dawn, though you couldn't tell by the sky. Clouds formed an impenetrable wall across the vault of the sky, so darkly aspected they had no shape to them, they were simply manifestations of Shadow. The wind was polar, worse ashore than afloat, tearing at the land as though its most fervent desire was to scour it down to bare and bloody rock. Waves, too, attacked with a rage he'd never seen before, and as he blearily blinked his eyesight into focus, he saw a promontory off the coast give way, a towering slab of rock calving free as an iceberg does from a glacier, undercut beyond the ability of the main body of the pillar to support it. The basalt split partway up its length, bowing outward like a piece of paper being folded, tumbling to the surf in that eerie slow motion that truly massive objects seem to have, landing one atop the other in a jumbled pile that was almost immediately swept by another legion of waves, as determined to do the same to the rest as the tower was to defy it. There was a natural rivalry between the elements; wind and water and land were always in opposition to each other in an eternal struggle that none could win. But here and now the battle was joined with a blinding hatred, a desire for mutual annihilation, that took Thorn's breath away.

Not that he had much to lose. He lay beyond the tide line, in sand made soggy by rain alone, pummeled so hard his body had to be a single awful bruise. Every part of him was sore, to the extent that lying brought as much discomfort as moving. There was as much noise as on the ocean, the crashing surf vying with the rolling thunder of the wind to such an extent that he doubted even shouted voices could be heard.

He levered himself up, realized with the first movement that he'd made a major mistake, but persevered nonetheless until he'd regained his feet. His stomach was a knot, probably from hunger, though the very thought of food filled the back of his throat with bile. Starving he may be, there was no way he'd keep down even the smallest scrap.

He saw a figure staggering along the seafront, a scarecrow man whose rags and tatters made Thorn feel ashamed of his own clothes, protected by spells, left dry and unmarked despite the hurts inflicted on their wearer.

It was Shando, his voice even more of a ruin as over and over again he screamed Morag's name.

"Shando," called Thorn, the Daikini pivoting as if his back had been stroked by a hot lash, staggering stiff-legged to maintain his balance.

"Bastard Peck," was the retort, raw with grief, "you *killed* her!"

Thorn should have expected the blow. Perhaps he did, in some secret inner part of himself, and chose to accept it as partial atonement for their mutual loss, he really didn't know. Hadn't the energy to care, as the man's fist caught him across the cheek and stretched him full length on a dune that wouldn't be there on the morrow.

Shando put both knees to the Nelwyn's back, landing on him with his full weight, using his hands to press Thorn's face into the sand. He was ranting, words that made no sense except as a mad expression of his loss. Thorn thought of dying there, but his own conscience wouldn't allow him the indulgence.

Sand was far more porous than stone, and there wasn't the additional obstacle of any binding spell. In less time than it took to tell, permission was asked and granted and he felt his substance flow into the earth, leaving behind a dim wail of frustration as Shando saw his prey sink out of reach. The man tore at the dune face with such fervor that nails ripped and his hands turned bloody in a vain attempt to follow, but Thorn was already pushing himself laterally along the beach, senses questing for sign of any other survivors. One in particular.

He thought that would be Elora.

But the lifelight that drew him once more into open air was Khory's.

He knew his surprise showed as he pressed hands to earth to push the whole of him into view, but she didn't seem to mind. Hellsteeth, she didn't seem to *notice*. He wondered if she really hadn't a clue, or was simply being courteous. She still held the sword she'd taken off the slain old Lion in Angwyn, and he had the wry sense that the weapon had bound itself to her in much the same way as she had to him.

"We need to find the others," he said, receiving a solemn nod of acknowledgment in reply.

Turned out not to be so hard an accomplishment. A shout came whizzing along the shore on the wind, a hawk-eyed look in that direction revealing Taksemanyin waving both arms upraised in greeting. He and Geryn had joined forces to save Elora—though once they were in the water, it was the Wyr who'd done most of the work. On the beach, it was Geryn who insisted on offering her the shelter of his arm, despite the fact that the Wyr's fur would have proved more useful in that regard.

Shando approached while they were clustered at the head of the beach, where dunes sprouted sea grass and sand began its transition to proper earth. Khory met him with drawn sword.

He was calmer, in appearance and manner, but the set to his jaw, the way he carried himself when he related to Thorn, most especially the dangerous gleam from behind his eyes, bespoke a wound that would never heal.

Thorn knew the words would sound hollow, but had to say them nonetheless.

"I'm sorry."

The Daikini blinked. His expression didn't change. He couldn't come any closer, not with Khory's point an inch from his throat, but neither did he back a step away.

"You're a welcome sight, Shando," said Geryn, rising to step around Khory and pointedly offer his hand.

Shando blinked again, released a huge breath as though laying aside some monstrous burden, then angled his body to face the Pathfinder and shake his hand.

"Where d'y' go from here?" he asked.

"Only way we can," Thorn said. "North beyond the end of the peninsula. Same basic plan as before, only a different direction."

"Won't they follow?"

"How? Weather's near as wild within the Bay as without, certainly more than any ferry can manage. To catch us, the Maizan'll have to circle near the whole circumference of the Bay; even walking, we should be well clear before they come close."

"Not the Maizan I'm thinkin' of, wizard." The way he said the word, it became as cruel a gibe as "Peck" often was.

"This is sacred ground. First-growth forest, Shando, that dates back to when this land was born, consecrated to Cherlindrea. I don't think the Deceiver can touch us here." Unbidden, though, came the remembrance of that Faery Queen, snared by the Deceiver's Web within Elora's hall along with all the rest, her perfect features stretched into an idiot's grin, eyes lost in a wonderland that left her helpless while her power, her very *essence,* was stolen by her captor.

"If y' say so." Subtext, as clear as if he'd shouted it: *But you've been wrong before, Peck.* "Me, I'm thinkin' I'll be makin' my own course." And doing so alone, that too was made plain.

"Don't be bloody daft!" The heartfelt protest came from Geryn.

"I'm no lander, lad. I'll follow the shore till the weather slips, try my hand with a signal fire or maybe a skiff, make my way home."

"You'll be missed."

"Better this way."

"Is there anything we can give yeh?" Geryn asked, upon the realization that Thorn wasn't about to speak.

Shando returned a small grin, that actually encompassed the Nelwyn, accompanied by a sidelong glance. Personable enough on the surface, but with jagged, bloody edges beneath, man made shark.

"Nowt y'll be willin' t' offer, am I right, Peck?"

"I would have saved her if I could."

"Y' should ne'er ha' put her in harm's way at all."

"Food, Shando?"

"I'll find my own, Pathfinder. Same as I'll make my own way."

Thorn watched him stride away, with the exaggerated gait of a man used to walking on loose sand. Geryn said nothing, but there was condemnation in his eyes as they flashed back and forth from Shando to the Nelwyn. Khory didn't relax her stance, sheathe her sword, until the man was out of sight beyond a natural jetty formed by an age-old rockfall. Geryn's back was hunched, arms wrapped snug about himself, the quintessence of chill, thanks to a cold that had to reach his bones. Elora wasn't much better; she was just too far gone to show any sign beyond a bluish cast to her skin that gave her the appearance of dulled chrome; Taksemanyin tried as best he could to wrap himself about the pair of them, tucking both deeply into his chest and belly fur, combining the mass of the dune plus his own body to blunt the wind.

Alone among them, Thorn was dry, his clothes fresh as the day they were made. Most embarrassing.

He cast his eyes upward, following the rise of the cliffs to their crest.

"Time for us to go as well," he told the others.

"We need rest, Peck!" snapped Geryn.

"Agreed, but this isn't the place for it."

"We're well above the tide line, we'll be safe enough."

"Against a normal surge, a normal storm, perhaps. It's a risk I refuse to take."

"Suit yehrself." The young man wasn't willing to move.

"Have you no wits whatsoever, Trooper?" Thorn spoke with nearly a snarl, surprising himself as much as his companions with his vehemence as Geryn became the lightning rod for a whole host of pent-up rage and frustrations. As the words boiled from him Thorn scrambled within his skull to regain at least a semblance of control, lest rage manifest itself with a tangible display of power. He needed the Pathfinder as he was, not transformed into a newt.

"There are Powers at play here far beyond our comprehension. Believe me, I *saw* it happen. So did she," his arm lashing out to indicate Elora, who visibly flinched, which in turn prompted warning glares from both males.

"I don't really *care*"—he spaced his words with deliberation, as much to gain time to restore his own inner equilibrium as for external effect—"how you feel right now, Pathfinder. About me personally, or my decisions. All I require is obedience. If that's beyond your desire, then by all means join Shando."

"What gives y' the right t' decide for the Sacred Princess Elora, hey?"

"A debt. A vow."

"Whether she wants it or not? Shouldn't that be her choice?"

"Elora Danan?"

"She won't hear," Ryn said calmly.

"Is she hurt, then?" Geryn, concern plain in his voice as he shook free of Tak's grasp and knelt before her.

The Wyr shook his head. His ears were never at rest, they reacted independently to every wayward sound, no matter how slight. His eyes responded only to those sounds that merited closer scrutiny. At the moment their focus was shared by Geryn,

Thorn, and Khory. The Nelwyn had his sorcery, the Demon-Child a good sword, but Ryn had fangs that would do any predator proud, with claws to match and a speed and grace that demanded respect. Should a battle flare between them, a victor might well emerge, but that triumph wouldn't be worth the price. To remind the others of that, Ryn bared his teeth, ostensibly in a yawn, stretching his lips up and away until his canines were exposed to the gum line.

"Nothing bruised, nothing broken," he reported. "I wager she came out of the water in better shape than the rest of us combined. Except"—and here, he indicated Khory—"perhaps for her." She had her back to the gathering, her eyes roving what passed for a horizon, sweeping a constant circuit of trees and sea and shore.

"I don't much like you, wizard," Ryn continued, to Thorn, "but you have a point. Staying in place is asking for trouble. And while I like a good scrap more than most . . ." He let his voice trail off; nothing more needed being said.

Geryn, true to talent and training, found them a way up the cliff, a narrow switchback trail that, fortunately, soon gave way to a sloping meadow. It was a hard climb, as much due to the steepness of the pitch as the distance they had to travel, and there were frequent rest breaks. Their pace was defined by the slowest among them, Elora, and there was no change in her withdrawn manner as grassy, windswept fields gave way to groves made up of dwarf trees, stunted and twisted by the constant blasts off the ocean.

If anything, the land here was even more folded than the southern peninsula, forcing them to traverse a series of deep rills that created a topography most akin to an accordion bellows. It was a trek that soon reminded Thorn of an early conversation he had with Maulroon, on his first visit to the Islands, when he wondered how far it was from one village to another just down the coast.

"As the crow flies, as the boat sails," the big man had said, in all seriousness despite the gleam of humor in his eyes, "not so far. Following the shore trail, though, y're talkin' near a hunnert mile, easy."

In direct line, over the space of the whole day, Thorn knew they hadn't come more than a couple of miles, yet it felt like ten times that as they trudged up one murderous slope and down the next, in an extreme slow-motion repetition of what the schooner had gone through at sea.

After the first ridge, which acted as windbreak for any weather blasting in off the water, there was a marked evolution in ground cover. Grasslands along the crest became true forest once they began their descent on the far side, the trees growing in height and breadth as they continued inland.

They were in a spectacular stand of timber, that was obvious from the very start. Thorn and the others stood on the meadow, looking up country toward the mountain fastness of Doumhall—the ancient peak that dominated the entire Bay, one that wouldn't have looked out of place among the continental spine—taking in the level plain of treetops that filled the space between, not realizing until they proceeded onward that many of those trunks stood hundreds of feet tall and that their journey was in no way going to be as easy as it first seemed.

The sole saving grace was the realization that it would be just as difficult for anyone trying to follow.

Thorn soon gave up trying to sightsee. Not that he was jaded or uninterested, quite the opposite; he simply couldn't endure the cricked neck from constantly bending his spine near double in vain attempts to see what soared above them. The trunks themselves were powerful things, he saw more than a few so big around that all five of them with arms linked and outstretched couldn't surround it, larger in fact than the floorspan of many a Nelwyn house. They rose up bare of branches for half to two thirds their length mainly because the trees were clustered so closely together that too little sunlight reached past the inter- laced canopy of leaves and nettles.

Occasionally, they came upon a tree that had been over- thrown by some combination of circumstances—say, whose lo- cation on a slope had been undercut by erosion to the point where it could no longer be supported, especially in any sort of wind. There was little sense of the tempest they all knew was still raging, both trees and the ridgelines provided a more than adequate bulwark, but there was likewise a constant agitation across the crowns of these forest giants. In this instance, when the wind pushed hard, there was no foundation left to withstand it, and so, down the tree went. The trunk formed a monstrous bridge across the ravine, which they happily used to save themselves time and effort, and discovered along the way that it was still very much alive, sprouting a whole line of fresh branches that over the centuries might well become full-fledged trees in their own right.

The contrast between Elora and Khory couldn't be more striking. Geryn's focus was the trail, finding them the easiest, quickest route to get them where they wanted to go; to his dismay, that left Elora in Taksemanyin's charge, and the Wyr proved as solicitous of her well-being as a border collie, save that he always let her rest when he sensed the need. She progressed in much the same manner as a cow or sheep; when nudged along her way, she went. No questions, no problems, in a stolid, plodding, functionally mindless gait that never really varied. Khory, on the other hand, couldn't stay still, or on the trail. Her vitality appeared as boundless as her reserves of strength; she would spend some time pacing Geryn before sashaying up the ridge, or down a ways, to closely examine some piece of flora or fauna that caught her gaze, before dropping back to Thorn to ask him about it. She was nothing but questions—what is this, where did this come from?—bludgeoning him with a barrage as infuriating as it was genuine, to the point where he would as cheerfully throttle her for her enthusiasm as he would Elora for her equally total lack of it.

There'd been little change in the degree or quality of the light. It was much like a winter day in the far north, where time was measured by levels of murk. Thorn's internal clock told him it was late afternoon when a concerned Geryn took advantage of the latest rest stop to hunker beside him for a quick conference.

"Know this country, does yeh, Peck?" he asked.

"By reputation. The only maps are too superficial to do us any good, I'm afraid. Beyond that, it's my first visit. Why?"

"The forest's somethin' special, am I right?" Thorn noticed the Daikini couldn't keep wholly still; in his own way, Geryn's senses were as alive and questing as Taksemanyin's, save that he used eyes as his primary receptors, where the Wyr preferred ears, searching the gathering dusk as though some attack were long overdue.

"It's the trees themselves, the oldest of old growth. They're consecrated to Cherlindrea. Said, so story tells, to have been first planted by her own hands."

"Too damn quiet, an' yeh ask me."

"I was wondering about that," Thorn agreed.

Geryn gathered and released a slow and steady breath, deliberately taking his time, repeating it twice more before he spoke again and using the opportunity to sweep his gaze through the arc of a full circle around their resting place.

"Not a sign of life. Not among this world, nor the Veil Folk. Not deer, not lizard, not dryad nor nymph. Not a case o' them havin' moved on somewhere's else, it's as if they'd never been." He held out a leaf. There was a dusting of glitter along its edge, a crystallization that had barely begun on high but hadn't faded in his grasp.

"Frost," Geryn wondered, "am I right?"

Thorn touched his tongue to it, nodded.

"All the wet in the air behind us, won't be long afore we'll see snow."

"In a land that's never before known winter."

"So you say. Ain't speakin' f'r the trees, my point's if we're still in these ravines when it starts, tha's as far as we go." He puzzled a long moment. "Think tha's why everyone's skipped, mebbe? Seekin' warmer climes, like any other migratin' critter?"

"Might explain the animals. The Veil Folk aren't like that."

"Can yeh light us up a'night, so we can continue on our way?"

"I think we'd do better with some proper rest."

"I got an instinct says yeh're right, another shriekin' that's a mistake."

Thorn nodded, extended his hands. "Close your eyes," he told the Pathfinder, and touched both lids with fore and middle fingers, casting a spark of Power across the way to his companion.

"MageSight," he told Geryn, when they moved apart again. "Better vision than a cat, in anything less than absolute dark. More suitable than a torch. I'll offer the same to the rest so we'll each be on equal footing."

"Damn," Geryn responded in wonderment. "*Damn!* When this fades, it's be like goin' mostly blind."

"I'm sorry for that, because it will fade. The charge is temporary, and there's a limit to how often I can reenergize it. The body has a finite capacity, it can be taxed only so hard before it begins to break down. Superhuman strength will eventually burn out the muscles or shatter the bones; enhanced sight will make you blind. Each Gift has its price. The more you desire, the more you pay."

"Yeh go well enough."

"And it's cost me dear." He spoke with an edge that hadn't been intended and Geryn's face twisted a little, as though the Nelwyn had suddenly brandished a knife.

"Do best, I'm thinkin'," he said, brushing his trousers as he rose stiff-boned to his full height, "breakin' a trail along the central crest till we're past Doumhall. Rather stay high along the ridgeline than low, an' keep to the lee side of the range."

"Agreed. You're still not happy."

"Bein' watched we are, Peck. An' not by friendly eyes. Sooner we're clear o' this place, safer I'll feel. We ain't welcome here."

"That shouldn't be. There are no strangers in Cherlindrea's Groves. That's true the world over. Nothing of Shadow can endure here, nor any harm be done."

"Everything else about the damn world's dove straight t' hell, why should here be any different?"

Food for thought, as fatigue curled in about the muscles of his legs, the joints of his hips, like tendrils of a fog bank, despite his best efforts to banish it. The others were in considerably less discomfort, once he'd worked a small Dismissal to immunize them against the effects of fatigue. Unfortunately, the same rules of cause and consequence applied here as with the en-hanced sight he gave them all; his enchantment allowed them to use their physical instrument to its fullest extent. When it wore off, the need for recovery would be just as dra-matic. Thorn's problem was that he was starting from a far lesser plateau, well into reserves of strength and spirit the oth-ers had only begun to tap. His senses were as acute as ever, but the orbits of his eyes burned with strain, his joints cast off a constant ache, he moved with the gingerly grace of an ancient. In a way, he was the axle that kept their wheel turning, but there was less and less oil to grease the mechanism; metal had started grinding on metal, wearing it gradually but inexorably away. His challenge was to find them a place of refuge before that happened.

Geryn's right about the silence, he thought as he tried to find even a semblance of beauty in the perpetual twilight.

He had walked such stands as these often; Cherlindrea planted them where she pleased and they flourished in spite of local conditions. Normally, there was a humid warmth to the groves, as the sun warmed the air beneath the overhanging canopy, which in turn prevented it from slipping away as day progressed toward nightfall; in addition, heat was given off by the decaying matter scattered across the floor, everything from fallen leaves to fallen logs. Sound carried a goodly distance and it wasn't uncommon, if a visitor walked with care, to hear evi-dence of the creatures who dwelled within. Many was the night when sprites and spirits themselves would come to visit, drawn to his power as a moth to a candle flame. He'd danced at his share of their circles, helped them be born, and helped them gen-tly die. These were among his favorite places, because in atmos-phere they most reminded him of home. They were places where he felt at peace, finding a simple joy that brought renewal to his soul as the rest restored his body.

Here, though, he found desolation. A semblance of what was, form without substance. To the surface eye, his Out-Sight, all the elements seemed as they should be: the trees were as sturdy as ever, the earth as firm beneath his feet. Yet they were hollow. It wasn't a case of the Veil Folk hiding from strangers; as Geryn said, it felt to him, too, as though they'd never been.

He wasn't aware that he was whistling, until he caught looks that mixed amusement and surprise directed his way from the others. He couldn't help a weary smile—weary because even the muscles of his face felt overburdened, as though he were re-shaping soft lead—at being caught. It was something he did when he was lost in thought, drove the brownies positively wild, made them join in themselves, which in turn, because their voices were in no way a match for their desires, sent the eagles winging for maximum altitude, well out of earshot. It was a measure of his profound fatigue that not only was he beyond an emotional response to the memories of his lost companions, but also that he didn't notice.

Simple tune, at least at first. Descending thirds, and he paused a moment to listen to the notes rebound through the gullies, echo fading past echo until the air was once more still. It was no tune he remembered hearing, but something that seemed to flow naturally from him as he grew into a life as a sorcerer. Like sorcery, the melody built on what came before, growing in complexity with every refrain. And like magic at its best, it was wholly extemporaneous, an expression of purest intuition, leavened by his deepest feelings.

A somber cast to this recital, reflecting a mood as sunless as the sky, that absorbed him so completely he put a foot wrong and came near to tumbling off the trail.

With a start, he recovered wits and balance, to find Elora Danan standing before him, a doughy waif, with a haunted aspect to her eyes that was starkly at odds with the well-fed flesh that encased it. She had no notion of how her clothes were meant to be worn; Thorn had the sense from her that she blanked while being dressed, standing before her maids nearly naked and emerging properly and exquisitely outfitted, without the slightest clue as to how it was managed. Still, she'd tried to arrange them as best she could. Not terribly successful, from the perspective of either comfort or aesthetics.

Her eyes were very large, the only burst of color on a body that was a casting made flesh.

"Yes, Elora," he said gently, flicking his gaze past her to Taksemanyin and Geryn, watching concernedly. This was the first time the child had taken the initiative since they'd come ashore.

"I know that music," she said. Her voice was broken, with a huskiness reminiscent of Shando, her larynx as cruelly and thoroughly savaged as her spirit seemed to be.

"Something I used to whistle," he conceded, "when you were very young."

"It's my fault," she said, bleakness spreading like oil across the sea from her eyes to her voice. "I should have given Willow what he wanted. If I hadn't fought, none of this would have happened."

"Stop it," he said.

"Look at me," she cried, her tone disconcertingly as deep as his, "I'm cursed, the world's cursed, I never meant for anything bad to happen, I was just so *scared*!"

"There's no shame in that." He took her by the shoulders. A mistake; she broke his hold as though his hands were coated with acid.

"What do *you* know, Peck?" and she made that last word as foul an obscenity as any he'd heard, so harsh in speech and intent that he actually flinched. "Don't you *dare* touch me," she cried with a large portion of her own imperiousness. "*You* brought me to this, nothing about my life was wrong until you showed yourself."

Everything was wrong, child, he thought, though it would have been better to have spoken it aloud.

He was about to, but he never got the chance.

He heard a scream from above, and was gripped by a staggering discontinuity of vision as he was wrenched from himself and cast into the raging consciousness of Bastian, glaring cold-eyed at five people below, frozen in place by the suddenness of the eagle's attack.

"Oath-Breaker," he heard Rool cry, from his perch on Bastian's shoulders.

"Betrayer." This, from Franjean, riding Anele.

"Demon!" they cried together, even more of a curse than Elora's "Peck" had been, a word meant to hurt worse than any weapon.

His vision bifurcated. In the same moment he saw himself as the eagle's back arched, her great wings belling outward to break her madcap descent, and beheld through his own eyes Anele's extended claws, lunging for his face.

CHAPTER 13

THORN DROPPED AND ROLLED. REFLEX TOOK HIM down, wits sent his hands scrabbling for a hold as he dropped over the lip of the trail. He had no doubts that the eagles were trying to kill him; that was clear from the manner of their approach and the furnace fury in their minds, but he had no intention either of giving them that satisfaction or harming them in return. He snagged a sapling, second-year growth, scraping layers of skin from his palm as he used the momentum of his fall to pivot him back toward the trail, working hands and feet like a hedgehog to get him there, trying to protect himself while keeping track of the unfolding fight.

Geryn sprang to Elora's defense, but Anele executed a magnificent turn over the tip of one wing and used the other to swat the charging lad aside. Their bones may have been hollow, but the eagles were a match and more for Thorn in size of body and they could strike with the force of a respectably sized bludgeon. Anele would have dropped on the Daikini, stabbing for his face with claws and beak to maim him, but Khory leaped from her perch on the slope, sword leaving an afterimage in its wake as she aimed a double-handed slash for the bird. Anele backpedaled furiously, making yet another impossible midair maneuver to avoid the blow. She saw at once the DemonChild's speed, so Anele made no attempt to climb to safety; she broke off the engagement by wheeling toward the ravine and jinking away through the trees.

Ryn wasn't so fortunate. He scythed Elora's legs out from under her to bring her down, and clear her out of harm's way—the child had neither his reactions nor his experience; she stood frozen by the intensity of the ambush, dumb and upstanding as a post, the perfect prey. But when the Wyr turned from her to Bastian, he was met by an arrow from Rool's bow. No ordinary dart; that was obvious from an impact that threw him from his feet as though he'd been roped from behind. Brownies, too, had their secrets, generally choosing weapons that stung and annoyed, preferring to harry and humiliate a foe rather than do him actual harm. But when pressed, they could be as deadly as any, striking with poison that could drop a Daikini in a matter of steps or, as now, imbuing their missiles with a portion of their own life force, to give it a striking power far exceeding its diminutive size. At its ultimate, a brownie could trade his life for that of a foe, and Thorn had no doubt that was where this engagement was meant to end as Bastian's claws opened bloody stripes across Tak's flank before the eagle surged skyward for a second attack.

Thorn lashed out with a gust of wind, using it as he would a punch, Bastian squalling in surprise and dismay as he found himself pushed away from his quarry. Rool, always better at a physical scrap than Franjean, managed another shot, but Khory used her sword to block it, her blade slicing the thorn in twain and thereby dissipating its force. She didn't stop there but charged forward herself, compelling Bastian to follow his mate's example and flee down the ravine.

"Damnation," Geryn cried, clambering sloppy-legged to his feet, with huge snuffling noises as he tried to stem the flow of blood from his nose. "Those birds, Drumheller, they were the ones traveled wi' yeh!"

"Yes," was the flat reply.

There was no hint of a geas, or a glamour, not the slightest whiff of entrancement. They came at him of their own free will, possessed by a rage that bordered on hatred and allowed not the smallest hint of mercy. Not for him, nor for Elora.

"What has happened?" he breathed. But the question was rhetorical, for InSight had already presented him with the answer, embodied in that one awful word both brownies and eagles had cried at him: "Demon!" He had become one with Khory's sire in order to bring her into the world, accepted that Bonding fully and freely and thereby branded himself as cursed and outcast in the eyes of all the Veil Folk. It would be the same with the Daikini, if they learned what he'd done, for those who willingly consorted with DemonKind were considered the most wicked and damnable of creatures, wholly beyond forgiveness or redemption. They attacked Elora because they feared he had corrupted her as well. There was nothing he could say to persuade them differently, because a signature of DemonKind was their mastery of the arts of deception; for their own survival, they would assume his every word a lie, and every gesture a trap.

At least, the brownies had escaped Elora's tower; that was something. But it hadn't been a clean getaway, for one of Franjean's arms was wrapped tight to his body—that was why he didn't use a bow against them—and there was a wicked scar across Bastian's back that hadn't wholly healed. Likely wouldn't, from the stench it left behind him. They weren't clean wounds; they cast an infection deep into the bodies that would quickly consume them.

He didn't know if he could heal them. Worse, he knew that if he called them back, he wouldn't get the chance. If they saw him, they would kill him.

He snuffled himself, nostrils taunted by the faintest tang of smoke on the air. His mind was on other things; he didn't notice.

"Very nice," he told Khory as he passed her.

"Sword knew what to do," she replied, "I just helped."

He stopped and stared, truly *looking* at her for perhaps the first time. She was right-handed and that sleeve had suffered from all their travails, to the extent where she'd finally torn it off at the shoulder. The lines of her arm were smooth; this was a body that had always been healthy, and then honed to its keenest edge; that was clear from the easy movement of her muscles. There was a knotwork tattoo about the biceps, deceptively simple at a glance, representing the endless life cycle of birth and rebirth. Toward the wrist, covering the lower half of her forearm, a far more complex and delicate filigree, as though the engraver had sought to replicate a pattern of black lace on her skin. A startling contrast, to find so overtly feminine a decoration on such a determinedly strong figure. Whoever the woman had been, she had defied easy typecasting.

In that, she and the DemonChild were disturbingly alike.

Khory spoke out of the side of her mouth, offering only a fraction of her concentration while devoting the rest to sentry duty. She lounged loose-limbed against a boulder, her sword lying at the ready across her lap, positioned so that she had a clear view of the scene below while remaining protected by a tight clutch of trees from any attack from behind. She might be overwhelmed, but Thorn doubted she'd ever be taken by surprise. It was a comforting thought.

Ryn had shifted sideways where he lay, to clear himself from Elora. That was all he could manage. Thorn could see from the shallow, tender way he breathed that the impact of Rool's bolt had broken bones, and he knew from experience that Bastian's slash would be bad. Elora was on her knees, close beside the Wyr, a smear of darkness—the neutral twilight stole away even the scarlet of fresh blood—across her front, in stark opposition to the argent purity of her skin.

"He's hurt," she said lamely as Thorn approached.

"Any pain?" the Nelwyn asked as he hunkered beside Ryn.

Eyebrows raised in an apparently universal expression of incredulity. But his answer was as to the point as Thorn's question.

"Hurts to breathe, hurts to move—those parts of me that still can, I mean. Leg's numb below where I'm cut. Probably loss of blood, I've no sense of poison. Think I'm leaking like a sieve."

Thorn placed a hand gently on the wound, shook his head in relief.

"It's a mess, but he missed any of the major vessels. Your fur ate up most of the force of the blow; Bastian hadn't accounted for that when he struck."

"Lucky me."

"Very much so, Wyr. Any of the rest of us'd be holding our guts in our hands and wondering how to put them back inside."

"Nelwyn . . . !" Ryn hissed warningly, with an urgent flash of expression toward the side where Elora knelt.

"Was that supposed to be me, then?" she asked, in a very small voice.

"Very likely. As was I, for Anele and Franjean."

"He knows 'em," said Geryn, joining them. "Traveled with him, those gobshite lamb swipers." There was a metallic thickness to his voice that told Thorn he was still bleeding, so the sorcerer fished about in his pouch for a vial and a clean square of cloth. A drop of liquid, a hurried incantation, and he handed the dressing up to the Pathfinder, telling him to hold it over his nose and breathe deeply.

"Same for me, please," requested Ryn, good humor belied by the evident weakness of his voice.

"I wish."

"Oh joy."

"Not to worry, I can pull you through. I'll need some time, is all."

"Drumheller, we may not have any."

"Say again, Geryn? What are you talking about?"

"Take a breath. Couldn't smell before, 'cause o' the crap in my nose, but it's plain as death now."

He didn't comprehend what the Pathfinder meant at first, as he took in a heady mix of evening scents. Growing things, old and young, sprouting from a rich, loamy earth, touched—faintly at this point, thank heaven—by the salt tang of ocean air.

"Someone's lit a fire," he said without thinking.

"Tha's a fack."

Thorn rose to his feet, wondering if his face had gone as pale as Elora's.

"That can't be," he said.

"What's happening?" Elora asked.

"Torch, perhaps?" he wondered, knowing that was hopeless.

"Close enough t' smell, close enough t' see. I'm thinkin' this is a ways off still. Thank the Maker."

"But coming our way?"

Geryn shrugged. "Can we afford to assume dif'rent?"

"It can't be," Thorn repeated, as though his words alone would make it so.

"Bugger that, Peck," scorned Havilhand. "I seen the greatest city of the coast turned t' ice an' spun crystal, an' a fair, decent woman tore inside out b'fore my eyes. If nothin' else holds true no more, why should this?"

"What does he mean?" Elora, again, fright skittering across the body of her voice.

"Hopefully, nothing," Thorn told them both, "but it's best we move."

"I can't," Ryn said matter-of-factly. His senses were keener than Daikini; Thorn needed only a glance to see that he knew the truth.

"Khory," Thorn said, "once this dressing's applied, he's all yours."

"If the eagles come again, Drumheller?"

"One crisis at a time, please. You can manage him, none of the rest of us can."

"I'll carry the sword," offered Geryn, to back away with up-raised hands and an apologetic mien when Khory thrust it emphatically into its scabbard and tightened the sling that bound it across her back.

"My apologies, swordsmistress," Ryn said with unaccustomed formality, and a turn of phrase Thorn associated more with a

Princess like Anakerie, "for the inconvenience. And"—accented now with a shrug that was quintessentially him—"for bleeding all over you."

"Your blood, fuzzy," she said, slinging his arms forward across her shoulder, "keep it to yourself."

It hurt the Wyr when she rose, there was no way he could hide it, his choked grimace sparking a tiny outcry from Elora, as though his pain had struck a resonance in her.

"We have to move fast," Geryn told them.

"We might as well put a blade through Ryn's heart right here and now," Thorn snapped back at him, "and have done with it!"

"Jus' sayin' what's what, is all!"

"High ground, bare ground, that's the drill. Find us the quickest way."

Geryn took off at a jog, moving as easily through the growing night as he would in bright sun.

"And don't thank me," Thorn muttered beneath his breath, "for the MageSight."

"Thank you," a voice said softly from the side.

"You're most welcome, Elora Danan."

"I told the sea to stop," she said, after they'd walked awhile.

"I was wondering about that. What gave you the idea?"

"It was so awful below. I was so sick, I thought I'd heave out my insides. Still sore." She rubbed herself across the belly, leavening the memory with a wan smile until that brought her hard up against the memory of Morag's end. She blinked very rapidly, until Thorn handed her a cloth for her tears.

"I can imagine."

"I wanted it to stop. Suddenly this way came to me. Next I knew, I was on the deck, screaming my head off. *Is* that how things are supposed to work?" she asked with sudden urgency and a sense from her that it wasn't how she wanted it to be.

"I don't know," he answered honestly. "No one does, really, I suspect. Some powers, like some people, don't like being told what to do." Elora flushed a little, at the memory of how she'd treated her own servants. "They prefer to be asked. Pride of place and being are not exclusive to the Daikinis, or to brownies, or any single race." He smiled. "Not even Nelwyns. We each have our wishes, our imaginings, but they're all colored by experience and prejudice. They're right for one, not necessarily for another. There's craft to magic, as there is to monarchy. You start with the gift, as you might a claim to a throne; the trick is learning to use it properly. Mastering energies," he waved a hand, leaving trails of languid rainbows from the tips of his fingers, "mastering people, mastering yourself.

"The Twleve Domains are ruled by prideful folk, on both sides of the Veil; none among them are comfortable with the idea of an overlord, no matter how sacred. That's the trouble with prophecy," his smile turned ironic to point the comment, "always too damn ambiguous!"

"You never used to curse."

"You never saw me in a bad temper."

"You're the one who made me laugh." There was a sense of quiet discovery to her words, a pale echo of the wonder Khory had exhibited earlier, as she labored to make connections between the decimated images in her memory. Thorn was impressed, as much by the effort she was making as by her success.

"We all did, in our way. You made it easy."

"Why'd you leave me?" The ache of loss was naked in her tone, as it was in his when he replied.

"I thought"—a shrug—"my work was done. I had a home, family, responsibilities. I'm a Nelwyn. The adventure may be a great one, but the parts we play in it are supposed to be small, like us, that's the way it's always been. You were where you rightly belonged, among those best able to protect you."

"Good thing you left, you might have shared their fate."

"Or saved them. Elora, what happened that night, do you remember?"

She shook her head, slowly, purposefully, considering the question, truly seeking an answer.

"I was warm, snug abed, then I was burning. The fire that claimed Bavmorda had come for me, that's what I thought. I couldn't move, not any part of me." She held out her arms and gazed at the transformed skin with a sad smile. "My skin was cast metal. I couldn't even speak. I was thrown through sky, through sea, through the heart of the world, through stars in the heavens; I became a star myself. Everything I was, was torn away. . . ."

Her voice trailed off and she was silent for a time. Thorn didn't try to press her, but wondered instead how closely the truth of her journey resembled his brief fusion with the Demon. If that was so, if she'd also encountered those unworldly creatures, that would explain why the brownies were so ready to believe the worst of her. Frustration was a sour, bilious taste in his mouth; it was like being blind and trying to visualize the face of the world from a handful of random spot-flash images.

But why should I expect it to be anything else? he thought. *We're rational beings, how can we make sense out of chaos? Even the way we frame the question invalidates it.*

"Then," she said at long last, her voice as remote as the memory, "I was cold. Freezing. Screaming. I was hungry, I was hurt, I was scared. I was *so* scared. My bed was gone, Tir Asleen was gone. I was somewhere different, someplace strange."

"The palace in Angwyn."

"The courtyard, actually." She nodded. "They built me a house, then they built me the tower. Elora's Aerie. They were always nice to me . . . but they were always afraid. All things considered, I guess they had good reason."

"Bollocks."

They'd been climbing all the while, along a track whose shallow grade made it seem far easier than it turned out to be. Thorn's legs felt held together by rubber bands, and those badly frayed; he doubted Elora fared much better and didn't want to think about Taksemanyin. Even Khory was showing the strain.

"Your friends are angry," Elora said suddenly. "I saw them with you in the tower." She flushed, which had the effect of underlying her silver skin with a hint of rose gold like the promise of a sunrise. "I called them 'bug men.' "

" 'Awful little bug men,' to be precise." Then, more seriously, after a small sigh's pause: "I placed them in harm's way, and left them there."

"To save me."

"Things happened too fast, I couldn't do both."

"Why am I so important?"

"Blessed if I know. But I think you are."

"Nobody ever asked me if it was what I wanted."

"I'm not sure our approval is required."

"That isn't right, Drumheller."

He looked at her. "No offense, but that never seemed to bother the Sacred Princess Elora."

A small smile touched the corners of her lips.

"No," she conceded slowly, stretching out the "n." "It didn't."

They were traversing a middling ridge, a subordinate offshoot of Doumhall Mount that ran along the peninsula to its end at Duatha Headland, and as they neared the top none had any notion which way to go next, whether it would be better to walk the crest for a time or descend the far side.

Geryn was waiting. He was scratched all over, bark scrapes and nettle cuts from climbing a tree. Whatever he'd seen hadn't made him happy.

"Yeh have to run," he told them without preamble, puffing like a bellows. "F'r yer lives!"

Thorn followed the angle of his body, and beheld a roseate glow that reached from shore to shore across the peninsula.

"No," was all he could say, in absolute denial.

"It's burning, Peck. Fast as a wildfire, trees candling like they was soaked in pitch."

"No."

With a terrible violence, born wholly from fear, the Daikini yanked him off his feet by the shoulders, till their faces were level.

"I've *seen* it, damn yer maggoty eyes! Don't matter that this is s'posed t' be impossible, that *nothin's* s'posed t' torch these woods, they're burnin' jus' the same! An' us with 'em, we don't go now! Fast as we're able."

"Where?"

He swung around, shoving Thorn bodily toward the looming peak.

"Crest line's good the whole way," Geryn husked. "Made sure o' that myself. It's a bear of a climb, but there's a bulge in the rocks, forms a natural break, more stone than trees beyond, no fuel for a decent burn. Reach that wall, then the slopes o' Doumhall beyond, we're good f'r another day."

There was sound now, that hadn't been heard from within the ravines. A crackling that boot soles make striding across a bed of dry nettles and twigs. Smoke was thickening as well, reminding him of autumn nights in the village, with the scent of a score of hearthfires spicing the breeze.

"Can you manage, Khory?" Thorn asked, after shaking himself free of the Pathfinder's grasp. Geryn was growing more agitated by the moment, as though his body were shot through with lightning, so full of energy that he could hardly contain himself. He wanted to run, he couldn't abide the delay.

"I run," she said flatly, "he dies."

"So set him down," Geryn snapped, "do him quick, as a mercy, an' let's be off. Damnitall, the *time*!"

"No!" This cry came from Elora.

"He risked his life for us," she protested further, rushing to help as Khory eased her burden down. "I owe him mine! We can't just leave him."

"He can't go, Highness, we can't stay, simple a' tha'!"

"He's right," agreed Ryn.

Thorn knew that, had rationality marshaled like a conquering horde inside his head to provide all the arguments and justifications needed for the decision. But there was a wild giddiness within him as well, a residue of the Demon's chaos that flew in the face of presumed common sense, a resonance of the healing madness that gripped him up on the Scar. He felt as though he'd walked away from so many friends and companions, always for good and noble and necessary reasons, he couldn't bear another such. He wanted the fight.

"Bollocks," Elora said, closing the subject as far as she was concerned, though Thorn knew he could probably overrule her. She was trusting him to save them, trusting him to give himself the chance to try.

Geryn tried to make the decision for them, by yanking Elora by the arm and tucking her close.

"Be daft an' die, if tha's yer will," he told them. "I'll not weep for fools. An' I'll sure not let the Sacred Princess burn with yeh!"

He got the words out but didn't make it farther than a single step before Elora wiggled her legs between his, in a move she'd seen Khory make, and tripped him up. They sprawled together, but she planted a foot against his flank and heaved him clear. His recovery was quicker, but she had a knife, drawn from the deep folds of her bundled gowns, which she'd been carrying like a talisman since coming ashore.

"Don't *do* this, Highness," he implored. "I beg yeh!"

"Don't touch me like that. Ever."

"I'm sorry, I just want to keep yeh safe. *Please.*" He was edging fractionally closer, a crabwise sequence of tiny motions that Thorn recognized too late to be of help, as his warning cry coincided with Geryn's lunge for Elora's weapon.

She flinched and slashed wildly; he got a hand on her but also caught a shallow gash along the opposite forearm for his trouble. Had it just been the two of them scrapping, he likely would have overmastered her, but Khory's sword hissed clear of its scabbard, the reinforcement prompting an immediate backpedal from the Pathfinder as he scrabbled beyond their reach, tumbling ass over teakettle to the base of a small depression.

"Does she mean so little," he raged, recovering his feet, "that yeh'll let her burn?"

"She means so much," Elora answered, surprising them all, "that they'll let her make her own decision, and accept the consequences."

"Fools!" The Pathfinder turned full face on Thorn, dark emotions plain as he worked himself into a violent state. "T' place yer trust in the Peck when all he does is leadja from disaster t' disaster! Yeh saw what hap'ned t' the shipmaster; d'yeh want the same fer yehrselves? If there's evil come t' Angwyn, by the Blessed Bride, I say it's *him!* Aye, Peck, it's *yer* doin', all the horror tha's fallin' on the land, damn me fer not seein' tha' from the

start an' stoppin' yeh when I had the chance. Yeh say yer tryin' t' save the Sacred Princess; well, I'm askin' if *stealin'* her ain't what brought down curses on all our heads? Shoulda figured yeh were in the dungeon fer good reason an' by God *left* yeh there! Yeh care nothin' fer Angwyn, yeh care *nothin'* fer her!" In any other situation, they'd be at blows by now, the Pathfinder trying his best to beat any and all foes to bloody pulps. But his rage could find no such release so long as Khory blocked him with her sword, which left him nothing to turn on his foes save parting words, and with them he was gone. "Demon yeh were named, it's Demon yeh are an' I pray yeh *burn* fer it!"

"You're wrong," Elora cried as Havilhand pumped himself for all he was worth along the steepling rise. "He's wrong," she said again, to Thorn and the others.

"We won't burn, then?" From Ryn, all naive innocence, with intent to amuse.

Thorn looked him in the eye, having already decided to stop their hearts before the flames claimed them.

"No," he said simply.

"Well, that's a relief. Nor die neither?"

"Can't promise that, I'm afraid," was Thorn's response, and now he smiled.

"Now you tell us!" The Wyr rolled his eyes for dramatic emphasis.

"Into the hollow," Thorn instructed them, all business. As Elora passed he touched fingertips to her arm, the barest brush touch. "Thank you," he said. "Truly."

Traditional fire sounds now, like drum heralds before an advancing line of battle, bringing with them the first flashes of heat. All the humidity was vanishing from the air; Thorn could feel the skin of his face tighten as the scene was sucked dry of ambient moisture. The stand of trees was still too thick, the trunks stood too tall, for them to get a decent view of the approaching conflagration; by the time they saw it in full, it would be upon them. Conditions were changing with dramatic speed, as though the hurricane that was battering the coast had turned its attentions full on the land.

The hollow wasn't so terribly deep, Thorn could see over the top simply by standing erect, but there was nothing better available. Khory set Ryn in the deepest part, taking up position on one side, with Elora lying beside him on the other, both snuggling as close to the Wyr as they were able.

An explosion caught Thorn's eyes, downslope in the neighboring ravine, and he watched a sinuous, serpentine shape—colored as though blood were made molten and leavened by pure gold, so that it gleamed from within with an intensity to shame the sun—dive into the trunk at its base. His eyes followed its progress up the heart of the tree, although at first nothing could be seen by the naked eye, until the wood itself began to glow. Every leaf burst alight and then dollops of raw fire leaked into view, the way a smithy might use a white-hot bar to sear his way through a plate of metal. Fountains of flame rocketed from the ground, as the roots were consumed, and with a tremendous *whoumpf* of expanding gas the tree itself instantaneously combusted, brilliantly ablaze from floor to crown.

"Bastard," Thorn snarled, yet again in helpless rage as the firedrake leaped to another target.

He was sweating. In the matter of seconds it had taken the tree to die, the fire had pumped the temperature a score of degrees, from autumn to summer. He pulled a bottle from his pouch and upended it over the hollow, not so much to drench anyone lying within or the ground beneath but primarily to remind them what it felt like to be wet. A pool wouldn't save them, when the smallest breath of that superheated air would scorch their lungs worse than a cauterizing iron, and the water itself would be heated to a rolling boil.

His cloak wasn't big enough, so he borrowed one of Elora's, shaking it out to cover the whole of the depression; a spray of water went on it as well.

One big advantage in a fast-moving fire such as this, he knew. Its intensity made it a horror almost beyond imagining, but its very speed made it one that didn't have to be endured long, where a more leisurely blaze might be around awhile. On the one hand, speed and intensity were the hallmarks of a brush fire;

they didn't occur in oldest-growth forests. On the other hand, Cherlindrea's Groves didn't burn, period. Fact of nature, like the rising of the sun. Presumably, that was where the firedrakes came in, happy to consume what a match couldn't possibly ignite. Which meant, ultimately, that all bets were off.

The Deceiver's doing, of course, his actions gradually establishing a recognizable pattern as he took what was normal and violently twisted it back upon itself. Casting order into chaos, setting one natural force at deadly odds against another. Firedrakes represented one of the primal forces of creation; according to one legend they were born with the universe and swam in the molten hearts of the stars themselves, while another belief held that it was they who burned the holes in the fabric of the sky that allowed the heavenly radiance to shine through to the waking world below. Kin to dragons, some theorized; but where the one was considered to be the quintessence of thought and reason, these were beings of raw and untamed passion, quicksilver emotions to go with their protean flesh. It wasn't known if they were intelligent; like Demons, their minds worked in ways neither Daikini nor Veil Folk could comprehend. The only surety was that they were a power to be reckoned with. Only a first-rank mage would even consider summoning one, because only the most absolute and all-encompassing of wards could contain their tremendous heat; the problem was, firedrakes apparently hated in equal measure being confined. From the moment of manifestation, they were reputed to fight like berserkers to break free, with consequences to the world if they did couched in the more dire and fearsome terms. Among all the sorcerers Thorn had ever met, the histories he'd ever heard told or read himself, these terrible creatures were considered without exception to be the bear best left sleeping in its den. To be ever avoided and *never* disturbed.

Yet the Deceiver had summoned and unleashed, not a single such horror, but an entire clutch.

"Madness," Thorn breathed because he still couldn't believe it was actually happening. "Madness!"

Nothing gentle about sight or sound any longer. He knew it

was time to get under cover, but the sight held him with the attraction of a cobra for the mongoose. There was no way to see far, the forest grew too tall around, preventing the spectacular vistas that should be the stock-in-trade of such a vantage point, but what was in sight before him was rapidly becoming an inferno. Wind hotter than the breath of a dragon, more appropriate to a desert where the only scrap of moisture is what lives within your own body. A roar like an avalanche, as though all the furnaces that ever were had been brought together in this one spot and stoked hot enough to consume the world.

A hand tugged his trouser leg—Elora—and he ducked beside her, the child hurriedly brushing stray sparks from his hair before they had a chance to do some mischief.

"I can spell you all to sleep," he said. "That would make this easier."

"If it's not an essential requirement," Ryn answered, for them all, "I think I'd rather watch."

Thorn lay on his stomach and sank his fingers into the soil, already warming to the touch. There were root networks below, winding around the rocks that composed the ridge, and he knew the firedrakes would happily try a jump from them to the people above, given the opportunity.

He went to work on their clothes first, recalling what it was like on Morag's schooner, with the wind howling, the seas booming over the deck. They'd been soaked to the skin, soaked, it seemed, *through* the skin, every particle of their beings saturated with water. As then, so now. Remember the wet, was his injunction, cast into the earth as well as their clothes. This was a place of generous weather, it had to be to support such luxuriant growth. The sea air created an environment of near-perpetual dampness, and when there weren't actual storms to soak the landscape, the fog did its best. He chanted of winter, cool time, rainy season, showers falling every day, saturating the earth, a time that was rich with both the promise and actuality of life. He didn't neglect the air in this, but reminded it of how cool it was on a spring morn, possessing more than a bite still of the winter just past, crisp and invigorating, far removed from the oven without.

He didn't speak, there was no point as the leading edge of the blaze swept over them. He'd seen battles where thousands had come together in a clash of arms that rivaled the heavenly thunder; they were nothing compared with this. He'd stood on the slopes of the continental divide, with titanic explosions of thunder tearing at the sky so close above it seemed like he could reach out and touch the cloud base, where the shock of the discharge was felt as much as heard. Also nothing. They were caught up in a reverberating barrage, where the ordnance was trees being blown to bits by the resin that was their lifeblood being instantly heated to vapor—like the pops made by a log on the household hearth, magnified a millionfold, beyond the capacity of ear or mind to accept.

He felt a trickle of warmth along his back, as though a line of hot wax had been dripped the length of his spine, and he redoubled his efforts, calling forth visions of the great waves that smashed the boat and the desperate struggle to survive after the schooner's destruction. He could feel Elora shake beside him; the lesser trembles may have been fear but mostly he was certain it was remembered cold, her garments so sodden they plastered themselves to her silver skin. His were no better, as this enchantment shunted aside the one that normally kept him dry. Problem here, if his teeth chattered he'd lose the rhythm of his spell and that would be their doom. There was no margin of safety, they were in the heart of a true holocaust, balanced on the most razor-thin of margins. As Geryn counted on his legs to save him, so were the rest dependent on Thorn's will.

He was weeping with effort, taking enough breath to get through a single repetition of the spell, each cycle leaving more of a hollow sensation in his chest. Nelwyns didn't run, weren't built for it, that was a Daikini affectation, but he'd seen the Tall Folk when they met for games, especially those who attempted the distance races. He looked worse than they . . .

. . . and thought of the time he crossed the Roof of the World, the greatest of mountain ranges, with peaks so high no living thing could reach the summit. Rashly, he'd given it a try and found himself driven back when he reached a point where the deepest of breaths still left his lungs starving for air. *Strange,* he remembered thinking, with a scholar's detachment and a warrior's frustration (then as now, he didn't like losing), *to feel like you're drowning, when you're a continent removed from any decent body of water.*

Same sensation now, as he worked himself ever harder to less effect. Ultimately, he would reach the point where his diaphragm had no more strength to expand his lungs, or his heart to manage another beat. His gamble had been that the fire would blow past them long before that moment. Only it seemed to have stalled.

He wasn't surprised.

Elora swiped his arm.

There was a faint glow beneath the surface of the sand that put him in mind of a foundry, where a forger had trickled a current of molten metal into a mold. A more fierce, actively hungry radiance than he'd see from a volcanic lava flow, because that liquid rock began to cool the instant it emerged.

There was no cast-off heat from the firedrake; the wards Thorn cast were holding fine. The opposition was merely making its presence felt.

"This is different from the ocean," Elora said in his ear. She spoke in a normal tone, which meant he shouldn't have been able to hear a word—he could barely make proper sense of his own thoughts—but he understood her fine.

"Yes," he said, not trying to be rude but not having the voice or breath to spare.

"That was natural, this is something else."

"Yes."

"Willow's doing."

"The *Deceiver's* doing, Elora. Whatever face that creature wears, it isn't Willow. It was never Willow." He had to pause every few words to chant the next passage of his spell, which made his speech halting and disjointed. He couldn't even spare the effort to project his half of the conversation through mind-speech; too much of his focus was required to sustain his work.

"But the deception worked. On me. On those who possessed the power to know better. Cherlindrea above all would have known a lie. If she accepted him, some part of it—some part of him—must have been true."

"Impossible!" But beyond that protest, he had no argument to refute her logic.

The both of them watched the gleaming sinuosity beneath them, while it in turn cast enough of a glow to highlight all their faces in turn.

"You never answered my question, Nelwyn."

Another mystery defying simple solution.

"Nothing to say worth the speaking of it. I'm sorry," he added. *Or,* he thought, *the sparing of the breath.*

"It must be nice to be a piece of gold," she mused. "At least then you'd have some sense of why you were valued. Do you think this fire means Wil—" She caught herself, offered a shy demi-smile of apology. "I mean, our adversary"—and Thorn tossed a look her way at the deliberate choice of the plural pronoun, her smile broadening a fraction more in return—"has given up on taking me alive?"

"No," was his flat reply. "But you'll forgive me for not putting your supposition to an empirical test."

"You don't look well, Drumheller."

He had no energy to spare for a shrug, much less a spoken reply. There was a burning in his body that had nothing to do with the fires outside, hot wax turning to acid, coursing along the pathways of his heart and nerves, lacing itself between the cords of muscles until every act of living was accompanied by its own special lash of pain. It was endurable, but it was also getting worse.

"Is there anything we can do?" she asked.

" 'We'?"

She met his gaze, without attempting to hide the fear behind her eyes, but also without taking back a word of her offer.

"I'd like to try."

"As you wish, most Royal Highness."

She clutched his arm and at first he assumed it a burst of second thoughts.

"I'm Elora Danan," she told him, and he responded with a grin of approval, taking a last breath before flinging aside the cloak and rising into hell.

The world was fire. On every side, seemingly close enough to touch, flames rose to form a roof above them; the ground cracked and seared as badly as any slab of meat. Trees remained mostly as residual afterimages, defined by the ever-shifting shapes of the firedrakes that consumed them, those that hadn't yet been blown to bits radiating shimmering bands of heat, up the visual scale from golden yellow with scarlet highlights to a brightness so intense it was wholly bereft of color.

Amidst this inferno, Elora was likewise transformed. Her skin was an ideal reflecting surface and the fiery elements around them restored a warmth to her appearance that had been lost, painting her in wild mixtures of the hottest colors until it seemed to Thorn that she was herself composed of living flame.

Through the fire moved the firedrakes, as serpents would through water, with the boneless sinuosity of eels, kept at bay by the boundaries of Thorn's wards but never straying far, always returning to press here, nudge there, testing, ever testing, for that fatal hint of weakness that would allow them entry.

Elora couldn't help herself, her hand leaping forward of its own accord to touch the nearest one, Thorn's reacting as quickly to snap her back.

"You hurt me," she said, rubbing her wrist where his fingers had left their mark.

"I'm sorry." His head was pounding, the glare like spikes through his eyes, and he despaired at the arrogance, the *madness,* that had put him in this place, in this hopeless fight. Of their own accord, Geryn's accusations sounded in memory.

Peck, he heard, a chorus of voices, slippery and melodious, caressing with warmth, **Peck Peck Peck Peck Peck**

The catcalls rose and fell, gaining in mockery as the words themselves crashed against him like hurled stones. He'd heard the diminutive his whole life; it was part and parcel of a Nelwyn's lot, whether as gentle derision or true insult.

"Stop saying that," cried Elora, only to have her own words thrown back at her in the same dissonant musicale.

Foolish little fleshling, and before their eyes a number of the creatures flowed together to briefly form the image of something much greater, whose true nature was achingly beyond their ability to comprehend, before dissolving again to their normal state.

"What was that?" Elora asked, more entranced than afraid.

"Tales tell of a monstrous celestial Unknowable—some beliefs refer to it as the Phoenix—alpha and omega, beginning and end and beginning of all, the fire that consumes yet brings forth rebirth."

"It's so beautiful, it's *all* so beautiful."

He had to concede that was true.

To pit your mortal strength against us, they heard further, with chitters of laughter.

"Got that right," he said, and Elora heard the effort in his voice.

"No," she said to him, and then she turned back to the flames to repeat herself, *"no!"* It wasn't a command, he realized, she wasn't imposing her will on the flames as she'd tried to do with the water. Instead, more of a statement of opposition. "This is wrong," she continued, "why do you wish us harm when we've done none to you?"

Our nature.

"To burn the world to ash?"

Yes yes yes yes yes yes yes

The firedrakes were giddy with delight at the image, swirling so fast and brightly across the field of Thorn's vision that even closing his eyes didn't help, scarlet and gold stripes branding themselves across the inside of his lids. The heat was so intense here that the last of his strength couldn't wholly shield them any longer; he felt baked, and didn't want to think of how Taksemanyin felt under his fur. Around them, the fire had coalesced into a whirlwind, a vortex of unbelievable proportions that no longer needed any outside wind to push it along; here was a monster that created its own, a juggernaut engine of absolute destruction that pulled air to its center just like a hurricane, stoked it hot enough to vaporize steel, and spat it away to carry flames to new tinder. Such a blaze as this would cast a glow to rival the icy radiance of Angwyn, and hurl its superheated poison to the top of the atmosphere, along with smoke sufficient to blot out the day.

"Then you would cease to be," Elora noted simply. "For what would sustain your fire, once there's nothing more to burn? If even the hope of life is gone, where then the promise of rebirth?"

As she spoke she held out her hand once more and to his shame Thorn found he hadn't the strength left to hold her back. She passed the boundary of the wards as though they weren't there, without disrupting the matrix in the slightest. The barest tip of her finger touched the nearest firedrake, stroking its back as it slipped past the way she might a cat, and it arched with a rapture of its own at the attention.

Another twisted knotlike and came straight for her, diving into the child's body as if flesh itself were no barrier between them. Thorn's heart near to stopped as he believed he was witnessing in her what he'd seen destroy the tree earlier. Worse, by passing through her, it circumvented the wards as well, which meant the rest of them were likewise condemned.

Elora began to glow from within as the firedrake slid beneath her skin as it did beneath the earth. The child swayed in time to a music Thorn couldn't hear, suddenly possessed of a boneless grace that had to come from the creature within. Her hair radiated out from her skull, as though she were moving underwater, to burst alight, separate strands of flame that miraculously burned without consuming. Only Elora's smile, the one he remembered from when they'd first met, kept Thorn from a reaction that would have destroyed them all. She was silver before; she'd become the essence of sungold, flush with the majesty of the dawn. When she looked at him, there were no more whites to her eyes; all he saw were cobalt pools against a background of flame.

She held her hand before her, as if seeing it for the first time. Fist clenched, then released; in its hollow was a tiny shape with wings, and Thorn felt an awe that hadn't touched him since the birth of his first child.

Now his hands moved forth with a will of their own, forming a cup beside Elora's, unspoken invitation for the tiny fire eagle to step from her to him. And so it did, clawed feet leaving sizzle marks on his flesh with every step, as though to make plain a difference between him and Elora.

He looked into the creature's eyes. Somehow, that wasn't hard; though the little thing could be enclosed within the globe of his hands, its head smaller than his thumbnail, when he raised it up before him, the sight of it seemed to fill the field of his vision. One eye was sorrow, the other joy, both brought forth their share of tears. He held his father's hand at the moment of his death, and his son's the moment after birth. His nostrils filled with the scent of wildflowers, the bouquet he'd made for his wife when they met on Courting Day; and tasted the acrid tang of ozone and sulfur that reeked in Bavmorda's sanctum. He felt an ache that swept out from his heart with such force that he thought it had broken and this was the final moment of being before the Dark claimed him, for all that had been won and lost before, and what remained to be.

He blinked, because the bird was no longer where it was; it had slid back to stare at him from Elora's eyes, and bid sad, smiling farewell with her lips, its crest encompassing her head to give it a gravitas and maturity that no span of human years could equal.

It had touched him, but been one with her.

He stood in darkness, and thought he'd gone blind.

Elora stood before him, lambent silver in the night, which thankfully proved his fears wrong, but brought forth a whole new host of horrors in their turn once he realized she was stark naked. That was about all the time allowed him for that set of worries, because he took a reflexive breath to fill his lungs to bursting . . .

. . . and dropped to all fours like a man accursed, more sick than any living being had a right to be as he found himself flooded with the stench of charred wood and ravaged earth.

Khory held him till the spasms passed while Elora fumbled in his pouch for water. He tried to tell her that was no use, the bags' special properties worked only for him, but the shape of the bottle on his mouth, the cool spring flow across his tongue, made crystal clear how pointless that was.

"It went away," Ryn said in wonderment. "The fire. Just like that."

"Elora?" Thorn husked.

"I have no idea," the girl told him. Her mouth worked, her eyes alive with a twinkling brilliance that was a fair match for the merry light in Ryn's eyes; she gestured with her hands, using all the tools of her physical being to pound her thoughts into something she could express, only to end in a sigh of defeat. "I have no idea," Elora said again helplessly. The words, the very concept, made her laugh. She couldn't stop herself, she was too ridiculously happy just to be alive.

"Makes us a pair, then," he tried to say, to comfort her, but her laughter was infectious although his came brokenly, chortles separated by huge gasps of breath. Ryn joined in as well, although he winced almost as much, as the movements of his chest tweaked his wounds. Only Khory stayed silent, watching the three of them in puzzlement while the paroxysm of relief ran its natural course. Thorn tried to explain, but he couldn't find space or breath to get the words out between guffaws. To his amazement, as the echoes of their laughter faded in the distance, her lips creased upward in a small smile.

He reached out to her and, when she hesitated, unsure of what was being asked of her, took hold and pulled her into his arms, holding her close as tears flooded his cheeks. He'd laughed so hard he was crying. And not alone, either, as he felt himself and Khory gathered into Elora's embrace. Blindly, because he knew the Wyr couldn't rise, Thorn reached out a hand to Ryn.

And there they stayed, a circle of life, of hope. Of victory.

It didn't last, it wasn't meant to. Thorn found his spirit willing, albeit under protest, but his flesh, far weaker, and he needed

Khory's assistance to once more stand erect. He had both cloaks in hand as he rose, and held them out to Elora.

"Actually," Elora said in a smallish voice as she wrapped the water-and-smoke-sodden wool about her, "I wouldn't object to those clothes you offered earlier."

The view from the reef was desolation, to match the bleakest soul. Only a few trunks had survived the holocaust; they stood like cenotaphs in a random scattering across a starkly barren landscape. It was a moment when Thorn wished he had no use of MageSight, and knew the others felt the same. The slopes had been seared to the bare rock, in some places layered with ash as deep as a Daikini knee. The ground was cracked and blistered, burned free of moisture down to bedrock; about their hollow it had been fused to gleaming glass, in a circle of false ice that fell away from them on every side for a score of body lengths.

"What stopped it?" Ryn asked. They were all speaking in hushed tones, as if in a church; it seemed like sacrilege to make a sound in such a wounded place.

"Elora did," Thorn replied, all joy fled from him, as it had when he beheld the ruins of Tir Asleen.

"Then I guess you really are the Sacred Princess," Ryn said to Elora.

In the midst of tucking shirt tails into her trousers, she gave him a look that would have made a firedrake quail.

"I'm Elora Danan," she said. "For what that's worth."

"Tonight, gentle friend," Ryn said with considerable charm, "it's worth the world, at least to me."

"They would have done this to the whole of the world, Drumheller," Elora said as she took in the enormity of the destruction and compared it with what might have been.

"Outside and in." He nodded agreement. "Cracked it to its core, burned everything they could, that's a surety. That's"—a reflection on his face of what the snake had told them—"their nature."

"Where's the sense to that?" she demanded of him. "To utterly destroy the world you mean to conquer?"

"Well," Thorn considered, "they wouldn't stop of their own

accord. So either the Deceiver assumed himself capable of doing the job, or . . ."

"That, my friends," noted Ryn from where he lay, "is a disturbingly ominous pause."

". . . he assumed we would."

"Helluva way to take the measure of your opposition, Nelwyn, an' y'ask me."

"Our foe is a creature of extremes, Ryn. Mad without question, but in no way stupid."

"We're not safe here, Drumheller," Khory told them.

A point he readily conceded. "But we can't move till Taksemanyin's able."

"Have you the strength for a healing?"

"Each time I think not, I discover there's more in the reservoir yet. Besides, Khory, a trek along this ridge to the top of Doumhall won't make me any stronger."

"Think the Pathfinder made it?" Ryn wondered aloud, speaking the question that Elora had feared to ask.

"Well, we formed something of a firebreak," Thorn told him while setting out some food for the others, and the tools and medicines needed for the healing. "The blaze swept around us on both sides like a tidal wave of flame, claiming everything below this crest and as far up the south slopes of Doumhall as there was fuel to burn. If he stayed to the reef and climbed as hard as he ran—"

"Oh!" A strangled gasp from Elora interrupted him, accompanied by a clutch of her hand on his shoulder so tight he winced and worried of a powdered bone.

A stag stood beyond the smoothness of the fused earth. It was a magnificent beast, standing as tall at the shoulder as Khory, with better than a dozen points to each of its widespread antlers. It appeared immovable, feet planted wide apart, head bowed under what must have been some impossible weight. There was a majesty about the animal that was matched only by an indomitable will. If the forest had a king, this was truly he.

"Stay," Thorn told the others, but he might as well have saved his breath, because Elora took flight with that very word, as though she'd been waiting for its cue, only her trousers in place as she raced to their visitor.

Khory held out the shirt that had been left behind. Thorn snatched it from her and strode after the girl. He knew what he would find. Elora stood so straight and still she might have been a statue, or someone who'd just felt the lash of a whip. She was crying. He wished he had tears enough left to join her.

"I wanted to spare you this," he said. "That's why I told you to stay."

The stag's whole body had been swept by the breath of the Devil incarnate. Not enough to kill, not quickly, not decently. It had been seared from crown to hooves, skin made raw, blackened flesh, meat fresh off a grill. There was no pain, beyond that awful, initial caress of flame, because the neural receptors had been burned away. That would quickly change as infections leached into the muscles and sinews and organs beneath. Its blood was probably already thick with poison, far beyond the ability of liver and kidneys to process. The shock would wear off, the euphoria fade, and in the madness of its pain, the animal would dash itself to death.

As if she heard those thoughts aloud, Elora said once more, "no," in that same, strangely still and resolute voice with which she'd addressed the firedrakes.

"There's nothing to be done, save put the poor thing out of its misery."

"You're a sorcerer." She rounded on him. "You're a healer. You mean to do it for Ryn, why not for the stag?"

Because I'm alive, he wanted to say, *because I have limits. I'm tired and I'm weak and I'm not even sure I can save the one, much less both.*

But nothing emerged save a slow nod of acquiescence, because when he came right down to it, the bedrock of his being, he didn't want to make any such choice. He wanted to save them both.

Gray dawn, gray day, another in a series of monotonous dawns more suited to the polar realms than once-temperate

Angwyn. The air had a bite to it that heralded snow, but Thorn knew even a proper sheeting of the stuff wouldn't make this land look any less wretched. Light brought no improvement, only more evidence of how primal a catastrophe this had been.

Thorn held out an apple slice and the stag's broad tongue snatched it into his mouth. There was rage in the beast's eyes as he beheld the ruin of his domain, and a resolve that boded ill for those responsible.

Thorn sat because he had no more strength to stand, with a body held together by strings like some badly constructed puppet. If someone else did the work, he could perform a semblance of major movements—walking, for one—but initiative was beyond his grasp.

The stag nuzzled his nose against Thorn's ear, his ragged hairs making the Nelwyn tickle, and was rewarded with another piece of fruit. He wasn't a pretty beast, by any standards; Thorn drew the limit at cosmetic work, preferring to let Nature herself finish that job. His coat was a frazzled patchwork of old growth and new, the skin beneath as tender and pink as a newborn's. He'd be in a really rotten mood for the next while or so, as the regenerated nerve endings grew accustomed to their new envelope of flesh; every sensation would be amplified to the point where the brush of a branch along his flank would seem more like the lash of a barbed whip. Nothing to be done for that, especially in the wild, part and parcel of the natural process of healing. Thorn hadn't given the stag any guarantees with his work, only a decent chance.

Ryn wasn't much better off. His bones were set and healing, the great wound itself closed, but he moved with an evident care that was at odds with both his normal demeanor and his physical grace.

Thorn heard the hiss of Khory's sword being drawn, sensed the sudden tension in his companions, but he didn't care as closed eyes presented him with a wholly different view of the scene. Anele cocked her head, tightened her turn, to grant him a better view, and their breath seethed in unison at the sight.

"We do appear a pathetic bunch," he spoke aloud.

"Leave you on your own one damn minute," Rool groused from ahead and below him, "you just go straight to hell."

"You," Franjean offered haughtily as Thorn restored vision to his own eyes, "smell."

"It's been a busy night," was the Nelwyn's deadpan reply. "We've not had time for our toilet. Or breakfast, for that matter."

"Is that to imply some obligation on our part, hey?"

"Perish the thought. Khory," he called over his shoulder. "Sheathe your blade, we're among friends." He turned a more baleful gaze back on the brownies. "I trust."

"So did we." Rool didn't back off a step. "You left us, remember?"

"*You*, as I recall, ran from me."

"What did you expect, with the stench of Demons about you?" Franjean took a delicate step forward, followed by a snort that would do an elephant proud. "Still there, thick as ever. Risk our souls simply by talking with you."

"Then don't."

"See if we care."

"Then go!"

There was a silence. There were some shrugs.

"Eagles won't let us." This from Rool.

"And why is that?"

Rool cast him a sour look, a streetwise hustler before the magistrate. "They seem to feel we did you wrong. We saw you with the stag. Anele, she could see how done in you were, none of us thought you'd last through a single healing after standing up to those flaming whatchits, much less two."

"There were moments last night when I'd have agreed with you."

"Could have turned her down." He gestured toward Elora. "Had every reason."

"It wasn't a matter of reason, Rool."

"Yah. That's the point, they say. You chose from your soul. If that hadn't changed, the Demon taint didn't matter."

"You disagree?"

The brownie's voice and manner turned deadly serious.

"Drumheller," Rool said urgently, "use your InSight, look through our eyes, with our hearts—"

"I have."

"Then you see, you *know*! Franjean's too kind when he says there's a stench of Demon on you, its nature's tied tight to yours, as yours is to that one's!" He jerked a thumb at Khory. "Damnedest thing, she's as much yours in spirit as any natural child. It marks you, and not kindly. On the face of it, none of the Wee Folk will take you in, nor heed your entreaties—nor ours, for that matter, should we stay with you. Figure our reaction was extreme, you've seen *nothing* yet! Outcast and anathema, you've made yourself, across all the Realms. Among the Veil Folk, they'd as soon kill as look at you; that's the way it's ever been with Demons."

"They're wrong."

"They won't listen, they'll care less."

"Ever stop to think," Franjean interjected, "you and the Demon weren't no accident? Big, empty dungeon, coulda chosen any cell, why that one, hey? Maybe the Deceiver, he pushes you down a path intended to cut you off from every natural ally?"

"I've thought that." From the very first.

"Ever think, maybe, he plants a seed of Shadow in you—"

"There's a seed of Shadow in us all."

"Don't talk platitudes with *me,* Peck, you know blessed well what I mean! Demon Shadow is different."

"So is this child, Franjean," and he indicated Khory. "The Demon's impulse didn't come from the Deceiver, it grew from Elora. I choose to believe that what's of me, and her, in Khory is stronger and more lasting than what's of the Demon. I choose to have faith."

"Brownies!"

"Elora Danan," Thorn said, by way of polite introduction in answer to her outcry of delight, "may I present my sometime companions, Franjean and Rool."

Franjean offered a courtly bow, Rool a nod of the head. She folded herself into a switchback of calf and thigh and body, dropping her backside to her heels and resting her chin on her knee with that jointless ease so common to the very young, even when they're a bit plump.

"I saw you in my aerie."

"And we, likewise, lady."

"I spoke harshly, to you and of you. For that I ask your pardon. And as well for not knowing you sooner. My memory may be a sieve now, but then I had no such excuse. I owe the pair of you so much, you deserved much better. But then"—and her eyes turned hooded—"so did everyone in Angwyn."

"Point to you, Drumheller," Rool told him after raking his eyes across the girl, "she may be worth the effort after all."

"Thank you," she said with a twist of her old asperity. "I think."

"Should I assume the eagles won you free?" Thorn suggested.

"Damn near thing it was, too. Hey!" Rool roared suddenly in his biggest voice, jumping and waggling his arms like a pip-squeak dervish. "Keep your damn distance, you damn, horn-headed lummox!" And the stag, appropriately startled, backpedaled a few steps with a snort of surprise. He'd been intrigued by the little animates and stepped over to investigate further, to see if they might prove edible. Another downside of so fast and ferocious a healing, it left all concerned, physician and patient, ravenous.

"Thought we were done when the Night Herons rolled out of their roost."

"My stick-leg birds!" Elora cried. "Are they all right?"

"The Night Herons?" Thorn was unsure whether to be astonished or aghast. "Yours, Elora?"

She was genuinely puzzled. "Well, they rooked in the tower. No one seemed too eager to shoo them away. . . ." She paused until the hoots of derision from the brownies ran their course.

"That's a game worth seeing." Franjean chortled.

"Get thee gone, wicked wingie." Rool affected a high-pitched voice and fey manner, flicking a hand at the wrist as though brushing off a dust mote. "Be off, we'll have none of *your* rough sort about."

"How long have they been there?" Thorn wondered.

"As long as I have, I guess—what's so funny, you two?" She got no satisfaction from her demand, as it sent the brownies into even greater paroxysms of hilarity. Ryn and Khory exchanged a glance of confusion and decided to stay well clear; this was a confrontation best left to the principals. "Certainly," Elora finished to Thorn, deciding herself that her best course was to ignore the little perishers, "as long as I remember. We'd roost in my garden together. I'd feed them in my tree. I think I sort of liked them because no one would come near when they were about."

"None would approach, Princess," Rool said in his matter-of-fact way, "because herons are known to favor the taste of human flesh."

"They're creatures of *evil*, Princess," Franjean told her in his most schoolmasterish tone.

"Not mine."

"It isn't as if they have any bloody *choice* in the matter, you know. They're *born* that way!"

"Which condemns them forever, Franjean? You were wrong about Drumheller . . ."

"That remains to be seen."

"But you're willing to take that risk. The herons can't learn a different way, they can't change?"

The brownie struck an attitude. "I don't believe my ears. I can't talk to the child, she's impossible."

"They did me no harm, ever!"

"Some of *us*, missy," and Franjean waggled his sling for emphasis, which reminded Thorn of healing work still left to do, "weren't so fortunate!"

"Who looked after them?" Ryn asked suddenly.

"Never thought of that," Rool conceded. "They're predators, they live for the hunt. All I've ever seen or heard of 'em, they only eat what they've fresh killed."

"Not in Angwyn," Elora told them. "Not the ones in my tower."

"Must've given the locals pause, I'm thinking," Rool continued, letting his thoughts choose their own path, "to see their

Savior Princess consorting with such abominations. Why didn't anyone do anything about it?"

"Actually," Elora said, "I don't believe anyone knew, outside of my Vizards. From a distance, to anyone looking from the ground or even the palace itself, they're just birds. They only came to visit when no one else was around."

"No one else," Ryn prompted, "besides the Vizards."

Elora nodded.

"They knew," the Wyrrn said. "But they didn't tell."

"Can't be certain," from Franjean.

"Given Elora Danan's position at Court—and what happened to his wife and son—the King would have acted immediately to protect her from even a hint of threat."

"You speak like you know him."

"Not necessarily," Franjean interjected, saving Ryn from any reply. "Your precious king sanctioned the presence of the Maizan in Agnwyn, why not the herons as well? Maybe he believed they'd protect her."

"Nobody," was Rool's retort, "is *that* naive. Present company excepted."

"Enough," Thorn said quietly and, to his amazement, was obeyed. He tried not to let the unexpected achievement go to his head. "We need shelter, we need food, we need rest. Find those, and you can all argue to your hearts' content."

The stag huffed, pawing the ground with a forehoof before using his horns to shunt Thorn around until he was facing the mountain fastness of Doumhall.

"Returning the favor, are you?" he asked the stag, who offered another sharp exhalation that might have been agreement, might even have contained a breath of amusement.

"It is the easiest road," Thorn noted.

"Too easy, do you think?" asked Ryn.

The Nelwyn shrugged. "Prudence dictates we assume the worst, namely that the Deceiver must know we've survived his holocaust. We can't afford to wait for his next move, whether he comes for us himself or uses more surrogates. There's no decent path along the shore, and following any other route means slug-ging our way up and down these gorges. Anybody here feel up to that?"

The silence included even the wind, which chose that mo-ment to pause.

"Right, then, it's decided. To Doumhall we go!"

And with stately tread, the stag led them on their way.

CHAPTER 14

THEY THOUGHT THEY'D HAVE A VIEW ONCE THEY reached the Doumhall heights, the opportunity to properly gain their bearings, but the whole summit of the ancient peak was occluded by the storm. The cloud base settled in about a third of the way up the main slope, and if the winds below were any indication, there was no going any farther.

As it turned out, the stag had no interest in leading them high but picked his way instead along a track that meandered around the broad eastern flank of the mountain. The fire had flowed as Thorn had surmised, cresting across the valleys like a storm surge against a beach, though its greatest intensity appeared to have been concentrated on the hollow where Thorn and the others had taken refuge. The stag set a gentle pace, for his own comfort as much as theirs, but it was soon apparent that had they followed Geryn's lead, only Khory could have possibly escaped alive.

They had to stop more than once, and well before the end, the DemonChild had placed Thorn across her shoulders. He hadn't complained before she picked him up, but he didn't protest either; in truth, his hips were an ever-tightening knotwork of pain and not even spells could keep away the surety that bone ground on bone. Elora looked to Ryn, who lamented being denied the option of switching to a purely four-footed incarnation to make his journey easier. She wasn't in much better shape, devoting her focus mainly to placing one foot safely and surely before the other. She hadn't been hurt, but she was as exhausted as any of them and the stresses of the past days were beginning to make their presence felt, oozing through cracks in the walls she'd built to protect her inner self.

"According to story," the Wyr said, to pass the time, "the world has two ways of ending, in fire or in ice."

"I'm done with endings, I want no more of them," Elora said, refusing to be cheered.

"No problem there, Highne—" He caught himself before she could cast a rebuke. "Elora. Since you proved yourself so adept at chasing away the one, all that's needed is to banish the other."

"I didn't chase anything, you nit! I just talked to them." Despite herself, she flashed a smile of remembrance. "I wish you'd seen them as I did. There were so many textures to their flames, it was if a piece of the sun in the sky had been brought among us and given life."

"Who's to say it wasn't?"

"Who, indeed? They weren't . . . of *us,* do you know what I mean? Not Daikini, not Nelwyn, nor Waking World, nor Veil Folk. We speak so casually of Gods and Powers, yet when I touched them I felt a kind of purity that we can't even dream of."

"An essence transcending mortal physicality."

"You've *seen* them." She clapped delightedly, losing all her hard-won maturity and reminding them all she was still very much only a girl, on the merest cusp of adolescence. "You *know!*"

"Know, perhaps. Seen them, not what you have, nor the way

you mean. They're a Mystery, that's why the word in this context has a capital. What?" he asked suddenly, at the stark alteration in her expression, as though an inner torch had been doused.

"You're talking like a tutor."

"Knowledge does that. Ask the brownies, sterling exceptions that prove the rule."

"I don't think so," scoffed Franjean, from his perch on Thorn's pouch.

"All the airs but none of the learning?" asked Elora. "That isn't very nice. Or, I think, very true." And Rool made a very rude gesture he'd picked up on a military parade ground.

"Stop a moment, Khory, will you, please?" Thorn asked.

A moment later he was riding behind Anele's eyes, enjoying once more her superb view—even circumscribed as it was by the lowering roof of storm clouds—of the world below.

"There's something about this place. . . ." he mused, sharing his thoughts with the great eagle, as always.

"Good, bad, indifferent?"

"Not sure. You?"

"I'm definitely good"—beat—"when I'm not bad. But indifferent, never!"

"You're developing a far too human sense of humor."

"Ah. Forgive me, mage, I had no idea 'humor' was the sole prerogative of you two-leg walkers. Or, for that matter, what you call 'humanity.' "

"Well, it is. The one, anyway."

"And as for the other?"

"I stand suitably corrected." He sighed, sobriety restored.

"Not see what you want?"

"Can't see what I want. The perspective's not right, I need more altitude."

"Not here, not while that city glows and these winds howl."

"How bad do you think it is in there, Anele?"

Now it was her turn to sigh as she measured the power of her wings against that of the storm. She didn't like to come out wanting, but she liked dissembling less.

"Franjean says you stink of Demon—not because you shared a cage with one; he says the taint's a part of your soul."

"I can't deny it, much as I'd wish to."

"Smell much the same to me, old duffer, for what that's worth. But then I key off visuals mainly. Far as Bastian and I are concerned, that wind, *that's* a demon. It's a whirlpool of air, drawing anything it snares to the heart of that damnable city. We heard some wing-born"—and her voice took on a coloration of sorrow—"crying as they were swept past. For help, for mercy. For death. Couldn't offer any of it.

"The vortex sweeps you in, tighter spirals, faster winds, takes all you have just to hold position, there's nothing left to maneuver. Try to go sideways, you end up being swept along until you're right back where you started. You get tired, you lose a little more air; eventually, there's nothing left. And you're lost.

"Going to play hell with migrations, Drumheller. This maelstrom lies smack across one of the major flyways."

"When you and Bastian broke away, when I came to Angwyn, did you mark anything of this peak?"

"All who fly the Bay 'mark' Doumhall, Drumheller, same as the mariners and seafolk do. It's the clearest landmark on the entire coast."

"Have you a distinct memory, Anele, may I see?"

The eagles had been much higher that day, the last full day of sun, and her keen gaze found for him in an instant precisely what he'd been searching for.

"Thank you," he said, as he returned wholly to himself.

"As always. And apologies to the Wyr, from me and Bastian both."

"He'll be more receptive, I think, when he's full healed."

"Fair enough."

"Blessed Bride," he said in a marvel, after Khory set him on the ground, so beside himself he was talking more like Rool. "It's no mountain. I mean, no *natural* mountain. It's a fortress!"

"Drumheller," Ryn asked incredulously, "are you saying somebody *made* this place?"

"Looks that way, yes."

"I thought it was a bedtime story," Ryn was shaking his head in wonder, "something passed down by the Kings in Angwyn to make them seem better than they were."

Once upon a time, he told them, as they continued on, content for the moment to follow the stag's lead—since he, of them all, appeared to have a destination—Gods walked the world. It was a far wilder time, so the story went, and the Powers in play more elemental, composed of utterly primal forces. No subtlety to being or deeds, they displayed a raw, untamed strength that boggled the mind. Wherever they strode, they left their mark, but they were giants in stature as well as accomplishment and those who came after too small in every dimension to comphrehend the wonders they had wrought.

This was one such place.

"Doumhall Mount," the Wyr proclaimed, once the varied, good-natured comments concerning peoples' stature, or lack thereof, had run their course, "seat of the ancient fortress of Angwyn."

Thorn picked up the tale, relating what he'd seen in the eagles' memories.

"You can't tell from the ground; even looking at the mount from out to sea isn't much help because of all the growth that's gone on about it, obscuring the clean lines of the structure. But from the air, from high above, the look of the place suddenly comes apparent. It's the symmetry, you see. The slopes fit too neatly together, they drop too smoothly to the water—hellsteeth, take the mountain itself! You have to go all the way to the continental spine to find anything near as big. Sure, it looks much the same as the rills and ridges that make up the coastal range, only it's three times their size."

The stag picked up its step, to a faster walk, and they hurried to keep pace as it led them through a series of folds in the rock that turned out to be far wider in actuality than first appearance. The whole mountain was an artful blend of optical illusions, and Thorn grabbed at a firefly of memory, of an early voyage with Maulroon when the big man showed him twists and turns in the rivers where it seemed that the water ahead simply . . . ended.

For mile upon mile as they approached, rock walls loomed before them, forming a barrier none could pass. Until they found themselves rounding a sharp bend to discover the stream continuing on as broad and powerful as ever. No wall, merely a chimera of the eye, and it was much the same here. Folds in the rock that, to the distant and casual observer, might be taken for the natural deformations were transformed on closer scrutiny to passages and sally ports, ramparts that stood so tall they put Cherlindrea's woods to shame.

"Is this a door?" Thorn asked in wonderment, bending back so far to see its lintel that he nearly toppled onto his back.

"No moat," commented Ryn, gazing at a parade ground beneath arching drapes of stone that could hold the whole of the Maizan Horde, with room to spare.

"Of *course* there's a moat, you lumping ninny of a hairball." Franjean was in rare form. "You just call it the Bay."

"How old do you think this place is, Drumheller?" Elora asked, as they passed within.

Franjean beat him to the reply—Rool stayed with the eagles, who despite the magnificent space preferred to remain outside— and delighted in it. "Might as well ask, milady, how old's the world."

As they progressed, earthen floor gave way to flagstones, each spanning greater dimensions than the foundation plan of a good-sized Daikini town house.

"Is the whole mountain hollow, d'you think?" Ryn wondered.

"Very likely."

"Must be hell to heat."

"Quite easy, I'd wager," and all eyes went to Khory, as this was the first she'd spoken since coming near the peak. "You can feel it in the bedrock stone, lava streams relatively close beneath the surface."

"Makes sense," agreed Thorn. "Probably thermal springs as well, scattered through the interior."

"What," Ryn exclaimed, "are you saying this is a volcano?"

"All of the assets, none of the liabilities," Thorn told him cheerfully. "If it had any tendency toward eruption, I suspect people would have heard by now."

"Wouldn't be the first time a builder screwed up his location."

"Whoever they were, Taksemanyin, they're long gone—from this place, from the world."

"No offense, Drumheller, but I suggest we follow their example."

"Something wrong?"

"Perhaps I'm like the eagles, I've never been very comfortable under a roof."

"We need the shelter, Ryn, and the rest. Our friend didn't bring us here by accident," and he indicated the stag, standing patiently to the side. "I say, let's have faith in him, as he did in us to save him." He cast his thoughts to Bastian.

"Weather's lowering. Fair day, wicked night."

"Have you a place to rook?"

Bastian made a dismissive noise. "Not close by, thanks to those firedrakes. Safe haven in a tree places us too far up the coast to do you any decent service. If there's any shelter on these crags, here on Doumhall proper, it's above the cloud line. I can taste the ice forming. We go there, we'll freeze."

"Doesn't leave much in the way of options."

"Rool feels much the same."

"Will you come inside, then?"

"Don't look for us, trust us to find you."

"Take care, my friend."

"Always. You, the same."

He returned to himself to find Khory watching him intently, hunkered down on her heels so they were on the same level. In the distant background, Ryn and Elora busied themselves finding fuel for a fire.

"The eagles aren't happy," Franjean told her, tucked in close to Thorn's side and hoping the information would satisfy the DemonChild enough to make her stroll away.

"What's your problem?" she asked him levelly, at which point the brownie went spectacularly ballistic, a fireworks display of arms and legs and speech, all working wildly at once as he charged forward, uncaring of the size differential between them.

"You!" he squawked. "You you *you*! I know you for what you are, dissembler, and where you rightly belong—which *isn't* in the company of decent folks."

"Odd," Thorn couldn't resist interjecting, "I've heard much the same said about you, Franjean."

"Oh"—the brownie turned the most exaggerated look of dismissal on Thorn—"how *droll*. I am so struck to the quick!"

"Would it were so, that we might have ourselves a little peace."

"You—you're standing up for this, this *thing*?"

"Khory is quite capable of 'standing up' for herself. But she's as much my friend as you are and deserves the same respect and courtesy."

The brownie's mouth gaped as he struggled to find an appropriate, preferably lethal, rejoinder. Gaped wider (in appearance, like a fish gobbling for food) as nothing came, not the slightest flash of inspiration. His teeth came together with a sharp and resounding *clack* and he spun on his heel to stalk stiff-legged away, muttering determinedly that he'd have no more truck with such foolishness and ingratitude.

"Why do I suspect that I will pay for this, in full measure?"

"What else are friends for, mage?"

"Surprised me, too, saying that," he told her honestly, face turning into a frown that betokened mostly confusion.

"Did you mean it?"

Took a deep breath before replying, because he still wasn't wholly sure. And decided, in that breath, to cast rationality away, as he had with the deer, and let his instincts speak for him. *The High Aldwyn,* he thought, *would be proud.*

"Wouldn't have said so, otherwise."

Since none of the others knew how, Thorn had to light their fire, and in any other venue it would have been a most impressive blaze. But they were crouched in a hearth that stretched wider than a jousting pitch and stood half as high as a cathedral. The chamber itself was beyond superlatives. Elora's Aerie fell far short of the ceiling and the King's Palace could have been lost in a corner. The walls rose in a gentle arch, but the scale of construction was so huge that Thorn couldn't easily tell which elements were due to the ravages of time and which were ornamentation; it was too hard for the eye to wholly encompass the scope. A single glance wouldn't do; too often, he was forced to scan from side to side to take it all in. He heard a jest from Ryn about what it would take to light the room—one of the towering trees from Cherlindrea's forest would do nicely, with a firedrake to set its crown alight—but the truth appeared both more prosaic and breathtakingly beautiful. As the comparatively minuscule fire they'd laid in the hearth cast its glow outward, that light was caught by crystalline threads in the very fabric of the rock. This wasn't simply a reflection, the light was somehow absorbed, each thread energized throughout its length in the same way that heat flows down a strand of metal until the entire piece is warm to the touch. The threads cast no direct light—the shadows were still primarily cast from the fireplace—but that was because the source was too weak. For Thorn and his companions, they established a background ambient texture that sparkled like a starlit sky, an everchanging panoply of color and intensity. Were the hearth in proper use, the room would have been awash in brilliance.

"Hoy, Franjean," called Ryn as Thorn sliced vegetables for cooking (under the circumstances, with the stag close by, he thought it inappropriate to serve any kind of meat), "you Wee Folk are supposed to know all there is—"

"About everything worth knowing, yes," the brownie deigned to reply, from his distant perch midway up a fireplace cornice.

"Anything about where we are?"

"There's the obvious, that one could fit the whole of the Royal Angwyn kitchen into this single hearth."

"We know they built big."

"Gods don't like to think about the Gods that came before. You Daikini are supposed to have the exclusive market on mortality."

"And I'm sure," Elora interjected smoothly, "if Ryn were Daikini, he'd feel properly humble."

"Ever wonder, though," Ryn went on, "about what comes after? In their day, think of those who dwelled here. Were they the ones who made the world? What were they like, to make their homes of mountains? Where'd they go? How would they feel to be forgotten? How will we, when it's our turn?"

"Brownies, cretin, are *never* forgotten, so long as the memory of one of us lives, so live we all!"

"My point, exactly. What happens when even the memory dies?"

"Somber thought, Ryn," Thorn said, "for so generally merry a folk."

"It hasn't been a merry few days, mage. People lived here, now they don't. Same was said of Nockmaar and Tir Asleen and now Angwyn. The world turns, but where does it go?" He shrugged, suddenly, disarmingly, disturbingly human in stance and gesture, as though another had stepped forth to live for a time within his skin.

"I swim, I hunt, I play," he said, "I try to do none lasting harm, and think nothing amiss in asking much the same in return. How many folk in that city across the way walked their waking days by the same rules? How many of my brethren will suffer from the storm that killed Morag? *Mortal* I may be, Peckling"—and he rounded on Franjean as he spoke, with a thread of real anger laced through his words, "but does that give Gods and Goddesses the right to rip my life to shreds as though I was no more than a piece on their game board? If they want a war, let them find a place to do it that leaves the rest of us the hell *alone!*" He finished with a shout that boomed and echoed off the stone rafters and took a long time to fade away.

"Bavmorda was no God," Thorn said simply. "She was a woman with tainted dreams—and the desire and ability to make them real. And for all the fanfare, Elora's no God, either."

"No God," the girl said, trying for humor but coming up short, because her description of herself was what she believed to be the truth, "no dreams, no desire, no ability."

"I don't know," Ryn continued helplessly, waving away the plate of food Thorn offered and a cup of steaming broth as well while he paced back and forth before the fire, as though he were in a cage. "I've heard the stories. If this Bavmorda was such an abomination, why'd the Great Powers have to drag that Nelwyn into it? What's'isname?"

"Willow Ufgood," Elora told him softly, and then, more softly still, her memory of the tower haunting her features, fading the rich, dark blue of her eyes, which turned inexorably toward Thorn, "my protector."

"Why any need for a Sacred Princess at all? Why didn't they simply slap Bavmorda down and have done with it?"

"Why not ask them yourself?" Thorn said, draining the last of his own cup.

Ryn looked puzzled a moment, before noticing that Thorn was looking past him, as was Khory. Even Franjean had fallen silent. Only Elora, staring into the heart of the flames as though she might find the transcendence she'd touched oh so briefly with the firedrakes, paid not the slightest heed.

The great, vaulting hall was empty no longer.

Throughout their trek up from the beach, they'd remarked on the emptiness of the forest, not an animal to be seen or heard, as though none had ever been. Now they knew why.

All stood before them, from the smallest bugs and lizards to full-grown mountain cats and highland rams. Birds and beasts together, hunters and prey, amongst their own kind or mixed in with others, some standing alone, others with families clustered close by, the very old and the barely born. They stood and stared, with an air of patient expectation, and the thought came to Thorn that he had come into some fantastical court, with this multitude the jury.

Dead center—in the room, in the gathering—was the stag, and as Thorn rose to his feet and started forward, so did he. Only the beast's aspect changed with every deliberate step, flesh and sinew running like wax or mercury, turning him to fox and owl and raven and mouse and spider, so that by the time he finally came to stand before the Nelwyn he had manifested the form of every creature present.

Including, at the last, a passable imitation of a Daikini.

He was tall and he'd seen better days; the one constant throughout his ongoing metamorphosis was the legacy of his burns, and in each instance he wore them as a badge of honor. The hair of his head had been reduced to scrappy stubble, his beard the same. The day's travel had weathered his skin some, but it still possessed the roseate pink of a baby's flesh and he held himself as though the very touch of the air was an irritation. He still wore horns, though not so huge on a human head as when he was a stag. They formed a sleek curve up and back from the flanks of his skull, each with three nasty, sharp points.

"Why?" he demanded, without preamble or introduction.

"I don't know," was all the answer Thorn could find.

"This was a blessed place," the man said, his voice as raw as his flesh, and there was a pain in it that had nothing to do with his wounds. "All within lived in peace and harmony."

"I know. I'm sorry."

"The balance is broken. The land screams because its spirit is no more."

He saw Cherlindrea, as silver in her way as Elora had become, that glow dulled, the bright glory of her eyes as ensnared by the Deceiver's lies as her body was by his web of evil.

"We are all of the world," Thorn said, with a passion of his own. "In our way we have all suffered. But we survive, we persevere. As Franjean said, about his own folk—so long as one of us lives, there is hope. From that hope, rebirth."

"Words!" the StagLord shrieked, hand flashing up and down faster than the eye could follow, changing as it swept across Thorn's face to grow a brace of claws in place of fingers. He felt a sting and saw blood fly but otherwise took no notice of the strike as the StagLord raised his hand—truly a human hand once more, as normal in appearance as Thorn's own—to show its scarlet fingertips to the assemblage.

"Is that what you'd prefer?" he asked of the taller man, after quelling Khory with a silent glare. She'd crossed almost the whole distance to him, starting the instant the StagLord raised his hand, gathering speed with every loping step in a charge that would have ended with her plunging past him, her sword slicing across him level with his shoulders to claim his head, and into the heart of the gathering beyond.

"That there be war where once was peace," Thorn continued, without making any effort to stem the flow of blood down his slashed cheek. If the StagLord was bothered by Khory's aborted attack, as Taksemanyin placed himself bodily in her way and pressed her—gently, insistently, inexorably—back toward the wall, it didn't show.

"If such is your hope," the StagLord replied, "it comes too late." And a rustle of agreement made its way across the assemblage.

"We come as friends!"

"What was once given freely, manling, must now be earned."

He thrust out his right arm, and Thorn's blood leaped forth from outstretched fingers, becoming the rough-braided body of a whip, to rake diagonally across Elora's back from shoulder to hip.

"If you would regain your rightful place amongst us," the Stag-Lord thundered, "you must prove yourselves worthy." This time his cry was echoed by a susurrus of voices from the assemblage, redolent with a rage and a hunger for vengeance that allowed little chance for mercy.

The fire was blazing more brightly, far beyond the capacity of the combustibles that had been found for it, reaching up and outward to the side as though the hearth were remembering the way things were when it was young and well used. Too late, Thorn saw that Elora sat too close; he couldn't go to her; he dared not turn his back on the StagLord, sensing he'd be impaled within a brace of steps, but aware as well that it was too hot for Ryn or Khory to try either.

The whip slash left a wicked trail across her shirt, and should have cut her to the bone—but as they watched, the stain faded away, until there wasn't a mark on her shirt. The cloth was as pristine as when it first was woven and by implication the skin beneath as well.

"She is the great Betrayer," accused Cherlindrea's forest consort, taking her immunity to his attack as proof positive of his indictment.

"Not so," denied Thorn, with passion to match.

"All came to pay her homage."

"And were deceived. As was she."

"More words."

"True words!"

"Spoken by one who would say anything to save her!"

"I saved *you!*"

"And that has earned you the right to be heard, and judged fairly."

The blood whip came now for him, his vision flooding scarlet as tendrils stabbed through his eyes and poured fury into every particle of his body. The StagLord thrust himself forward, hands grasping Thorn beneath the armpits and lifting him high overhead until he was poised on the tips of the man's horns. The energies of the blood whip arced around and through them both, spread-eagling Thorn and stretching his extremities to their utmost until joints began to pop from their sockets; his mouth had likewise gone wide as flesh would allow, teeth bared to such an extent he thought all the component parts of him would tear apart, his expression twisting into a rictus of unbearable agony that he knew was but a fraction of what the StagLord had endured running through the fire.

He and the StagLord had shared blood, now they shared life, the skeins of their pasts rising from every orifice, right down to the pores of their skin, and Thorn found himself in the depths of the primeval wood, moving with stately grace on four hoofed feet, secure in his speed and strength, and the deadly prongs that tipped his antlers, to keep him safe. Wherever Cherlindrea had a grove, there was he able to roam, moving with the ease of thought from one to another regardless of the distance between them. On solstice and equinox he and his lady met for a moonlit dance, casting through a myriad of forms in celebration of the diversity of life within their realm. Sprites and fairies streaked the air with rainbows that were in turn lit from within by an array of cascading sparkles, creating the same riotous patterns of glittering diamonds that could be seen watching the moon cast its glow across the ocean surface. Even in the depth of winter, their bower was bedecked with garlands, and from the elemental passion of their love came a surge of renewal for both the woodland and the creatures who dwelled within.

When Cherlindrea was ensorcelled, it was as though the heart had been cut from both her consort and the land he nurtured. It had been a struggle to shift halfway across the world to this grove, and he arrived to find the firedrakes already at work. He'd wasted no time, but rushed to the defense of its inhabitants. There'd been none of the Veil Folk to rescue, trees were empty of dryads, ponds and streams of nymphs; no elves, no fairies, no pixies, nor nixies, brownies, or trolls. Only the denizens of the waking world, and those he herded with increasingly reckless desperation to the hoped-for refuge of ancient Angwyn. The firedrakes tried to stop him, for the sport of living prey excited them even more than the joy they found in simple burning, but here his strength stood him in good stead. And to the surprise of the elemental fire creatures, his rack proved as formidable against them as any corporeal foe.

But the woods about him had become a hollow place, bereft of any aspect of the divinity he worshiped, and far poorer for the loss of her. He wasn't the first to share her arbor; his desperate fear was that he would be the last.

"I," Thorn cried, each word a hoarse shout, like a man uttering his last testament. "Fight. For. What. I. Believe!"

"And what is that, manling?"

Pain vanished; with it, all support, as the StagLord cast him to the stone floor. He'd been pulled so taut that nothing about his body felt like it fit together any longer, not jaw, not teeth, sentences emerging as though he had marbles in his mouth.

"Elora Danan spoke for your life," he said from all fours, as though he were the beast here. "Doesn't that count for something?"

"You speak with passion for the Betrayer, mortal. Say you nothing for yourself?"

"She's no more your betrayer than I am."

"Have a care, lest you condemn yourself."

"Slain by friends or foe, the end's the same. I'm sorry for the damage that's been done here. But you're not the first to suffer so, nor—heaven have mercy—the last, and of a certainty nowhere near among those who've suffered worst! I don't know why the patterns have been broken, perhaps that was necessary to re-form them in a new and better way. But it's done. Wish all you please for something different, the world is as it is, we have to make the best of it.

"For myself, that means I'll fight. For Elora Danan, against the Deceiver. You've seen my heart"—and he regained his feet to confront the StagLord full in the face, as though there was no longer a size difference between them—"both when I healed you and now, with this judgment. And through me, my friends. That is truth. We are not your enemies, lord, and that child is all the hope of the world!"

"How noble a sentiment, Peck," intruded the Deceiver's voice, too familiar by half, the sound of it stabbing at Thorn like a dagger, as resonant here as it had been in Elora's tower.

At the same moment a shape flashed past the corner of Thorn's vision and he sprang toward it seconds too late to catch Bastian and Anele before the eagles' broken bodies, bound cruelly in a barbed capture net, bounced on the flagstones. He had his knife out by the time he reached his friends, and he used a dollop of Power to add keenness to the blade, strength to his swing, as he slashed at the mesh. All he saw was blood, and the eagles' rapidly dimming eyes; all he could think of was the anguish of losing another that he loved, and how much their strength was needed for the coming battle. He never stopped to consider why he'd felt no hint of any attack over the link he shared with the two great raptors, if not from them then surely from Rool. He saw what he was supposed to see; out of fatigue, out of fear, out of love, he never turned to InSight to make sure it was real.

Too late, as he touched the net, he realized he'd been tricked and the sight before him, an intentionally cruel illusion. The strands flowed out and up and over him, the barbs reversing themselves to stab through clothes and skin and fill him with a poison that numbed his limbs and flooded him with an agony that far surpassed even what the StagLord had just put him through. In the meantime the eagles' forms altered as well, legs and necks elongating, bills stabbing outward into something best resembling a rapier, bodies swelling to twice their original size, with wings whose span surpassed the height of a tall Daikini.

At first look, Night Herons appeared black, but it was really the darkest of blues, noticeable only as highlights at the tips of their feathers, or when sun or firelight touched them just so. Their accent colors were an equally dusky red. They were the essence of sorcerous power cast into a semblance of flesh.

One of the pair stooped for the StagLord, who used his whip to fair effect, raking it across the body of the creature. The heron staggered in flight, a raw lesion opening across its breast, but that blow had taken all that remained of the whip's power and it sizzled to nothingness in the StagLord's grasp. He'd meant it only as a delaying tactic, however, and took the moment's grace to shift back to his cervine form. Without the slightest hesitation, he stabbed forward, catching the heron across the throat with crown and royal antlers, before finishing the job with his brow set in a lifting strike that opened the predator from abdomen to throat. He belled his challenge as he cast the already decaying carcass aside, but the triumph was brutally short-lived; as he reared up on his hind legs to rally all his domain, he was struck from every side, by so many crossbow quarrels that it seemed in that one appalling instant as though he'd been turned into a living pincushion.

His legs collapsed as he landed, folding at knees and shoulder and sending him crashing partially to ground before Thorn, who fought against his own bonds in a futile attempt to go to the stag's aid. Somehow, the beast twisted a foot into place and began to struggle upright.

There was a tumult toward the rear of the huge chamber, and a pair of horses burst into view, one black, the other white, the same color as their riders. The woman reined in her mare as the scene came fully into view, but her companion spurred his own mount into a full charge, sending animals scrambling frantically from his path. Some snarled defiance, a very few made reflexive moves to attack, but snipers from hidey-holes scattered high along the walls cut them down with ease. Panic swept the assemblage with the consuming ferocity of a wildfire, and here and there across the vast space some of the animals broke for freedom.

Thorn was bawling defiance, it was all he could do, make these idiot sounds; the poison had severed the linkages between mind and voice, stripping him of the ability to express himself with any coherence. The StagLord knew what was coming and he was determined not to be found wanting. The Castellan leveled his spear, his stallion eating the distance between them. It seemed so easy. The stag stood much as he had atop the reef, legs splayed, chest heaving—only in this instance, each pump of his heart sent another helping of his life pouring through a skin festooned with iron quills. There was blood on his muzzle and streaming from his mouth, together with a crimson froth that meant his lungs had been punctured. He was angled away from his attacker, preferring in this last moment to share his glance with Thorn. There was no regret in his dark eyes, only a grim anticipation.

At the moment of contact, the StagLord spun with a speed and strength that none suspected were left in him. The spear was bang on target, punching through the solid bone of the beast's shoulder, through both lungs and the noble beast's indomitable heart. Simultaneously, though, the stag raked its crown the length of the horse's flank.

The stallion screamed like a woman, a high-pitched ululation that resounded through the hall, freakishly gaining in intensity before it began to fade away. There was a cry from the Castellan as well as the animal reared and pitched itself aside, allowing no chance for its rider to leap free before crashing down atop him.

It was as though that fall was a signal. The archers lay down an indiscriminate fire, as quickly as they could reload, choosing what they saw as the most dangerous targets among the gathering, namely the great, fanged predators. But neither cats nor wolves—nor anyone else, for that matter—stayed still to be massacred. The whole floor began to move, in every conceivable direction, as though it were a pool of water suddenly unleashed down an open drain.

Through that living chaos surged the Princess Anakerie, urging her mare with more care than the Castellan had shown but no less determination, reaching him more quickly than any of his men. The StagLord was dead, as was the horse, and Anakerie's ragged cries went unheard at first, amidst the howling, rowling cacophony of roars, yips, squeals, squawks, and chitters, not to mention the scrabble of every kind of foot upon the stone, as the animals all fled. And the more than occasional scream, as each side took its toll of the other.

Stillness returned to the room without warning. Looking about herself, Anakerie could see a fair share of bodies, but less than nothing compared with the multitude that had been, and she couldn't help a shudder at the memory of the exodus of animals from Angwyn only a few nights before.

"I need a *healer*!" she roared again, hooking her arms beneath the Maizan's shoulders and bracing a foot against his saddle, the better to heave him free. He was a mess, one leg slashed multiple times to the bone, a wicked gash along his flank as well, so sodden with blood that she was sure a major vessel had been severed, while the other leg was visibly broken above and below the knee. She stripped a belt from her harness, wrapped it tight about his thigh, as snug to the crotch as it would go, then twisted it again and again until the pulsing stream slowed to the merest trickle.

"Damn you, Peck," she snarled at Thorn, making no attempt to hide the raw fury on her face, "for what you've done."

"No fear, my dear," called the Deceiver from the hearth, " 'twill soon turn out aright."

"Mohdri's dying, wizard, can you do something about *that*?"

"At the moment, regretfully, no," the Deceiver said.

Thorn cursed the fact that he was draped away from the hearth, with no idea what was happening there. The poison had crippled his InSight, he couldn't see through his friends' eyes. It had been years since he'd last been headblind and it wasn't a treat.

"But your Peck's a healer, brought stag and Wyr both back from the brink. Make him an offer he can't refuse, I'm sure he'll see his way clear to offer you similar service."

She took Thorn by his bonds, hauling him hard and high, ignoring the grimaces as its barbs stabbed him.

"Fair deal, Peck," she said, "the Castellan's life for yours."

He wanted to ask why she cared so much, for someone who had to be her deadly enemy, and ask as well what force her pledge had in a room full of Maizan. So it was probably for the best that he couldn't say a word.

Instinct once more spoke for him, with the only movement he could manage, the barest nod of his head.

Once released, he tried to take a moment on the floor to gather his wits, but a rough hand grabbed him by the scruff and set him upright.

It was Geryn Havilhand, in the leathers of a captain of the Red Lions.

Khory and Taksemanyin had been separated and moved to opposite ends of the great fireplace, there lashed in place against the massive andirons and watched by guards with ready swords. Elora hadn't moved from where she knelt before the fire; only now that blaze stretched from one end of the hearth to the other, the tips of its flames vanishing above the lintel. Before her, in the heart of the inferno, stood the Deceiver.

As tall as before, as beautiful, the picture-perfect hero—and yet . . . to Thorn's eye there were pieces missing. A softening around the edges, as though the figure were somehow losing definition, the way an object might look to someone with weak eyes. Thorn's were perfect (bless his powers); the wrongness wasn't his, but the Deceiver's. His eyes looked a fraction more hollow, as did the drape of skin below his cheekbones, and the skin itself had lost a measure of resilience. Whatever had happened since the aerie had visibly diminished him.

"For what it's worth, Nelwyn," the Deceiver said, "I meant for none of this."

"Is this some plea for absolution?" He spoke slowly, rounding his words as though he had trouble speaking. "Am I supposed to care?"

"Always, you judge me," the face remaining no less perfect in fury. And he understood his foe meant more by "always" than these past days, another piece for his mosaic, making no more sense than the rest. "As the StagLord did you. Have a care, lest you share his fate as well." Then, calm returned, the mask slipped once more back into place. "Do your work, little sorcerer," the Deceiver said dismissively, "while I do mine."

Thorn turned to Anakerie. "Let Elora Danan go, I'll save your prince."

"Waste of breath, Peck," the Deceiver said over its shoulder, throwing the words directly into Thorn's mind, where no one else could hear them. "She's not the power here."

"What's this, then?" Thorn asked of Geryn as he was escorted to the fallen warrior.

"I'm a soldier of the King. I swore an oath," the lad replied proudly, as if that explained all.

"And you, what's your excuse?" he demanded of the Princess as she unlaced Mohdri's helm.

Geryn cuffed him soundly. "She's Princess Royal," he admonished, "an' yeh keep a respectful tongue in yer head, Peck, or suffer for it!"

"I'm Princess Royal of the Realm," Anakerie replied, with a formality of speech Thorn hadn't expected, at odds with her brusque, matter-of-fact battlefield manner, "and I too swore an oath."

She pulled Mohdri's helm free—and therein, Thorn thought, lay perhaps part of the answer. It was a haunting face, defined by planes and angles so sharp they might have been cut by a master stonemason, as many edges to his features as to his personality; in feature, in body, here was a man distilled to his quintessence, pale of skin, with hair of white gold. As little color to his eyes, even allowing for the significant loss of blood.

He's not good enough for you, he thought, shifting his gaze from one to the other, and wondered if Anakerie read that in his face because she flushed and turned her hawklike gaze away. *But I can see why you might think otherwise.* Because for all the cruelty and calculation that swam in the turbulence of the Castellan's spirit, there was also true feeling, a regard for this woman, possibly even love, that surprised the Maizan above all.

"Please," she said, and he knew it cost her to say so, "he's dying."

"Stop stalling, Peck!" snapped Geryn, with a not-so-gentle clout to the shoulder. "And yeh'll na' be needin' these!" With a thrusting twist of his short sword, he severed Thorn's belt and quickly sidekicked the pouches out of reach.

No matter. Thorn's offside hand came out of his vest pocket closed about a pair of acorns: one for each of them, followed by a solid punch to shatter them to bits. He kept them as keepsakes, to remind him of a time when both the power and the ability of a sorcerer were still mostly dreams. But they served a practical purpose as well. The acorns were a very basic magic, not the sort of thing any foe worth the name would expect. For the same reason, he practiced his old sleight-of-hand tricks; every scrap of knowledge, no matter how seemingly trivial, was an asset, never to be discarded. Because a body never knew when it might come in handy. Unfortunately, he had no idea what to do with the snipers, or the guards watching Khory or Ryn, or most especially how to deal with the Deceiver. His only certainty was that once he began his work on the Castellan, Elora was doomed.

"I'm glad you've found your heart's desire, Geryn," he said. "I pray this lays your ghosts to rest."

The Daikini's blade lightly touched his lips. "No sweet words, Peck," Thorn was warned, "lest yeh lose the tongue t' speak 'em, get my meaning?"

"It's your destiny, Elora Danan," he heard in his mind from the hearth, and knew the Spell of Dissolution was once more being woven.

"To reach out your hand across the Domains, and know your will is Law; that's not so horrible a thing? To wipe away hatred, fear, greed. They are prideful folk, they require a strong will to master them. Not yours, I'm sorry to say"—and there was true regret in the words—"but every prize of value has its price."

Thorn couldn't help himself; he turned and saw the two figures separated by a boundary of cold flame. The Deceiver had a small advantage of height on Elora, though in manner he seemed much taller, with a commanding presence that matched the Castellan's. His hand was outstretched, his body curved forward along the back in eager anticipation, Elora's matching him in every gesture, every expression. Fire rippled in the Deceiver's grasp and leaped across to hers.

"I won't beg, Nelwyn," said the Princess. "But I won't let Mohdri die unavenged."

He faced her. "That's not salvation happening over there, Highness, it's doom!"

"Your word against his, and he's her protector." And in an undertone she cast toward him over the link they shared, *And the power, Drumheller. Both here and in Angwyn.*

He took another look, without a care for the blade that Geryn lay across his throat hard enough to draw a line of blood. Elora had her arms wrapped about herself, the Deceiver's wrapped about her, as though the one were enclosing the other, and about them all swirled a nexus of flame, become a living being all its own. Thorn heard the chatter of teeth, clamping his mouth tight upon the realization they were his own, and used a portion of his own magic to stoke the hearthfire within his flesh against the growing cold. There was an air of tension about Geryn, shared by the Maizan Thorn could see, born of the sudden fear that they were all to be frozen now as Angwyn had been.

"The way of the world is so hard, Elora Danan," crooned the Deceiver, almost as though he were speaking more to himself than to another, with a wilding change to his voice that struck

Thorn with that same disconcerting sense of familiarity he felt in Elora's hall. He knew the face of Willow was a mask, but wondered more than ever about what lay behind it. "So much pain. So much grief. You want none of that. Accept the pattern laid out for you, let things happen as they were ordained. Embrace the fire, let it burn away all troubles, all cares; be one, little spirit, with the oblivion that should have been yours at birth. Let us be One."

They all watched, even Mohdri with the last scraps of consciousness and life left him. Thorn had never seen so artful a seduction, never imagined such a thing possible as the Deceiver spoke longingly, lovingly, of all the secret places in Elora's heart. It was as if that abomination knew the child better than she did herself, as it wove a glorious tapestry of desire with thread drawn from Elora's soul. Another figure came into being before them both, facing the fire, a gossamer frame at first, whose general size and proportions approximated Elora's. But with each caressing phrase, with each new strand drawn outward from the child, the simulacrum grew more real, taking on shape and form and substance until it seemed as though the hearth had become a mirror.

It was then that Thorn, with blinking eye and shaking head, realized that the Deceiver had nearly faded away. The outline of the creature still remained, but it had lost almost all substance, to the point where it had become as translucent as a pane of flawed glass, through which could be seen only the inferno that it had created, making it the embodiment of living flame. The same delicate threads that had been drawn from Elora now emerged from the Deceiver's own flesh, striking forth like cobras to claim their prey.

Thorn's mouth opened, to cry a last denial . . .

. . . but it was Elora who spoke.

It was the voice that came to her on Morag's schooner, her legacy of the storm, erupting from the bottom of her belly with a strength none present, and the child most of all, ever suspected she possessed, a cry of defiance coupled with a fierce lunge forward from the flames. She smashed through her likeness, the creature combusting at her touch, momentum and a lack of balance sending Elora tumbling to the floor. A fortunate fall, because right on her heels came a terrible gout of flame that spewed forth from the Deceiver's outstretched hands like the Wrath of Ages, incinerating with cold whatever lay before it. The bodies of the StagLord and the castellan's horse were most notably in the way; they twinkled under an instant coating of hoarfrost, like objects frozen beneath a cloudless winter moon. Then their own weight proved more than their fragile, crystalline substance could bear, and they shattered.

A cry from above announced the fall of a sniper, blown from his perch as though shot from a catapult, with force enough to send him to a landing better than halfway across the immensity of the hall. That same moment Anele stooped for Geryn's eyes, dropping from the roof with wings folded tight to her side in a classic attack, throwing them wide at the last possible instant, using both the sound of wind slap and the shock of the air to disorient her target for the moment she would need to strike. He'd have lost them for sure then, had Anakerie not been a fraction faster than the eagle and kicked the young Daikini's legs out from under him. Anele scored his helm, and one claw left its mark across his forehead, but he got away with his sight, with his looks, with his life. And the knowledge that his princess had saved him.

He was up in an instant, cloak rolled over one forearm as a shield, sword in hand to give better than he got, but the eagle was gone. He turned to lash out at Thorn, but the Nelwyn had followed her example. After that, he had more pressing concerns.

Khory was free, Franjean's doing. Taksemanyin was loose as well (accomplished all by his lonesome). Geryn looked to the sniper posts along the wall, called for suppression arrowfire, but heard only echoes of his own voice in reply.

"Elora Danan," Anakerie screamed as the sounds of battle built upon themselves, until the resonant shell of the hall made it sound as if an army was engaged within, "find her, you'll find the Nelwyn! I want him *alive!*"

Thorn had already reached her, skibbling along the floor like a bug to keep from being noticed in the confusion, praying with all his heart that Elora hadn't been caught in the eruption of icefire. She had much the same idea, going the other way. Neither knew the other was so close at hand until they had a sudden meeting of minds.

"Ow!" in unison.

Thorn felt as though he'd been clonked by a hammer and was sure his skull had been cracked right straight through to the brainpan. He was also starting to suspect that Elora's silvery exterior wasn't just looks anymore. She gave the lie to that by grabbing his hand—his was chill as ice, hers surprisingly warm—and hauling him bodily toward Khory, leaving eagles and brownies to cover Ryn.

"You should have stayed a farmer, Nelwyn."

He knew what was coming, the Deceiver's voice was that of a magister pronouncing sentence of death. He moved to break Elora's hold on him and give her as hard a shove as he was able to throw her well clear, but she proved herself a step ahead of him, pivoting one way as he went the other to place herself between him and their foe. In that instant, as he realized what she'd done and cried out in futile protest, another gout of flame exploded from the Deceiver's hand.

He thought they were both dead.

But the flames passed her by, and him as well since he stood right behind her.

"Bless my soul," was what he said. What he did was pitch his acorn up and over, as he would a ball, right into the heart of the inferno.

There was a tiny, brilliant, absolutely blinding pop of light, and the flames stopped.

They became solid, in an ongoing cascade of petrifaction that rushed headlong back the way they'd come to engulf the whole of the magical fire that filled the hearth. The Deceiver had time for a look of true astonishment, and then, with a congratulatory tip of the head to Thorn, that false face began to laugh. The echoes of it lasted long after the entity itself had turned to stone.

It was as though, for a moment, when the duel was done, Thorn had become the only living thing in the room. He heard no other sound but his own breath, was aware of no other reality but the thunderous beating of his heart.

Too easy, he thought. *We're not done yet, are we, you and I?*

He cast about for a weapon, anything that inspiration would bring to hand as a hammer to smash the statue to powder. What came instead was Geryn, and Thorn dropped flat in a diving roll that tripped up the Daikini and sent him sprawling. Trained fighter that he was, Geryn was on his feet before he stopped rolling. Unfortunately, he found himself facing Taksemanyin. The Pathfinder made a fair try, but while he had training and heart, the Wyr far overmatched him in skill. Geryn lunged, to find his sword batted aside, then had to scrabble desperately aside to avoid Tak's counterslash, the spike blades missing by the proverbial hair. Dumb luck worked in Geryn's favor then, as his clumsy tumble brought his sword around faster than Ryn had anticipated; this time, it was the Wyr who had to hurl himself through a wild evasion in order to avoid impalement.

In the heat of the engagement, Geryn had forgotten about Thorn. The Nelwyn had a blade of his own, but he and the boy had been good companions on the trail and he couldn't bring himself to use it. Geryn saw the knife, thought for that instant he was done, but it was Thorn's fist that dropped him. Ryn scooped up the Pathfinder's sword, grasping it with the awkward grace of one long and well trained in its use, but who hadn't held the damn thing in an age, using the threat of it to keep the Maizan cautious while he and Thorn made tracks for their friends.

Whether from anger or exertion, Elora's sweat-damp skin seemed to have developed the ability to glow. It made for a startling visual, the child's hair streaming like a silver pennant as she scooped up a cudgel and laid into the nearest Maizan with a vengeance she must have been storing up for years. Her problem was, enthusiasm and desire were no match for training and experience. She got in one good swing, regrettably blunted by the warrior's body armor, and then another Maizan looped her about the legs with his whip.

Ryn took care of him, whipping his blade two-handed across the man's belly with force enough to lift him off his feet and bend him double. Thorn caught the other one struggling up, and stroked the man's throat with his blade—no mercy for the Maizan as he'd had for Geryn—springing clear with Elora before the blood could fountain.

Khory faced a pair, and they were very good. For the initial exchange, she had just enough skill to hold her own. She used the andiron for cover, sliding back and forth between her foes, touching one blade, then the other, calling on the agility of her body to save her when the sword couldn't manage. What she saw, she learned; what she learned, she put to immediate use; in a brace of heartbeats, the Maizan realized they were facing a woman who would soon be a match for both.

They were brave, they weren't fools. Pressed suddenly from two sides, they scrambled clear and cast about for either reinforcements or weapons to drop their foes from range.

The same applied to Thorn. He swept the room as the Maizan formed themselves into a double line of skirmishers, spreading wide enough to block the fugitives away from any exits. There were pikes among them, and bows; their losses thus far had been mostly due to surprise; they weren't about to let that happen again. Someone among them spotted Anele as she soared across the scene; arrows were in flight before the warning shout could form its first echo. Deadly shots, too; she avoided being hit only by tucking her wings tight and turning herself into a feathered missile, booming out of her madcap descent behind the cover of Khory and Tak's bodies. The DemonChild took a silent cue from Thorn and plucked the eagle from the air, tucking her close to her side, both arms wrapped tight about her. Anele didn't like being carried, but she saw the wisdom of the moment and held her peace.

"Lay down your weapons," called Anakerie. "I won't offer twice."

For emphasis, one of the Maizan loosed a shaft for Khory's leg to cripple her, but Ryn, with the blistering speed they'd come to take for granted, slapped it down with a sideswipe of his own blade. Thorn had sidled behind the two taller figures as well, drawing Elora with him, until his back was to the wall; he had no idea whether what worked in the dungeon would apply here. There, in addition, he'd had the Demon's strength to help. But there was also nowhere else to go.

"Elora." He was gulping breaths, working himself into a state of mindless terror. "Do you trust me, girl?"

"I think so, yes."

"Step behind me, then." And when she'd done that: "Wrap your arms about me, and hold tight."

"I'm afraid, Thorn."

It was the first time she'd called him by name. He gave her clasped hands a comforting squeeze, adding a sideways kiss to her cheek snugged right beside his own, a burst of tears sliding from her face to his as though there were no separation between them.

"So am I, little moonshade."

"Now what?"

"Remember the tower?"

Her jaw dropped, his hands lashed out to grab Khory by the belt and Ryn by his back fur—a hefty handful of both—and Thorn heaved the lot of them backward with him into the wall.

CHAPTER
15

"Are we safe?" Elora asked, when at long last they emerged into an upper gallery.

In that initial surge, as they were immersed completely in the ancient rock, they were almost lost, as everyone panicked at once, only to be swiftly, ruthlessly cowed by a grim-edged snarl from Thorn.

"Be *still*!" he'd told them, mandating absolute obedience. "Cue your movements to mine, let me take the initiative. The stones here are far older than the palace and a lot more hard of hearing; they didn't answer when I asked for permission to move through their domain. They may not appreciate trespassers. But if we don't make too much of a rumpus, I think we can pass in safety."

"And if you're wrong?" Ryn had to ask.

"Then let's pray we never know what hits us."

Their sanctuary was close to the mantle walls of the fortress, the shell of the mountainside, and from the exterior sounds not terribly far beneath the mantle of storm clouds. The cold was piercing, and this time Thorn was without his infinitely stuffable pouches to provide them with food or clothing.

"Depends on your perspective," Ryn said, in answer to Elora's question, ruffling his fur from top to toe to rid it of any residue of their passage through the rock before dropping into a bearlike seat and reaching out to gather the girl close to his body, where she'd be warmest. She folded herself into a tight little huddle, burrowing so deep it seemed she wanted to disappear. But she was really too big for that, and he, for all his height, not big enough.

"We're loose, Princess," he finished, "but we're freezing."

"I'd say no," Thorn replied to them all, "not so long as the Maizan have Geryn to lead their hunt. As a Pathfinder, he knows his business."

"False friend," Khory condemned him.

Surprisingly, Elora spoke up for the lad. "I don't think so," she said.

More surprisingly, Thorn agreed.

"He said it, he swore an Oath. He's a soldier of the King. And by Royal Proclamation, I'm a wanted man. His duty's plain, especially when it's the Princess Royal who tells it him."

"Now there," noted Ryn, "is a piece of work."

"Yes"—Thorn nodded—"she is."

"Do you do that often," wondered Ryn to Thorn, "strolling through solid rock?"

"I'm learning as I go," he confessed, "much like Khory and her sword."

"Demon skill," accused Franjean, having clambered down from Anele's shoulder. "Decent folk should have no truck with it!"

"Care to shout any louder, shrimp? I'll lay odds the Maizan didn't hear you that time."

"I need no lessons in etiquette from some overstuffed baby toy in need of a major haircut!"

"How about some lessons in common sense! We're on the run here, Peckling, the goal is *not* to advertise our location!"

"Enough," Thorn told them, "the pair of you! Anele, take Franjean, would you please, and find us a way off this rock?"

"What then?" Elora asked, a tad plaintively.

"That's *your* choice, isn't it, Princess?" Once more, from Ryn.

A gusting backdraft—with a squawk of protest from Franjean that he wasn't properly secure, plus an announcement that *he* would be in charge of their mission—proclaimed the eagle's departure.

"I'll keep watch, Drumheller," Khory said, and was acknowledged with a nod, though Thorn's eyes never left Elora Danan.

Recent days hadn't been kind to her, throwing her physical trials that sorely tested folk in far better shape. She sat against Ryn with back and shoulders slumped, too weary to hold herself erect, hands clutching nervously together between legs that had no idea where comfortably to go. She tried sitting with them straight out before her, bent knee up in the air, bent knee flopped out to the side, cross-legged. She even considered amputation.

"I'd rather run," she said, the raccoon circles under her eyes so pronounced, as were the hollows of her sockets, that she looked like she'd been soundly punched.

"Sensible girl."

"Don't feel it, Wyr."

"Like unto died, my girl—"

"I'm not *your* anything, thank you very much."

"Figure of speech, do you mind? Like unto died anyway, when I saw you face that flame."

"She wasn't the only one," added Thorn. "Elora Danan, whatever possessed you?"

"I'm immune," she said matter-of-factly. "At least, so you've said. To spells and such. I think."

Thorn let out his breath in a great gust. "Quite possibly," he conceded. "But that was no time for an acid test."

"You'd have died, otherwise. Besides"—she groped for words — "it was the only answer that made sense. If I'm so important to this Deceiver, he can't very well kill me. Where's the sense?"

"Gods," Thorn whispered, simultaneously aghast and awestruck by what she'd done. "You have no idea, not the slightest conception."

Ryn understood as well, but his way of expressing himself was to enfold her in a snuggly hug.

"It worked, though, didn't it?" Elora asked them.

"Yes and no," Ryn replied when it became obvious that Thorn wasn't able to.

"I saw through your masking spell, right off, Drumheller," she said.

"You did. Forgive me, but that's like striking a match and comparing it to the sun, thinking that because you can puff out the one, the same goes for the other." He held up a hand to forestall any objections. "It may well be you can, that's not what I'm saying. Elora, the Deceiver caught you twice, in your own aerie and in the hearth below."

"And I broke free of him twice!"

"Through you, he slew a dragon. They make legends of feats like that and he did it"—snap of the fingers for emphasis, the sound so sudden and sharp, so close to her eyes, that the young girl jumped—"as easily as that. He ensorcelled the heart and soul of the Twelve Domains, and they didn't even know it was happening. He called up firedrakes and turned them loose on Cherlindrea's Grove. And very likely is the force that destroyed Tir Asleen." He leaned toward her, his voice supernally still. "There is strength in him, and knowledge, and cunning, beyond all belief. Bavmorda wanted you dead. This one means to put you on, body and soul, like a suit of clothes. Your saving grace, even after all that's happened, is that he thinks you are nothing. That's your salvation, child, not some precious 'immunity.'"

Thorn turned away, rolling in a circle on the balls of one foot as though searching for an open window, a possible sight of sun, the taste of fresh air. There was a haunted, hunted quality to his voice and manner, and the image touched Elora, resonating off his own thoughts, of the Nelwyn once more riding that impossible wave of Power, dancing above the Abyss. As though she'd been called by name, Elora found herself rising to her feet and striding clear of Ryn's embrace.

"The true horror," Thorn told her without looking, pulling off Anakerie's silver clip and shaking loose his hair, "is that if we survive this day and make our escape, the Deceiver won't be played for such a fool again. You'll have to learn to face him on his level, there'll be no going back."

"You'll save me," she said, meaning that simple declaration of faith to be a reassurance and a comfort. She didn't expect a look from him as though she'd thrust a spear through his heart.

He smiled, nodded, put the face she'd seen deep away, so quick a transformation of his features she told herself she could have been mistaken.

"What are you doing, Drumheller?" Ryn asked as Thorn dropped to one knee and rubbed a palm gently across the stony floor, brushing aside the layerings of dust, newer films of frost, and stray patches of snow, to feel the primordial rock directly.

"The thing about wielding magic," Thorn said, in a sudden and deliberate change of subject as he cast forth his InSight into the depths of the ancient fortress, "particularly on the magus level where the Deceiver appears to operate, is that the actions have reactions. More intense the one, likewise the other. Drop a stone in a pool, it's much the same—the ripples bounce off the shore and return to you. One set of interactions. But there's another, equally critical, which is what the devil's *happening* on shore. Could be nothing. Could be an earth movement that'll bury your stone under an avalanche.

"You're quite right, though, Elora," he noted suddenly. "You did break the Deceiver's glamour."

"Twice," she reminded him, prompting an answering grin. She stood very straight, with hands clasped beneath her chin, big-eyed and very young.

"What made you do it?"

She worked her hands, roving her gaze anywhere but toward his face. His never moved.

"First time, it hurt. It just felt . . . *wrong.*"

"And now?"

Her eyes swam with tears, but she fought to master them and the sobs that went with.

"You worked so hard, you gave so much of yourself to save the stag."

"You asked me to."

"You'd have done it anyway."

"So?"

"It was a giving thing, a *healing.* When I stood on Morag's deck, in the storm, I was so charged up inside; I was being hit, I wanted to hit back, for all the times I couldn't when I was growing up. I was the *Sacred Princess,* but nothing I said or did mattered! Go here, do this, wear that, speak the lines written for you, be our puppet!"

"You hit your servants."

She blinked furiously and her back went even straighter than before, as though she'd been called to account and it mattered very much how she responded.

"They didn't like me," she said.

It was a reportage of fact. The sorrow came after. No tears or sobs or trembles about the mouth; dramatic, yes; histrionic, not at all. She'd discovered within herself a kernel of true pride—*This is me,* it said, *warts and all. This is a wrong thing that I did and I must take responsibility for it*—and it gave her a center of being she'd never known before.

"I did it because I could," she went on. "And because no one told me different. In the tower, in the hearth, *I* was weaker. The Deceiver didn't ask what I wanted. He *told* me—this is what you are, this is your destiny, take it. I order, you obey. It was like he offered glory without price. I speak, the world trembles, it costs me nothing. It's no wonder his fires burn cold, Drumheller, there's nothing of warmth, nothing of true life in that abomination.

"Can't I just run away and hide somewhere?" she asked in sudden desperation. She thought she knew that answer, but he surprised her.

"Of course." She knew he meant it, knew as well that he'd yield up his life if that was what was necessary, because it was what he once wanted most of all.

"Drumheller," asked Ryn in a strange voice, picking up the hair clip from where Thorn had set it aside, "where'd you get this?"

"It's the Princess's," he replied absently. "Anakerie's. She left it in my cell, back in Angwyn. If not for her, I'd have likely died there, or been consumed by the Deceiver's ChangeSpell. Why, Ryn?"

"I—" the Wyr began, then broke off as Thorn's expression changed markedly, as though the Nelwyn had heard an alarm bell beyond the comprehension of his companions.

"What?" Ryn demanded, rising to join them, one arm going protectively across Elora's body while he gathered his muscles for a fight. His other hand took up his sword.

"Something's afoot."

"Maizan?"

Thorn shook his head, crouching himself low to the stone, fingertips caressing its scrabbly surface as if it were the most delicate piece of rice parchment, ready to crumble at the slightest puff of breath.

"Firedrakes started it," he said, so quietly they had to strain to hear. "They're distant cousins—from the rough-'n-ready, side of the neighborhood—of the rock silkies who live within the worldcore. Those resonances I spoke of." This, to Elora. "The mountain's beginning to stir."

In that moment Thorn found himself called to Bastian's eyes. The eagle was high in the stone rafters of the great hall, very quiet, very still, as he and Rool had been from the start. Nothing had moved below since Anakerie led the Maizan in headlong pursuit of the fugitives. She hadn't wanted to leave Mohdri, but since Thorn was the only one with even a prayer of saving the Castellan, finding him was of the utmost necessity. A pair of guards were left to guard their fallen commander.

Through Bastian's eyes, Thorn watched as both warriors were speedily, silently slain. The Deceiver did his work well. A call from within the hearth brought both men close, weapons at the ready; they'd seen their quarry disappear into stone and were quite prepared to see them reappear from same. Tough men, confident men, the kind who survived by never making mistakes. They made none here, by their lights; their loss was that they were playing far out of their league.

They gave the petrified tableau what they thought was a decent berth. It wasn't enough. Two puffs of frigid flame in both their faces, a reflexive breath of air turned cold as naked space, their lungs instantly freeze-burned, so that even if they managed to overcome the paralysis of their diaphragms and draw another breath, the bronchial membranes would be so badly seared that no oxygen could be transferred to their bloodstream. They suffocated, gasping for air in a room that was rich with it.

Mohdri saw, and to his credit tried his feeble best to avenge them. There was no change to the icon, unlike a decade before when Bavmorda burned herself free of the same trap. Whatever lay imprisoned within simply passed into view, in much the same way that Thorn and the Demon moved through walls. On emergence, it had no form, it looked to be a random coruscation of energy from someplace far beyond human ken; with each step forward, though, it coalesced into a more presentable figure until once more the Deceiver had reclaimed the face of Willow Ufgood.

Anakerie had left a blade by the Castellan's side; with the last of his strength, Mohdri thrust up and out with it, straight through the center of Willow's chest. The Deceiver wasn't bothered in the slightest as he took a couple of steps backward to clear the rapier from his body. Then the slightest of taps shattered the flash-frozen blade to glittering dust.

"Ah, Mohdri," the Deceiver said in false sorrow, the words possessing a cold so awful it seemed to those watching like they came from somewhere beyond the lights and warmth of creation, some pitiless realm that long ago forswore gentleness and mercy. "Never deceive a Deceiver. I thought so much better of you. Was I not clear in my commands? I wanted—I want—the Nelwyn *alive*. As whole in mind as body. Did you think without him, I'd be more easily controlled? Or even banished? Wheels within wheels, was I to be your cat's-paw, as you were mine? The means by which the Maizan could seize Angwyn without a battle? I should have kept you on a tighter rein. Now I suppose"—and the smile was terrible to behold—"I shall."

Mohdri tried to call for help, but the Deceiver's hand across his mouth put a stop to that. There was none of the delicacy that was used against Elora Danan—there wasn't time, for either of them—the filaments burst free of the falseling's flesh like ravening wolves after fresh meat and plunged immediately the Castellan's, burrowing deep into body and soul. The big man began to glow, a lambent radiance that lit his skin from within, his eyes going wide as he found himself lifted from where he lay until he and the Deceiver floated face-to-face. And from there into a last embrace.

The watchers thought, from what they'd seen before, they knew what to expect. Between themselves, Bastian and Rool agreed on a course of action: They would wait until both principals were deep into the spell, then the eagle would stoop and Rool hurl a bolt with all the strength left in him. If that didn't do the trick, Bastian's claws would either slay the Castellan, thereby depriving the Deceiver of a corporeal host, or at the very least leave him one that was a maimed cripple. They had no illusions of their own fate in this enterprise. For them, it seemed a fair exchange.

Only the past turned out not to be prologue. Whether from desperation or some sense of impending danger, the Deceiver acted with ruthless efficiency. At his touch, Mohdri stiffened into death; within another heartbeat, there was nothing left of the shape that called itself Willow Ufgood.

Hale and healed, Castellan Mohdri filled the chamber with laughter, as resounding in its contempt as in its triumph.

Then he looked straight at Bastian.

Flame shot from his eyes—nowhere near as impressive a blast as what they'd seen before, more than able to finish them nonetheless—but all it did was strike naked stone. The eagle dropped like a rock, throwing sense and caution to the winds as he fought to avoid destruction. How Rool managed to hold on, the brownie never knew, much less how in the bargain he was able to empty his quiver, sending shaft after tiny shaft straight for their foe. Here, the Deceiver's overconfidence worked in their favor, for the first impact blew him off his feet and the second sent him crashing through the crystallized shell that had been his prison. It shattered as if he'd been a wrecker's ball, and he dropped in a boneless heap.

Bastian wheeled over wingtip and pumped into the hearth after him, Rool standing to his full height on the eagle's back, arm at full extension, bow drawn taut to his ear. A good day, a good way, to die.

It didn't happen.

Bastian's approach was so extreme he needed an equally frantic evasion to keep from smashing himself on the cold stone. That, in turn, nearly precipitated his passenger to disaster, as Rool found himself taking flight; fortunately, another wild twist of the body and quick stabs with both feet managed to save both the brownie and his weapons.

The Castellan was gone. Into the wall, dancing himself through the stone as Thorn had done.

Only his passage wasn't so courteous as the Nelwyn's and the mountain didn't like it.

Not so much a rumble, but a low, tearing groan, felt more than actually heard, that made Thorn scramble bolt upright, face almost as pale as Elora's ensorcelled skin.

"He's coming for me," Elora cried, face stamped with the shock of a girl faced with death and worse. Then her expression hardened with resolution and she said, in a much older voice, "I'll run, Thorn, but I won't flee."

He understood the difference and gave her the best smile he could (not much, sadly, because he thought he knew the odds) as encouragement. This battle would be his.

Ignoring Khory's outcry, he stepped away from the others and into the stone.

That's when Geryn and the Maizan found them.

It was a wild fight above, no less so below, as the Pathfinder bulled forward into a collision that bounced Ryn clear of his

charge. Geryn lunged after him, determined on a different outcome than their earlier duel, with a pair of wild sword swings
that struck sparks and gouged chips out of both stone and steel.
Elora Danan was on his back before he could go farther, latching
on like a monkey to do what damage she could with voice and
fists. He was well armored and well schooled; it wasn't much.
But the distraction allowed Ryn to recover his own blades and he
came back for Geryn without hesitation. At the same time the
leading element of Maizan and Khory entered the fray themselves and the battle was joined with a vengeance.

There was nothing pretty about the free-for-all; it was a
bloody, brutal business, more on the order of a street brawl, with
kicks and punches being exchanged far more often than swords
were crossed. There was no room to be fanciful with a blade, for
fear of hitting one of your own, which in turn proved a further
disadvantage to the Maizan. True, they had numbers on their
side, but that meant Khory and Ryn could stand back-to-back—
with Elora between their legs—and strike pretty much as they
pleased.

The eagles broke the battle open. Bastian and Rool were the
first on the scene, with the brownie unleashing yet another en-
hanced shaft, so supercharged it left a burning trail through the
air in its wake, to hurl a Maizan bodily into the mass of his fellows. The last sight for one was Bastian's claws before his eyes,
the last sound for another the eagle's hunting cry before an awful tearing sensation stole away his life. Anele, striking from the
opposite direction, took as deadly a toll.

From her sanctuary, Elora had no decent sight of the melee; for
her, it was mainly a matter of avoiding stray kicks, until Geryn
took himself a nasty header after the confluence of a misstep on
some blood and Ryn's fist to his face. Strung from his belt was
Thorn's knife and, most importantly, his pouches.

The girl was off like a ferret, staying low and moving fast, ignoring the thumps and bumps collected along the way as she
scrambled for her prize. A slain Maizan dropped on her; she
shoved him over on top of Geryn without a second thought,
skipped her plan ahead a couple of steps as she ran eyes across

his struggling body as he tried to muscle free. Decided to forgo any attempt at the knot, went for the main belt buckle itself, with the hope in passing that maybe the Pathfinder's pants would fall down at a critical juncture. The buckle was easy, getting the belt was not; Elora had to use both her own feet as a brace and haul with all her might. Had Geryn's help in that regard, for the moment he shoved the corpse on top of him aside was when she found clearance to yank the belt, and the pouches, into her arms.

She'd gotten turned around in the struggle—or the body of the fight had moved on without her—and found herself on the fringes of the scrap, with the whole troop of Maizan between her and her companions. Geryn had figured what she'd done, he blocked one way, and a fast flash over the other shoulder brought Anakerie into view, at the head of a whole new band of black-clad warriors.

Which was when a pair of leather-clad arms rose up from the floor to yank her into the body of the mountain.

Mohdri to her left, one hand clutching her by the hair. Drumheller to her right, but she had no notion how to move to him. For her previous jaunts, the rock she'd passed through had been an all-enveloping glob of nothingness. Like swimming underwater, only without even a hint of light to show the way. Strange, how something so fundamentally solid on the outside should have no sense of it from within. There was a resistance to shifts of her body, the only indication that she was in a medium more dense than air or water, but infuriatingly nothing of substance for her to brace herself against or function as an anchoring point.

Now, however, the blackness had grown color, brilliant strands of energy sizzling outward from the two sorcerous combatants as though they were weavers in a race to see who could craft the more eloquent tapestry. Mohdri completed one, a small patterning of knots and sigils, and radiance flared from it to Thorn, who thrust out with his hands in a forward-pointing steeple to form a wedge to break apart the force of the Castellan's attack.

Without—coming to Elora as rippling waves through the rock,

the way a gusting breeze might stir chop on still water—this exchange manifested itself as a line of powerful explosions, bulging and fracturing the wall above the battling warriors, turning the attention of all from one mode of survival to another as shards the size of houses calved from the face.

Within, Thorn wove a reply of his own, a double hand's worth of strands that seemed to take a winding, leisurely course through the brightening dark toward their target. Mohdri appeared not to notice as he unleashed yet another bolt of force, and Elora couldn't help an outcry as she saw this one wasn't to be deflected so easily. Thorn hissed with shock as a portion of it broke past his defenses to turn near half of him to ice. Elora had seen the images from Bastian; she knew what that awful cold could do, and feared she'd see Thorn's body split asunder. But he proved to be made of sterner stuff and cast off the scourge.

Elora felt her head twisted, her body forced to follow, the Castellan's hand, as used to breaking horses as warriors in battle, drawing her hair so taut she was sure it would tear loose from her scalp as he made sure she had to look at him.

"Yield," she was told, with a force that had never been denied. Not an offer, a command.

"No." She wanted to sound braver, but couldn't find it in her.

"Elora Danan, you know not what you do. This is for the best, for the world as it stands and for generations yet unborn."

The horror of it was, in that blinding moment of contact, breaths mingling, eyes so close her own hand couldn't fit between them, Elora believed him. Every word rang true, the pronouncement as immutable a fact as the dawning of the world. This was no place for her, no role she could play. The Castellan, and the Deceiver who wore his shape, were the personifications of Power; what right had she to stand against them?

So much easier to give up. It was what she wanted, with so much of her heart she was certain she would not survive the breaking of it.

She couldn't do it. Not out of contrariness, or some sense that she was tired of being pushed around. But because this was wrong. As the Deceiver was wrong. She knew this the way she knew the fact of her being. This was Evil before her, and she could not be a party to it. A part *of* it.

So, in the barest whisper, her reply was, "No."

She stood at the gates of her own soul, and gaped with awe when, at his first onslaught, they shook, they splintered, they cracked—but above all, they held. A small measure of her worth, but enough to give her heart, to give her hope.

The Deceiver had no chance to try another. This was the opportunity Thorn had been waiting for and his tendrils caught Mohdri by the extremities, to bind him fast, and in that moment came the inspiration Elora needed, that there was indeed a mass within this ephemeral solidity for her body to push against. It stood right before her.

Legs came up, and she was thankful for her ability to fold as she placed her feet flat against his armored chest. He still had a hand on her, the other tearing at Thorn's strands as though they were composed of acid, burning through to the unseen parts of him without doing a whit of harm to his corporeal flesh. Her first heave brought no joy; she wanted to bite him on the wrist to make him let her go, but the steel facing on his gauntlet would have broken her teeth. So her next kick put both heels in his eyes.

He was human enough to reel at that impact, and that was all she needed.

She flailed wildly, without a proper sense of direction, but Thorn was too occupied to come to her aid. Elora gaped as the texture of his features began to change, losing all sense of flesh as they took on the aspect and then the fundamental nature of the ancient stone that surrounded them. She could still discern his features, but only as striations within the rock. At the same time a great and terrible sound came to her, a basso profundo note that seemed to originate in the core of her own being, as though she was a chime that had just been struck. Accompanying it was a modest radiance, the same kind of glow she saw when for fun she would hold her hand before a candle flame to see how it lit up her skin. She remembered Thorn's analogy about the match and the sun because that was how she felt now, comparing herself to him as he blazed unbearably bright. The shape of him was a mold that was now being filled with metal heated beyond incandescence. She could bear the sight, Mohdri could not. He snarled and struggled frantically in his bonds. Elora knew they wouldn't hold him long, and as well that they wouldn't have to.

"We know *you, Deceiver,"* she heard issue from Thorn's mouth, but it was nothing that approached human speech. She thought of rocks the size of continents grinding together to shape raw sound into words and felt the faintest itch at the back of her own throat as a resonance of the Power that gripped Thorn prompted her to speak as well.

"As you have marked us, so shall we you!"

In the blink of an eye, the stone around them was transformed, the whole heart of the mountain changing state from solid to liquid, as though some monstrous grate had been removed, to allow the fire at the heart of the world to claim this new territory.

Elora cried out with startlement, but there was no fear in her, any more than there had been on the hillside when the firedrakes came at her behest. She swept an arm across her front, argent immersed in golden glory, and grinned delightedly at the eddies and swirls of flame left in its wake. She thought this might be a place to stay and play forever . . .

. . . but Thorn caught her by the arm.

Another columnar slab of stone crashed free, taking them with it, pitching them from an immaterial realm to one that was all too tangible, and Elora cried out as a chunk of basalt clipped her leg.

The mountain wasn't groaning any longer; it had woken with a roar to shake the heavens and the earth. The floor split before them, one side cast up, the other down, two voices lost in the shriek of shredding stone as Thorn and Elora were carried apart. What had been a level passage was remade in a twinkling as a flight of jaggedly uneven steps, more appropriate to the giants who built this place than those who roamed it today. At the same time huge sections of the wall fell away at the sides, admitting the tempest on the one, and giving a view straight to a roiling lava flow below the other.

The main body of Maizan were a fair way below, cut off from their prey by a wide crevasse of granite that the lava was rapidly filling. All thoughts of the chase had given way to a quite natural instinct for self-preservation. Elora herself was on a fair-sized platform that curled off out of view in the direction of the mantle wall. So far as she could see, she was alone; there was no sign of any of her companions, not Khory or Ryn, the eagles or the brownies.

"Drumheller," Elora called, a genuine fear for the Nelwyn accenting her girl's falsetto.

"I'm here!" was his reply from above. He cast his gaze over the drop and as quickly ducked back until his heart slowed its snare-drum cascade. He hated heights. Not when he was riding the eagles, that wasn't the slightest problem, but looking out over such a precipice . . .

He shook his head angrily, a bulldog of a man, and lunged a shoulder forward with his head this time, for all the good that did. With both their arms outstretched, there were body lengths between them.

"I'll find a way up," she cried.

The devil you will, he thought. And then: *Why am I always doing this?* Finally, aloud: "Stay where you are. It's just a plug of rock here, your ledge is the way to safety. I'll come down."

He'd forgotten the other heron. He was hanging by his fingers, scrabbling with toes for a flaw in the facing he was sure he'd seen before committing himself, wondering if Elora could catch him should he simply drop, the air gusting thick with sulfur from the rising lava, which in turn was making it too hot to breathe, when a brace of knifepoints stabbed him in the back.

He had no words for the pain; even the luxury of a scream was denied him as the bird tried to pluck him from his perch. He didn't dare let go, even to defend himself, but was rapidly losing strength enough to hold on. It stabbed with its beak, to punch through the back of his skull, but he ducked his head aside and got a face full of rock splinters instead.

The eagles saved him. There was nothing left in Rool to power his bolts; he could only hold on, with Franjean spread-eagled on top to hold him in place, while Bastian and Anele tore at the heron with beak and claws. It was a suicide charge. The essence of those accursed birds was so foul that drawing their blood was tantamount to a sentence of death; being wounded by them made that a certainty. But their intervention gave Thorn the opportunity he needed.

He had one acorn left to hand. With a feral grimace, he popped it right into the Night Heron's mouth.

It shattered quite nicely on the step below.

So would have he, in his own way, had Elora not answered his unspoken query. Not a catch, in the proper sense of the word, since the impact carried them both to their backsides, but he wasn't about to complain. His only regret was an inability to return her heartfelt hug when she near squashed him with happiness.

"Well," he said with a wild smile at odds with his deadpan delivery, "that was exciting."

"You could have been killed," she raged back at him.

"Every day, in every way." She thumped him in the shoulder, not seriously but hard enough to be noticed.

"What happened here?" she demanded. "What's *happening?*"

He spared a look around them at the growing conflagration.

"There's a soul and spirit to these mountains, just as there is to each of us. The Deceiver is their enemy as much as ours; I told them he was here and asked for their help against him."

"Drumheller," she cried, aghast, "you've set off a volcano!"

"Some tigers, little Princess, aren't ridden quite so easily as others."

"Is he dead, then, the Deceiver? Is this over?"

When he didn't reply, she had her answer.

"At least we're safe," Thorn offered. "That's a start."

"You call this *safe?*"

"If we go quickly, the mountain will do us no harm. I made sure when I opened the crevasse to put our foes on one side and friends on the other. The Maizan can escape, but they can't follow."

"I thought the herons were my friends," Elora said softly.

"And so they were, child," he responded. "*Yours,* not mine."

Then they heard Geryn's voice.

"Elora," was the call, thready with physical stress and not a little fear. "Elora Danan!"

He'd evidently been caught on a separate outcrop, as Thorn had, only his had dropped away from their step; worse, it had begun to separate from the main rider, opening a gap wider than Geryn was tall. He must have leaped for the wall when he felt the ledge split loose beneath his feet; he'd found some handholds but the rock above offered no decent purchase to continue his climb. And since it was a straight fall to the lava flow below, a descent was wholly out of the question.

"Damn!" Thorn snarled at the sight.

"There must be something we can use to save him," Elora cried, burrowing frantically into his pouches. "Why don't you have a rope in here!"

There was, of course, and because it was what she truly desired, it came to her hand complete with a grappling hook.

"Elora Danan," came Geryn's call again, audibly weaker than before, "help me!"

Thorn reached for the rope, but Elora wrenched it from his grasp.

"It's my fault he's down there, Elora," Thorn told her. "I thought I'd controlled the temblors better, to leave us all in safety."

"Do you want to argue, Drumheller, or save the man? You're fighting off the Night Heron's poison, you're not strong enough for this. Will the rope hold him?" she asked.

"Don't worry about that," Thorn said as he jabbed the hook into a crack on their step, and Elora pitched the line over the edge. "The stone will split before one of my ropes breaks."

She didn't know how to climb, she certainly hadn't the muscles for it; what she managed then was slightly better than a controlled collapse, leaving rope burns on hands and feet and thighs as she dropped to another jarring landing on Geryn's ledge. She held fast to the end of her line while warping a length of it close enough for the Daikini to catch hold; afterward, it was a simple matter for him to swing over to join her.

"Are yeh mad, girl?"

Her smile was a mix of bravado and stark terror. "Aren't we all?" she replied.

"Drumheller," he called out, "I have the rope. Haul up the Sacred Princess, I'll follow after!"

"He can't," Elora told him. "He was hurt by the heron, he's too weak."

"Where the hell are the others, then?"

"I don't know. But I *do* know that this promontory is too unstable for us to wait. I thought I could manage on my own," she confessed; "I was wrong, I'm sorry. So either you go first or we go together."

"I'll have yer heart, Drumheller," Geryn hissed, as he secured the line snugly about Elora's torso in a harness hitch, "for allowing the Sacred Princess to place herself in such danger."

"It was my choice, trooper," she said with surprising formality.

"Yer too important," he told her sternly, to her face. "Yeh should know better."

That said, he pulled her snug to his back in a rescue carry, with her legs wrapped about his waist and her arms around his shoulders.

"Hold tight," he told her.

"Thorn's rope'll break before I let you go." He paused a moment at her words, for there was something in them that made him believe that she was speaking an absolute truth.

"Perhaps yeh *are* 'Sacred' after all," he muttered, and let the rope take the strain of their weight as he stepped off his ledge and swung toward the wall.

There were cries from far below as a new figure joined the Maizan, perfect features stricken with concern as he beheld the tableau, a hoarse cry echoing over the crackling growl of the stone as the Castellan called for a bow.

"We hurt him," Elora cried exultantly as she looked over her shoulder to see Mohdri sway and nearly collapse, held erect by a Maizan at each shoulder. "Drumheller, we *hurt* him!"

"Hush, girl," Geryn snapped, propriety cast aside as her excited wrigglings set the both of them to spinning on the line, "or you'll hurt *us* in the bargain."

He tightened his grip, braced his boots once more on the sheer wall, but never got the chance to start climbing on his own, as he found himself being drawn speedily upward. A glance upward showed him Ryn and Khory on the rope, while Anakerie stood beside Drumheller, visible over the crest of the precipice.

Anakerie was staring at Mohdri, lips parted in horror at his miraculous recovery. None of the Maizan with him had been inside the Great Hall when he fell; none knew how badly he'd been injured.

"I tell you true, Keri," Thorn told the Princess, for her ears alone.

"Don't call me that, Peck, only my brother's allowed to call me that. Goes for you as it does for Mohdri . . ." She stumbled on the Castellan's name.

"He is not what he seems, Anakerie. He is no friend." She turned her face to him and he felt an irrational desire to wipe away the giant bruise that discolored a fair piece of it. "I'm sorry."

"I shouldn't be here."

"You'd rather be with them?" Thorn refused to believe that.

"My place is with my people. I'm the Princess Royal, Drumheller. The King no longer sits his throne," she couldn't bring herself to say aloud what she most feared, that her father was dead. "I must take his place. Especially since the only political or military force worth the name that's left in the land is the Maizan."

"You *know* what leads them."

"It's *because* of what leads them that I'm needed most."

"Thorn," Elora called as she and Geryn cleared the lip of main riser. *"Drumheller!"*

The second cry was full of startlement, as Geryn's hand locked on one of her wrists as tightly as any vise and he swung her swiftly, smoothly around into a painful hammerlock.

His voice rang out: "Release the Princess, dogs!"

Thorn was the first to find voice enough for a reply. "Geryn, what are you doing?"

"Fair exchange, wizard; one Princess for the other."

"You deceived us!" Elora's young voice cracked with outrage.

"It worked, didn't it."

"You were never in any danger!"

"I learned to climb afore I learned to ride. Hush now, an' it please you. I'll do none harm if I get what I came for."

"Another lie? It gets easier as you go along."

"Stop this foolishness, boy," Ryn told him. "There's no other way off this rock, without you come with us. And whatever you may believe, Keri's no prisoner here."

"I thought you pledged to serve me," Elora spat at her captor, with more than a flash of her old imperiousness. Then, her yell turned into a squealed yelp as Geryn tightened his grip.

"I pledged to serve Angwyn, Sacred Highness. And the personification of Angwyn is the Princess Anakerie."

"Over to you then, Keri," Ryn called to her. "Tell the young Captain to let her go."

Elora chose that moment to make her bid for freedom, attempting a hammer kick to Geryn's knee that she'd seen Khory use on occasion to good effect. She wasn't a trained fighter, though, and Geryn was; he blocked her attack and hurled her bodily away from him, into a stumbling spin that sent her crashing full-tilt into Ryn. In that same movement, he had his own blade clear of its scabbard and swung it in a wide, sweeping arc to make Khory keep her distance as well.

"What I believe," the Pathfinder cried as he launched himself towards Thorn, "is that *yeh're* the cause of all this misery. All was right with Angwyn—an' the world—till I brought yeh within its walls!"

"Geryn, *no!*" The cry came from Anakeri, her movements as quick as his as she three herself into his path.

The young man stared in horror as his Princess crumpled to his feet, the act of falling pulling her body clear of the blade that had impaled it. He'd run her right through.

"Put down your sword, Geryn," Ryn said, in the calm, implacable voice that he boasted of using to scare off killer whales.

Instead, the Daikini lunged for him, hard and fast, presenting a whole series of roundhouse swings with his saber that drove the Wyr quickly back to the wall. The Pathfinder had good strength and speed, and he swung with a near-berserker intensity that would not be denied. He gave Ryn no opportunity to duck underneath his guard and reach him without being cut. Strangely, Ryn didn't appear to mind.

"Let it go, Pathfinder," Ryn offered a final time, "and we'll all leave this place alive."

"I swore an Oath," Geryn said. "And you've made me betray it!"

When the Wyr finally chose to move, he was a blur of mahogany, using one shoulder to deflect the blade hand while the other caught Geryn in the chest. By rights, the Pathfinder should have been bowled over, but instead, it was Ryn who reeled a step or two away, with a fresh wound in his flank. Geryn brandishes the sword that had stabbed Anakerie, streaked crimson with her blood and Ryn's, as was the hand holding it.

The Pathfinder lunged forward, using sword and a knife drawn from his belt to drive his opponent further back. Despite those best efforts, he found himself unable to reach either point or edge past Ryn's defenses. He'd drawn his last of the young Wyr's blood.

Ryn moved once more to the attack, this time taking no chances, striking at Geryn as he would a shark. His muscles and skills had been honed in the great deeps, against pressures that would crush a Daikini, his claws (the natural ones) shaped and sharpened to breach skin that served as well as armor. A spinning side kick took Geryn down the first time, with force enough to jar his belt knife loose from his grasp. Elora as quickly grabbed it out of his reach. The Pathfinder had another though, this one from his boot. Didn't make a difference. Another lunge, and a willingness to suffer a superficial slash that barely broke the flesh, brought Ryn in close again, to deliver a murderous succession of blows to the body, and leave his foe only the blade that had done the initial damage.

Ryn offered him his life a final time.

"I'm a Captain of the Red Lions," was his reply, "we don't surrender to the likes of you."

With a speed that would have done Ryn himself proud, Geryn slashed through the rope binding Elora, then sprang from his fallen Princess, using the same movement to disengage the grapnel and take it with him; Ryn's outcry was matched by those of his companions as the two figures disappeared over the edge. Ryn threw himself after them, stretching himself full-length on the slab, with his head extended past the edge, though he dreaded what he'd see below.

Geryn and Anakeri had landed on the small outcrop.

"You son of a *bitch*!" Ryn raged, which got himself a roguish grin from Geryn in reply.

"I'm a Pathfinder," he said, brandishing the rope. "We climb as well as ride."

"Throw back the rope then, I'll haul you up."

"Now where's the sense o' that, I ask yeh?"

"We're not your enemies, damn you! It's the Maizan you should be fighting!"

"Made my choice, furball. Swore my Oath. I'll be true to both."

He tied the rope expertly about Anakerie's torso, then anchored the grapnel in a seam in the rock.

"Keri," Ryn roared, "don't let him do this!"

"She's beyond hearing," Geryn said. "My doing. Saving her life's how I'll make amends."

"Drumheller's a healer, you've seen him work!"

"Yeh. Truth, I don't know anymore *what* I've seen. He tells me Elora's protector is the enemy; my own kind tell me the reverse. Yeh say the Maizan're the enemy, yet my Princess, she rides with 'em. Back in the forest, them brownies what attacked us, they called Drumheller, 'Demon.' "

"They were wrong."

"So yeh say. Me, I've seen the Princess ridin' with the Castellan. She loves him true." He dropped her off the ledge, controlling her descent by looping the line about his own body. "The King's gone. Angwyn's hers now ta rule. With her people, that's where she rightfully belongs."

He started a small swing, moving Anakerie through a gradually increasing arc, that took her well out over the lava field in one direction, but ever closer to the waiting Maizan and their Castellan in the other.

"There's a proper order ta the way of things, Drumheller," he said as he worked. "Yeh've cast it into chaos, an' the whole world besides. Whatever fate comes for you, it'll be as well earned as well deserved. So far as I'm concerned, Anakerie is well rid of yeh an' my only regret is I can't save the Sacred Princess in the bargain."

Above, Rhy turned to Thorn, demanding another line.

"That perch isn't big enough," was the Nelwyn's reply, "and far too unstable."

"I don't care, I have to help her!"

"Then *leave* her!" Thorn's expression was as fierce as the larger, bulkier Wyr's, neither figure willing to be swayed. "Geryn's her best chance, her *only* chance. By staying, you put our lives at risk as well!"

"He's right," Elora said, placing herself between them. "The mountain's awake, and angry beyond Drumheller's ability to manage it. *I* can feel that. So could you, Ryn, if you took the moment to care."

"They have her," Khory announced casually.

"Bless the Maker," Ryn said thankfully, then looked around sharply as Elora plunged to her knees at the edge of the slab.

"Geryn," she called, "throw us the rope, we'll pull you up!"

Again, that wild smile from the young man.

"I don't think so, Sacred Highness. But I thank you for the thought."

"Drumheller!" she cried, full-voice.

"There's nothing I can do." Sorrow was stark on his face, and fatigue as well. Sorcery wasn't an option any longer; he stood by act of will, his body could do no more, his reserves had been drained dry, as had the Deceiver's.

The ground shook again and with another awful *crack* the face of the slab opened before them, calving clear as cleanly as if it had been quarried. Against such a terrible noise, Elora's scream should have been a little thing, easily buried, but all present heard her nonetheless.

As though she'd passed a portion of that strength to the man below, Geryn's voice came back to them just as clearly, with a smile to it that made Elora wail and turn away to bury her head on Thorn's shoulder.

"For the Princess Royal," the Pathfinder cried as the cliff gave way around him.

His last words, before the fire claimed him: *"For Angwyn!"*

To the ear, Doumhall's death throes sounded like a game of bowls, with balls the size of mountains. To the eye, it was a great, glowing cauldron of raw fire as the elemental heart of the world fountained into the sky. The peak itself had collapsed in the night to form a monstrous caldera, easily a mile across, canted upland from Duatha Headland and the King's Gate—and frozen Angwyn beyond—and lava poured from the summit to complete the destruction of Cherlindrea's forest begun by the firedrakes. The molten rock filled in the serrated rills and spread mostly to the side as though to form a wall.

Of the Maizan there was no sign, which was hardly a surprise since they'd been on the south side of the peak when it blew, a comparatively safe venue but one that allowed them no chance of pursuit. Thorn sensed the Deceiver wouldn't be following either, at least not right away. Too much had happened too quickly; the fiend had actually been hurt, as well as his host form; he'd have to recover before making another move.

So would Anakerie.

So would he, though he prayed everyone around him would stay healthy for the immediate future. He had his limits, too.

Ryn was hunting, Khory sitting sentry near the cave wherein they'd taken refuge. They'd traveled far enough north to pass the fringes of the storm. There were clouds above, turned to scattered streamers by the high-altitude winds, and beyond them he could see the sky itself and all its welcome stars. This was still primeval land, they wouldn't find settlements for another few days; once they crossed that threshold, Thorn knew they'd have to move as hard and fast as the wind.

It was a hard climb to find Elora, perched atop the hill where she had a decent view south of burning Doumhall. The effort quickly left him breathless and he was huffing long before he reached her. He brought a steaming mug of broth, fresh from the cookpot, and she wrapped her hands around the mug to warm them before hazarding a sip. She sat as huddled into herself as she could manage, back to a standing stone, legs pulled close to her chest.

"I wish I had the opportunity to return this," he said, mostly to himself, fingering Anakerie's silver hair clip.

Elora gave him a sidelong look, then returned her eyes to the distant burning mountain. "No more use for it?" she asked.

"I have use for it."

"You like her, the Princess." Elora didn't wait for his reply; she was already certain of the answer. Instead, she said, "I never had the chance. She ran away from home right after I arrived."

"Her father wanted her to be the first of your vizards."

Elora's face twisted. "I'd have rather had a friend. She ran away. By the time she returned to Angwyn, the patterns of our lives were both set."

"Not anymore. Patterns, I mean," when Elora cocked a questioning eyebrow. "Yours and hers both are broken."

"Mine, hers, the whole wide world's. So everyone's fond of telling me."

"We've all been humbled, Elora. It's what comes next that matters. The order of the world—the fundamental *way* of things—has changed. Perhaps permanently. We either accept it, or try to set things right."

"I bet you'd rather be home, tending your beets."

"Corn, and barley, thank you very much. And wheat. Burglekutt grew beets."

"Is she a friend, Drumheller, or foe?" Elora asked after another cautious sip of soup and a lick of the lips at its delicious taste.

"Yes."

"That's no answer."

"No."

She gave him a look to see if he was making fun of her. His in return told her that was as good as she was going to get on the subject.

"I hope she's all right."

"So do I."

"It's my fault," she said. "If I hadn't tried to break loose—"

Thorn took a long breath, then let it out as slowly. "Geryn chose his fate when he left us on the reef, before the firedrakes. You trusted me with your life, Elora, wholly and without reservation. He couldn't. Not then. Not later. He'd marked a path for himself, built himself a structure to define the shape of his days; he couldn't bear to tear it down, nor conceive of how he'd survive the aftermath of such destruction."

"Will we? Survive?" she asked after a time.

"We'll try."

"Will we win?"

"I don't know."

"Any idea how?"

He considered for a bit, then said, "Not the slightest."

She laughed aloud. "Then how can we fail?"

Her laughter faded and she sniffed, very much a girl who'd hardly begun the journey of her life.

"I miss my bear," she said, with true sadness.

"I beg your pardon?"

She shrugged, tried to cover her sorrow with a smile. "My bear. I had it in my arms when I came to Angwyn. The only thing that came with me from home." Her voice broke on the word and she sniffed loudly. "Wasn't much to look at. Singed all over, poor thing, one eye gone, an ear torn to shreds. I didn't know better, I'd say it had gone to war." Her smile broadened. "I used to look at him, in bed at night, and think to myself—you figure this is something, Elora my girl, you should see the *other* guy!"

An impulse drew Thorn's hand to his pouch. Even as he reached inside he had a flash of InSight about what would be waiting. And remembered as well that last exchange with the Demon.

"Evil abides," he had said, in despair.

Silly little mage, had been the reply—**so does good.**

The bear did indeed look the worse for wear. The fur had been brushed and clean—he knew from the touch that it had been by Elora's own hand, this was a treasure she entrusted to no one—but soot had been baked into its fabric, making him a very dirty blond. The fabric over one foot had worn away and been replaced. From the odd shape—it no longer matched its fellow—it was clear that new stuffing had been added as well, by a seamstress with more desire than skill. It was indeed missing an eye, and an ear had been savaged, with companion scars down the side of its head. But the eye that remained looked back at him with the rough-and-ready confidence of a survivor.

"Bear!" Elora said in a whisper, not daring to believe the sight.

He handed it to her and she cradled it with the gentle passion of one true friend for another.

"How?" she asked Thorn.

"You've Khory's sire to thank."

"The Demon?"

"I think it snuck it into my pouch before our escape."

"What a world"—she marveled—"where Demons offer kindness." Then she looked from bear to Nelwyn.

"He's yours, isn't he? You made Bear for me."

He nodded.

"I couldn't be with you, so I left him in my place. I thought it was a dream. I suppose"—and he looked skyward, letting memory sweep him along like the wind—"where dragons are concerned, dreams are reality and reality a dream."

"You know, I always told myself that it was Bear who saved me."

"Well, I asked him to look after you."

"Thank you, Thorn. With all my heart."

Her eyes turned once more to the newborn, ancient volcano in the distance.

"Why is there always fire?" she wondered.

"That which cleanses, that which consumes, been a part of your story from the start, I'm afraid. One of the Realms. Fire, I mean."

Her head turned a fraction to her left, looking past Doumhall toward the glow that could no longer be seen thanks to the volcano's fury. "The ways the world ends, that's what Ryn said—in fire or in ice. Ancient Angwyn claimed by one, young Angwyn by the other."

"The world's far from dead, Elora. Both fire and ice have their role in the preservation of life as well as its destruction."

"What the StagLord said, is everyone's hand against us?"

"Very likely, I'm afraid. New relationships, new alliances. It'll be a time before the dust settles, while new heads claim their respective crowns. Afterward, everyone's going to choose up sides. Some might join the Deceiver willingly, others may well be overthrown. Some will decide the safest place is on the sidelines and wrap themselves in neutrality. The best, I hope, will cast their lot with you."

"It's a war, then."

"Against the Shadow, yes."

Her eyes were blinking very rapidly, the distant glow of Doumhall giving her tears the aspect of the raw lava flowing down the mountain's flanks.

"I didn't want Geryn to die," she said softly, after a silence.

"Nor I. But that's the way of things sometimes."

"I keep seeing his face—not the way he was at the end, but when we were friends, on the boat and on the beach, when he kept trying to keep me warm."

"Good. So long as you remember, the good in him lives on."

"Like the brownies said?"

"Like the brownies said."

"Thank you for saving me."

He stretched his arm across her shoulder, and drew her close.

She snuggled like a cat again, like his own daughter, fitting herself as best she could to his lap, and he stroked her gleaming hair.

"I did my part," he told her, "as did we all. But when it counted, Elora Danan, you saved yourself."

Then, for what felt like the first time in a lifetime, he let a smile of true joy crease his weathered features, and he sang the hope of the world to a deep and gentle sleep.

GEORGE LUCAS is the founder of Lucasfilm Ltd., one of the world's leading entertainment companies. He created the *Star Wars* and *Indiana Jones* film series, each film among the all-time leading box-office hits. Among his story credits are *THX 1138, American Graffiti,* and the *Star Wars* and *Indiana Jones* films. He lives in Marin County, California.

CHRIS CLAREMONT is best known for his seventeen-year stint on Marvel Comics' *The Uncanny X-Men,* during which it was the bestselling comic in the Western Hemisphere for a decade; he has sold more than 100 million comic books to date. His novels *First Flight, Grounded!* and *Sundowner* were science fiction best-sellers. Recent projects include the dark fantasy novel *Dragon Moon* and *Sovereign Seven*™, a comic book series published by DC Comics. He lives in Brooklyn, New York.